10/06

INCAS

BOOK III
THE LIGHT OF MACHU PICCHU

A. B. DANIEL

TRANSLATED BY ALEX GILLY

A TOUCHSTONE BOOK
PUBLISHED BY SIMON & SCHUSTER
New York   London   Toronto   Sydney   Singapore

Touchstone
Rockefeller Center
1230 Avenue of the Americas
New York, NY 10020

International rights management for XO Editions: Susanna Lea Associates
Copyright © 2001 by XO Editions. All rights reserved.
English translation copyright © 2003 by Alex Gilly

TOUCHSTONE and colophon are registered trademarks
of Simon & Schuster Inc.

First Touchstone Edition 2003
Published by arrangement with XO S.A.
English language translation published by arrangement with
Simon & Schuster UK Ltd.
Originally published in France in 2001 as *Inca: La Lumière du Machu Picchu*
by XO S.A.
For information regarding special discounts for bulk purchases,
please contact Simon & Schuster Special Sales at 1-800-456-6798
or business@simonandschuster.com

Manufactured in the United States of America

10 9 8 7 6 5 4 3 2 1

Library of Congress Cataloging-in-Publication Data is available.

ISBN 0-7434-3276-2

INCAS

BOOK III
THE LIGHT OF MACHU PICCHU

Tropic of Cancer

Atlantic
Ocean

Panama

Orinoco

Equator

Quito
Tumebama
Tumbez
Cajamarca
Hatun Sausa
Lima
Cuzco
Titicaca

Amazon

Madeira

Paraguay

Pacific
Ocean

Tupiza

Tropic of Capricorn

1,000 kilometers

Farthest extent of
the Inca empire

PART ONE

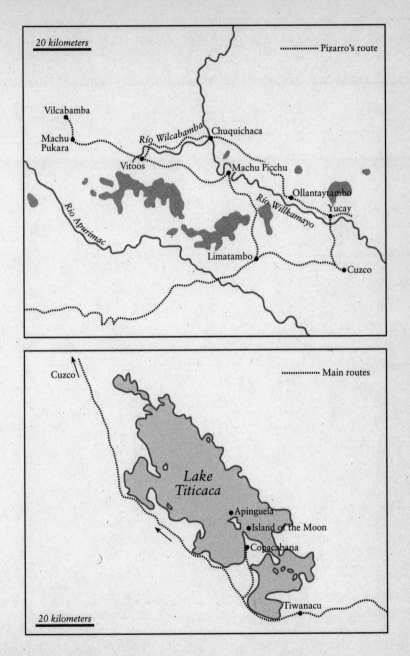

ONE

Cuzco, May 1, 1536

No one took any notice of Gabriel squatting at the corner of Gonzalo Pizarro's *cancha*. It was approaching noon.

The tunic he had been wearing for week upon week was grimy enough not to draw attention, and he had rubbed clay into his cheeks to camouflage his blond stubble. To the Spaniards, he looked like yet another squalid Indian in rags, one of the many who now populated Cuzco's alleys. And with his square hat, with its odd, pointed angles, pulled low over his face, he looked, to the Cuzco Indians, like some peasant come from Titicaca. A small bronze club hung from a leather strap under his *unku*, and in this humble weapon he had invested all his hope.

He had arrived in town at daybreak, having traveled by night to avoid the endless stream of warriors called to arms by Manco and Villa Oma, and he had walked from Calca without stopping. He had become lost once or twice in the darkness, and his trip had taken longer than it might have. But his rage and suffering had driven him on, forbidding him any rest.

Only now, as he squatted at the base of the vast, sun-warmed wall, did Gabriel become aware of the hunger and fatigue that caused his limbs to stiffen. Yet the thought of heading off in search of a meal and rest never once crossed his mind. His eyes remained fixed on the *cancha*'s door. He would have time enough later to eat and sleep, should those things still hold any meaning.

He was here to kill Gonzalo. It was his sole remaining duty.

For the better part of two hours, he saw only servants and a few courtesans coming and going from the Governor's brother's house. For

Gabriel, they were for the most part new faces, men whose demeanors and dress were still redolent of Spain: They stamped their heels into the dust with all the manifest arrogance of recently arrived masters.

Gabriel was extremely tired, could barely keep his eyes open. He trembled sporadically from thirst and hunger. Yet nothing on earth would have convinced him to give up his watch in favor of finding food and water. He fantasized about the moment when he would strike Gonzalo, at last ridding the world of the man's wickedness. He took a few coca leaves from the cloth pouch slung around his neck next to his skin and chewed them deliberately until his hunger dissipated.

The dwarf's terrible tale still lingered in his mind: "Gonzalo entered Anamaya's room while she slept. She only woke when he already had his hands on her. She cried out; they fought. Manco wanted to kill him on the spot, but Anamaya feared that the Strangers would seek their vengeance against the Emperor. So instead, we fled Cuzco before dawn . . ."

Gabriel had been turning these abhorrent words over and over in his mind for days. The words had become images that provoked an icy hatred in him, a fury that stung his nerves more than actual hunger or thirst. With each breath of air, he drew in his vengeful plan as though it were nectar. His eyes remained wide open, his swollen fingers tight around the hilt of his bludgeon.

He sweltered in the afternoon heat. The sun befuddled him, and eventually he fell asleep, his mouth full of dust, without Gonzalo having come out of the house. He sunk into a nightmare. He saw Anamaya, cold, distant from him, her face hardened with determination. She wrapped her arms around her gold husband and said to Gabriel:

"We must take up arms against the Strangers—against you— because only our love and courage will keep the Mountains and our Ancestors from slipping into the void. I shall be at my gold husband's side when he fights, for that is my right and proper place. You must distance yourself from me, my love . . ."

He wanted to protest, to explain to her that they couldn't confront each other as enemies. But although his mouth moved, no words came out. He made a heroic effort to be heard. He begged, implored Anamaya to soften her hard gaze. Nothing. No sound, no cry escaped his mouth. He woke so suddenly that he heard himself sob. Haunted as he was by Anamaya, he didn't immediately recognize his surroundings.

The feeling of helplessness that he had experienced in his nightmare followed him into wakefulness. And then, as though driving a dagger deeper into his own chest, he recalled the answer he had given her after their passionate night together at Calca:

"So, we must fight each other. If during the battle your place is at Manco's side rather than mine, Anamaya, then it means that I have become a Stranger in your eyes. And if that's the case, then my place is with the Strangers."

Anamaya's lips had trembled with hurt. Stroking his cheek, she had murmured:

"You are the Puma, my beloved. You are the only man who can reach me, whether here in this world or in the next. You are the one and only who can touch my heart and show me the joy of the world."

Gabriel smiled, not realizing that tears were running down his clay-covered cheeks.

Yes, there was no doubt that she loved him as much as he loved her.

And yet, it was impossible between them. The distance was too great: The sad realities standing between the sorceress wife of an Inca lord, dead many years past, and a Stranger who was nothing, even among his old brothers-in-arms, were too many and too much.

All that remained for him was to kill Gonzalo.

And it would be a welcome gift of destiny should he die at the same time.

What he had been waiting for finally occurred just before night enveloped Cuzco.

A great commotion woke him from his reverie. Terrible cries pervaded the alleyways. Gabriel sat up, his knees cracking, his thighs painfully stiff. A swine emerged, its mouth wide open, an enormous, hairy pig as black as night, a true Andalusia *serrano,* weighing fifty pounds at least. It bared its tusks sharp enough to gut a horse.

From behind it burst a herd of others: at least thirty, running with their heads down, bawling as though their throats were being slit. The males stormed straight ahead, crashing their heads into the *cancha*'s wall, while the big-bellied sows dragged their udders through the dust. A dozen terrified piglets squealed from behind and scurried between the legs of the inept, yelling Indians, these last trying as best they could to herd the foul-smelling drift.

These mud-splattered peasants—recently promoted swineherds—thrashed their long sticks through the air; yet they dared not use them to strike the pigs' rumps. Rather, they seemed ready to bolt each time a piglet bumped into them. A crowd of locals, gathered at a judicious distance, looked on, laughing at this strange cavalcade.

Gabriel let out a roar as he bound into the middle of the alleyway. He kicked a few plump pig rumps, grabbed a young male by the ears, and thus blocked the chaotic flow of ham. The pigs stopped dead in their tracks, instantly ceased their squealing, raised their snouts, and gazed around complacently.

The swineherds, flabbergasted, gazed suspiciously at the newcomer. Gabriel greeted them in Quechua to reassure them. But when he asked where the animals were bound, he met with silence. He realized that his accent must have bewildered them as much as his attire, the dried mud flaking off his face, and the green coca juice dribbling from his lips. Eventually, one of them pointed at Gonzalo's house.

"They're for the Stranger. They're his animals. He had them brought from Cajamarca. He plans to eat them."

The man seemed amazed by the idea, though his tone remained deferential. In a flash, Gabriel understood that chance was smiling upon him.

"I shall help you," he said. "I know how to manage these beasts."

It still required unusual effort to get the entire herd through the *cancha*'s narrow trapezoidal door.

And once inside, the pigs continued to cause quite a stir: The excited animals alarmed the Indian servant girls, bolted around the courtyard, knocked over and broke several jars, and annoyed the horses being groomed.

Gonzalo's house hadn't changed much in the two years since Gabriel had last visited. Solid doors now divided the rooms—doors finely worked by Spanish carpenters—and a bridle-rail had been erected in the courtyard.

Gabriel abandoned the pigs and stood in the center of the yard. He had only been there a short while when he heard shouts and laughter approaching. He recognized that hated voice.

A small group appeared, including Gonzalo wearing a ruffled shirt, velvet breeches, and shining boots. The others were a couple of his courtiers. They took no notice of Gabriel, mistaking him for an Indian, and continued their frivolous play. One of them grabbed a young servant girl by the waist, up-ended her, and brought her face-to-face with the fiercest piglet, introducing them. Before the swine had a chance to charge her, however, Gabriel whipped out his studded club and brought it down hard on the idiot's arm, forcing him to release the young girl.

"By the blood of Christ!" cried the fop. "You damned monkey, you almost broke my wrist!"

Gonzalo and his friends were furious and they made to strike the stranger, but when Gabriel threw back his hood, they stopped dead in their tracks. He rubbed away some of the mud from his cheeks with the back of his hand, revealing his identity.

After the initial shock, however, Gonzalo quickly recovered his old sarcastic aplomb.

"Well, well, isn't this a pleasant surprise! My friends, allow me to present to you Gabriel Montelucar y Flores, who has come with the swine. Well, my dear fellow, it seems that you have found your place at last!"

The others had already unsheathed their swords. Gabriel ignored them.

"Rumor had it that you'd disappeared, run, or even died," continued Gonzalo, feeling himself to be on a roll. "But no, here you are, alive as can be and filthy as ever, I find. Am I to understand that my dear brother Francisco has at last decided to be done with you?"

Gabriel's eyes shone with violent rage. Gonzalo and his sidekicks instinctively took a few steps back.

"Hell awaits you, Gonzalo," snarled Gabriel, swinging his club. "The day has come for you to take your place there."

"*Hola!* If you think that you're going to frighten me with that . . . implement!" guffawed Gonzalo.

"I'm going to crush your balls with this implement, Gonzalo. You're out of luck. I'm not one who waits for God to punish scum like you. I shall have the pleasure of doing it myself."

Gonzalo's companions tried to hide their fear, tightening their mouths. Gabriel lunged forward. His bronze club clashed against their swords and he flung them aside with a fierce backhand swipe. Gonzalo jumped back and pulled a dagger from his breeches. He made a short, awkward thrust at Gabriel's arm. But his blade sliced through nothing and, meeting no resistance, he lost his balance. Gabriel ducked to avoid the other blades whistling through the air and simultaneously dealt Gonzalo a severe blow to the thigh.

Gonzalo crumpled in a heap, screaming in pain. Gabriel made to continue his attack, but a sword sliced through his *unku* and brushed past his ribs. He rolled to the ground as the two Spaniards whipped their swords through the air above him. He held them off with his club, but its handle, repeatedly gashed by their blades, was weakening.

He thought of the horrible powerlessness he had seen so many times when Inca warriors had had their weapons destroyed by Spaniards. Like them, he would soon have nothing with which to defend himself. But suddenly an idea occurred to him.

He let out an enraged cry and windmilled his club like a sling before releasing it at his nearest enemy's face. The Spaniard had no time to dodge, and the bronze bludgeon slammed into the side of his face, smashing his jaw, and splintering his bones with a loud cracking sound. He collapsed, already unconscious, while the other man froze in terror. Making the most of their stalling, Gabriel dove onto one of the piglets panicked by the fight, picked it up, and brandished it at arm's length, like some strange, wriggling shield, just as his assailant lunged forward to run him through. The sword plunged through the animal as though it were butter, and so deeply that the weapon became stuck. Heaving with all his might, Gabriel flung the piglet across the courtyard, and the sword twisted deeper as it landed with a thud, tearing the poor animal's guts out. The beast squealed in agony as Gabriel kicked the now disarmed coxcomb in the gut. Then he threw himself at Gonzalo and grabbed him by the throat like some crazed demon.

"It's over, Gonzalo," he growled. "It's all over for you, the world has no use for your kind!"

Hypnotized as he was by the eyes popping out of Gonzalo's asphyxiated head, Gabriel didn't hear the voices or the footsteps approaching from behind. A steel-capped boot clobbered him in the ribs, and it was surprise as much as pain that made him lose his breath.

He let go of Gonzalo's neck and fell across his legs. Another blow, this one to his head, almost knocked him out cold before he had a chance to pick himself up. He was hardly conscious of someone holding his hands behind his back. His rage and frustration gave him one last burst of energy. Gathering all his remaining strength, he tried to get up, hoping that whoever it was would finish him off for good.

But the back of his neck exploded in pain, and he fell into blackness.

The liquid dark first turned a confused red before brightening into a lucid pain. His head felt as though someone were hammering nails into it. Gabriel was astonished to discover that he could feel his hands and that they obeyed him. He ran his fingers over his face. He opened his eyes, letting them adjust to the blinding light. He took stock of his surroundings.

He was lying on a beaten dirt floor. He recognized the room: It was the same one that he had stayed in a long time ago now, before Don Francisco had ordered him to leave Cuzco.

Still stunned, he sat up.

A man as round as a barrel was carefully hammering shut a shackle around his right ankle, its chain fixed to the wall. He worked with astonishing precision, despite his size. Gabriel noticed that his black eyes showed neither cruelty nor pleasure, but rather weariness. Four others surrounded him and gazed upon their prisoner with grim, menacing eyes.

"What's your name?" asked Gabriel.

"Enrique Hermoso, Don Gabriel, but my friends call me Kikeh."

"Well then, Kikeh, do what you must do, and don't worry too much."

Kikeh sighed and continued with his task. Gabriel grit his teeth. He tried to distract himself by examining the others, whom he did not know. They wore new thick leather vests emblazoned with the Pizarro coat of arms: a pine and apples girt by a pair of bears walking on slate. Also new were their halberds with sickle-shaped blades, which they held carelessly against their shoulders. And it was with no real surprise that he saw them make way for a large man wearing a well-groomed beard and a spotless starched lace ruff: Don Hernando Pizarro.

"I shall be finished this instant, my Lord," said the fat man.

He brought the hammer down onto the shackle one last time, but it slipped and came down on Gabriel's ankle instead, bruising it horribly and drawing a cry of pain.

The jailer chortled awkwardly and said, "Well then, with this chain on his paw, Don Hernando, he's not about to cause any trouble, much less dance a saraband!"

"Just so, Enrique," said Hernando, amused. "Rather we shall invite *señor* Montelucar y Flores to a dance of our own devising."

As the fat man rose to his feet, breathing heavily, Gabriel stood also, gritting his teeth to smother any hint of the giddiness gripping him. His leg was so painful that it barely held him up.

Hernando shook his head.

"The passing of time has seen little change in you, Don Gabriel. I leave you hot under the collar and I find you exactly the same some thirty months later! Although, looking at your dress, you have changed somewhat after all. Now you are even lower, even closer to the manure that is your proper place!"

Gabriel spat blood.

"Very well," Hernando said, "and that explains the stench floating about since your arrival."

One of the men in the leather vests made to move forward, but Hernando held up his hand.

"This time, Montelucar, you shan't be able to count on Don Francisco to save your skin. I am master here now. My good brother the Governor was so happy to see me back from Spain that he very officially nominated me lieutenant-governor. What's more, the scales have at last fallen from his eyes in regards to you. He has learned how you abandoned the mission with which he had entrusted you."

"It won't help you," said Gabriel, leaning against the wall. "A grandiose title can never hide the mediocrity of its bearer. Pig's shit you are, and pig's shit you will remain, Don Hernando."

Hernando slapped Gabriel hard in the face with his gloved hand, splitting his upper lip and sending him to the ground.

"You're in no position to be insolent, you whoreson dog!" spat Hernando. "I could crush you like the insect that you are this very instant. I could leave your fate in Gonzalo's hands, whose most fervent wish is to gut you with a spoon! But that would be too good for you. In Toledo they were particularly insistent on the importance of trials. Well then, I'll give you a trial, my friend, in due and proper form! That way all of Spain shall know why we hanged the bastard excrement of the Montelucar y Flores family. All of Spain shall learn the name of the crown's first traitor in the new world!"

An odd snigger came from Gabriel's bloody mouth.

"You'll have to run your trial quickly, Hernando. Your charming brothers treated Manco and his people with such amiable courtesy that the Inca are now baying for blood. Manco and his generals have amassed tens of thousands of men in the valleys north of Cuzco. I saw them with my very own eyes. There are more than a hundred thousand of them! Tomorrow or the day after, they'll be twice that, and they'll be here."

His words had the desired effect on Hernando's men. They looked at one another, their gazes hard and grave. And Hernando uttered a laugh a little too disdainful, too obviously defiant.

"Well, that's what I call news! If those wretches imagine that they're going to take back their city with sticks and stones, then they shall be cut to pieces once again. If I were you, Don Gabriel, I wouldn't place too much faith in them. And since those savages can't save you from your inevitable fate, I suggest you turn to prayer!"

TWO

Cuzco, May 3, 1536

His cell lacked even a straw mattress. The jailer had left him a jug of water and three ears of boiled corn in a corner. But he hardly touched them in two days. He slowly opened his eyes and saw a fat man coming to check if he was still alive.

"Don Gabriel?"

"I'm here, Kikeh. At least, what remains of me is here. . . ."

"I'm so sorry about . . ."

Kikeh mimed the motion of a hammer missing its mark. Gabriel languidly raised his hand and uttered a suffocated laugh.

"I thought you more dexterous than that. So, I assume you didn't do it deliberately, then."

"Of course not, Don Gabriel, I promise you! I even went so far as to disobey Don Hernando's orders by leaving you your . . ."

The jailer pointed at Gabriel's *chuspa*. Gabriel had chewed all the coca leaves it contained to alleviate the pain radiating through his muscles. He had chewed so many leaves, in fact, that the bland paste these formed in his mouth had swollen to the size of an egg.

"Thank you, Kikeh," he said quietly. "Now please let me be."

But the fat man instead cradled his neck in his hand and poured water into his mouth. Gabriel could smell the tart stench of the jailer's sweat and, in his extremely reduced state, this human closeness seemed so miraculous to him that tears welled up in his eyes.

Then he was alone once more.

His fatigue had diminished somewhat, but it had given way to a nausea that he couldn't shake, not even when he stretched out flat on the floor. Sudden bouts of fever left him shivering and curled up on himself at the foot of the wall, his fingers clenched around the links of his chain as though he were holding on from falling into the void.

He was frightened of falling asleep. Yet he nodded off frequently into dreadful deliriums. He was subjected to a series of images so palpably real that he could hardly believe that they were dreams.

He had a lucid vision of himself on his horse in a saltpan whiter than linen. He saw his bay's legs snap as they broke through the salt crust into a hole. He had forgotten the name of the desert. Water gurgled between his horse's hoofs and its broken legs. The animal looked at him imploringly with its big, round eyes. He saw himself remaining completely immobile for a long time, his arms wrapped around his animal's head, the sun scorching them both. Then he saw his dagger suddenly piercing the horse's throat.

A deluge of blood—far more than the animal could have actually contained—streamed from the wound without coagulating in the sun, a flood of boiling blood engulfing everything.

Now the sun was immense, so big that it appeared to swallow up the entire horizon of the earth so that not one shadow remained. Gabriel wanted to protect himself from it by climbing into his horse's carcass. But when he peeled away its skin like that of a fruit and opened its gut, he morphed into an animal himself, into a wildcat capable of dodging death.

The madness of his dream brought him intense pleasure. What he was now living and seeing was no longer shackled to reality. The sun was once again distant and gentle. The desert had disappeared.

Each time he made another catlike leap, he was overcome by the extreme joy usually particular only to children. He looked at his own shadow, his own fabulous, feline silhouette slinking along against the fields and dusty roads. His body was covered in a thick pelt of short hairs, and he felt them brush past the leaves on the highest branches. Rocks felt soft and padded beneath his claws. He was carried like a bird by the breeze and his beloved.

Gabriel glided above the endless blue of Titicaca. He lay on his side on its shore and listened to the Master of the Stone's lesson. He watched him play with a sling stone and fling it high into the air. He was astonished to see it remain suspended, as though it were as light as a feather. The Master of the Stone grinned at him. It was a warm but sad smile, a smile in which Gabriel made out a wish never uttered.

Then he heard a laugh.

Anamaya appeared, clad entirely in white. She was clasping a gold statue that seemed alive, almost human. She extended her hand toward him and called to him.

"Gabriel!"

Her voice was gentle, musical, and he couldn't resist it. The ferocious feline went to her.

As he lay down beside her, he realized that the golden man had disappeared. Now Anamaya was naked, fragile and beautiful. She offered herself to him, and he burned with desire for her. She showed no sign of fear. She wrapped herself around his feline body and kissed his muzzle. He could have destroyed her with his fangs. She didn't feel his claws when he put his paws on her body.

For a while they were lost in an allaying happiness. Then Gabriel saw, over Anamaya's shoulder, the golden man watching them from the shadows. He was twinkling like a star in the night.

The statue addressed Anamaya without moving his lips. She left Gabriel without a moment's hesitation. She didn't even turn around when he let out a raucous growl, the cry of a savage and fatally wounded animal that echoed over the mountains.

The violence of his own cry sundered his soul. He opened his eyes.

His tattered clothes were stuck to his chest with his own sweat. He had a bitter, pasty taste in his mouth. The pain that had been assaulting his head ever since he had been beaten and kicked in Gonzalo's courtyard returned with a vengeance.

Later, benumbed, he couldn't tell if he had dreamed all this or if insanity was gaining on him. Had he the strength, he would have prayed to God to let him sleep until the end of time.

A bitterly cold dawn brought a strong wind that woke Gabriel. The narrow dormer window was covered in frost, the harbinger of winter.

By the frail light that precedes sunrise, Gabriel discovered what a wretched state he was in. His filthy tunic was torn to shreds, barely cov-

ering him. His body ached from head to toe. He felt his face with his
fingertips; it was still swollen from all the blows he had taken. The skin
around his ankle under the iron was chafed raw. His nausea had faded,
but his head felt as though a host of drummers had taken residence
inside and were beating a call to arms.

He carefully placed his swollen lips on the edge of the jug, and at
last slaked his thirst. The ears of corn brought by the jailer two days
previous were shriveled now. But the hunger racking him was too
strong, and he devoured them feverishly.

Only then did he realize that the drumming he could hear wasn't
coming from his own temples or from his throbbing body. They were
real drums, their tempo increasing, and being played closer and closer.

He recovered his lucidity and strained to hear what was going on.
He stretched his chain as far as it would allow toward the window and
heard the first cries in Spanish rise from outside his cell.

"The Incas! The Incas!"

The narrowness of the dormer window limited his range of vision.
At first he saw nothing; he heard only an increasing number of panicked cries rising from the predawn shadows around the town.

"The Incas! The Incas!"

Then a riotous explosion of trumpets and human cries drew his
attention to the eastern hills overlooking the town. What he saw chilled
him more than the freezing wind whipping past his face.

It looked like a forest of bushes or hedgerows being shaken by the
wind, but in fact he could make out arms, spears, and banners rising
from its thickness: He was looking at thousands of warriors silhouetted
against the breaking sky.

The vast Inca army had completely surrounded Cuzco, covering the
crests of all the hills surrounding it like some giant, monstrous snake. It
was as though the wind had whisked away the greenery from the hilltops during the night and had replaced it with this massive, multicolored crowd, now howling like madmen.

The beating drums and the deep wail of horns and conch shells
grew louder. Panicked Spaniards emerged onto the streets.

After his initial shock had dissipated, Gabriel found himself admiring this extraordinary spectacle. So, Anamaya and Manco had gone

ahead with their plan. The bitter prospect of revenge warmed his heart. He completely overlooked the fact that the army on the hill represented as grave a danger to him as it did to the few hundred Spaniards in Cuzco.

And in fact, it mattered little to him if he perished during the attack, the justified attack. He preferred to die by the hands of warriors commanded by Anamaya than by those of Hernando and Gonzalo.

He remained standing by the window for hours waiting nervously for the attack to begin. He underestimated neither their overwhelming force nor their rage.

To his surprise, the great Inca army still hadn't attacked the town by midday.

By then, the ranks of warriors had swollen to the point where one could no longer differentiate one brightly colored tunic from the next, and they appeared as a single, compact mass. They hadn't relented with their deafening din. But Gabriel no longer heard any cries from immediately around his jail or indeed any movement at all. Cuzco seemed abandoned.

Then he heard the bolt being drawn back on the other side of his cell door. He stood absolutely still, holding his chain in his hand.

His potbellied jailer appeared holding a large hide gourd in one hand and a *manta* containing cornbread and boiled potatoes in the other.

"Kikeh!"

"Don't welcome me so kindly, Don Gabriel. I don't deserve your gratitude."

"I would welcome the Devil himself in these circumstances, my dear Kikeh. Never before have I understood so clearly how one's own existence is affirmed by the presence of another."

"Please, no philosophizing, Don Gabriel. I never understand it at moments like these. Or at any other, for that matter."

Gabriel noticed the fear twisting his jailer's face. Kikeh examined each corner of the room as though he expected to find an army of Indians there. He threw his load at Gabriel's feet.

"You'll have to make do with this for the moment," he mumbled. "I'm sorry to say that it's all I could lay my hands on."

"Ho!" protested Gabriel, "I'm meant to be tried, not starved to death!"

But his jailer's laugh was joyless.

"You must have heard them. Those savages out there, I mean. You should be grateful that I thought of you at all before disappearing!"

"You're fleeing? Are the Spaniards abandoning the city?"

"Oh no! No one's fleeing. It's too late. But I've found myself somewhere to hole up in before those Indians cut me to pieces."

He approached the window and glanced at the hills.

"You don't see nothing from here. They're everywhere. They cover the southern mesa like ants. They've already captured two cavalrymen trying to get through. They cut off the horses' hooves and their riders' heads."

So, thought Gabriel, Hernando's pride and underestimation of the Incas has turned against him.

"What's odd," said the fat man sadly, "is that they haven't attacked yet. I guess they have a reason. I don't want to be around when they decide to reveal it."

"Something odd happened to me too, Kikeh."

"What?"

"Suddenly I don't feel like dying anymore."

The jailer stared at him with a look of boundless surprise.

"What do you expect me to do? I've given you all I have. But don't worry, it'll last you until they fall upon us. And when that happens, being hungry will be the least of your worries."

"In that case, I thank you, Kikeh."

Gabriel's calm resignation surprised the fat man once again, and his small, black eyes grew wider.

"Stop thanking me the whole time. It bothers me more than if you were haranguing me. Here, take this."

He drew a packet from his filthy doublet and handed it to Gabriel.

It contained a thick slice of ham wrapped in pork rind. The smell of fat stoked Gabriel's hunger. He looked up at the jailer's back as he headed toward the cell door.

"You're going to thank me again, aren't you," he grumbled.

"No. I'm only going to pray that your life be spared."

Kikeh stopped short, still with his back to Gabriel.

"I was told that you don't believe in God, Don Gabriel."

"I believe in him enough to pray for you, friend."

The door closed. Gabriel remained still, transfixed.

He felt fear rising up through his limbs, and he held the slice of ham between his hands as he murmured something under his breath.

Perhaps even a prayer.

THREE

Cuzco, May 6, 1536

The jailer had it wrong.

The Inca warriors didn't attack after all. Not that day, nor the next, nor the day after that.

They remained on the slopes and hilltops. Their numbers swelled continually until they covered the entire plain to the south of the city. At night, the thousands of fires they lit ringed Cuzco like jewels in the night. But they had stopped their shouting, and their drums had fallen silent. And this silence, this waiting, weighed perhaps even more heavily on the Spaniards than the cacophony that had preceded it, and every now and then Gabriel heard a demented bawl from someone who could no longer stand the wait.

Indeed, after two days of silence, he himself began to grow impatient for battle. But at least the pause permitted him to recuperate and gather his strength a little, despite the minimal amount of food that he cautiously allowed himself each day.

Because he was worried that Gonzalo's henchmen might profit from the general confusion and come and cut his throat on the sly, he slept only in short spells. He spent his time fashioning himself a crude weapon: He carefully broke the water jug, making sure to preserve a long, thick shard still attached to the handle. He spent hours mechanically sharpening it against the stone wall. But this repetitive activity left his spirit empty, and his thoughts wandered constantly to Anamaya.

He was no longer haunted by nightmares, but he still dreamed of his beloved's face, of the unique scent of her skin. Anamaya's musical laugh echoed around his head like a song he couldn't stop humming. He closed his eyes every now and then as he polished the increasingly sharp shard and imagined that he was in fact caressing the nape of his beloved's neck or stroking the small of her back.

How happy they might be at this very moment, he thought, had she fled with him away from this chaos to the shores of Titicaca.

But alas, as soon as he opened his eyes again, his dream was chased away by reality, by the irons bruising his leg, by the straw mattress rotting in the corner beneath the cold dagger of light passing through the window set in the thick walls of his prison.

Anamaya was far away in the mountains. She was the living hope of a people to which he, Gabriel Montelucar y Flores, a Stranger come from afar to steal their peace and their destiny, could never belong. The Incas' very survival depended on their taking Cuzco, on their destroying all the Spaniards without exception and regaining the power that they had given away. Gabriel would have to die along with the rest of his compatriots. Soon he would be nothing more than a memory to her, one that Manco and the influential priest Villa Oma would gradually succeed in erasing from her mind.

How had he ever been able to believe even for a moment that he could have done differently, that he could have simply held her hand as one does an ordinary woman's and, thus joined to her, pursued happiness?

If God exists, then he was punishing Gabriel for his delusion, and if he doesn't, then Gabriel was simply paying the price of his own naïveté.

Gabriel scratched his skin until he drew blood to prevent himself from wandering into the useless mire of his doubts.

The shard that he had painstakingly polished for the last two days now appeared to him as the most ridiculous, grotesque piece of work ever undertaken. The forgotten hole into which he had been thrown was a far worse fate than having his throat cut. What use had he for a weapon? The Pizarros wouldn't even bother to stick him with a blade. All they had to do was totally forget about him, let him succumb to hunger and thirst, abandon him to the fury of the Indian warriors, and their aim would be accomplished.

Enraged, Gabriel hurled the shard against the cell wall. It shattered and became dust once again.

Gabriel stood stock still for a moment, shocked by his own action.

Then he rolled himself up into a ball, wrapped his chain around himself like a blanket, and sought the oblivion of sleep, his final refuge.

A trifling noise woke him. He recognized the creaking; someone was surreptitiously trying to lift the heavy wooden block that barred his cell door.

Instinctively, he propped himself up on his arms. He silently picked up the links of his chain and held them in his fist like a flail. His earlier resignation had evaporated in his slumber, and he felt the urge to fight permeate his body. Pride dictated that he defend himself with enough fury to destroy his attackers.

It was so dark that he couldn't see the door open, but he did feel a slight movement in the air. He couldn't know how many they were. Crouching with his back flush against the wall, he forced himself to breathe slowly, deliberately, and tried not to think about the fact that he was living his last moments.

Suddenly he heard the squeak of someone opening the shutter of a dark lantern. The yellow light of a tallow candle traveled across the walls before settling on him. When its beam reached his face, the light shuddered, as though the person holding the lantern had started with shock.

"Gabriel!" exclaimed the person in a low hushed voice, a voice that Gabriel nevertheless recognized even before he made out the fringe of the long cowl beneath the lamp. "Gabriel, don't be frightened, it's only me."

"Bartholomew! Brother Bartholomew!"

"Dear friend," whispered Bartholomew, his smile evident in his voice.

The monk, to banish any lingering doubt, thrust his strange, joined fingers into the scanty beam of the dark lamp.

"God's blood!" exclaimed Gabriel. "You are the last person I expected to see here tonight!"

"Which is why I take care to show myself in the light before you assault me."

Gabriel laughed and let go of his chain.

"A wise move!"

But when the monk offered him a hug, Gabriel pushed him away saying, "It pains me to forgo your embrace, but I think it's best that we don't."

Bartholomew slowly ran the light over Gabriel, examining him from head to toe.

"My poor, poor friend. What a state they have left you in."

"Yes. No doubt I foul the air twenty leagues from here!"

"Here, take the lamp. Shine it on me," whispered Bartholomew. "I've something outside that will make you human again."

He returned a moment later carrying a large basket.

"Some things to eat your fill of, Gabriel," said the monk, setting the basket at Gabriel's feet, "and also water, enough even to wash yourself with, as well as a few salves to treat your cuts and bruises."

"Why, there's enough to wait out a siege. . . ."

"You've never spoken a truer word! But we'll talk about that later. First, eat until your hunger is broken."

Gabriel shook his head with feeling.

"Last night, I had resigned myself to dying alone, like a dog, with no one to prevent the vermin from picking my bones clean. I thought that the last human face I would see in this vile world would be the pot-bellied jailer's—who isn't the worst of men, by the way, although far removed from Erasmus and Socrates. And now, here you are! And I feel strong enough to pull this chain from the wall with only my bare hands!"

"God indulges us in his own ways, Gabriel, even if you choose not to notice," quipped Bartholomew, offering him a waterskin full to bursting. "And now it seems to me that it would be in both our interests were you to wash yourself a little. But I regret that I am so indifferent to clothes that I didn't think to bring you something to replace those rags!"

"Don Hernando came to tell me about your return and subsequent arrest," explained Bartholomew while Gabriel tore roasted llama meat from the bone with his teeth.

"'Brother,' he said to me in the sweetest voice, 'that man deserves nothing less than death. And I'm sure that death is what he will shortly receive. Nonetheless, we know that a hasty verdict offends Christian charity. So we're going to indulge that bastard with a trial. And you're the only person here that I can think of who is morally irreproachable enough to conduct it,' he said, and that is how he made me your judge."

Bartholomew chortled quietly as Gabriel gulped down water and slaked his thirst. The monk went on.

"Don Hernando returned from Spain more conniving than ever. He found himself in an extremely uncomfortable position in Toledo. The Pizarros' methods have shocked a great number of people in court. The Queen and her suite in particular were especially moved by the story of Atahualpa's end."

"I should hope so!"

"Oh, you know, it didn't result in much. He was still awarded the order of Santiago even though you and I both would have preferred to see him sent to rot in the prison where we met."

They both smiled at the memory.

"So I asked to interrogate you immediately," continued Bartholomew. "They tried to dissuade me, using the pretext that you had to be given some time alone to repent. That told me that they had no doubt caused you dreadful harm."

"And what exactly do I stand accused of?"

"The attempted assassination of Gonzalo. But also of treason, for having disobeyed the Governor's order to follow Almagro's expedition to the south."

"Oh yes, that fine mission! It consisted of helplessly watching Almagro wreak horror everywhere he went. You cannot imagine what I witnessed in the south, Bartholomew. You say that the court in Spain was distressed by Atahualpa's execution? They would vomit like sick dogs if they could see what my eyes saw week after week! The gallows birds following as Almagro raped and massacred the Indians as though they were nothing more than rats. Children, the old, women, the sick . . . those bastards spared no one. I watched them decapitate corpses. For hundreds of leagues, they burned and pillaged every village they came across."

"Yes, I've heard tell about it."

"I was there. And there was nothing I could do. When I tried to protest, Almagro simply aimed a crossbow at me. Try to imagine what it's like to spend day after day amid all that horror, without being able to stop it or even ease the suffering. Imagine the shame of being taken for a murderer, to be cut from the same cloth as those dregs of humanity now sweeping through the south, rabid in their hunger for gold!"

"Why are you saying that? You did nothing."

"Exactly. I didn't help spread the horror, but I didn't stop it either, which is just as bad. Henceforth, the peoples of this land will see Spaniards as all the same."

Gabriel vehemently pointed at the red glow of the Inca fires through the dormer window.

"For the thousands of warriors surrounding us, howling at the tops of those hills, there are no longer any good Strangers or bad Strangers. In their eyes, we all deserve to be annihilated. This is what Hernando's diplomacy has brought upon us; this is what giving free rein to Almagro and hellhounds like Gonzalo has caused."

"Well, I see that you omit at least the Governor from your list," said Bartholomew with an appeasing gesture.

Gabriel uttered an acerbic growl and rose to his feet. He walked over to the dormer window to breathe a little fresh air, pulling his chain behind him.

"Don Francisco is no brute," he conceded, "but he knows how to turn a blind eye when it suits him. And it often suits him."

The first light of dawn was emerging on the eastern horizon, although barely discernible for all the Inca fires illuminating the sky. Thousands of fires set the surrounding hills aglow, as they did every night, and their light reached even unto the walls of Cuzco. Gabriel caught glimpses of silhouettes moving about here and there.

"I think that your trial will be forgotten," remarked Bartholomew, after having joined Gabriel at the window. "I'm going to help you escape, Gabriel. I'm going now to find some tool to break your chain with. In all the confusion presently gripping the city, no one will notice your escape."

"Thank you, Brother Bartholomew. But please don't harbor any illusions. Whether locked up in here or free in the city, we're all doomed to the same fate now. Our hour of judgment is upon us."

Both men stood in silence for a moment, spellbound by the river of flames linking the hills together.

"There're maybe two hundred thousand of them," murmured Bartholomew suddenly. "One has to wonder what they're waiting for."

"They're simply waiting until we have no chance of resisting them."

"Or until we all starve to death. There is less and less food. I had to steal what I brought you tonight, and you won't see a basket as full as that again. Today, a knight called Mejía was absolutely determined to charge out of here and cut himself a passage through to the plain. He was immediately unhorsed. They decapitated him, then sliced clean through his horse's hocks."

"What defenses has Hernando ordered?"

"He plans to assemble the cavalrymen and charge the enemy, to try to breach the wall of Incas and fetch reinforcements."

"How many horses does he have?"

"There are about sixty in the city."

"What madness."

Bartholomew gave him a piercing look. Since Gabriel said nothing further, he asked, "Why do you say that?"

"Oh, one only has to give it some thought. But milord Hernando Pizarro is too convinced that he faces mere savages, and so he deigns not to think. I know a little of their war chiefs. They are very well aware of how we fight, and they know our weaknesses. They're waiting for exactly that, a grouped charge, still to this day our one and only military tactic."

"Perhaps because it has until this day always succeeded."

"It won't this time. The Incas will let the cavalry pass without really trying to stop them. At the most, they'll offer some feigned combat. And what will happen in the meantime? Two or at most three hundred Spaniards will be left in Cuzco to face a hundred thousand Indians with nothing better to defend themselves than their swords and their wits. The battle won't last a day, Bartholomew. Manco's men are formidable in hand-to-hand combat. Their sling stones pierce the thickest armor and shatter our swords. I tell you, the miracle that was Cajamarca will not happen again!"

"What other solution is there?"

"To make peace! To restore to Manco all his Royal rights, and to return all the gold stolen from him. But that will never happen, and in any case it's too late. The Incas won't want to parley. Why would they, when they can crush us like ants?"

Bartholomew nodded in agreement. But his voice changed in tone slightly. "Don Hernando pretends to believe that you have become Manco's agent, his spy, and that you helped him escape, and helped organize this siege. . . ."

". . . And that I've hidden away an enormous statue made of solid gold, not to mention an Inca princess said to be the gold statue's wife," interrupted Gabriel with a bitter snarl.

"It's true that the oddest rumors are starting to spread about you," sighed Bartholomew. "But then, seeing that you returned here disguised as an Indian peasant, as well as your violent attack . . . Gonzalo has had a nasty limp ever since, and you well and truly shattered the skull of one of his best friends. Why were you so savage?"

Bartholomew's demeanor grew suddenly distant, and the monk displayed the detached curiosity that so often in the past Gabriel had suspected hid dark intentions.

"Is this the beginning of the judge's interrogation?"

"Gabriel!"

"At this late hour, I can confess everything to you with total candor, Bartholomew. My greatest regret is having missed my mark. My club should have crushed Gonzalo's head, not his companion's. For that, I will gladly accept my punishment."

"I fear I still cannot fathom the reasons for your hatred, dear friend."

Gabriel hesitated. Outside, above the hills, the sky grew paler and paler. The Inca warriors seemed more active than usual.

"More than a year ago now, while I was far away, Gonzalo tried to rape Anamaya," he said in a muted voice. "That was the infamy that caused Manco to flee. He realized that neither of them was safe in

Cuzco. Gonzalo, of course, didn't boast about this particular exploit of his. You couldn't have known."

"Dear God!"

"Gonzalo, unfortunately, caught Manco and flung him in irons. As for Anamaya, she managed to escape with her friend the dwarf. She hid in the mountains and organized the rebellion. Her first aim was to free Manco, who was suffering the worst humiliations here. I knew none of this until later. Then, when I learned that Manco was being kept prisoner by that madman Gonzalo, I assumed that Anamaya was also in his hands. The mere thought was unbearable. I immediately left Almagro's expedition, where in any case I'd had my fill of atrocities . . ."

"I understand, I understand," said Bartholomew, placing his hand on Gabriel's shoulder. His voice was warm and friendly once again.

Gabriel moved away from the dormer window and, in a few succinct words, described to the monk how he had tried to cross the salt pan to reach Cuzco as quickly as possible, how his horse had died, and how he himself had only been saved at the final hour by Katari, the Master of the Stone.

"I was dead, and he brought me back to life. Literally."

"Katari . . ." murmured Bartholomew, moved, "ever since I met him, I have always believed that that man would be consecrated as a saint were he one of us. It is as though he has some prevision into our mysteries. He taught me my first words in Quechua, and I his first in Spanish. Merely gazing upon him, I realized that he was that rare thing, a pure soul. I will gladly meet with him again, if it's God's will."

"Ah!" exclaimed Gabriel, hardly listening to the monk at all, "I came to in the most beautiful place in the world! An enormous lake, almost a sea, which the locals call Titicaca. The surrounding mountains are the highest that one can imagine, they wear a permanent blanket of snow and, on certain days, their peaks reflect on the surface of the lake, as still and pure as a mirror. And yet, the climate is as mild as that of Cádiz! The people there are peaceful and kind. I daydreamed of returning there to live with Anamaya. I dreamed of fleeing there with her. . . ."

He fell silent. The nightmare that he had lived over the past few days returned to the forefront of his mind like a punch to the gut. He wished that he could speak frankly to Bartholomew about it, but something held him back. Perhaps his pride wouldn't allow him to admit that he dreamed of being an animal. So he confined himself to describing his arrival in Calca, and how Manco's warriors were already gathering from the farthest reaches of the Empire of the Four Cardinal Directions.

"It was there that she declared her love for me, but also told me that it was impossible for us to remain together, for a war was about to erupt. To tell the truth, Bartholomew, what she told me with her kind words and kisses was that, in her eyes, I was different from the other Strangers, and that . . ."

"Gabriel!" exclaimed Bartholomew, "God's blood, Gabriel, look! Almighty God . . ."

Gabriel stopped short, then bounded for the window, his chain clinking loudly behind him. He unwittingly uttered a cry of amazement.

In the pale glow of dawn, he saw that the fires had come down from the hills, as though the Indian warriors' river of fire had broken its banks. Suddenly the piercing sound of horns erupted, causing the air to shiver, and immediately after horrendous cries rose up into the sky.

"They're attacking," murmured Bartholomew blankly.

"Look up!" said Gabriel. "Look at the sky!"

A thick cloud of arrows streaked across the sky, so densely packed that it seemed like a giant blanket lifted from the ground. The two men heard terrified cries in Spanish rise up from the alleys nearby and saw the thousands of arrows whistle toward the ground. Bartholomew instinctively retreated from the window. But the archers were too far, and the *cancha* in which the prison was located was still out of their range. Gabriel was now oblivious to the cries. He watched in a daze as the blanket of death came down from the sky, covering the roofs. The thousands of arrows making impact made a dull, drawn-out, tearing sound, clearly audible despite the panicked Spanish cries. Drums began rolling, replacing the searing sound of horns.

"I must go and join Hernando," said Bartholomew.

Gabriel caught him by the arm and said, "Wait a moment. It's too dangerous. Something is about to happen. . . ."

He had barely finished his sentence when an odd, throbbing sound thickened the air, echoing even into their chest cavities, as though some god was trying to drown out the cries and agonized moans of those wounded by arrows. Yet they could see nothing.

"Stones."

Indeed, a storm of sling stones now succeeded the shower of arrows. They were flung not from the distant hills but from the great fortress of Sacsayhuaman overlooking Cuzco, in the immediate vicinity of the city's houses and alleys. The stones flew much farther than the arrows. Gabriel and Bartholomew listened silently to the dull thudding as they came hurtling down against the roofs and walls. The sound increased in loudness, indicating a greater volume of stones being launched. There were so many now that some crashed into one another in midair. The storm lasted for what seemed like an eternity. The Spaniards' terrified cries grew louder, and the war cries from the hills increased as though in response. Another salvo of arrows came whistling down, now mixing with the stones, creating a deadly storm. It felt as though the sky were literally crashing down on Cuzco, as though the firmament were at last acting to exterminate all the living, engulfing life with a wicked determination that would only end when nothing remained but motionless piles of corpses.

"I must go!" cried Bartholomew.

"Then carry this over you," exclaimed Gabriel, shaking all the contents out of the basket and placing it upside down on the monk's head. "It will offer you some protection."

Bartholomew opened the door, then froze.

"Dear God," he murmured, making the sign of the cross.

Smoke was already rising from a dozen of Cuzco's thatched roofs. Flames began bursting upward here and there, as though some invisible hand were stoking them.

"The sling stones," explained Gabriel, "that's what they were for. The sling stones are setting the thatch alight."

"They're going to burn the entire city!" cried Bartholomew.

Gabriel yanked on his chain, enraged.

"Find someone to release me from this damned chain!"

"Don't worry, I won't leave you here to burn alive."

The monk quickly embraced him.

"Do you promise me that?"

Despite the quick nod from the monk before he disappeared into the smoke, Gabriel doubted that he would ever see him again.

The wind fanned the flames well into the night. The entire city had become an enormous pyre. Only a few of the houses around the great square were spared, either because they were out of the fire's reach or because of the courage of the Indian allies, who doused the fires with water at the risk of their own lives.

At dawn, the smoke had become so thick that at times it was impossible to see a wall or alley that lay just ahead. The acrid smoke penetrated lungs like poison, tearing them apart. Men fell to their knees, unable even to cry out in pain, so little breath did they have left. All the horses were terrified. They snorted furiously, shuddered at their withers, and rolled their bloodshot eyes, their nostrils quivering and their chops trembling. A few bit their masters, others neighed with terror.

The storm of arrows and stones never relented, whistling through the smoke. They crashed into walls or thudded into the flesh of the abandoned wounded. Their suffering didn't last long.

Inca warriors, their mouths masked with cotton, and using the thick smoke as cover, slipped silently into the narrow roads on the edges of the city. There, they erected barricades, laid down tree trunks, and set up palisades that they had built in advance. They blocked all the exits from the city one by one, making sure that the barricades were too high for horses to clear.

At Villa Oma's orders, small groups of Incas penetrated even farther into the city. They finished off any wounded they came across, then scaled the walls of the *canchas* burned to cinders. Canary women and children, the terrified whites of their eyes piercing through their blackened faces, begged them for mercy. But Manco's men spared no one.

For the first time, the Incas were fighting with the taste of victory in their mouths.

"I've waited a long time to see this," gloated Villa Oma, giving Anamaya and Manco a smile—a very rare thing from him. "Emperor, it is truly a great joy for me to be able to at last present this battle to you. I hope that your father the Sun and all your ancestors are celebrating as we are."

They were sitting on the highest tower of the sun fortress, Sacsayhuaman. Cuzco revealed itself before them in the gathering light of dawn, a massive, unbroken pyre. Warriors whipped their slingshots around unflaggingly, hurling stones that they had placed in their campfires the night before, then removed and wrapped in cotton. The friction of the air sufficed to ignite the cotton as the red hot stones flew through the air. When the projectiles hurtled into the roofs of Cuzco, the very dry *ichu* took only a moment to ignite.

Today, all the Ancestors of the Other World were with Manco. The wind picked up again before night had lifted, quickly fanning the blaze. The flames grew and grew, stretching to the sky and writhing like giant snakes slipping from roof to roof. Then all the *canchas* of upper Cuzco caught alight at once, as though the fire had become liquid.

The warriors unleashed another volley of stones. Thousands of stones whistled over the flames onto the roofs of lower Cuzco, which promptly ignited like a cornfield at the end of a very dry summer. The fire jumped across the alleys, the gardens and courtyards, sparing nothing.

With his hands resting on a stone wall as broad as road, Manco laughed gleefully.

"Look, Anamaya! Look at them run like rats, our almighty Strangers! Don't they remind you of insects when they sense death singeing their antennae?"

Anamaya nodded in agreement. Manco's analogy was apt. The Spaniards and the few Indians who remained loyal to them, including Canaries, Huancas, and members of other nations, were running in every direction in total disorder, their only purpose being to avoid the beams collapsing beneath the flaming roofs. But as soon as they appeared out in the open, safe from the flames, a blizzard of sling stones and arrows would fall upon them. Anamaya could already make out a great many corpses, as well as the crawling bodies of dozens of wounded whom no one dared to rescue.

The Spanish horsemen were gathering in the great square, which was the only place that was safe from both the fire and the barrage of stones and arrows, for it was too far from the towers of the Sacsayhuaman fortress. Anamaya tried to pick out Gabriel's blond hair amid all the movement of those distant, twitchy silhouettes. But the Strangers were too closely packed one against the other, and in any case their faces were hidden by their morions. Others now arrived on the square, screaming and protecting themselves as best they could by placing their shields above their heads.

"What do you think, *Coya Camaquen?*" asked Manco, looking at her closely with an amused look on his face. He knew exactly what she was feeling.

"I think that it is a momentous battle and, like all battles, it is a terrible thing."

"We are going to win," said Villa Oma indignantly, "and you don't seem pleased."

"We haven't won yet," replied Anamaya quietly. "At the moment, all we've destroyed is Cuzco, *our* Cuzco, and not the Strangers."

Her remark cut Villa Oma to the quick. He swept his hand angrily out before him, indicating the mass of Inca troops surrounding Cuzco.

"Look out there in the plain, *Coya Camaquen.* Look at our warriors covering the hills. An ant couldn't get past them. Do you really think that they can be defeated?"

"For the moment, all our warriors are outside the city, while the Strangers remain inside it."

"It will not last. I shall give the order shortly. Our troops will soon sweep into the streets of Cuzco. Take a good look at the Strangers over there on the square! By this evening, not one of them will remain alive."

Villa Oma was almost shouting. Anamaya said nothing. She knew what the old Sage, drunk with violence, was inferring. She tightened her lips to prevent herself from asking the question that had been burning them ever since Gabriel and she had separated at Calca. If Gabriel were indeed the Puma, then what would happen if he died?

"Anamaya's right," said Manco dryly, snapping her out of her reverie. "I am pleased by what you show me, Villa Oma. But it is still too early to celebrate."

"Then wait for this evening!" growled Villa Oma with a hint of disdain. "Look! Look over there. . . ."

He pointed at the first wave of warriors entering the streets and erecting barriers to prevent the Strangers from fleeing on their horses.

"No!" ordered Manco firmly. "No, we shall not enter the city tonight. It's still too early. More warriors will soon arrive from Quito. When they do, we shall attack . . . and win."

"But my Lord! There are already two hundred thousand of us, whereas there are only two hundred of them!"

"I said no, Villa Oma. We must continue to weaken them. We must cut the water canals to the great square. We must starve them and make their every moment unbearable, until they try to break out into the plain, which you've flooded so their horses will be useless. They will fall into our hands, and we will sacrifice their riders to Inti. Fear, Villa Oma! They must die of fear!"

Villa Oma's face twisted with rage. But he said nothing. In silence, he watched the city burn, watched the men scurrying and screaming through its streets. Anamaya made out his lips trembling and his fists clenching as though involuntarily. The priest used all his strength to hold himself back from striking Manco.

"Villa Oma . . ." she began in a conciliatory tone.

"You shouldn't be here, *Coya Camaquen!*" squawked the Sage with vicious irony. "If the Strangers are indeed as dangerous as Manco claims, you are putting yourself at grave risk by remaining here on this tower. You must return to Calca immediately."

Anamaya turned her back to him and allowed her blue gaze to lose itself in the sky above the rising smoke and flames. She could at last allow her heart to feel the terrible anxiety that she had been suppressing.

Yes, she was trembling for Gabriel!

Yes, she hoped with all her strength and from the depths of her soul that he, and he alone, would survive. And not only because he was the Puma foreseen by the great Huayna Capac, but because he was the man she loved, and to live without him was not living at all.

FOUR

Cuzco, May 1536

As helpless as a dog at the end of its chain, Gabriel listened to the death cries of the victims outside and watched the city burn. When the smoke reached his window, he retreated back into his cell. He tore up what remained of the rags of his tunic and wrapped them around his face. He suffered terrible coughing fits, bent double. He had long since given up hope of seeing either the jailer or brother Bartholomew again.

Indeed, hope had left him some time ago, and all he thought about now was being able to breathe and surviving.

Half of Cuzco was already ablaze when he heard the much-feared thuds: The sling stones were now reaching the roof of his prison. The warriors were now within range. The dull sound repeated itself perhaps ten times. Ten volleys. And then a stone pierced through the thatch *ichu* of the roof and landed close by him.

Almost immediately, thin plumes of brown smoke began to rise from the log beams supporting the roof. A little flame sputtered to life and jerked about, growing. Like a golden snake, it reached the peak of the roof, zigzagged hesitantly for a moment, then slithered down the opposite side and ran along the walls. Within a minute, countless other flames were born, joining the first.

Then, all of a sudden, the thatch burst into flames.

Before Gabriel had a chance to react, the flames came roaring down from above him, as though they were trying to caress the ground. They forced him onto his knees. In only a few seconds, the heat became unbearable.

Gabriel cursed his chain, cursed Hernando and all the Pizarro brothers. He lay down flat on his stomach, trying to protect his face, but the heat burning his back was excruciating.

Growling like a wild animal, he saw entire sections of burning thatch collapse, sending sparks in all directions on impact. The flames doubled in size, but were now being drawn to the air outside, and they took the smoke with them. Gabriel thought of the water that Bartholomew had brought him.

He crawled along the ground, braving the heat that burned off all the hairs on his hands. He tore the leather strap holding the wood cork out of the first waterskin with his teeth and splashed the water all over his face and shoulders. He drenched his entire body with water until every skin was empty but one. The cold shock was so extreme and brief that it left him trembling, his teeth chattering. He was still just conscious enough to catch a glimpse of the thatch giving way directly above him. His movement limited by his chain, he dodged the burning thatch as it fell as best he could and curled up at the foot of a wall.

And then suddenly, as quickly as it had ignited, the fire went out.

Only a few flames continued to lick around the beams overhead, disturbed by a wind that carried away the smoke in tortured spirals. Cool air managed to find its way through the burning walls.

His arms and hands in agony, Gabriel grabbed the remaining waterskin and gave in to the urge to drink and splash more water on himself. It was the last of his water, but too bad.

Exhausted from fear, he stretched out on the ground and gave thanks for the little bit of coolness that the wind bestowed upon him.

Now the smoke rose up above Cuzco's walls, veiling the sky like a storm at twilight. The smoke was like a physical manifestation of all the cries for help, all the death moans, all the sounds of death and destruction that rose from the city.

Gabriel closed his aching eyes and ran his tongue, as dry as old leather, along his blistered lips.

He wondered how many of the Spaniards were still alive.

He felt as though he already had one foot in the kingdom of the dead.

That night, like those that had preceded it, the air was thick with the wails of trumpets, war chants, and the furious insults shouted down at the city by a hundred thousand Inca warriors. The terrible cacophony echoed beneath the incandescent sky and pierced through smoke as thick as storm clouds, as though the Devil himself had extended the canopy of hell over Cuzco.

Exhausted and aching from head to toe, Gabriel dozed for a long while, hoping to find respite in the stupor of sleep.

A cry that stood out from the rest made him open his eyes.

He was unsure of what he saw before him. Three faceless silhouettes stood stiffly on the wall above. He could make out only their torsos and limbs, and he could see their spears and clubs.

Nothing moved for a moment, and he thought that perhaps he was still asleep, lost in a nightmare. Then another cry shot out of the shadows. One of the silhouettes raised its arm, and threw something at him. A stone, a large stone with a rope attached! It bounced next to Gabriel's leg, and immediately he stood and shouted, "I am not your enemy!"

The three men hesitated, surprised at hearing their own language.

"I am not your enemy! I am with the *Coya Camaquen!*" cried Gabriel.

He instantly sensed the Inca warriors' hesitation. One of them said something incomprehensible, then waved his arms at him. Gabriel repeated, "I am not your enemy!"

He yanked on his chain to show how he was bound. One of the men gesticulated and spoke some words that Gabriel still couldn't understand. Another Indian nervously shook the rope so that the stone attached to its end rolled between the Spaniard's legs.

Gabriel instinctively grabbed the rope and pulled it toward him. One of the warriors, meanwhile, let out a cry. The other two dodged quickly aside, and the rope went limp in Gabriel's hands. One of the men on the wall collapsed as his companions cried out, already twirling their slingshots. The warrior fell like a sack onto the floor of the prison cell.

When Gabriel looked up again, the two warriors had bolted into the ocher night. The man who had fallen next to him was already dead, a quarrel from a crossbow so deeply embedded in his chest that only its end was still visible.

But Gabriel hadn't the time to be surprised. His cell door creaked open and an indistinguishable form, like some black ghost, slipped into his roofless cell, holding a small cranequin* crossbow in his hand.

Gabriel stepped back, the chain clicking between his legs. His visitor let out an irreverent laugh.

"Well now, my friend, you don't recognize me?" said an instantly recognizable voice.

Gabriel was tongue-tied with surprise. The silhouette took two cautious steps forward.

"*Hola*, Gabriel! Have they torn out your tongue already?"

"Sebastian . . . Sebastian!"

"Here at your service, your Grace!"

His tall, proud, black companion, a former slave, drew nearer and carefully set his crossbow on the ground. Then he candidly embraced Gabriel. He was no more concerned with sullying himself than Gabriel was. His only clothing was a sort of leather skirt to which was attached his quiver of arrows and a long dagger. He was otherwise completely naked, his black skin spattered with gray beads of sweat mixed with soot.

"Sebastian, disguised as the Devil!" cried Gabriel with relief.

A broad grin of white teeth gleamed through the haze.

"This is the best dress possible, given the present situation. For once my black skin is an asset, and I'm making the most of it!"

Gabriel laughed so heartily that it was as though he had just gulped down cool, fresh water. Sebastian prodded the Inca warrior's corpse with his foot and said, "Well and truly dead. I arrived just in time, didn't I?"

"How did you know I was here?"

"Brother Bartholomew, of course. He told me that I'd find you stuck here like a rat. It took me some time to make it, because I had to get my hands on this. . . ."

Sebastian pulled a steel awl and a little hammer from his leather skirt.

---

cranequin: a crossbow fitted with a removable windlass or rack-and-pinion winding mechanism.

"Your fat jailer friend proved reluctant to be found. Still, he's a cheerful fellow, the kind of man I like. He confided in me that he had to father six children with six different Indian girls before one of them gave him a son. In any case, he had this damned awl, which is the only way to break your irons. Without it, all I could do is rip out the chain from the floor, and you'd have to carry it about with you."

Sebastian set about breaking the irons as he spoke, setting the awl against the shackle that held the irons to the chain and striking it with small, precise blows with his hammer.

"Don't move, I'll be finished in a moment. Watch the walls and make sure that our Inca friends don't return to surprise us with their company!"

The tinkling sound of his irons opening was, for Gabriel, more precious than the chinking sound of gold. As soon as they were off, he immediately breathed easier.

"There, you're free," said Sebastian, affectionately taking Gabriel by the wrist.

"Sweet Jesus, I was sure that I was going to roast like a chicken between these walls," said Gabriel, massaging his ankles, which suddenly felt as though they were being pricked by a thousand needles. "I am deeply grateful to you, Sebastian."

"By God, you smell like roasted flesh!" said Sebastian with an amused grimace. "Come, we must go. But first . . ."

He drew his dagger and kneeled down beside the dead warrior. Without flinching, he plunged the blade into the corpse's chest.

". . . I must take back my arrow," he explained. "It's too valuable, we've not enough munitions to waste."

"Where are Hernando and the others?" asked Gabriel, avoiding looking at what Sebastian was doing.

"In the *cancha* on the great square. It didn't burn. Don Hernando placed slaves on the roof to put out fires as they ignited. A dozen were killed, but now we're all sheltered there, and the horses too. There, I'm finished."

Without showing the slightest emotion, Sebastian wiped the blood off the short arrow with the dead man's tunic.

"Come, I'll lead you," chuckled Sebastian. "I look forward to seeing the surprise on their faces when they see you alive and walking about!"

"Like this, in these rags?"

Sebastian's hearty laugh rung out over the cacophony of the city under siege.

"No no, my Lord! I've something far more proper than that!"

To Gabriel's astonishment, Sebastian didn't take the shortest, most direct route back to the great square. Quite the opposite: In total silence, and with feline agility, he took the small alleys around the square, smoke still rising from the burned-out roofs of the houses lining them. They came out onto a road that Gabriel recognized as the one leading to the palace of Hatun Cancha. Sebastian stopped before a door made of guanaco skin and pushed it open. The skin was still fresh enough to have survived the blaze.

"Wait in here a moment," whispered Sebastian, closing the door behind him. "Don't go anywhere, I'll be right back."

Sebastian disappeared into the smoke. Gabriel didn't recognize the *cancha*. Like most of the other buildings in the city, its roof had gone. Its masonry, however, seemed to have survived well and was decorated in the Spanish manner. Recently built walls covered in dun-colored roughcast joined the long Inca walls, so that the space was surrounded by an unbroken barrier. Doors and windows had been fitted, real European doors and windows, giving the room a familiar feel.

"All's well," whispered Sebastian when he returned. "I just wanted to check that we have no unwelcome visitors."

"Where are we?" asked Gabriel.

Sebastian's laugh was as tinkling and as clear as a child's.

"Ho! Where are we! Why, we're in my palace, of course!"

"This is yours?"

"Have you forgotten that I'm rich? A true Croesus!"

Gabriel shook his head, smiling wryly. He looked at Sebastian, almost naked and holding a crossbow, and it was hard to imagine him as the owner of this palace.

"If the truth be told, I'd forgotten. And I'd forgotten precisely *how* rich you've become . . . what a house!"

"Oh, it's much better when you see it with its roof and furniture," grumbled Sebastian, leading him in. "Come, let's not stay here."

There was a smell of stale smoke in the room they entered, a smell of soot and ash. Of the wooden furniture, there remained only the leather seats of the chairs, and they were all cracked, as well as a few corner irons from a table and a candelabra's dented base.

"What a waste!" lamented Sebastian.

He pushed aside the charred debris of a bed and a carpet of *mantas* stitched together. The broad flagstones underneath weren't particularly exceptional. But before Gabriel had a chance to express his surprise, Sebastian wedged an iron bar between two flagstones and levered one, and then two more, open. By the faint light of the stars and a crescent moon that was at last finding its way through the banks of smoke, Gabriel made out a heavy wooden trapdoor.

"Lend a hand," said Sebastian, "it's as heavy as three sawhorses."

The trapdoor seemed to open into a well of darkness. Still, Sebastian made his way in. He felt his way through the darkness until he reached the bars of a wooden stepladder. He felt around with his hand until he found a piece of candle and a lighter.

"We'd better go quickly. There's no reason to let anyone see us!"

A few moments later Gabriel found himself absolutely flabbergasted. His evident surprise gave Sebastian a feeling of deep satisfaction. They were in a cellar, an underground space that was both a comfortably appointed room and a warehouse chock full of clothes and weapons.

"Rich is what I am," chuckled Sebastian, "and in a city like Cuzco, one might well say that the political situation is far from stable. I could find myself poor again tomorrow, either by the Indians' hand or by a change of mood in the Pizarros or Almagro. And if there's one thing that I've learned from life, it's that black is what I am and black is what I shall always be. In other words, I'll always be a little bit the slave! So Prudence, God bless her, dictates that I don't reveal my treasures for all to see. You're the first person to enter here, and you see before you my insurance for hard times. In other words, what you see here in this cellar is an illusion. It doesn't exist."

While Sebastian climbed back up the ladder to close the trapdoor properly, Gabriel, amazed, took stock of the treasures accumulated around him. There were a few trunks filled with new clothes: fine shirts, doublets, split-sided stockings, and even bolts of velvet, cambric, and linen waiting for the tailor's knife. Coats of mail padded with leather and cotton hung from odd porticos. Morions were piled up in baskets. Four saddles, richly decorated with silver, sat on trestles, and a large box contained swords, daggers, and two cranequin crossbows. Gabriel couldn't see gold anywhere, but he was sure that a few ingots were doubtlessly hidden away somewhere even more discreet.

"I can't believe my eyes," he confessed, amazed.

"Come, I've something else to show you," replied Sebastian.

They went to the far end of the cellar, lighting their way with the candle. A narrow passage led into a cold room. Gabriel heard running water without being able to see it.

"Look," said Sebastian, raising the candle so that its feeble light revealed a natural pool in the stone. "It's absolutely freezing, but at least we can wash ourselves, then rest until dawn. What's more, we can barely hear the Incas here, with their cries and jeers. And tomorrow, you can choose yourself a fine tunic and a sword worthy of you. You'll cut a splendid figure!"

"Sebastian . . ."

"Now now, Gabriel, don't argue with me. It gives me boundless pleasure to be able to offer you these trifles, and I will be tenfold happier when I see the surprise on some of our friends' faces when they see you walking about tomorrow, well and truly alive, ha ha ha!"

At dawn, it was dressed in clean clothes, with new boots on his feet and a thick leather tunic and chain mail covering his shirt, a Toledo sword embellished with a silver-encrusted guard hanging against his purple velvet breeches, that Gabriel left Sebastian's house. Smoke was still rising from the city. At least half of it was in Manco's warriors' hands.

The two men had to twice return the way that they had come, running as fast as they could, dodging sling stones, before they managed to reach the Spaniards who were entrenched in the only *cancha* still standing on the great square. Thick sheets, like enormous sails, had been hung with vast quantities of rope above the courtyards, to protect them from the stones and arrows. Soldiers stood guard at the entrances, using unhinged doors as shields, and they immediately let Gabriel and Sebastian enter. Gabriel didn't recognize any of the faces and, in the jampacked interior, no one paid him any attention.

Gabriel walked among the soldiers for a while, observing their worried faces, before suddenly hearing Hernando's voice ring out. He stood between his brothers Juan and Gonzalo, facing a small troop of cavalrymen. Gabriel watched as he struck a hastily drawn map of the city spread out on a large table before him with his finger.

"According to the Canaries, all the alleys in the north of the city are now blocked by barricades between eight, ten, or even twelve *codos* high.* In any case, far too high for the horses to clear. And it's the same here, in the east, and here, in the south. They didn't waste any time. . . ."

"They're tightening the noose, I tell you! They're going to cut our throats like pigs!" cried a man, the back of his doublet burned through so that his shirt could be seen.

"Let's not turn into poltroons because a few flames singed our asses, Diego!" cried Hernando.

"The barricades in the northern part of the city are the most worrisome," intervened Juan Pizarro, "because they prevent us from charging against the Sacsayhuaman fortress. And it's from up there, unfortunately, that the Incas are barraging us day and night with slings and arrows. It is unbearable! It's as though we were mere ants being gazed upon by giants!"

Hernando, irritated by Juan's disillusioned tone, interrupted him with a gesture.

"Brother, it's no time to wax lyrical. From now on, we must be especially careful about how we move about. We can no longer leave this *cancha* in small groups, or else we'll crumble under a hail of stones and might lose our valuable horses. We'd best wait patiently and check our rage, and then mount a massive charge toward the plain in two or three

---

codo or *codo normal:* an archaic unit of measurement used in Spain before 1590, roughly equaling 56 centimeters, the distance from the elbow to the tip of the middle finger.

days. Let's be clever and play on their nerves. Let us lead them to believe that we're weak and terrified, then break through their siege, shattering their lines as though they were made of glass."

"Weak and terrified! Listening to the cries that have risen from this city over the last few days, let me tell you that we'll have no trouble convincing them of anything! We *are* weak, and they know it. How can you be so sure of your tactic, Don Hernando? There are two hundred thousand of them and two hundred of us with no more than fifty or sixty horses!"

"That's fifty more than we were with my brother the Governor at Cajamarca, my Lord del Barco! There, we defeated Atahualpa's hundred thousand warriors in a few short hours. It was God's will, and he gave us our strength. Never forget that a Spaniard with a good sword can cut down ten Indians like a peasant scythes wheat, whereas they need fifty arrows to pierce through your leather and cotton breastplates. Contrary to what my beloved brother Juan suggested a few moments ago, we are not ants, gentlemen. And so what if we're frightened? It's a good thing: It makes our balls bigger!"

Gabriel came farther into the room, a room that stank of soot, sweat, and fear, and met Bartholomew's surprised and direct gaze. Gabriel gave him an amused smile and put his fingers to his lips, motioning him to say nothing, while a young man, his eyes sunken from lack of sleep, protested vehemently.

"But Don Hernando, I don't understand! Why wait for tomorrow or the day after to charge? Why not charge right away and get ourselves out of this death hole?"

"Because we must not fail, Rojas. Given the numbers, we will have but one chance. These last few hours have made us weary. Look around: Whether horseman or foot-soldier, we all need some rest. And so do you, my dear Rodrigo, perhaps more than anyone—you can hardly stand!"

"Staying holed up in here, Don Hernando, means giving them the city! Giving them the city means condemning ourselves to die like rats! And now you suggest to us that we waste our time sleeping!"

"No, Rojas, we won't be wasting our time. We will annoy the Indians by *not* moving. They'll wear themselves out shouting and throwing their stones!"

"And what will stop them from simply coming here and burning us alive tonight? There are tens of thousands of them, Don Hernando. If they want to, they can jump over the walls into this *cancha* like fleas jump into a priest's habit!"

"But they don't want to, my Lord Barco!" growled Don Hernando, growing livid with irritation. "Don't you see that they're content to remain at the other end of the square hurling stones at us? If they weren't frightened of us, of our swords and horses, then we'd all be already dead! They're frightened of us, del Barco! There may be thousands of Indians, but they are thousands of *frightened* Indians! One charge, I tell you, one charge, with all our strength pulled together, and we will throw their rank and file into panic."

"You delude yourself, Don Hernando," interrupted Gabriel in a quiet voice. "We aren't at Cajamarca. You were there, but so was I. I have just come from outside, and I can assure you that the fear that you say overwhelms the Inca warriors doesn't exist. On the contrary, they are quite determined. Looking upon your faces, my Lords, and without wishing to offend you, I say that fear reigns in here rather than out there!"

Standing his ground, Gabriel met the astonished gazes as each man turned to face him.

"Fucking hell!" spat Gonzalo. "Who freed him?"

He took a couple of steps toward Gabriel. He was still limping from their last encounter. Juan grabbed him by the elbow to both help him stand and hold him back.

"I am as overjoyed as you are to find myself still alive," said Gabriel, glaring at him before bowing especially low, the mockery of his gesture clear to all. "Having regained my liberty by my own means, Don Hernando, I forgive you for taking it from me and I put myself at your service for the fine battle that awaits us!"

Gonzalo shoved Juan aside and reached for his sword. But Gabriel's was already out of its scabbard.

"I could fight my Lord your brother, Don Hernando, and we could well disembowel each other. But may I suggest that the moment is ill chosen. After all, you need as many men as possible and, in any case, no doubt there will be a great many opportunities to die in these coming days. Don Gonzalo might even choose to do so himself!"

"Brother!" cried Gonzalo in a hoarse voice. "You cannot allow this mongrel of a spy to join us! You cannot take on this liar and murderer! He will betray us at the first chance he gets!"

"Why don't you shut your stupid mouth, Gonzalo?" replied Gabriel. "There's nothing to betray here except honor. Or have you so little of that left to realize it?"

"Enough!" cried Hernando. "We will settle our scores later. Do not think that you have escaped justice, Montelucar!"

"It is not in my nature to flee justice, Don Hernando. It's just that one encounters it so rarely around here. I believe that I've proven that to you on more than one occasion."

"My Lords! Don Hernando! Don Gonzalo!" interrupted Bartholomew, raising his deformed hand. "This is not the time for your squabbles. Whatever grievances you hold against Don Gabriel, you must admit that he has fought the Indians as often, if not more often, than any man here. His advice must therefore be of some worth. Why not listen to him?"

"Very true," agreed Juan Pizarro, looking at Gonzalo. "Brother Bartholomew gives wise counsel. Let us leave our differences aside and join forces. Once the battle is over, and if we win it, then we will have plenty of time to study Don Gabriel's defects of character!"

When Gonzalo made to reply, Hernando sighed and stopped him with a wave of his hand, then asked, "Since you are so erudite, Montelucar, why don't you enlighten us with your wisdom: How should we deal with your Indian friends?"

"They have been observing us for years now," declared Gabriel for the benefit of all and ignoring the gibe. "They have learned what our weak points are and how to put our horses out of action. The days when they panicked whenever we charged, and when they let us cut them down like hay, are over. They know how to sling their stones so that they break our arms or our horses' legs. As for hand-to-hand combat, they are far superior to us; they are far more agile, and far more efficient. . . ."

"What grand news!" spat Gonzalo. "You're not telling us anything we don't already know."

"What they are waiting for, what they are *hoping* for," continued Gabriel, totally ignoring Gonzalo, "is that our arrogance gets the better of us and we give in to our impatience. They're hoping that hunger and thirst will drive us into the plain, at the mercy of their troops. They hope that once again we will simply throw our cavalry at them, just as you have suggested, Don Hernando, in an attempt to break their stranglehold on us and escape beyond the plain. The difference this time is that they are expecting it, my Lords! I promise you that any path we take out into the plain, we will find their resistance unusually light, until we start falling into their traps, into the pike-lined ditches that they have built, and grow confused among all the hidden obstacles that they have assembled. Go ahead with your charge as you intend, Don Hernando, and our horses will all have their legs broken before we have even brushed an Inca neck with our swords!"

Gabriel's speech had its effect. He had effectively said out loud what others had been thinking. A long, discouraged silence ensued.

"What do you propose we do, Don Gabriel?" asked Juan Pizarro eventually.

"Take the fortress!"

"You've lost your mind," laughed Gonzalo contemptuously. "It's impossible!"

"It's the only useful thing we can do. It's absolutely necessary. You know as well as I do," said Gabriel, turning toward Hernando as though Gonzalo didn't exist, "that without the fortress, there would be no siege."

"Oh really? And how do you plan to take the fortress?" sneered Gonzalo. "By jumping over its walls? Its tower and walls are at least forty-five or sixty *codos* high. Not to mention the barricades that block all its approaches."

"We can destroy it this very night."

A murmur rose from the men. Gabriel caught sight of them glancing at one another, of their heads dropping with disappointment. Even Bartholomew looked unconvinced. Gabriel raised a hand and placed it emphatically over his heart.

"My Lords, I have not lost my mind, nor do I want to lead you to certain destruction. I understand your fears. But the truth stands before us, more naked than ever. Either you die prudently or you die in battle. And it's not only that prudence is shame and fighting is glory. . . ."

"And now he sounds like my brother Francisco," said Gonzalo sarcastically to no one in particular.

". . . and it's prudence," continued Gabriel, still ignoring Gonzalo, "that will spell certain death for us, whereas attacking might well bring us victory. And a fair few of us may even survive."

In the silence that followed, all eyes once again on him, Gabriel stared Gonzalo up and down.

"Thanks to Don Gonzalo, I am indifferent to death. So this is what I suggest: Tonight, I will set fire to the barricades. I will go alone if I have to. We will see what happens."

"Brother, it's a low trick!" roared Gonzalo. "He simply wants to escape and join the savages!"

"Don Gonzalo," said Bartholomew with some feeling, "reveals how little sense he possesses. If Don Gabriel had intended to flee after having broken out of your prison, surely he wouldn't have come to tell you about it!"

An unpleasant smile broke out on Hernando's face even before Bartholomew had finished. Hernando put his hand on Gonzalo's arm.

"What you propose suits me perfectly, Don Gabriel! I am curious to see how you fare. Perhaps someone here will lend you a horse. And if any of the gentlemen here care to accompany you, then I will let five go, no more. That way it won't be too great a disaster."

"I am delighted, Don Hernando, that some sense has come to bear on your ardent desire to see me take leave of this world," said Gabriel affably.

"My dear Don Gabriel, if at last you wish to make yourself useful to your King and to bring some glory to Our Lord, who am I to stop you?"

"I'm coming with you," Sebastian assured him a moment later.

"No," said Gabriel with a smile. "Although it amused me to play off the Pizarros' bad characters, I'm far less sure of succeeding than I pretended."

"They, on the other hand, are sure of your failure, Hernando most of all. The way he looks at you, you would think that you were already a corpse."

"Bah. Let them dream."

"I'm coming with you," repeated Sebastian with a severe look, "otherwise you'll have no horse. Who else is going to dare offer you one?"

Seeing that Gabriel was about to protest further, Sebastian added, "And you're not the only one who wants to show these gentlemen what loyalty and courage is."

The two friends looked at each other for a few moments before Gabriel, moved, took Sebastian's hands in his.

"I am most indebted to you."

"You've paid your debt in advance . . . well in advance, dear Gabriel. And there's nothing I enjoy more than baiting the Devil himself in your company. Come now, I want to show you my horses."

The *cancha*'s inner courtyard, which had been carefully covered with canvas, had been transformed into stables. The thick smell of horse urine and dung assaulted their noses, and flies buzzed about in dense clouds. As soon as Sebastian and Gabriel entered, a few of the horses drew fearfully away, and a moment later all the animals began neighing, stamping the ground, and rolling their big, frightened eyes back in their heads, lurching violently into one another. They were all huddled together with no real space to speak of, and clearly they were still terrified by the fire and the fearful cries from the hills. Their fear was visible on their quivering, unkempt withers.

Sebastian whistled softly, and a superb mare, her coat white as snow, approached somewhat hesitantly, with neck bent and head forward, as though looking for a comforting hand.

"This is Itza," said Sebastian, stroking the animal's muzzle. "You see, I'm not like you, I give my horses names."

"What does Itza mean?"

"I don't know. But back when I was a slave, when I didn't dare even look a white man in the eyes, I met an old conquistador in Panama who spoke to me as a man rather than an animal. And he always said that word: *Itza, Itza,* as though it was some magic spell. I thought it suited this lady perfectly; she's lively, as quick as a flash, yet she's gentle. And here, we have Pongo."

"I'm not going to ask you about that name."

A gray gelding came out in front of the other horses, but without drawing closer to the two men. It stood back a little, watching suspiciously as Sebastian stroked the mare.

"Pongo lost his balls, but he retained his bad character. And yet, we get along well. You shall ride Itza, I'm sure that she'll take to you."

Without warning and as though on cue, the mare left Sebastian's caressing hand, turned to Gabriel, and rubbed her head on his chest.

"What did I tell you?" chuckled Sebastian.

"Do you think any other cavalrymen will come with us?" asked Gabriel in a serious tone, but not before having returned Itza's affections.

"What's important is not how many cavalrymen join us, but how many of our Indian allies. They will prove far more useful."

"No, that's not what's most important," said Gabriel, grinning.

"Oh no? Then will your lordship care to enlighten me what is?"

"It's having an African like you as a friend."

That night, after endless arguments, fifty Canary Indians and three Spanish cavalrymen volunteered to accompany Sebastian and Gabriel. The rest of the Spaniards formed a silent row and watched as the *cancha*'s door was opened. The only sounds were those of horses' hooves on the flagstones and Bartholomew's prayer, while out on the hills the Incas kept up their caterwaul.

Don Hernando was closest to the door. He smirked as he bowed slightly and said, "Good night, Don Gabriel."

"Have no doubt," said Gabriel in an equally even tone, "it will be a good night. And if you cannot find sleep, I suggest you glance over the walls. You might enjoy the spectacle."

The men made the most of the darkness and of the fact that the Incas weren't expecting anyone to leave the *cancha*, and they reached the first barricade with no difficulties. It blocked the largest of the alleys leading to the Sacsayhuaman fortress. The Incas had tied thorny faggots of wood to the log barricades, the thorns sharp enough to tear out the belly of any man or horse.

The warriors' cacophony out on the hills covered the click-clack of the horses' shoes and harnesses. The animals' necks and heads had been carefully wrapped in cloth to protect them from stones, and their hocks, cannon bones, and chests were armored with thick leather. But all the gear weighed down the horses and slowed their pace.

When they were nearly at the barricade, they suddenly heard the dirgelike tone of a *pututu* shell. A lookout had spotted them; he had sounded the alert. In the space of a second, Inca warriors swarmed out onto the tops of the burned-out walls of the surrounding *canchas*. Gabriel had just enough time to raise his shield to protect himself from the first volley of stones. He let out a berserk cry and, with his head down, urged his mare on at an irregular trot, staying close to the walls and holding his sword high to cut away at the Incas' feet and legs.

Behind him, the Canaries bound up onto the walls with bewildering agility, already swinging their clubs and bronze axes. As the blizzard of stones ended, a terrible mêlée began on the walls as the Canaries and Incas engaged in hand-to-hand combat, both sides crying out horrendously.

"The oil, the oil!" screamed Gabriel to Sebastian.

As he turned Itza around in circles by the barricade, whipping his sword through the air like a scythe, Sebastian and two of the Spaniards smashed a large jug of oil against the barricade. It only took one spark from a flint-and-steel to set it alight. A huge yellow flash erupted, blinding them, and someone cried out with joy, "Santiago! Santiago!"

By the intense glow of the burning barricade, the merciless hand-to-hand fighting on the walls resembled some fiendish dance by men possessed by the Devil. The Canary warriors cried out with demented joy as they hacked through their opponents as though the Incas were mere scarecrows. The blackened walls became gummy with blood and guts, and the dead piled up atop one another.

Gabriel, horrified, looked away and howled out the order to fall back at the top of his lungs.

"The next barricade!" he cried. "We must burn another immediately, before they see what we're about!"

He pressed his knees lightly, urging the fine Itza into a gallop, the other Spaniards and Canaries following behind him.

And so it continued throughout the night. The barricades in one alley, and then another, went up in flames. The same slaughter repeated itself four or five times. Their task became more difficult with each new barricade they came to. But they had managed to draw close enough to the fortress to clearly make out its dark walls looming above them. Despite the men's exhaustion, and although half of the Canaries had fallen, Gabriel was determined to destroy one last barricade. By destroying this one, he hoped, the road leading directly to the fortress would be clear by morning.

But things went differently this time. The Incas were expecting them now. Their volleys of stones and arrows were thicker than ever before and far more difficult to weather. The Canaries, reduced and slow with exhaustion, struggled to climb atop the walls. Barrages of stones hurtled into their faces and legs, breaking their bones and their forward motion.

Gabriel pushed his agile mare to the limit and, miraculously, she bound over a ditch hidden under branches and earth that the Incas had dug in front of the barricade. But the two cavalrymen following him weren't so lucky. Their horses fell into it, breaking their legs. Gabriel heard their terrified neighs and he pivoted Itza around just in time to see a barrage of stones descend upon his companions.

"Sebastian!" he cried.

"Over here!" replied the African giant just as loudly. He was single-handedly fighting back a pack of Inca warriors.

"They're too many, Gabriel! We have to retreat!"

But it was too late. The Incas were now rushing forth by the dozen, howling like demons. Gabriel abandoned his attempt to get to the barricade and instead charged to help the two wounded Spaniards, whom the Canaries could no longer protect. Blood streamed from his sword. Suddenly, Sebastian cried out again, surprising him, "Watch out! Gabriel, watch out for the fire above you!"

The Incas were firing burning arrows from the top of the fortress, and the arrows fell upon them like shooting stars slamming into the ground. The Canaries, suddenly petrified, stopped in their tracks, and terrible howls of pain rose up into the sky as arrows found their marks. Men waved about madly, their shoulders or chest on fire. Out of the corner of his eye, Gabriel noticed the Incas on the ground retreating. Another salvo was coming from the fortress.

"Damn the Devil, they've trapped us!" cried Sebastian. "We're stuck between the barricade and the . . ."

He never finished his sentence; a burning arrow slammed into his leather breastplate, and the cotton padding immediately caught fire. Sebastian tried to stamp out the flames with the back of his hand, but the roundel of his armor impeded his movement. His horse panicked and began galloping in circles, and the motion of the air only fanned the flames as other burning arrows slammed off of the horse's flanks. Gabriel came galloping up and drew his dagger. He cut away the burning sections of Sebastian's leather armor, flinging them to the ground.

Then something remarkable happened. Everyone, Spaniard, Canary, or Inca, saw it.

Another volley of burning arrows came down upon them, yet not one touched Gabriel or Sebastian. They didn't even need to raise their shields to protect themselves. Arrows fell around them, breaking on the flagstones or the walls, but not *on* them, as though deflected by some invisible force.

Gabriel's white mare launched into a gallop, as tireless as he. They charged the Inca line. Many retreated, but the braver among them twirled their slingshots. Yet, like the arrows, their stones disappeared into the night without touching Gabriel or Itza. From the defensive circle into which they had retreated, the Spaniards and Canaries watched as Gabriel charged the Inca lines at full gallop, his blade pointed out before him, without touching a single warrior. Looking like some guardian angel atop his perfectly white steed, Gabriel forced open a passage for himself without shedding a single drop of blood. The Incas, petrified with either fear or amazement, offered him no resistance, and soon there was a clear passage through the alley.

"Follow me!" Gabriel shouted to his companions. "Follow me, there's no danger!"

His men came out of their shock and ran after him, crying, "Santiago! Santiago!" Not a single Inca tried to stop them, and not one arrow or stone fell upon them.

For the rest of the night, it wasn't fear, hatred, or violence that churned in Gabriel's gut, it was a strange, intense, and irresistible urge to laugh.

*   *   *

The heroism of that desperate night was quickly dispelled the following day.

Around midday, not long after Gabriel had dozed off despite the relentless noise from the Inca drums and his great hunger, he was woken by shouts and a great commotion. He grumbled sleepily and was about to leave the shady corner near the horses where he had found refuge when Sebastian, his arm and shoulder now in bandages, appeared before him, along with Bartholomew. Both men looked grave.

"How are you feeling?" asked Gabriel the moment he saw them.

"Like a bride does the morning after her wedding night!" growled Sebastian.

"Are his burns serious?" Gabriel asked Bartholomew.

"Serious enough to cause him pain for some time to come," sighed Bartholomew with resignation. "But what I fear most is that his wounds may become infected. I need to treat him with an olive oil salve, but finding that here . . ."

"I'm not some delicate maiden. My wounds will wait patiently with the rest of me for better times," protested Sebastian somewhat irritably. He pushed Gabriel back into his shady corner and continued. "As for you, my friend, it's best that you remain inconspicuous for a time. . . ."

"Why? What's going on?"

"We're out of water," announced Bartholomew, "except for a very few casks. This morning, the Incas destroyed the stone conduits that supply the fountains on the great square."

"And why does that prevent me from showing myself?" asked Gabriel, astonished.

Sebastian looked at Bartholomew. Hunger and fear had hollowed their faces just as much as it had the rest of the Spanish contingent. Fever had dulled Sebastian's usually lively disposition. He was suffering from a nervous tic in his wounded arm. As for Bartholomew, the skin on his face was as gray as his faded cowl. His skin was stretched so tight on his temples and hands that one could see the details of his bones. Both men looked embarrassed when Gabriel repeated, "Well, why does it?"

"Certain people feel that our barricade burning expedition last night vexed the Incas," murmured Sebastian, "and that, without it, they wouldn't have thought to cut the conduits."

"Who can believe such a thing?" said Gabriel, furious.

"Anyone Gonzalo can persuade to listen. What's worse is that the Canaries carried out a reconnaissance mission just now. The Incas have already rebuilt the barricades. All of last night's efforts were in vain. We can no more reach the fortress today than we could yesterday. . . ."

"What of it? Of course they're going to rebuild the barricades," cut in Gabriel. "And we'll just burn them again and again! Are they not laying siege to us? What can we do but fight? Or else, negotiate peace with the Incas. I certainly wouldn't regret it. . . ."

"It's not just the barricades."

"Oh?"

"No. It's also what happened."

"Oh yes? And what happened?"

His question met with silence. Gabriel at last became aware of his friends' deep embarrassment.

"Fucking hell, are you going to tell me what this is all about?"

"You know very well," murmured Sebastian, turning toward the horses.

"I know nothing!"

"People are saying all kinds of odd things about last night," said Bartholomew softly.

"Such as what?"

"That you rode Itza through the hail of stones and arrows with impunity, while others fell."

"What of it? We were lucky, very lucky, that's all."

"No, that's not all," said Sebastian.

"Sebastian, you're wounded. You were frightened and you allowed free rein to your imagination. It's only natural."

"Protest all you want, Gabriel, I know what I saw, and there was nothing natural about it. Itza returned without a scratch, whereas I have just spent the last hour seeing to Pongo's wounds."

"Would you like to hear the rumor that was spread this morning?" interrupted Bartholomew. "Gonzalo is telling anyone who'll listen that both the Devil and the Incas are with you. Those who were with you last night swear that they saw Saint James himself rise from you. Some even pretend that the Sacred Virgin cleared you a passage."

"Well, I didn't notice any saints," said Gabriel with ill-humor. "And now I hear this rot . . . all that happened last night was a fight, too many people died, and that's it."

"No. Even the Inca warriors saw it," contested Sebastian, "that's why they let us go. In any case, you know it very well, you drove them back with your sword without even touching them."

"Sebastian's not the only one to have seen what happened, Gabriel," continued Bartholomew. "I've spoken with the cavalrymen whom you saved as well as with the Canaries. They all agree: The flaming arrows and the stones spared you as though by miracle. Are you protected by God? Or is it . . . is it thanks to your friends among the Incas?"

"Brother Bartholomew, with all due respect, you have lost your mind! I know how susceptible the Inca warriors are to anything that smells of magic during combat. All I did was play on that susceptibility! I pretended that I feared neither their stones nor their fire. And it worked. Furthermore . . ."

But Gabriel's voice lacked conviction and his tone was unnatural. He could see both the doubt and the incomprehension in his friends' eyes.

". . . Furthermore, I was lucky. It was luck, that's all. . . ."

In truth, he wasn't so convinced himself. Sebastian was right: He *had* felt something strange happen to him during the battle. He had felt as though he had been imbued with strength without limits. But how could he admit such a thing without appearing mad?

"You must believe me," he repeated in a muted voice. "It's true that I don't care whether I die or live. But there was no miracle and no magic last night."

"In your eyes, maybe so. But for those suffering here who don't want to die, it's not so simple," replied Bartholomew. "They are not so proud as to consider meeting Death as a fine moment, Gabriel Montelucar."

"What do you want me to do to convince you, Brother Bartholomew? Shall I go out into the alleys unarmed and prove that the Incas can slay me as much as they can any other man?"

Bartholomew answered by raising his joined fingers to his face and deliberately making the sign of the cross before admonishing Gabriel. "We don't ask so much of you. God will decide what path you take! But until he does, have the humility to behave like anyone else and lie low. Don Hernando has forbidden any further action. That goes for you too."

They left him, and Gabriel remained lying on the ground. He gazed over at the massive stones of the unbreachable fortress and then beyond at the mountains. He laughed privately at his so-called luck or his divine protection. "Where is she?" he murmured to himself. "Where is she?"

But the gods who had spared his life the previous night now refused him the answer that would have restored him his taste for it.

Over the following five days and nights, Cuzco was but a maelstrom of pandemonium, death, and suffering.

The Inca warriors had learned from the Spanish attack during the first night, and they not only rebuilt the barricades so that they prevented any cavalry charge, but they dug more hidden ditches in front of them and they posted guards above them day and night. Furthermore, in order to terrify the Spaniards and deny them any rest, they didn't let an hour pass during which the doleful wails of their horns and sinister drumming didn't succeed the chants and jeers of their warriors. Day and night, the archers and slingshots on the high walls of the Sacsayhuaman fortress took turns bombarding the great square and the last *cancha* in which the besieged remained holed up like rats.

Hunger, thirst, and the complete impossibility of rest—the endless din forbade even the possibility of sleep—drove the men mad. Some shrieked deliriously with their eyes closed, others sobbed like children. Some took to praying so incessantly and with such vehemence that Bartholomew didn't dare accompany them in their piety. Others remembered desperate methods adopted during Governor Don Francisco Pizarro's earliest campaigns and took to roasting earthworms and drinking their own urine, even begging others for theirs.

On the fourth day, realizing that he wouldn't be able to restrain the

demented, bloodthirsty men much longer, Don Hernando acquiesced
to his brothers Juan and Gonzalo's request to lead twenty foot soldiers
in a charge to retake Gonzalo's house on the other side of the great
square, where they hoped to find a few of the pigs that they had
brought from Cajamarca, along with some beans and perhaps even
some corn flour. Gonzalo forbade Gabriel to join the expedition, so
Gabriel, along with a few others, formed squads to guard Gonzalo's
troops' rear and protect them from a flanking maneuver by the Incas.

It was only after four hours of fighting that Juan's and Gonzalo's
horses, trampling over Inca corpses, managed at last to enter the building. But the only pigs they found were dead ones, the animals' carcasses
infested with maggots and left to rot. They found only one cask of flour
in the cellar that had been overlooked by the Incas. However, the dis-
covery of a fountain full of fresh water, a basin fed by some invisible
source like the one in Sebastian's house, caused them to cry out with
joy.

That night, the victory, although slight, restored some hope to the
Spaniards. The Incas could no longer pound all of the Aucaypata, the
great square, with stones. Men were ordered to fetch from Gonzalo's
house every sheet, tablecloth, and carpet that they could find. And the
house was as full of fabric as a Cádiz warehouse.

They worked feverishly throughout the night, and their exertions
made them forget about the cacophony from the hills, their hunger, and
their fear. While cavalrymen took turns keeping the great square out of
Manco's troops' hands, foot soldiers, their thick-fingered hands more
used to the sword or lance, sewed together the various fabrics, while
others wove rope, raised stockades, or pulled free those few beams that
were still usable from the charred roofs.

Hernando's success had made him bold, and he was trying to break
the noose that was asphyxiating them. He sent his cavalry into skir-
mishes farther and farther away from the great square. But these actions
soon proved more costly than useful and threatened to weaken what little strength they had left.

The same thing happened in each skirmish. Horses fell into the
traps that the Incas had dug even in the terraces to the west of the
square, injuring themselves. Their riders were thrown to the ground

and were immediately assaulted by dozens of Inca warriors, or else literally buried beneath a hail of stones.

On the evening of the fifth day, Juan Pizarro was brought in and placed on one of the cots in Bartholomew's makeshift infirmary. A sling stone had shattered his jaw and, despite his courage, he moaned with pain as the monk dressed his wound as best he could.

Bartholomew enlisted Gabriel to help hold Juan still while he pulled the wounded man's jaw out so that the broken bones wouldn't overlap. Bandages and splints had been hastily prepared. By the time Don Hernando and Gonzalo had rushed to his bedside, Juan had fainted. Gabriel was astonished to see Gonzalo kneel by his brother's cot and stroke his forehead as one would a child. Tears welled up in his eyes, and his muttered words of comfort were lost before they left his trembling lips.

"Don't worry too much, Don Gonzalo," said Bartholomew in a low voice. "It's a painful wound, but not a fatal one. Your brother is as hardy as he is brave. He will be on his feet tomorrow, although still a little feverish."

"On his feet to do what, by the blood of Christ!" cried Hernando, clenching his wrist.

His eyes met Gabriel's. For once, they seemed to be imploring him for help.

They all looked at the gap between the canvas stretched above them and the *cancha*'s wall. Those in the Sacsayhuaman fortress had already prepared for night, and a hundred torches glowed from atop its walls. In dusk's failing light, the fortress's towers looked like a flame-colored dragon's head.

"It's up there that we have to go," murmured Gabriel.

"Up there? You know it's impossible."

"We must attack and take the fortress," repeated Gabriel. "It's all we can do."

"You go too far! Nothing is better guarded than those towers. The roads leading to it are so steep that the horses slip and are too slow to charge. We wouldn't cover a hundred paces before being massacred. The towers' walls are so high that one cannot scale them with ladders.

We would have to take the fortress from behind. But to do that, we'd first have to make it out of the city in one piece!"

"Don Hernando, you know as well as I do: There's no other solution. We must take Sacsayhuaman, at whatever cost."

"Another one of your follies, like your attempt to destroy the barricades."

"If we make it," continued Gabriel without listening, "we will gain control of the noose with which they are strangling us; we will turn it against them. Look at your brother, Don Hernando. How has his ordeal served us? There are only fifty cavalrymen left. It's our last chance."

Don Hernando had a grave look in his eye. His doubt and defiance of Gabriel were at odds with his hope.

"Let us first look after my brother," he muttered, "and then we'll think about it."

"Yes, look after your brother," said Gabriel. "We need every brave man we have."

For the first time, Gabriel saw in Hernando's glance something other than hatred and distrust. He thought he saw something not unlike respect.

Gabriel looked into Gonzalo's red, tear-laden eyes, surprised by how affected he was. But then the angel-faced older brother turned to him and spat, "You're the one who should die, not him!"

But Gabriel sensed how terribly the youngest Pizarro brother was suffering and said nothing.

FIVE

Ollantaytambo, May 1536

The sun's disk was immense.

It rested on the air still separating it from the western mountains like a huge, magnificent, golden bubble—one which could at any moment rend open and engulf This World as a father embraces a son returned from a long journey.

Anamaya stood facing it, wide-eyed on the steep steps in the royal city of Ollantaytambo. She felt its heat on her face, on her chest and belly. She felt the sun's breath enter her.

"Inti, O Inti, shine your light into our night."

The closer the sun came to the mountains on the other side of the valley, the larger it grew. Anamaya could hear the priests behind her, standing on narrow terraces so steep that they seemed to have been built directly above one another. They stood facing the sun amid tall stalks of ceremonial corn, the corn still green except for what was scattered among it that was made of gold, and chanted.

> O Inti,
> O Powerful Father,
> You have traveled the Universe and made the day burn,
> O Inti,
> O Compassionate Father,
> You turn red, you become blood,
> O Inti,
> May Quilla renew your blood,
> May She embrace You and allay You of Your weariness
> In the Shadows of the Other World.
> And we shall close our eyes,

We shall tremble like the stars until daybreak.
O Inti,
We shall tremble in the darkness and weep
Until You have rested,
Until dawn returns in the fire of Your gold.
O Inti.

Anamaya chanted the prayer with them as the sun grew heavier and floated gently down onto the mountains and then beyond, into the realm of the unseeable, leaving behind it a crimson glow as red as a heart cut open with a *tumi*.

The warmth within Anamaya's chest brusquely disappeared. A gentle but cold breeze came up from the mountains. The heavy stones of the buildings shone red in the gloaming, and for a moment seemed as supple and light as a child's skin.

And then an enormous shadow furrowed the depths of the great Sacred Valley. The river's surface lost its shimmer amid the soft green terraces, and now the furrow became a giant black snake, as cold as the eastern sky, which had already turned dark between the high peaks of the mountains. The narrow valley running down from them, ragged with sharp contrasts, yawned open like a mouth, slowly swallowing the silent shadow creeping up it, a shadow that was also engulfing the city's streets, neatly laid out as the pattern on a *manta*.

The *canchas'* roofs were already gray, and the smoke from the braziers in their courtyards rose straight, also gray. The silence in the city's narrow streets was gray, as were the terraces that fell away to the rivers, and the mountainsides disappeared into the same gray. And so the light faded until only one cliff face in the Sacred Valley remained illuminated with golden rays, as though Inti were applying one final polish to its stone with his red light.

For a few fleeting seconds Anamaya felt exalted, as though she were floating above everyone upon a pair of wings. She saw the darkened valley with bird's eyes, the slopes of the now pale and shortened mountains, the houses of Ollantaytambo, which looked like wooden toys carved for children.

And then, in a single stroke, the sun disappeared and even the sky turned gray and flat.

"O Inti," she murmured, "do not abandon us."

Silence lingered for a moment, as though everything in the world were falling under the same evening veil of sadness. Then she heard voices from the bottom of the steps. She looked down and recognized the man arguing with the guards to let him through. Her heart began to beat wildly.

She almost set off down the stairs to meet them before recollecting herself. She tightened all her muscles in an effort to hide her shivers. She yanked her *manta* tightly, too tightly, around her shoulders, and waited for the man to come to her. He was the young officer who had once escorted her to meet Manco at Rimac Tambo and who had helped her save Gabriel before the battle of Vilcaconga.

He had gained confidence since then, and the features of his face as well as his body had grown heavier, more battle weary. But even before he had reached her, merely watching him climb the steps as steep as a cliff face path, with his mouth slightly open and his shoulders drooping, she knew that he was bringing her bad news.

When he arrived at a step still five degrees beneath her, he kneeled and bowed his head.

"I am at your service, *Coya Camaquen*," he said, still catching his breath.

"Please stand, Titu Cuyuchi," she replied a little nervously.

What she saw on his face confirmed her fears.

"So?" she asked.

"May you forgive me my failure, *Coya Camaquen*, but we were unable to do it."

She forced herself to take a few deep breaths to still her beating heart, then asked:

"Do you at least know if he's still alive?"

"He was when we last saw him. But that was five days ago."

"Why didn't you succeed, Titu Cuyuchi?"

The officer waved his hand despondently.

"I had two men with me. As soon as the roofs of Cuzco stopped burning, I waited until the darkest moment of the night before running along the walls to the *cancha* that you pointed out to me. You were right, the Stranger was there. We recognized him by his dress, a peasant's tunic from Titicaca. He was tied to the wall with a chain. . . ."

"A chain?"

"Yes. That's what confused us. We stood there a moment, wondering how to free him. Then one of my soldiers was hit by an arrow and died. All we saw was a black shadow. It was a very confused moment. . . ."

"Did he say anything to you?"

"He said that he was your friend, *Coya Camaquen,* and that we shouldn't kill him. He hadn't understood that we had come to free him."

Anamaya said nothing. She turned her gaze away from the horizon, the last faint red tint still lingering over the west.

"We had to flee," continued Titu Cuyuchi. "We didn't even see the faces of those who attacked us."

"You didn't try again?"

"No, *Coya Camaquen* . . ."

There was a reticence in Titu Cuyuchi's tone. Anamaya looked at him closely.

"Have no fear, speak freely," she ordered him in a flat voice.

"The following night, the Strangers, with help from the Canaries, set fire to our barricades. They killed many of our warriors. I fought on the last barricade, where we managed to repel their attack. I saw him there. He was on a horse, and wearing Stranger's clothes, and . . ."

"And?"

But Titu Cuyuchi again hesitated before replying. His gaze wandered over to Anamaya's shoulder, and then up beyond it. As she turned around, she heard the Master of the Stone's soft step as he approached them. She was almost relieved that he was there. She repeated her order in a harsh voice and loud enough for Katari to hear:

"Speak, Titu Cuyuchi."

"He rode his white beast and fought like an immortal from the Underworld! He sliced through our warriors as though nothing counted for him, not the deaths on our side, nor those on his. And then something odd happened. We had encircled the Strangers in front of the barricade, and our warriors on the great tower of Sacsayhuaman were bombarding them with stones and flaming arrows. But the arrows and sling stones swerved away from him. I saw it with my own eyes, *Coya Camaquen!* Our warriors were so unnerved that they stopped fighting and let him pass."

Anamaya shuddered and shut her eyes.

"Are you sure that it was him?"

"Yes, *Coya Camaquen.* I saw him as clearly as I see you now. He tried to plunge his blade into my belly! He was alive and free."

The officer hesitated, but then a smile lit up his severe face. He looked Anamaya directly in the eyes. "But he burned our barricades in vain, *Coya Camaquen.* We rebuilt them the very next day. The Strangers no longer dare to come out of their hole. They will soon be defeated, and the Emperor will be able to return to Cuzco."

"Thank you, Titu Cuyuchi. I know that you did everything you could. Now go and eat and rest. . . ."

Night had fallen on the alleyways of Ollantaytambo by the time the officer went back down the steps. Anamaya was frozen. She didn't dare look at Katari, lest he see the tears in her eyes. He drew near her, put his hand on her shoulder, and said gently, "Your Puma is free, *Coya Camaquen.*"

"Free? Or dead? Who knows? Was what I did wrong, Katari? When I saw that the Strangers had imprisoned him, I ordered Titu Cuyuchi to free him."

"But the Puma always frees itself," replied Katari with a grin.

"Do you believe, as I do, that he's the Puma that Emperor Huayna Capac predicted would come?"

"When I treated him on the shore of Titicaca, I saw the mark on his shoulder. I put my hand on it, *Coya Camaquen,* and, like you, I sensed it."

Anamaya shuddered again. Night now veiled the mountains.

"I made a mistake, Katari. I can no longer make good decisions, because my heart confuses my spirit. I suffer from being apart from him, and yet I'm frightened of being too close. I accepted leaving Gabriel because Villa Oma asked me to. He hates him. But my fear of losing him grows with each passing day. Oh, Katari, am I frightened because he's the Puma or because the man I love is a Stranger?"

"I cannot tell you, *Coya Camaquen*."

"You agree with Villa Oma, don't you?"

"No. Villa Oma is no longer the sage who educated you. He is a war-hungry hawk now. He sees only violence before him."

"Help me, Katari. How can I tell what is true and what is false?"

"You must heed the Ancestors of the Other World."

"But I hear only silence."

The last hint of light evaporated from the top of the sacred town's highest building and the rocky peaks overlooking it. The first stars twinkled in the night sky, and torches lit the streets of Ollantaytambo. Anamaya felt the warmth of Katari's hand on her shoulder.

"If you will trust me, I think I know a way that your husband the Sacred Double will allow you to travel to meet the Emperor Huayna Capac," he whispered.

Anamaya could not tell through the darkness what it was that twinkled in the Master of the Stone's eyes. But his words echoed in her soul for some time after he had uttered them (and indeed, even in her dreams later that night), and for the first time in many moons she felt a glimmer of hope that wasn't immediately destroyed by anxiety.

"I will wait for you," she murmured to the night.

And she felt as though he had heard her.

SIX

Cuzco, May 1536

Gabriel didn't immediately recognize the man he saw approaching him on the evening of the tenth day of the siege.

In the half light that accentuated the shadows cast by the shielding canvases stretched over the courtyard, the man appeared only as a silhouette, albeit with an unusually large head. The silhouette approached cautiously, keeping away from the Panama slaves dozing on the rubbish-strewn ground. The ubiquitous filth made the place stink, and even the breath of the starving men stank as though they were already exhaling the foul stench of death. Gabriel, like everyone else, cursed the incessant pain in his empty gut, almost a burning sensation that never let a moment pass without reminding him that all he had eaten in five days was a shred of meat torn from a dead horse.

When the man was closer, Gabriel made out the scarlet feather rising from the morion that he held under his arm, as well as the large bloodstains smattered across his doublet. As for the abnormal size of his head, Gabriel perceived that it was wrapped in bandages with only small openings left for his feverish eyes, his hooked nose, and his mouth from which he now pathetically uttered, "Don Gabriel!"

His voice was so low and his words so ill-formed that they were nearly incomprehensible. Gabriel did not move from the empty barrel he was using as a chair when he returned the man's greeting with a barely civil nod and said, "Don Juan. Well then, I see that you're on your feet again. And that Brother Bartholomew has padded your head admirably. You shouldn't feel a thing the next time a sling stone slams into it!"

Juan Pizarro stiffened at Gabriel's remark, and the fever in his eyes gained intensity. Both men sized each other up for a moment. Gabriel didn't bat an eye. Then Juan raised his right hand in an appeasing gesture.

"Don Gabriel, I have come to make peace with you," he murmured in his unnatural, throaty voice.

Since Gabriel merely looked at him, saying nothing, Juan continued, pausing for breath between each sentence. "I know what drove you to attack Gonzalo . . . I cannot say that I blame you . . . I am not a stranger to the love of a woman, Don Gabriel . . . as you know, my wife fell to my lot in an unorthodox manner . . . yet I love her as though God himself had led me to her . . . my dear Inguill has often spoken to me about her friend . . . about your . . . about the woman whom my brother ill-treated . . . Gonzalo sometimes acts without thinking. . . ."

Gabriel waved away Juan's embarrassment and said, "Do not be mistaken, my Lord," he said sadly. "I have found no clemency for your brother. Indeed, I am afraid that, should the occasion present itself, my heart and my honor dictate I should take the same action again. . . ."

"In that case, you will find me standing before you, and for the same reasons. For honor and love are virtues I too carry, Don Gabriel. Whatever his failings are, Gonzalo is my brother, and I love him as such . . . and although it might surprise you, he loves me with the same absolute and burning sentiment, which I confess worries me at times: It's as though I am all that stands between him and his demons."

"Then lucky for him he is guided by angels!"

Juan was about to answer Gabriel's gibe, but a sudden bout of pain twisted the features of his face, and it was only after a moment that he managed to articulate, with bitter irony, "So be it, then, Don Gabriel. You would kill him and I defend him. Isn't there anything better to do until then?"

Gabriel gave a disenchanted wave in reply. This time, the grimace that appeared fleetingly on Juan's tense mouth was closer to a smile.

"Let us look to the moment," Juan continued, approaching Gabriel so that his mumbled speech might be better understood. "I have come to make peace with you so that we may make war together . . . Don Hernando called us together . . . the decision has been made to attack the fortress. It was your idea . . . even though I'm wounded, Hernando has nominated me as commander of all the lieutenants . . . this battle is mine."

"Very good," said Gabriel, now serious, "but don't commit the same error as our lieutenant-governor: Do not underestimate the Incas. I know their chief. His name is Villa Oma. He is both intelligent and tenacious, but above all, he dreams only of annihilating every last one of us. He derives his strength from this dream. Do not expect any sign of weakness from him, Don Juan. He would fight you with his stumps, were you to chop off his arms."

Juan nodded, or at least moved his head as much as his bandages allowed him to. Gabriel noticed sweat beading on his forehead despite the coolness of the evening.

"I am aware of this, Don Gabriel . . . which is why I want you at my side. You have the energy that I lack. If I falter, you will take my place."

As though to give physical substance to his words, he roughly thrust his morion into Gabriel's hands.

"I want it to be on your head . . . I cannot wear it, because of my injuries. With you under this feather, each man will know what to do."

"It is a great honor that you do me, Don Juan. I am most unaccustomed to it. Are your brothers of the same opinion as you?"

Juan lifted his aching head and met Gabriel's sardonic stare. He was barely audible when he said, "I told you, I came to make peace . . . and I am to pick the lieutenants. . . ."

He let a moment pass, then continued.

"Our companions want you with us, Don Gabriel. Certain of them believe that you are protected by the hand of God, and that the Virgin Mary is with you . . . others believe that it's nothing to do with God, but that you have acquired magic powers from the Indians, from your relations with them. . . . Your exploits the other night have made a deep impression on the men. . . ."

"God's blood, how can you lend credence to these fancies?"

"Because I saw the same thing with my own eyes . . . and I didn't arrive yesterday, like many of the men here . . . no, it started on the beach at Tumbez when we arrived . . . you should have died on that day."

Gabriel sniggered.

"I am far too indifferent toward God for him to even blink in my direction. As for the woman that you're thinking of, she taught me no magic, indeed, nothing of particular note, except that the Incas are human beings like you or I, that they are big or small, thin or fat, and that they suffer in both their bodies and souls thanks to us."

"Oh, what does it matter to us whether God or pagan demons grant you your power?" interrupted Juan, irritated and breathing shallow. "What matters is that our brothers-in-arms now both fear you and see you as some sort of talisman or good charm . . . they believe that, without you, we have no chance of succeeding."

"Oh yes? Only yesterday they believed that all was lost because of me."

"Do you accept my proposal, Don Gabriel?"

"If I refuse, it's back to jail for me, right?"

"I have come to make peace with you, not to threaten you."

Gabriel carefully set down the morion on the barrel. He absent-mindedly stroked its scarlet feather as he asked, "How do you plan to enter the fortress?"

Juan emitted an odd-sounding grunt and screwed up his eyes. Gabriel realized a moment later that this was the closest he could manage to a laugh.

"By any way you think is best!"

Gabriel smiled, almost with Juan now, and traced an indistinct shape in the dust with the point of his boot.

"We must trick them. We must make Villa Oma and his lieutenants believe that we're trying to flee. . . ." He described a circle around the shape in the dirt representing the fortress. "Here, the Carmenga Pass. It leads out of the city to the northwest and avoids the fortress. It will be a formidable task to reach it, and a greater one to climb it; it's a true, steep-sided ravine. The Incas will rain death down on our heads, but if we succeed, then we will be out of their range of vision—they will no longer be able to watch our every move. We can then take a long detour and approach the fortress from behind. There are a number of doors there that may well prove accessible."

"Then we shall do it. . . ."

"Don Juan, no illusions! My hands can produce no miracle. Our chance of success is as thin as our stomachs."

"Well, as there's no banquet planned for tonight, I think each man will have plenty of time to pray."

Gabriel felt deeply troubled as he watched Juan Pizarro walk away, his step heavy and irregular. He had just accepted to serve his mortal enemies without a word of real argument (for, in the depths of his soul, he was as frightened of his invulnerability in battle as were his comrades-in-arms).

But he didn't regret it.

He even felt strangely joyful.

Dawn, and fifty horsemen were on their knees, with a hundred or so Canary and Chachapoya warriors looking on, impressed. The Incas, of course, hadn't let up their terrifying racket once throughout the night. Now, Bartholomew made his way through the close files of Spaniards, giving the benediction to each forehead with his joined fingers.

Juan, his head wrapped in fresh bandages and wearing real armor on his chest and thighs, received the benediction fervently. Don Gonzalo was kneeling beside him, his long, fine hair cascading down onto his steel armor decorated with fine gold chasing across his shoulders. He wore a scowl on his face. His lips hardly moved when he uttered the prayer of the benediction.

Hernando stood watching the ceremony from a little farther back, standing in front of the foot soldiers who would soon face the siege on their own. He was murmuring unconsciously to himself. He was the first to notice Gabriel arrive at the entrance to the courtyard, leading his white mare. He already had a round shield attached to his left arm, and he held the scarlet-feathered helmet against his leather-padded coat of mail with the other.

If Hernando's face betrayed nothing, then Gonzalo's, who stopped short midprayer, turned distinctly pale. His eyes grew wide and his mouth closed on the Paternoster. Gabriel thought that he was going to rise to his feet and challenge him. But Hernando's imperious gaze weighed upon his younger brother. The prayers ended and the horses were brought forth. The cavalrymen glanced at Gabriel. Some bowed their heads, saluting him, others crossed themselves one more time, but none dared approach him, and instead they mounted their animals.

Gonzalo was lost in the general movement, while Hernando helped

Juan clamber onto his gelding. Gabriel in turn donned his morion, pulling the strap tightly beneath his chin.

"You were in my prayers, my friend," said Brother Bartholomew as he approached Gabriel. "What's more, I saw you praying yourself earlier, when you thought no one was watching."

"I hope you're not going to denounce me. It would damage my reputation. Yet still, Brother Bartholomew, you should be happy for me. Didn't you explain to me that one doesn't have to believe in order to pray?"

"You believe more than you admit to yourself."

Bartholomew placed his wooden cross against Gabriel's chest. His eyes were sunken deep in their cavities, and exhaustion made his face appear ten years older.

"Be careful. Watch out both ahead of you and behind your back," he said in a lower voice. "Gonzalo is furious that Juan insisted that you go with them. Try not to provoke him."

"Don't worry. It's widely known that I'm protected from everything and by God himself."

"Don't blaspheme! It's pointless."

"Brother Bartholomew, if God does in fact exist," said Gabriel, looking directly at the monk with the utmost seriousness, "then today is that day for him to convince me of it. Not by preserving me from death, from which I do not shirk, and you know why, but . . ."

". . . but by purging the earth of evil in one stroke, preferably beginning with Gonzalo Pizarro?"

"By the faith, Brother, sometimes I wonder whether you are not inspired by God himself."

"My God," answered Bartholomew in a serious tone, "is not a god of vengeance who punishes by the sword, but a god of love and charity. And if you will heed my words, you would do well to heed his. As well as handling your sword properly when it's called for!"

Gabriel opened his mouth to make a sarcastic reply, but he saw that Juan Pizarro was approaching. Gabriel understood more from reading his dry lips than from his words.

"It's time, Don Gabriel . . . I have divided our cavalry into two groups. My brother Gonzalo is leading the second."

His eyes looked for approval, which Gabriel gave him with a nod.

"Let us go, then, with the grace of God!"

They approached the *cancha*'s door, barricaded with beams, in silence, as though they wanted to better hear the cacophony from the hills and the trumpets wailing from the fortress. Even the Canaries, normally so loquacious, said nothing.

Gabriel noticed Sebastian among the men removing the beams from the door, his arm and shoulder still wrapped in bandages, and smiled at him. For once, the African didn't return it. His serious expression had all the sadness of a real adieu. He approached Gabriel and stroked his mare's mane. She responded by nuzzling her head in his chest.

"Take care of her and of yourself, my friend."

"I shall bring you back some salve, so that you can come with us the next time," joked Gabriel.

Sebastian smiled a thin smile.

"Good idea."

At that moment Gabriel stood in his stirrups and shouted at the top of his voice, "By Saint James, tonight we dine at the fortress!"

Behind him, fifty voices answered with a thundering, "Santiago! Santiago!"

They were still shouting when the horses broke out into the great square, raising a cloud of dust through which the Canaries swarmed, also screaming, like a pack of wild animals.

Only moments after they had passed the last walls of the *canchas* and reached the lowest of the terraces at the foot of the pass, a salvo of arrows whistled over their heads. They had been fired from too far to be truly effective, and they thudded off the Spaniards' shields and horses' armored flanks without piercing them.

But now the Spaniards saw in front of them the line of Inca warriors, three or even four deep, blocking the road through the terraces to the west of the city. Juan turned to Gabriel. His eyes said what his mouth couldn't.

With his sword unsheathed, Gabriel shouted the order to increase their speed to a gallop. Itza immediately bound forward and stretched her pace, as though the command was all she had been waiting for. Her mane floating in the wind, she seemed to be floating toward the enemy, her hooves hardly touching the ground. The compact mass of flesh and steel that was the cavalrymen behind her moved as if in her wake, followed by the Canaries who, waving their axes and with their shields raised, ran on with astonishing agility, all the while howling at the tops of their voices.

For a second, perhaps two, the Inca warriors squeezed closer together, holding their spears out before them and their clubs in their other hands. But everything happened too fast, quicker than the sling stones that ricocheted off the Spaniards' breastplates and coats of mail. The Incas watched with bulging eyes as the horses bore down on them. The ground itself shook, and the hammering sound of the animals' hooves infiltrated their bodies like a vibration of fear. The twirling blades of Spanish swords seemed to hack the sun itself into shreds of blinding light. Inca mouths opened in agony as Spanish steel tore into their flesh and horses' hooves crushed their bones and staved in their chests, until the Spaniards had so cut up the Incas that their faces were unrecognizable as they cried out in agony, and the horses trampled not on stone or earth but on a yielding carpet of flesh and bone. Only then did the Canaries join the fray, adding to the general confusion. The ferocity of the battle doubled, and the dead fell quickly, yielding the way to the Spaniards while still their swords cut through the Incas.

The Inca lines had to give; some warriors flung their clubs at the Spaniards' heads before taking to their heels, others committed suicide by trying to thrust their spears into the horses' bellies or their riders' legs. But their heroism was futile.

Their chests and hocks now covered in blood, the horses extricated themselves from this tangle of death and galloped toward the first turn in the pass, beyond the reach of the slingshots.

His face covered in sweat and blood, his body aching from having swung his sword so much, his chest burning, and out of breath, Gabriel nevertheless continued shouting for the Spaniards and their allies to follow him.

He was exulted. His excitement rose up above his indifference, his distaste for life, and he felt a boundless sense of power.

"Santiago!" he cried once again, his voice hoarse from shouting.

And in the voices of the Spaniards and their allies as they answered him, in the whistle of arrows and clashing of arms, in the cries of agony or of triumph, in the din of battle and the thunder of horses' hooves, he heard the mountains, the stones, the earth itself confer the stamp of victory upon him.

But they had so far accomplished only the easiest part of the mission. The slopes of the Carmenga Pass proved as steep and difficult to scale as Gabriel had feared, and it sapped them of most of their strength.

For two hours they climbed up and up the steep, windy road. Sections of the path had crumbled away, leaving a space barely large enough for a horse to pass or even outright impassable scree or crevasses. So until the Canaries, as busy as ants, had finished clearing the scree or, squatting on their little square shields, bridging the crevasses, the expedition had to suffer the hail of stones flung down upon them from above.

Gabriel smelled the foul stench of fear rising up again from the Spaniards. Impatience and anxiety sharpened by hunger eroded the courage of even the hardiest among them. A stone struck a horse directly on the nose, injuring it, and it reared up in pain. It struck the horse in front of it with its forelegs, and threw its rider, who would have tumbled all the way to the bottom of the ravine had not two Canary warriors saved him. But the panic spread to all the animals in the vicinity, and the ensuing crush almost sent half a dozen horses and their riders plummeting down the cliff face.

"Dismount!" shouted Gabriel. "Dismount and hold your horses by the bit. Force them to lower their heads!" But, hearing the men murmuring in protest, Gabriel changed his tone and asserted as confidently as he could, "We will pass! We will pass, because we have to!"

Yet Juan looked doubtful. In truth, all the men were haunted by the same thought: That the Carmenga Pass would become a repetition of the battle in the Vilcaconga Pass during which, many years earlier and for the first time since they had arrived in Peru, the Spaniards had found themselves in such a precarious situation that Gabriel, who had been at death's door, had survived thanks only to his tenacity and love for Anamaya.

"It's the same situation," murmured Juan, closing his eyes as though trying to shut out a nightmare. "Them up there and us down here . . . and hampered by our horses."

"No," said Gabriel in a hushed voice so that Juan alone could hear him. "There's no one up there. The bulk of Villa Oma's troops are behind us."

"May God make it so!"

"I remember a rocky ledge, just below the summit of the pass. We can return to our saddles there and then follow the terraces to the northwest. They'll think that we're leaving the fortress behind us. They'll think we're just trying to get away."

Juan's only answer was to make the sign of the cross over his bandaged face.

"Watch out for the stones!" roared a voice. "Watch out for the stones!"

Gabriel instinctively raised his shield above Juan, whose thickly swathed head prevented him from wearing a helmet.

"Protect yourself, Don Gabriel," ordered Juan in a low voice.

This time, the stones fell so thick and fast that it seemed as though the entire mountain were avalanching down upon them. The Spaniards held their shields above their heads, but their shields cracked, and men shouted as their horses neighed in terror. Everyone, however, including Gonzalo, saw the avalanche of rock miraculously miss Gabriel and his white mare, even though they were at its center, and even though everyone else without exception had their thighs, backs, and shoulders bruised by the stones despite the protection of their shields and padded armor. And they saw that Juan remained as protected from the stones under Gabriel's shield as if it were a solid roof.

But no one dared breathe a word; instead they tightened their lips and prayed fervently.

When the avalanche of stones had at last come to an end, and they had reached the ledge as Gabriel had promised they would, they found that the Inca warriors who had been plaguing them from above numbered no more than fifty. The Incas didn't dare come close enough to use a slingshot, and the Spaniards only had to gallop at them briefly before they turned on their heels and bolted.

Gabriel listened to the Incas shouting to one another as they decamped.

"They think we're going back to Castile!" he announced to his compatriots with a laugh.

Their relief was as great as their terror had been a little while earlier, their chests swelled with laughter, and for the moment they were released from their exhaustion.

"Santiago! Santiago!" cried the cavalrymen before crossing themselves and lowering their eyes, as though they preferred not to know to what they owed their success.

Gabriel felt a chill settle on his soul.

He thought about what was to come, and the vision of it permeated his mind's eye as though he had already lived it.

It was only in the middle of that afternoon, after a number of detours, that they at last reached an uneven platform strewn with enormous black rocks from which a gentle slope led down to the back of the Sacsayhuaman fortress. The fortress's high walls were built of massive stones so meticulously fitted together that it was difficult to imagine how human beings had managed to place one atop the other. What was stranger, however, was that there seemed to be no Inca warriors at all standing guard.

Juan ordered them to stop and rest by a gurgling spring. Some overjoyed Canary warriors had taken the time to catch a few wild rats and even two llamas that had become separated from a herd—no doubt scattered by the battle—during the march to their present position. They carved up the animals and ate them raw since fires were forbidden.

For a long while, a curious silence reigned over the halted expedition. But after a few mouthfuls of meat, and the sickly taste of blood that they drank, even the most exhausted quickly recovered their energy and alertness. Gonzalo was the first to call for them to attack.

"It's time, my brother. We mustn't wait for night to fall. The Canaries have returned from their reconnaissance mission. The passages between the fortress's defensive walls are indeed barricaded but, as we thought, no Inca is guarding that part of the fortress. I suggest that our friend don Gabriel exploit his . . . unusual gift and accompany the Canaries to open a passage for us. He can send a signal when we are clear to charge. And as you are in no condition to lead one, dear brother, I suggest that you remain here with a dozen cavalrymen to reinforce us if we need it."

Gabriel smiled thinly at Gonzalo's irony. His eyes met Juan's, and he put his crimson-feathered morion back on his head as he nodded and said, "It's not such a bad idea."

Then he caught Gonzalo's shifting gaze, and what he saw in it gave him the satisfaction that comes only from the onset of revenge: He saw that handsome, cruel Gonzalo was frightened of him.

Gabriel approached the first undefended barricade on foot and surrounded by Canary warriors. It took them little time to breach it.

While the Canaries quietly finished dismantling the stone barricade, Gabriel jumped into the saddle. He silently urged Itza into the maze of natural rock and walls that were the first line of defense around the fortress's great ramparts and towers.

He constantly expected to hear an Inca lookout cry out the alert. But he heard nothing.

No one saw him or heard his mare's trot as he passed alongside the little hill that hid him still from the great wall. Soon, he made out the esplanade opening up before him, and he slowed to walking pace until he reached the edge of the vast, grass-covered space at the base of the fortress. He looked at the gargantuan stone blocks that made up its wall.

Gabriel's heart skipped a beat. No Inca warrior had spotted him; no stone or spear had been thrown at him. In front of him and to his left, the main wall followed a zigzag turn. In it, he could make out a large, trapezoidal gate that had been somewhat carelessly barricaded with stones and logs. Were they to breach it, they would reach the very heart of Sacsayhuaman.

He had seen enough: Sure of their coming victory, he yanked on his mare's reins and galloped back to rouse his companions.

"Everyone mount your horses!" he ordered when he was within shouting range of Gonzalo. "The road is clear! Don Hernando is distracting them on the city side of the fortress, and they are completely unaware that we are here."

As had been arranged, only Juan Pizarro and a handful of cavalrymen remained behind, ready to reinforce them if necessary. The rest galloped as quietly as they could behind Gabriel on his white mare. They bound over the dismantled barricade, hurtled past the Canary warriors, and charged the great trapezoidal gate. It was then that everything went horribly wrong.

They heard a conch sound from the top of the round tower. A furious clamor immediately erupted from the top of the great wall. Gabriel was about to launch across the terraces, which had been empty a moment earlier, when he was appalled to discover a hundred, two hundred, or even a thousand Inca soldiers assembled before him.

Before he had even managed to halt Itza's flying gallop, he felt the air around him quiver as the warriors twirled their slingshots so powerfully that they might have been hurling cannonballs rather than stones. A moment later, a hail of stones tore through the air, humming above him. The cavalrymen behind, still exposed on the esplanade, screamed with pain as they were hit. The horses stumbled against the bouncing stones, throwing their riders forward over their heads. Already there were Inca warriors swarming ahead to seize them.

Gabriel roared furiously, slicing through the air with his sword, and rushed back to help his comrades. His solo charge terrified Sacsayhuaman's defenders enough for them to move out of the way. Meanwhile, the riders who had been thrown tried to yank their horses back up or else abandoned them and instead jumped onto the hindquarters of their companions' horses and bolted back the way they had come.

But still, utter confusion reigned amid the Spaniards. The Canary warriors, surprised by the sudden appearance of the Incas, defended themselves poorly, and their hand-to-hand combat with the enemy obstructed the retreating cavalrymen. Furthermore, the ground was now so strewn with stones that the horses moved very gingerly. Only

Gabriel's mare maintained its gallop, and he charged down the Incas again and again in a futile attempt to force them back.

No one noticed how long this madness lasted.

The Spaniards, their frustration accentuated by their empty stomachs, continually beat pitiful retreats to the other side of the first barricade, and Gabriel had to harangue them five or six times to return to the fray.

But their forward movement was broken time and again by the hail of stones, long before they ever reached the massive wall. They were utterly unable to follow Gabriel's white mare, and each time they held their own horses back lest they break their legs.

More than an hour passed, draining them of their courage, and now the light was fading from the sky. Gabriel urged them to make one final, heroic effort. But he had only just come up in front of them when a bawl erupted in his ear. He raised his shield by reflex and saved his own life: Gonzalo had brought his sword crashing down, trying to cut Gabriel in half.

"Traitor! Filthy vermin!" screamed Gonzalo, a mad look in his eyes. "At last, we see your true colors! May you be cursed to hell for having led us into this trap!"

"Don Gonzalo!"

"Shut up, you goat turd! I saw you; we *all* saw you. The Incas leave you alone! You've learned how to dodge their stones and now you want to lead us right to them so that they can slaughter us at their leisure!"

Gabriel had no time to reply because Gonzalo was at him again, standing in his stirrups and waving his sword, screaming, "*Compañeros! Compañeros,* listen to me: This man is not Saint James come to save us, but a filthy traitor and a devil! Do not follow him! Do not obey him, or he will lead you to your death!"

The Spanish cavalrymen, deeply weary after all their efforts and all their disappointments, stared at the two men without being able to tell truth from the madness. Some crossed themselves, others dressed their calves destroyed by stones, still others pulled arrows out of one another's coats of mail or their horses' breastplates. But then the sound of galloping horses saved them from having to choose. Juan and his reinforcements were approaching at full pace.

"Juan!" Gonzalo shouted furiously. "My brother, you put out your hand to a viper and he's bitten you! Montelucar has led us to our perdition. He's the Devil himself! The Incas were expecting us; they had probably even been warned! We will never make it into the fortress! We must return to Cuzco before night falls!"

"Don Juan," exclaimed Gabriel, "don't listen to his rubbish! We still have one chance left. The Inca warriors are as tired of slinging stones at us as we are of receiving them; soon they'll be too tired to even lift their arms! We must assault them one more time. I'll go alone if I have to!"

Juan didn't hesitate. He pointed at the fortress with the tip of his sword and whipped his horse's flank. A moment later, the entire contingent was following in his wake, despite Gonzalo's protests.

This time, once he was past the first barricade, Gabriel urged Itza down the side nearest to the hill, where he had spotted a few rocks piled one above the other. His mare leaped up them deftly. He charged at the forward Inca line from behind, forcing them to rush back before they could turn and twirl their slingshots. His small, single-handed victory so inspired the Spaniards below that they roared with renewed hope.

A moment later, Itza's white coat beneath Gabriel's red feather appeared to be everywhere among the melee, and moving ever closer to the great wall. It was a marvel to the Spaniards, who began crying victory.

But then a horrendous volley of stones and arrows fell upon them from atop the great wall. Gabriel raised his shield like everyone else, and heard the deadly patter of arrows slamming into padded armor.

A brief, unnatural silence followed. Then a terrible cry tore through the air: "Juan! Juan! Oh, my brother . . ."

A hundred paces from Gabriel, Juan Pizarro fell from his saddle and crumpled onto the layer of stones now covering the grass. His bandage had come off, and the entire upper part of his skull was a bloody mangle of bone and brain. The excitement of battle had made him reckless, and he had lowered his shield, leaving his unprotected and wounded head exposed to the enemy's stones.

Gonzalo was already on his knees at his brother's side, his mouth agape as he wailed and sobbed. He drew Juan to his chest and cradled him like a child, but it was pointless.

Gabriel felt an icy blade cut his heart and his breath. Mechanically he urged Itza toward the Pizarro brothers, while all the other cavalrymen gathered around to protect them. They took up Juan's body and carried him away at a run. Gonzalo turned to face Gabriel, his handsome face twisted with grief and hatred.

"You killed him. You killed him, Gabriel Montelucar, you killed my beloved brother!"

Gabriel said nothing. All his hatred and biting sarcasm had left him. A moment later Gonzalo, overcome with grief, turned away from his foe and began sobbing like a child.

"I didn't fling the stone that smashed your brother's skull, Don Hernando, but it was I who insisted that we charge one more time. The final charge proved to be as futile as all those that had preceded it. Don Gonzalo is right to accuse me of bringing about your brother's death."

Hernando didn't answer. His hard, emaciated face was barely visible by candlelight. They could hear Gonzalo's wails of grief from the neighboring room, as well as Bartholomew murmuring a prayer.

It had taken them four hours to come down from the esplanade in front of the fortress to the *cancha* on the great square of Aucaypata, and they had carried Juan's body the whole way, despite constant harassment by the Incas. Gabriel was so tired that he could no longer feel his arms or legs. He couldn't even feel his hunger anymore. His fingers were numb and his hand swollen from having gripped his sword for so long. His eyes had trouble focusing.

"But it's not true that I hoped for, and orchestrated, our defeat," he continued.

Still Hernando said nothing. He seemed to be listening to the wails and the women's funeral laments that accompanied the Christian prayers next door. But then he said in a low voice, "Juan was the only person in the world that Gonzalo ever loved. He always loved him, and passionately. Rather strange, don't you think?"

Now it was Gabriel's turn to say nothing. But he remembered the words that Juan had spoken to him that very morning.

"Gonzalo has never respected anyone but Juan," continued Hernando. "No woman, no man. He obeys me, but only just. And now, Juan's death is going to make him even madder than he was before."

"The demons will be free. . . ." murmured Gabriel.

Hernando looked at him for a moment, surprised, then repeated, "The demons, yes . . ."

Next door, the last Christian rites had finished, but the laments continued still. Hernando made a weary gesture with his hand, as though he were trying to push away the thoughts that occupied his mind. A very thin smile spread across his lips.

"People tend to die in battle, Don Gabriel," he continued in his more usual ironic tone. "It's happened before. Especially when you lose the battle. I'm a good Christian, and my brother's death grieves me. But what grieves me even more is that, despite all your promises and magic powers, we are still on the *outside* of that damned fortress! It seems that the stones and arrows spared you once again, but never has a miracle seemed more useless to me."

"We shall see soon enough if it's magic or not," muttered Gabriel, wiping his hand across his face.

"Oh yes?"

"There's at least one good thing to have come out of our attack, Don Hernando. While we diverted the Incas at the back of the fortress, you at last managed to reach the base of its wall on this side. I noticed earlier that our people are camping there. . . ."

". . . For the moment. But tomorrow morning, the Incas will throw everything they've got at us to get us out of there. And they will succeed, because we haven't the strength to resist them for any length of time."

"No. At dawn, I will climb to the summit of the tower—alone—and I will open a passage for you."

"That would be madness, Gabriel."

Hernando and Gabriel turned together to look at whomever had uttered these words. Bartholomew crossed the threshold of the room and said again, "It would be madness. You'll never make it."

"There's a window halfway up the great wall. It can be reached with a good ladder. Inside, I'm sure there's a stairway leading to the base of the tower. The Incas have a way of getting up there: I'll find it!"

"You've lost your mind. By all the saints, today's action has sent you mad."

"Don Hernando, order the ladder to be built. I need to get some sleep. But make sure that it's ready by the first light of day."

"Don Gabriel, you'll be lying dead beneath an avalanche of stones before you reach even halfway up the ladder," remarked Hernando with cold circumspection.

"Well, I'm sure that my death will cause you little grief. On the other hand, I'm sure that you won't mind if I succeed, either. I've known worse deals, Don Hernando."

At first, Hernando looked a little surprised, then an odd little laugh came out of his dry lips.

"You are a strange fellow, Don Gabriel. Always this obsession with dying, then coming back from the dead! Always wanting to show yourself to be better than everyone else. Why, I may well end up sharing my brother the Governor's opinion of you, and admit that you have certain qualities!"

Gabriel ignored his comment and the sardonic look in his eyes. He took Bartholomew's deformed hand and squeezed it strongly.

"It is time to know, my friend Bartholomew. I must know! And this time, no one will have to follow me."

Gabriel hardly shut his eyes that night. Whenever he did snatch a few moments of sleep, it was despite himself, and the rest he spent in a waking dream.

The visions that thrust themselves upon his mind's eye pursued him relentlessly and never let his soul have a moment's rest. In them, he saw a rope tied to the crenellated ramparts of the round tower, the most forbidding one, and the rope's end floated gently in the breeze. And when his injured hands closed around the rope, he sensed that nothing could prevent him from reaching the top.

It was a cold dawn. The ground was almost frozen over, and the sky was as white as a linen canopy. Gabriel was holding a dirty blanket around his naked torso.

He had been woken by a soft hand caressing his forehead and

shoulders. He felt the hand's smooth skin and delicate fingers: a woman's hand, a forgotten gentleness.

When he opened his eyes and emerged from his deep sleep, his body still ached, and he looked into the young woman's face without recognizing her. He saw tears in her eyes and dust daubed on her cheeks.

"You don't remember me," she whispered with the slightest of smiles. "My name is Inguill. We met a long time ago, before Emperor Atahualpa's death. I was then a young girl serving the *Coya Camaquen*. She often spoke of you."

Gabriel sat up on his elbows, now completely awake.

"Did she send you?" he asked. "Did Anamaya send you?"

She shook her head, her smile broadening slightly.

"No. I am Lord Don Juan's wife." Her voice cracked as she continued. "Or was, until yesterday."

"I know. I regret it extremely. He told me about you."

He saw a combination of grief and pride in Inguill's eyes.

"He chose me as a slave, and yet he loved me as a wife. And I loved him. He was gentle with me. His Ancestors of the Other World didn't want him to suffer too much. It is well thus."

She nimbly reached into her *unku* and drew out a little jar, which she handed to Gabriel.

"We drew some milk from your goats for our children. I've brought you some. You must drink it before climbing up the tower. It will give you strength."

Gabriel grabbed her by the wrist.

"Why are you doing this?"

Inguill looked at him for a moment. She caressed Gabriel's shoulder with her free hand. Her fingers slipped over his shoulder blade and brushed over his birthmark.

"The *Coya Camaquen* is protecting you, and the Powerful Ancestors too," she whispered. "We all know that you are going to save us."

Gabriel tightened his grip around Inguill's arm.

"How do you know? Why defend me from your own people? It makes no sense!"

Inguill broke away and stood up brusquely.

"Drink the milk. It will do you good," she said simply before disappearing.

Only then did Gabriel notice Sebastian standing in the background and giving him a stony look.

"That woman speaks rubbish," he growled. "Climbing that damned ladder up their damned tower is the worst idea you've ever had, Gabriel."

Gabriel grinned as he rose to his feet.

"So, you no longer think that you saw Saint James reincarnate with your own eyes?"

"Oh yes, I do! At least, I saw enough to know that one of the two of you is an impostor. And I would happily put my money on it being Saint James!"

"Blasphemer!"

Laughing openly now, Gabriel embraced his friend.

"Look after Itza. She's a fine mare, and I'd like you to give her to me later, when this battle's over."

"I'll give you your mare and much more, your Grace, but first you must promise me one thing, by Saint James and the Sacred Virgin, by the Sun and the Moon, by my teeth and your beard and my own . . ."

"What?"

"Stay alive, damned fool."

The ladder was at least eight *codos* long, but still it only just reached the narrow window set high in the great wall. It took twenty men to raise it and hold it in the right position. They had made it out of roof beams and logs from the barricades, fitted together as best they could. They had run out of rope for the rungs, some of which were made from the shafts of broken spears and set so far apart that Gabriel had to pull himself up by his arms to reach them.

As soon as Gabriel was about four codos up, the ladder began to sway, so he was careful not to make any sudden movements. He climbed a couple more rungs, then heard people calling to him. He looked down and saw Sebastian, Bartholomew, Hernando, and the others on the ground dashing away from the base of the ladder. He immediately understood without having to look up. He bunched his head and shoulders tightly, hooked his feet solidly onto the rungs, and raised his shield.

As the stones slammed into his leather shield, he realized that he was almost enjoying their thudding sound. Some of the heavier ones struck the ladder, causing it to shudder. He had to hurry.

Grunting like a woodcutter, he ignored the projectiles and began scaling the higher rungs. The ladder squeaked horribly and sagged like a belly breathing too strongly. Gabriel kept his eyes fixed on the wall; he put any notions of up and down out of his mind and ignored the stones whistling past him, some smashing into his hip or onto the ladder, almost crushing his fingers. He climbed with his feet and knees and didn't hear the shouts and cries ringing out all around him.

His companions had taken his fatigue into account: They had assembled the last rungs closer together so that they were easier to climb. Gabriel felt as though he could practically run up them, and soon enough he found himself on the broad sill outside the little window.

The pale morning light barely lit the inside of the room, but still he could make out a staircase and a number of dumbfounded Inca faces.

The mere sound of drawing his sword from its scabbard sent the dozen or so Inca warriors scurrying back, even though they were all armed with slingshots and bludgeons. They looked at one another, doing nothing, their curiosity making them immobile as much as their surprise. Gabriel cried out in Quechua:

"Stand back! Stand back! I wish you no harm!"

Waving his sword about as though it were made of balsa wood, he took three steps forward. But the warriors took the corresponding number of steps up the staircase. Each time he advanced, they moved away, maintaining the distance between themselves and Gabriel. Then one of the Incas said, "It's the Stranger with the white beast!"

They stared at one another once again, utterly amazed, and Gabriel didn't know what to do next any more than they did. Then, wordlessly, the soldiers turned away from him and bolted up the steep staircase with astonishing agility.

Gabriel cautiously followed on their heels, breathing hard and holding his sword out in front of him. When he at last reached the light of day, he discovered that the rampart at the base of the tower was deserted. The warriors had run off to find their officers.

He could be seen from the neighboring towers. He heard shouting from them, and stones were slung. Yet none were thrown at him, only at the Spaniards still at the foot of the great wall.

Gabriel, encouraged by the ease of his adventure so far, walked around the base of the tower. He looked up and felt a shiver run down his spine: He knew, now, that Inguill had been right; everyone had been right.

There was no door or window that opened into the interior of the tower or led to its height, but there was a rope made of agave and *ichu*, of the sort that the Incas used to build their suspension bridges and as thick as a man's arm, hanging down the entire height of the building, as though inviting him to climb it.

He could now *see* with extraordinary certitude what he had seen in his dream.

His exhaustion and caution left him; his tense muscles relaxed. Unable to contain himself, Gabriel approached the top of the great wall, waved his sword and shield about, and cried:

"Santiago! Santiago!"

His companions down below, holding their shields close together, looked like tiny animals with dirty shells. Gabriel laughed like a madman and cried once again:

"Santiago!"

Then he flung away his shield, sheathed his sword, and took off his heavy coat of mail. He took a firm grip of the rope, a rope as miraculous as Jacob's ladder, and began his ascent. The thought that the Incas up above could cut it at any moment didn't even cross his mind.

But the exertion of hauling himself up four *codos* with his legs and torso at right angles to the wall, the soles of his boots slipping on the stone, and all his weight on his arms, was enough to bring him back from his paroxysm.

His legs felt desperately heavy, and his feet slipped twice when he set them poorly against the wall. Both times, he slammed into the wall with all his weight. He banged his knees and chest painfully hard and almost let go of the rope. He found himself short of breath once again, and his muscles began to tighten up. Both times he set himself right and continued his ascent. One *codo,* then another. He had six to go, perhaps more. He remembered Sebastian's words: "Not long from now, you will fly down to earth like a true angel, except that you'll be ballasted with stones!" He chortled to himself and paused to rest, but his body weighed so heavily on his arms that he preferred climbing.

He was almost halfway up the tower when he felt a tremor in the stone. He looked up; a rock the size of a footstool was hurtling down at him, bouncing off the wall. He didn't have enough time to protect himself so he simply closed his eyes.

Gabriel felt nothing except a movement of air as the rock brushed past his shoulder.

He opened his eyes just as the rock smashed into the flagstones of the ramparts below, exploding into dust.

"I *am* protected," he said to himself, his chest burning. "Anamaya is protecting me! She loves me and is protecting me!"

Suddenly, Gabriel was transported back into his frenzy. He no longer saw the stone wall of the tower in front of him, instead he saw Anamaya's blue eyes. He no longer felt the burning sensation in his lungs, or his exhausted arms, or his legs that would no longer bend. He climbed like a demon, like a monkey. The Spaniards below watched him scale the last *codo,* and when he reached the edge of the little wall that ran around the top of the tower they cried:

"Santiago! He made it! Santiago!"

Gabriel collapsed and stretched his body along the top of the tower, struggling to regain his breath. He didn't have the strength to lift himself up. He listened for the sound of Inca soldiers coming to capture him.

But the only sound he heard came from far off.

Finally, he sat up. He was alone; the top of the tower was deserted. There was a turret at its center that housed the top of a stairwell, and when he looked down, he saw that there were many flights, and that the steps were so narrow that one had to descend them at an angle. Gabriel saw no one. But he could hear voices rising up from the bottom.

He went back to the little wall at the edge of the tower. He cried out once again, he screamed at the top of his lungs—he had taken the tower, and they could all come and join him!

By midday, they were still fighting, and the Spaniards had taken a second tower. Gabriel never left the first one, and no one had come to join him. He grew horrified, but never weary, of watching the great spectacle of war. The ramparts of the Sacsayhuaman fortress were now strewn with corpses: at least a thousand, perhaps more.

Gabriel placed his aching hands on the little stone wall and saw that they were trembling. He couldn't feel anything anymore. He asked himself what madness had possessed him, how had he come to be like a drunkard emerging from his haze.

He didn't even dare think about Anamaya, nor did he believe the obscenity that she had protected him to permit this horrendous carnage.

The pestilent stench of death corrupted his nostrils.

Sebastian's affectionate words now seemed to have been addressed to some one other than him. Once more, he hoped that death would simply come and find him, that he wouldn't have to jump from the tower to forget the pleasure he had derived from being the catalyst of the present massacre.

"I thought I was master," he sniggered to himself, "when in fact I was nothing but a miserable slave."

But still he never looked away, not even for a moment, from the unflagging spectacle of men dying.

That evening, Hernando Pizarro gave the order to attack the last of the fortress's towers. It was the largest, but had been built hastily, and its stonework was less than perfect.

When the Spaniards were halfway up the ladders, the Inca general in charge of the defense of Sacsayhuaman appeared alone on the little wall at the top of the tower. Broad gold disks hung glinting from his ears, marks of his high rank.

Gabriel watched, appalled, as the general began to rub dirt into his cheeks so hard that he abraded his skin. The Inca warrior picked up yet more dirt from between the tower's stones and rubbed it into the wounds he had just opened, until his face was unrecognizable.

All the Spaniards now stood stock-still, their eyes fixed on him. The Inca soldiers, meanwhile, stood just as still. It was as though an icy wind had frozen everyone in place.

Then, the general stuffed dirt into his mouth, wrapped his long cape around himself, and stepped out into the void. There wasn't a sound until his body smashed into a pile of sling stones.

Only then did Gabriel hear someone cry out from behind him. He turned around to discover ten Inca warriors staring at him. He saw the hesitation in their eyes and the rope in their hands. One of them raised his long, bronze club, ready to strike.

Gabriel shook his head.

"No," he said in Quechua. "Don't bother." Then he slowly drew his sword from its scabbard and flung it over the little wall. "I won't fight anymore," he said. "It's over."

The warriors bound his hands together and led him into the night. As they went, Gabriel listened to his Spanish companions' drunken cries of victory floating on the breeze.

He had wanted to die.

He had wanted to live.

Now, he wanted nothing at all.

PART TWO

SEVEN

Ollantaytambo, June 1536

In the *canchas* out on the plain, in the fork between the two rivers, and on the slopes where the terraces and temples stood, in tiers, hundreds of fires burned. But there was no singing, no sound of drums, no cries of joy or drunkenness. The only sound was the murmuring of water, a haunting lament filled with sadness, that permeated Anamaya's soul.

The combatants crossed the bridge with the pace of the defeated. They went one by one, wordlessly, their expressions impassive and their heads bowed. By the hoary light of the full moon, their faces looked like tarnished silver. Deep lines of exhaustion crossed their foreheads and cheeks like so many wounds. Their *unkus* were torn to shreds and covered in blood and mud. Their limbs were weary, and their weapons dangled from the ends of their arms like useless toys. Even those carrying swords or those few leading horses taken from the Spaniards were deeply ashamed. They had lost.

When they caught sight of Manco and Villa Oma on the other side of the bridge, they slumped their shoulders as if the weight of their defeat had become too great to bear. But still Manco encouraged them with a little gesture or a few proud words as they passed. Then they disappeared into the night. Yet, despite their exhaustion, they found little rest.

Anamaya watched Villa Oma. The Sage's piercing gaze was lost in the distance, traveling along the length of the Sacred Valley to the hills over Cuzco. He seemed to be reliving the battle they should have won but didn't. His face was taut with silent rage.

For once, Manco was not standing in defiance of the Sage. His proud profile revealed only sympathy and encouragement for the warriors. Anamaya was surprised by this expression of gentleness, which had until now remained masked by the violence that had been corrupting Manco's heart ever since his humiliation by the Spaniards, or even, perhaps, since the day he was born.

Anamaya had hardly slept since Titu Cuyuchi brought her the news of Gabriel's disappearance. Whenever she felt herself about to fall asleep, she saw a vision of the Puma pass before her mind's eye. And during the day, she was tormented by chimeras of its shadow. She continued playing the role of *Coya Camaquen*, maintaining appearances and saying the right things, and everyone—including the priests and soothsayers who had come to pay their respects to her—continued to look to the *Coya Camaquen* for consolation or inspiration. But in the most private corner of her soul, she was a woman tormented by concern for her beloved.

And in this hour of defeat—worse because it was snatched from the jaws of victory—her concern for the man she loved was greater than any other, and she was almost ashamed of it.

"Come with me."

Katari's voice was so low it was practically a whisper, no louder than a bat flapping its wings in the night. Anamaya wasn't sure she'd heard him right. She turned toward him. The young man tilted his head slightly, his long hair flowing down to his shoulders. He didn't repeat himself, but motioned for her to follow. Anamaya banished her preoccupations about Manco and Villa Oma.

The two young people walked near the river, listening to its rumbling. They followed the low wall that ran alongside the water, its carefully fitted stones marking the river's sacred nature. Moonlight lit the path rising before them toward the city. There, they could see the hearths burning in the houses and temples, looking like distant stars belonging to another world.

Anamaya's beating heart slowed a little.

Now she could hear the water from the mountains gurgling in the canals that fed the fountains, and its music added a counterpoint to the deep rumble of the Willkamayo River.

Katari suddenly stopped in his tracks. Anamaya stared at his broad shoulders for a moment before following his gaze toward the western mountains, above which Quilla's perfectly round disk hung suspended.

The black silhouette of a condor began to emerge from the darkness. The mountain was shaped like a giant, watchful bird. A rock jutting out was its beak and head with one eye wide open, its ruff retracted between two powerful wings. Motionless, it looked as though it were staring down the Sacred Valley, protecting it, threatening anyone tempted to defile it.

After a long moment, Katari turned to Anamaya.

"It's time," he said simply.

Once again, Anamaya found herself admiring the young man's calm disposition and the radiant wisdom emanating from him, from his broad, muscled body, and from his eyes, slender like elongated flaws in a *huaca*.

She didn't immediately notice that sections of the rock had been worked by human hands. Rivulets had been cut for water, and countless nicks marked the base, a sign that men had been coming here for innumerable seasons to commune with the gods.

They passed into the condor's shadow and were hidden from the moon. Anamaya followed Katari confidently, despite the darkness, stepping where he had stepped.

They walked around an enormous flat shale stone set in the ground. Its shape seemed familiar to Anamaya. Embers glowed red in a small cavity carved out at its center, and Katari had little trouble rekindling them until he had a fire burning. Anamaya looked up and scrutinized four little niches carved into the rock. She had the impression that she recognized the place.

As she stood there, recovering her breath from the walk, she was overcome by a strange feeling. Katari was communicating with her without speaking. She was almost frightened by the ease with which she instinctively surrendered to the power.

"There's nothing to fear," he said gently.

"You were listening to my thoughts?"

Katari's laugh tinkled in the night.

"You should know that I listen to you even when I'm not at your side. . . ."

She remembered Gabriel lost in the Salar Desert. Her unease left her and she smiled back at him.

"You said that you could help me. . . ."

"I can. But first, all your fear must leave you. Also . . ."

Katari had already spread out his *manta* before him.

"Also?"

"We must be one to make the voyage."

"One? But I need you to make it. What do you mean, Katari? I don't understand."

"There is water, and there is stone," said Katari, "there is This World and there is the Underworld, there is the Willkamayo and there is the Way in the stars, there is Inti and Quilla, there is silver and there is gold . . . everything in the universe has its twin . . . but we can only see the one hidden in the heart of things if we know how to look."

Anamaya's heart had leaped as soon as Katari had started talking. In her mind, she added, There are Incas and there are Strangers. But she didn't dare say it out loud.

"I still don't understand," she murmured.

Katari glanced at her.

"You understand better than you say you do . . . but I can't explain it to you now. Simply remember that nothing you discover will be hidden from me. Do you trust me enough to do that?"

She watched him pull out a bundle of leaves from his *manta*. They had come from a forest plant, not a mountain one. He flung them onto the flames. A strong, acrid smoke rose up from the fire.

"You trust me enough to take me there," said Anamaya. "Let me give you what I . . ."

"I will guide you, Anamaya, and yet you will be the one taking *me* there."

She stared at the four niches and at the incredible outline of the rock in which they were encased. She smiled. She knew what voyage he was talking about.

Katari looked away from her. He closed his eyes and swung his head from side to side, using his long hair to fan the smoke in Anamaya's direction. He began singing a monotonous chant in a language that Anamaya didn't recognize. The smoke filled her nostrils and soon it and the song filled her head and even her entire body. She felt both heavy with sleep and alert, almost incapable of moving yet utterly light-weight. She saw him rise.

He sat next to her, holding in his hands a magnificent *kero,* a wooden vase incised with minute geometric patterns, the details of which she could make out with astonishing—even supernatural—clarity. A small volume of dark green liquid sat in its bottom.

Katari pulled out two smaller, undecorated *keros.* They were made of raw, unhewn wood, still in the shape of the branches that they had once been. Only the cavities within them had been worked by the hand of man.

He filled the two wooden goblets and handed one to Anamaya. They drank slowly, letting the liquid's soft flavor, not unlike that of unripe corn, permeate their palates and throats.

Katari's chanting had begun softly, like the distant murmur of a mountain stream; his voice had risen now, so that it almost drowned out the sound of the water coursing through the fountains. Anamaya's entire body became enmeshed in the chant's rhythm, from the buzzing in her ears to the dull thud of her heart. The song seemed to emanate not from Katari's throat, but from the rocks and water around them, and from the mountain itself.

She heard a more high-pitched voice rise above Katari's monoto-nous chant. Suddenly, she succumbed to a violent spasm, as though lightning were surging from the nape of her neck, down her back, and flooding each of her limbs. It happened again and again, and each time she surrendered to the sensation as though it were an amorous embrace. It was in fact pleasurable, and her pleasure took the form of a delicious explosion as wave after seething wave passed through her. Her belly felt hot, almost burning. Her happiness was so complete and so intense that she didn't measure its brevity.

Then the silence returned, and blots of brilliantly intense, glowing colors danced before her eyes.

The song had ended. All that remained was the sound of water streaming into the fountain, in the canal that ran along the Condor *huaca,* and rumbling in the river down below. But in the fraction of a second in which nature was suspended and all was calm, her perceptive faculties became so sharp that she could see, hear, feel, and taste everything through the hollow night. Her ears heard every fluctuation of the wind, from the slightest breeze to strong gusts. She felt it caressing her skin, and she opened her mouth and nostrils wide to gorge herself on it. Suddenly, a bird's cry echoed through the air. She hadn't heard that sound since childhood, when she lived in the middle of the forest. She inhaled the smells of the earth, the scents of its humus and dense vegetation loaded with nocturnal moisture.

She heard a shuffling on the stones nearby and opened her eyes. Katari was staring at the four niches in front of them. She looked at them, too, unable to see how deep they were. He reached for her hand, and she gave it to him without fear.

As they approached the rock face on their knees, a weak, milk-colored glow lit up one of the niches, as though it were emanating from the rock itself. They lowered still farther until they were crawling and their bodies were flush with the rock. The white light from the niche now engulfed them completely. Anamaya felt a continuous tremor in the rock. She couldn't tell whether the niche had expanded to allow them to enter or whether they had shrunken to its size. It didn't matter.

At some point, the feel of the rock on Anamaya's skin turned from a scraping friction to a smooth caress, and she felt as though all the weight and anxieties of her body were giving way to a very gentle mantle, as though her flesh and the matter surrounding it had fused. She heard distant voices echoing within her, saying that it was thus, once, that men had been born. But her rapture didn't allow her time to listen closely; limb by limb, her body was absorbed into the mountain, and the last human sensation she felt was Katari's hand wrapped around hers. She saw her fear off in the distance, a ball of flames traveling through the night, a ball of suffering in her mind, and the very great weight of the mountain brought her an unimaginable sense of lightness, as though one enormous mass were being stopped by another even greater one that would absorb it piece by piece, fiber by fiber.

She was stone. She was the mountain itself.

The strangest part was that she retained an unequivocal consciousness of herself. She was still Anamaya, but now an Anamaya enriched by an entire universe of sensations, one in which all things and all nature's aspects were agglomerated. Before she had time to delight in the feeling once again, all the fibers of her being began to surge like a thousand drums, a thousand trumpets, a thousand rivers, or a thousand stars hurtling toward a colossal explosion. And at the center of this sensation of abundance, she felt her being shrink into a tiny ball, the only purpose of which was to make the immense effort to extricate itself from the rock—as though, finding herself ingrained in the utterly immovable rock, she wanted above all to avoid dissolving into it and disappearing.

She heard Katari speaking to her in a very low yet clear voice from within. "Come, Anamaya. It is time."

She entered the other side.

Air.

The vibrations she felt were all that held her up, a gliding sensation, a lightness.

She was flying.

For the moment, she felt nothing other than delight, a sense of power coupled with one of absolute and infinite freedom. It seemed to her that she no longer had eyes to see, nor ears to hear, and that her body had become a fragile thing, like a *balsa* drifting on a river of wind.

You are the Condor.

For a moment, after the thought had occurred to her, she was struck by the strangeness of it. Then she realized that Katari was no longer beside her holding her hand. He was with her in her flight—he had become the Condor with her and for her.

She let herself go completely, feeling no fear or reticence.

She realized then that she had passed through the night and that she was watching the sun rise, that currents of air were carrying her higher into the sky. The world lay unfurled beneath her wings in all its magnificence; the winding river at the bottom of the valley, silver-scaled like the snake Amaru, the god of wisdom, who had come to her so often. He was everywhere in the valley, coiled around himself, nestled in the emerald bower of the forest.

She gazed at the distant mountains. She was as high as they. Salcantay's snowbound summit and all the Apus of the Andes offered themselves to her in their majesty by the light of the rising sun. She heard Katari chanting joyful incantations: *"Hamp'u! Hamp'u!"* And it was as though the mountains scintillated in the light by way of reply.

She recognized them, of course: the Young Mountain and the Old one watching over the city-that-cannot-be-named, where the young girl she had once been had been admitted many years earlier. She glided over the stepped terraces of harvest-ready corn and over the buildings of the city itself, where the tiny forms of priests and astronomers, soothsayers and architects, were emerging to begin the daily ritual of saluting Inti's return.

She could feel the gazes of the men below looking up at the Condor high in the sky, and she felt pleased by their fear and respect.

"It's here," she said to Katari, "that the Empire's secret of all secrets is hidden. The place that must exist beyond time is found here."

Katari said nothing, but she felt his joy, and she flapped her massive wings to carry them higher into the sky.

"Villa Oma took me there when he was still the one known as the Sage and could communicate with the gods. But he has lost his way and forgotten how to go there, and will never find it again."

"Look at the Sun triumph," said Katari.

They were above a stone in the heart of the secret city. The sun's rays were hooked onto it, as they were every day before spreading to illuminate the world and divide time. The stone had been hewn in ancient times to acknowledge the eternal momentum of the Young Mountain, Huayna Picchu.

They glided above it, caught up in the harmony that emanated from it. They were moved by the synchronicity between Man's wisdom and Nature's order that was evident here. The stone looked as though it had been cut to receive light, and the way it divided light from shadow was a prayer that silently echoed through the mountains. Its fragility was out of reach. Its beauty was memory itself.

Anamaya felt all her sensations pass through Katari at the same time, as though he were gorging himself on some intoxicating liquid— every temple, every terrace, every stone summoned in him the legend of the origins of the world, of its water, its stone, and its peoples.

The sun slowly warmed the muggy air. All the perfect sounds of life, from pestles grinding in mortars to the crackling fires stoked by women, from the frantic course of squirrels to the blood-flowers of orchids, converged and were unified in this perfection.

Anamaya climbed over the terraces and made out the invisible vein that crossed the Old Summit. It was the way she had taken many years earlier, when a condor had interrupted the priests as they were about to sacrifice a young girl. She remembered the look in the girl's eyes and the feel of her little hand clasping her own, and she remembered the childlike confidence and absolute trust that was implicit in that grasp.

As they approached the summit, their flight slowed and grew heavier. Her wings no longer carried her so well, and she felt suddenly very tired.

She landed just above the *huaca*.

She could hear nothing but breath—her own, Katari's, and the wind's.

"Look," said Katari. "Look into the depths of your own heart."

She automatically looked at the Huayna Picchu, its slender profile rising up before her. Her gaze fell into the abyss and was suspended facing the mountain, so that she could make out its every outcrop and crevice. And then, a terrible and familiar form loomed up suddenly from it: the Puma.

The mountain had become the Puma, or else the Puma had become the mountain in the same way that Katari and she had become the Condor. The magic spectacle fueled her passions, and she felt a river of all too human emotions flow through her. Gabriel, she thought to herself, at first timidly, and then with gathering conviction: Gabriel!

"It is he. He is in front of you, and he is waiting for you," Katari said softly.

Before she had time to understand or even think about it, she was overcome with joy. He was here, right in front of her, and all her fears evaporated with the breaking day.

She remained before the puma-mountain for a long time. She felt protected by its power. She understood now the meaning of Katari's profound intuition: Nothing could harm Gabriel. The Apus were protecting him.

When the sun had reached its zenith, she unfurled her wings and set off again.

With a single flap of her wings, they glided down toward the esplanade before the temples. They hovered above it, assessing the vertigo that seizes men lost between the bed of the Willkamayo, rumbling far below, and the snow-capped peaks of the distant Vilcabamba Cordillera.

A small stone stood by itself at one of the esplanade's corners. It had been expertly hewn, marking the Four Directions.

And it spoke.

The esplanade was completely empty, but had anyone been on it, they would have seen the odd sight of a condor facing the rock, absorbing the sun's heat. At least, that was how it would have appeared to those who could not see.

Only Katari knew that Anamaya had transformed once again into an innocent young girl, a pure and wounded child standing at the great Huayna Capac's side, and he in the twilight of his life. Katari saw her dressed in a white *añaco* held closed by a simple red sash, kneeling by the old Rock King, his gray skin trembling, his ragged profile turned toward the snows, toward the Underworld. He saw her leaning toward the King in perfect silence, listening to him speak.

Katari could hear every word.

> *You are with me, young girl with eyes the color of the lake,*
> *And I will never leave you while you watch over my Sacred*
>   *Double,*
> *After which everything will disappear, and he as well.*
> *You will see the Puma; he will bound here from across the ocean.*
> *He will only come to you when he leaves you.*
> *Although separated, you will be united as one,*
> *And when everyone has left, you will remain, and the Puma*
>   *will remain at your side.*

Together, like your ancestors, Manco Capac and Mama Occlo,
You will beget new life on earth.
There will be wars just as there have always been wars,
Separations just as there have always been separations,
And the Strangers, in their triumph, will know misery,
And we, the Incas, will have to know humiliation, we will
*   become slaves to our own shame before we understand the*
*   long journey that we have made, a journey that our*
*   Panacas, driven by the lust for war alone and no longer*
*   inspired by Inti, have forgotten in their destruction and*
*   madness.*
But we will not die.

Anamaya was in the old king's breath. Once again, she listened to him tell the story of the ancient times, of the creation of the world, of the confidence of the Incas born in the cradle of the mountains of Cuzco; she listened to him proudly tell of his military victories; and she listened to him despair over the war between his sons. He spoke about the ball of fire that had designated Atahualpa, and she remembered; he spoke of Manco, *the first knot of the future,* and she remembered.

I wanted to turn to stone, just as the Ancients of my race did,
*   and remain still on the soft, green grass of one of Cuzco's*
*   mountain slopes.*
War chased me away. I found refuge in the Secret City.
My stone opens to the Four Directions, just as I expanded the
*   Empire of the Four Cardinal Directions, and yet it's a*
*   humble stone, for it will be all that remains of the Empire, a*
*   stone to which the Sun will hitch itself.*
The Four Directions will remain in the heart of a pure man.
Today, there is already war between brothers, although they
*   don't know it yet.*
And there will be more war,
War visits the Sons of the Sun and war visits the Strangers: It is
*   the sign.*

> *The brother's blood and the friend's blood are shed far more than*
> *the enemy's: It is the sign.*
> *The stone and the waters vanish in the forest: It is the sign.*
> *The Stranger who worships a woman rather than his Ancestors*
> *is killed: It is the sign.*
> *No seer sees it; the priests are baffled; the Sun hides itself from*
> *the astronomers; betrayal insinuates itself as a friend of the*
> *people; the Ocean vomits Strangers on us, in ever-greater*
> *numbers. Soon it will be time for you to flee in order to*
> *preserve what has always been and what will always be.*
> *But you will heed the signs, and you will remain with our*
> *people until that moment when Inti has consumed the*
> *hatred dividing us, and only women singing their grief over*
> *all the spilled blood will remain.*
> *You will make no mistake.*
> *You will meet Him Whose Stone Stops Time and he will stand*
> *before me like you; but he will go to the place of origins*
> *whereas you will take the road to the city-that-cannot-be-*
> *named.*
> *You will know what must not be spoken, and you will not speak*
> *it.*
> *You will say only what must be and will be, and when it shall*
> *have been then two fingers of one hand, two fingers of one*
> *hand will unite you.*
> *You will be free.*
> *You will take my Sacred Double to the end of his way, and he*
> *too will be free.*
> *Only one secret will remain hidden within you. You will have to*
> *live with it.*
> *Never doubt me. Remain in my breath, and trust the Puma.*

Silence returned, save for the eternal speech of the wind and the river. Heavy black clouds filled the air and hid the sun.

Anamaya remained as still as Huayna Capac. Her hand was resting on the dying sovereign's body. Her old pain was young once again, and the loneliness that she had done away with now returned to grip her heart. She kept her eyes closed. She shuddered. She sensed the presence leaving without actually moving, heading to another shore, and she ached from being unable to go with it and live with it.

Katari put his hand on her shoulder and restrained her suffering.

The entire valley filled with fog, and they could no longer see the summits, the golden corn on the terraces disappeared, the ripe *quinua* turned gray, and the temples looked as though they had been built from water stone. Shreds of clouds streamed around them, as if in a slow dance.

Anamaya took her hand away from Huayna Capac's corpse.

She could see only the stone, but she wasn't surprised.

Katari's broad palm still rested on her shoulder. She was still sad, but she felt that her friend had stopped her from embarking on a dangerous voyage.

They both looked to the west, where a halo of light was still filtering through the clouds on the black horizon.

Then, the sky tore open as suddenly as it had closed. A rainbow's column stood in the central opening of the temple of the three niches.

"Come," said Katari.

Together, they rose into the sky.

Night had fallen on Ollantaytambo.

Katari and Anamaya were lying on the little wall that ran alongside the Willkamayo. Neither dared speak.

The sky was clear and the moon full. The condor-rock was visible in the light.

"I had a dream. You were in it," said Anamaya eventually, sitting up.

Katari didn't move, his eyes wide open and staring at the immensity of the star-speckled sky.

"I had the same dream," he said without looking at her.

"How do you know?"

Katari didn't answer out loud, but Anamaya heard his voice echo from within her, and in a flash she realized that the voyage that they had undertaken together had been real. Katari was right. She wanted to ask him if they had returned to their point of departure or if a day had passed. She looked at the moon, which was almost completely full, but didn't find the answer.

You will know what must not be spoken, and you will not speak it.

Anamaya let the words resonate within her, and she suddenly felt the full power of Huayna Capac's speech. No, she was no longer the terrified little girl who forgot the past, the present, and the future; nor was she the *Coya Camaquen* who had to continually struggle to understand the mystery. The world was in place: That which had been revealed remained, and that which was secret remained so as well.

They heard a dull rumbling sound from the north.

Katari sat up.

At first they wondered if it wasn't a convulsion of the earth, one that would shake the rock and lift the river out of its bed. But the rumbling gained strength, and they both realized its source at the same moment. It was coming from the mountain facing them, the one that rose above both the rivers, the one that stood guard over the Sacred Valley.

The mountain roared like a man being racked by violent pain. They felt it tremble, they felt the breaking point of its tension, and they saw an enormous block break away from the rock face, leaving a gaping cavity.

A thick cloud of black dust slowly rose up and permeated the night, and still the mountain quaked sporadically. Another almighty cracking sound signaled the breaking away of an entire side of the mountain, and Katari and Anamaya watched it fall away as best they could through the thick cloud of dust. After that, the mountain let forth two more agonized cries, howling against the scars that it was inflicting upon itself.

They watched the spectacle with utter fascination, quickly forgetting their own fears. This upheaval of nature wasn't some rage against Man. It came from farther away. Merely watching it was part of the secret.

The dust began to get in their eyes, half-blinding them. They were obliged to go to the fountain and wash out their burning eyes. Afterward, they remained by the fountain, waiting.

When the mountain had stopped making noise altogether, they turned around. The dust cloud was slowly settling, revealing the mountain's new form.

Anamaya cried out.

She saw Huayna Capac's face, clearly defined in the moonlight, revealed in the stone. It was his face as it had been at the hour of his death all those years ago, and as it had been during her dream—her flight—as a condor.

He was carved into the side of the mountain, as though some gargantuan sculptor had chiseled him there. He was the man of stone, a hundred times—a thousand times—bigger than those of flesh.

His eye was sunken into its cavity, and his thickset nose extended the straight line of his forehead, a mark of his resolve. A crack marked his mouth, and his chin was covered in a long beard of rocks. He was facing north, as though looking beyond the forest and toward the Secret City in its valley.

Anamaya knew then that the knowledge was within her.

EIGHT

Ollantaytambo, Choquana lock, June 16, 1536

His hands tied behind his back, his feet shackled with thick agave ropes that reduced the length of his step considerably, and guarded by a dozen warriors day and night, Gabriel had been walking for three days.

After his capture, he had been taken to a hamlet made up of wretched adobe houses beneath some arid mountain. He had been kept there for many months. The old woman who fed him didn't answer his questions any more than did his guards. His questions dwindled as time passed, and after the blind exultation of battle, he gradually slipped into an apathetic despair. He was no more master of his own fate now than he had been before, and he allowed himself to slide toward it without rancor, thinking that it could only be death. The thought that it would have been better had they killed him straight away had crossed his mind, but he quickly banished it as inopportune.

Three days earlier, they had come to fetch him at daybreak, and had told him that it was time to go. He had said nothing, and since then he had barely exchanged three words with his guards. They looked at him with an indifference with which he was now so familiar, and which he knew hid a deep curiosity as well as, most probably, fear. At sundown, he heard them discussing among themselves, but he was too exhausted to make the effort to understand what they were saying.

He woke as though from a dream.

For all those weeks, he had lived like a man possessed: surviving Gonzalo's revenge, then the burning of his prison, and avoiding the arrows and sling stones before taking the tower. He watched himself accomplish all these things in his mind, actions that had won him his companions' admiration, but he couldn't shake the feeling that he was watching a play being performed in the theater of his mind, in which a masked actor was playing himself. It was as though he, Gabriel, had been asleep throughout, as though he had slipped out of himself. When he found himself tied up once more, powerless, and being marched through this valley locked away in the mountains, it brought him disagreeably back to life.

He could see in front of him only the backs of the porters' bare legs, their muscled calves like knotted wood. They bore enormous sheaves of *quinua*, which made the broad Incan road ahead seem as though it had been transformed into a field being ruffled by a fickle wind. Gabriel exhaled all the air in his lungs; the sheaves shivered; he exhaled again; still they shivered. Suddenly, and absurdly, he felt an irrepressible urge to laugh. "I am the master of *quinua!*" he cried in Spanish. "I am the master of the grain!" He exhaled as though his lungs were the fountainhead of the winds. The Indian soldiers looked at him, clutching their spears and slingshots tighter: Had the prisoner gone mad? Gabriel laughed so hard that he broke out into a paroxysm of coughing and then stopped suddenly.

The river valley, which at first had been broad, became progressively narrower as they made their way up it. Cliffs now rose up on both its sides, at the bases of which fortresses had been built. The river meandered from one cliff to the other, from one fort to the next. Hundreds, or perhaps even thousands, of men wearing only their *hauras* were working to reinforce the forts, and they had formed long lines to pass down enormous blocks of stone while work teams erected walls and frameworks.

But it was only when the soldiers urged him to ford the river that Gabriel saw the magnificent spread of terraces rising up through the valley and, up above, an imposing building commanding over its entirety, no less fascinating for being unfinished. Whether it was a temple or a fortress, he couldn't tell—and in any case, he knew that the Incas no longer made the distinction between the two.

His breath was cut short.

In that moment, the exhilarating and painful conviction came to him out of nowhere that he was going to see her.

*   *   *

Nightfall brought with it a cool breeze. Gabriel, passing through the rectilinear streets, each one perfectly paved and lined by high, narrow doors leading into *canchas* under steep, thatched roofs, was struck by the bustling activity.

It was a city under construction, teeming with endless activity and people speaking to one another not only in Quechua, which he had mastered, but also in Jaki aru and Pukina, Kollasuyu languages of which he had learned just enough to differentiate between them. Many of the town's people had never seen a Stranger, and they struggled to hide their astonishment upon seeing him, with his long, tangled blond hair and the beard that covered his face after weeks of imprisonment and, before that, combat. Upon entering the town, his guards had moved in closer around him, as though they were worried that he might attempt the impossible action of escaping into the crowd.

They came to a halt before a *cancha* guarded by two *orejones,* as the Spaniards had taken to calling those Incan noblemen whose ears were distended by disks that before the conquest had been made of gold, but since were more often made of wood.

Gabriel was shoved into the building with little ceremony. He was familiar with its layout. The courtyard was full of soldiers. Behind them were the women, some busy preparing a meal, others gathered timidly together in little groups at the back of the courtyard just in front of the staircase leading up to the first floor shared with the neighboring *cancha.* Gabriel immediately recognized Manco sitting on his royal *tiana* in the center. He also recognized the emaciated and thin-lipped Villa Oma sitting on a bench to Manco's side, only slightly lower than the Emperor. Although his circumstances were greatly reduced, Gabriel felt that the young sovereign nevertheless exuded a far greater majesty and dignity than he had at the grand affair of his coronation on the Aucaypata in Cuzco. Gabriel couldn't help but be struck by the dark but inflexible will that Manco seemed to embody. The puppet-king installed on the throne by Don Francisco had died. In his place had been born a warrior who had almost defeated the Spaniards at Sacsayhuaman, and whose troops were still laying siege to Cuzco. But the one person Gabriel couldn't see was Anamaya.

A heavy silence filled the room.

Gabriel looked from the Sage to the Inca and from the Inca to the Sage. Gabriel had learned from the Incas not to speak too soon and to read the expression of his interlocutor's face before opening his mouth. Villa Oma broke the silence first.

"The Stranger must die," he spat, rising slowly from his *tiana.* There was fury in his calm. All those present were frozen in their places.

"He assaulted the tower at Sacsayhuaman. Many of our warriors died because of him. It is because of him that the noble Cusi Huallpa sacrificed himself. The Strangers pretend that he has magic powers greater than that of any of our soothsayers and that he is protected by their gods. These are ridiculous lies! Let us cut him into pieces and send them his skull; let us flay off his skin and make a drum with it and send them that too! That will prove our warriors are far more powerful than their so-called gods! We should have killed him long ago. Only our weakness prevented us from doing so. . . ."

Villa Oma turned toward Manco and, with an exasperation clearly too long suppressed, continued.

". . . And it was due to that same weakness that we relinquished complete victory over the mongrel Strangers!"

No one had ever dared attack Manco so directly and unambiguously in public. Gabriel was aware of the insult and, oddly, since it was his own life that was the subject of the argument, he felt a calm sense of detachment, as though he were an onlooker watching others decide his fate. He looked directly at Manco, ignoring the Sage, and said in a calm voice:

"I am more indifferent to my life than you are. My own people tried to take it from me, but God—or luck—let me keep it. You would take it for doing what soldiers do? Then kill me. It's not my place to say whether that is justice or else a pointless cruelty that would offend your gods as well as those of my own people."

Manco still hadn't said a word. He seemed lost in his own thoughts, almost completely inert. Villa Oma grew exasperated.

"Let us do away with him, brother Manco! It will be the sign that the people and the gods are waiting for to give us a brilliant victory."

"This man will not die."

Manco had spoken without looking at anyone in particular. Villa Oma was frozen in his fury. He raised his arm, pointing at Manco. But before he had the chance to affront the Inca, he was interrupted by a commotion at the *cancha*'s entrance. Two *chaskis,* streaming sweat, entered the courtyard and prostrated themselves before Manco.

"Speak," ordered the Inca.

Without raising his head, the older of the two began. "Emperor, we bring you news of a brilliant victory. Our troops have destroyed an army of Strangers sent by their *kapitu* to reinforce those we have surrounded in Cuzco. We killed many of their men and took many of their weapons and horses. These are being brought here, my Lord, as an offering to your glory."

Manco remained as impassive as he had been when Gabriel had been led into the *cancha.*

"Sage Villa Oma," he eventually said in a slow, measured voice, "must realize now that it isn't necessary to carry out injustices to ensure great victories."

Villa Oma's face was as green as the coca juice dribbling from his lips. But he said nothing. Without taking his leave, he cut through the crowd of astonished soldiers, shoved his way through the women, and swept up the stairs. When he reached the landing and was about to disappear onto the floor leading to the neighboring building, he wrapped his *manta* around himself, spun on his heels, and said:

"Manco, I have not forgotten that we are both sons of one father, the great Huayna Capac. Nor have I forgotten that you are the Son of the Sun. But Inti does what must be done to shine every day. Do you wish to bring eternal night upon us?"

The Emperor's soldiers moved toward the Sage following this insult. But Manco stopped them with a wave of his hand.

"Let him be," he said. "The Sage is no longer the Sage. Anger and hatred have overcome him, and his words are meaningless now, mere noises he makes when he moves his lips." Looking at Gabriel, he continued, "I too suffered humiliation at the hands of the Strangers. They wanted to take my wife from me, they treated me worse than a slave, worse even than a dog. But I kept silent, and in the secret places of our mountains, and with the help of our gods, I prepared for this war that we are going to win. . . ."

Manco's voice rose in volume as he spoke, and the murmur of approbation from his audience became a corresponding clamor, until the entire *cancha* echoed with their cries.

"And now," said Manco, once the clamor had died down, "I wish to be left alone with the Stranger."

He stood up suddenly, waving away the women who rushed forward to sweep the ground before him. He approached Gabriel and took him by the arm. The audience couldn't help but cry out in surprise, yet the Inca himself remained indifferent. He led Gabriel into another room, the largest and most richly decorated in the *cancha*.

Apart from that which passed through the door, the room was devoid of daylight. Gold and silver vases and animal statuettes sat in niches carved into the walls.

"You know, of course, the reason for my clemency?" said Manco dryly.

Gabriel couldn't hide his surprise.

"No, Lord Manco."

"No? And yet my reason is called by a name dear to your heart."

Through the shadows, Gabriel saw Manco's eyes flare up with anger. Only a moment before, the Inca had seemed as serene as the sage that Villa Oma had once been; now, the Emperor seemed to share his anger, and his eyes glowed with ire.

"Anamaya is the reason you live yet," said Manco. "If it weren't for what I know you mean to her, you would have been killed the day of your capture, and the dust of your body would now be fertilizing our fields. . . ."

"I know it, noble Manco. But I also know that you meant what you said to Villa Oma! You may hate me, but you cannot prevent me from admiring you."

"I am the Inca, Stranger! Remember that you look upon me now only because I wish it. Even your sentiments are not your own!"

Gabriel did his best to keep control of himself. He said, "In that case, you will allow me to keep the one thing that you cannot take from me: Silence."

Manco stared at him, saying nothing. Then he turned to leave the room. As he was about to pass through the door hanging, he turned, looked at Gabriel one last time, and spat spitefully:

"The Puma! The mighty Puma has come!"

NINE

Ollantaytambo, evening of June 18, 1536

Gabriel sank into the cold night.

He was dozing on his hard mat, listening to the sound of water running endlessly through the town, when an Indian slipped into the room that Manco had given him. No one had told him whether he was free or still a prisoner. His wrists had been untied and his ankles unshackled. He had been given two women to serve him and two Indians, taciturn Kollas, to protect him or perhaps guard him—he wasn't sure which. So when Katari slipped into his room, his heart leaped with joy: Katari was Bartholomew's friend, and above all it was Katari who had saved him on the shore of Lake Titicaca.

"Welcome, Master of the Stone! Are you here to bring me back to the world once again?"

To his great surprise, Katari said nothing and didn't even smile at his joke or make some gesture of friendship. His face, with its protruding cheekbones, remained completely impassive beneath his long hair.

"Follow me," was all he said.

Gabriel had been given a chance to wash and to throw away the filthy clothes that he had been wearing since the attack on the tower. He was now wearing a roomy Indian tunic made of alpaca wool. His muscles ached, and his body was stiff, as though he had just been in battle. He didn't question Katari, but simply rose and followed him through the heavy wool door hanging.

Katari spoke quietly with the two guards there, and they stepped aside. He stepped out onto the street, and Gabriel followed him past the silent *canchas*. Their sandals slipped silently over the flagstones. Katari crossed the great square without slowing and without saying a word, and soon they passed through a monumental gate. Gabriel following behind as they climbed up six platforms joined by flights of stairs. Then, despite the feeble light of the waning moon, Gabriel made out the base of a staircase before them, one that rose vertiginously in a straight line up the side of a hill. It was the hill on which he had seen the stepped terraces and massive structure when he had arrived that afternoon.

With each step he climbed, Gabriel shed the weight of both his exhaustion and Katari's odd attitude. He saw in the shadows beyond the terraces shored up with stones a building with many niches that he took to be a temple because of the quality of its walls. But his progressive shortness of breath, together with Katari's persistent silence, prevented him from asking the young man about it. Even when they reached the base of the massive walls enclosing the great temple that he had seen from the valley, Katari didn't stop or even slow down. The slope here, however, was a little less steep, affording Gabriel some small relief. Only when they reached a massive wall blocking the way farther up the hill did Katari stop.

Gabriel leaned against his thighs and breathed hard. When he had recovered his breath, he looked up at the Master of the Stone and asked, "Now will you talk to me?"

Katari said nothing, but at least his face had lost that neutral expression that Gabriel had mistaken for hostility.

"She is the one who will talk to you."

Gabriel lost his breath once again, but this time not from exertion. *Anamaya!* Ever since he laid eyes on Ollantaytambo, he had banished to a corner of his mind the thought that shocked his heart like a bolt of lightning: Seeing her, holding her . . . it was both so wonderful and so painful that he lowered his head and held it in his hands.

Katari pointed at the gentle winding path beyond the wall leading to the top of the hill.

"Go," was all he said.

He turned and disappeared without further explanation or even a good-bye. Gabriel looked at the path, then set off. Each step he took weighed on him. And he was trembling more than he ever had in battle.

*　　*　　*

Anamaya had been waiting alone in the little temple at the top of the hill since sundown. It wasn't visible from the valley, which was why she and Katari had chosen it. When they had told Manco of their idea, the Inca had listened without giving anything away before agreeing and sighing, "You know things that I don't."

So Katari had overseen the construction of the building, carried out by a small number of his Kolla brothers, so that the secret would remain so. It had been built in only one day: a simple supporting wall and a small building with four niches big enough to hold a man. Three nights previously, they had taken the Sacred Double there wrapped in *mantas* so that no soldier or priest or anyone other than Manco would know of it. The Sacred Double was now installed in the first niche, facing south.

Anamaya hadn't looked at the Sacred Double the same way ever since her great voyage. It was as though the knowledge that she had gained had quenched her thirst and done away with her anxiety. It was no longer he who held what she needed, but rather it was she who had to guard and protect him through the war.

And yet, when the last rays of sun had disappeared beyond the mountains behind her, when she found herself in the company of only the night's cold and wind, she couldn't help being overcome by the anxiety of waiting. Seeing Gabriel again, seeing him at last. She rose, stared into the darkness, and listened carefully for his step. She remembered how she had glanced at Katari when the *chaski* had brought the news that the prisoner was on his way. She checked her imagination from picturing herself running into his arms and holding him, or from imagining herself telling him all the things that she had kept to herself for so many moons. A jumble of Quechua and Spanish sat in her throat, and she felt the urge both to laugh and to cry.

She looked at the immobile, the eternal, Sacred Double, and some semblance of calm returned to her.

She took a short stroll outside the building. The breeze's murmur had grown as distant as those of the two rivers.

He will only come to you when he leaves you. Although separated, you will be united as one.

Those were the words of the great Huayna Capac. Did they refer to what had been or what was to be? Anamaya's blood boiled as she asked herself more questions than the prophecy had given her answers. There was another door on the other side of the door of knowledge, and then another, and so it continued until the end of life in this world until one reached the stairs leading to the Underworld.

A cloud hid the moon; the night turned pitch black. As the wind picked up again, Anamaya at last heard Gabriel's step. His silhouette appeared. She ran, not toward him but into the temple. He found her inside on the ground, her arms around the Sacred Double.

He slid down next to her.

They were unable to say a word or make a gesture.

They couldn't even look at each other.

The breeze picked up Gabriel's long blond locks and tangled them with Anamaya's black hair. They sat shoulder-to-shoulder, their skin barely touching. In mutual shock, they couldn't tell their own trembling from the other's.

Anamaya gathered herself first.

She slowly slid her honey-skinned hand onto Gabriel's shoulder, then let it slide between his *unku* and his skin. Slowly she ran her hand over his shoulder, and Gabriel's entire body shuddered at her touch. She traced out the mark of the Puma, knowing exactly where it was from memory, and scratched him lightly. He moaned.

Then she clasped her body onto his back and pressed her lips onto the mark that had been destined to him.

They rediscovered each other in the night.

Inchoate movements preceded any words between them: a giggle, a tear; Gabriel's hand furrowed deliciously through her hair, and then again, and again; Anamaya's nails scratched through his beard before she ran her palm over his cheeks, his chin, his entire face. They drew deep breaths of each other, touched each other, tamed each other with their fingers, their skin, their tongues. They struck each other gently, not painfully, but hard enough so that the marks they left roused forgotten senses.

Then, the length of their prolonged separation and of its corollary forbearance drove them into a furious embrace, and they caressed each

other almost violently, so that there was a brutality to their sweet pleasures. They rolled over each other like two young wildcats and bit each
other playfully, each one surprised by the fervor of the other's bite.
Gabriel had the advantage of superior strength, but Anamaya had the
reflexes of a forest animal and she slipped away from him just as he
thought he had her, only to jump on his back. He managed to turn
around and take hold of her; with a single movement, he made her
añaco slip to the ground.

They stopped and remained absolutely still.

She was naked before him. Their hurry to take each other dissolved
into the night. They stared at each other for a moment, and then it all
began again, hand in hand, lips to lips, but more slowly this time, each
gesture with a considered gentleness.

Anamaya held her breath as Gabriel's mouth approached her
breast. He kissed it as though he intended to cover every modicum of
her body with his lips. His desire was so deep and so intense that he
protracted it by being cruelly patient with her. Anamaya stretched
toward him and encouraged him, calling him to her not with words but
with soft moans—short, wordless cries that nevertheless conveyed her
desire for him. But he continued kissing her as lightly as he could
despite the urgency rising in his loins that was gradually wearing down
the measured pace of his exploration. Finally, she took his head
between her hands with such force that he brought his lips up to hers in
one movement. He kissed her forever, kissed her as though he were
drinking from a mountain spring after crossing the desert, kissed her as
one loves, as one breathes, as one lives—he kissed her as though he had
never kissed before.

Their clothes formed a bed on the ground, and they rolled around
on it. If it weren't for the different color of their skin, it would have
been hard to tell that they were two separate people. Yes, they wanted
to be *one*, the conquistador and the strange young girl from the forest,
the Spaniard and the Inca. In that moment, all they had was the other's
body, and Anamaya felt herself slipping into a place of happiness that
reminded her of her voyage with Katari. She came almost the very
instant he entered her, but as he persisted the dimensions of her pleasure broadened to include the universe itself, the stars and the streams

hidden in rocky mountain chasms. As for Gabriel, he was happy, and he thrust and thrust again and his roar filled valleys. He wasn't frightened of his body and all that was hidden inside it, and he felt able to push back all his limits. In one corner of his mind, he laughed at the irony of his past exploits: On his white horse, he had been but a boy; only now was he a man.

They became covered with sweat in the endless frenzy of their passion, and their sweat's salty flavor made them thirsty. The breeze picked up, the breeze died down, and the cold night reached them, but they didn't care. They stretched out the limits of the night, they smashed together like two stones, flowed like rivers, scratched each other's flesh like animals—they loved each other like a man and woman.

And even when, exhausted at last, they slipped into sleep, their love went with them.

They were lying at the Sacred Double's feet, their hands on each other's thigh, and with Gabriel's shoulder in the crick of Anamaya's neck. Their mouths were open, smiling.

They were happy and, because of it, beautiful.

The first rays of dawn grazed over the mountain ridges, waking Gabriel. He tightened his embrace around Anamaya. Together they sat up and watched as the world was reborn for another day: the fury of the waters flowing down the Willkamayo at the point where they were funneled through a narrow gorge; the narrow summit of the Wakay Willca.

As it emerged from night's shadows, Gabriel noticed the enormous shape in the side of the mountain facing them. He turned to Anamaya, a quizzical look in his eyes. She looked back at him without replying. But he felt the heat and even the light emanating from her, and without quite knowing why, he sensed that there was some link between her and the monumental and mysterious figure in the rock.

He drew her closer still, and she surrendered to him, but all the while keeping her eyes on Huayna Capac's face, for his words continued to reverberate through her mind like the rumble of the Patacancha River.

She spoke the first words between them since they had been reunited.

*   *   *

"Gabriel . . ."

The three syllables slipped from her lips as softly as a breath. Her soul was a seething cauldron: There was so much she wanted to tell him, and she didn't know where to begin, unsure of what he was allowed to hear. But then she succumbed to the urgency, and just as the light was now flooding through the valley and the mountains, so she had to feel herself flooded by his voice and reclaim it as she had his body.

"Tell me everything, Puma. . . ."

Gabriel described to her those appalling days when he had come to believe that the war separating them would never end, when he had given in to despair and had wanted only two things: to rid the world of Gonzalo and his henchmen and then to die. She smiled when he told her about the three Indians who had come to kill him in his cell, only to be thwarted by Sebastian's timely appearance. She displayed no emotion as she listened to his account of the battle, of Juan's death, of the strange feeling of invincibility that had risen up in him and that, along with his profound despair, had driven him to accomplish the most unimaginable and even absurd exploits.

"I didn't understand it then," murmured Gabriel, "and I still don't. I felt as though I were emanating light and as though I were surrounded by it. I'd heard silly talk of magic, you know, but I frowned upon it. Stories of arrows bouncing off of soldiers, of stones changing direction before hitting them and rolling harmlessly into the rocks. I don't believe those things any more than I believe in Don Francisco's beloved and very sacred Virgin. And yet, I had to suffer it; for although I myself didn't believe it, my companions, those few brave men as much as the rabble, did, and they looked upon me not as a hero—which is something I'm familiar with and which is in the end only a very human sentiment in which admiration and jealousy are mixed—but with a fear of the divine. But don't think that it made me proud. No, it only heightened my indifference, if such a thing is possible. When I flung my sword off the top of the tower, I felt like I was freeing myself. If I could have thrown my skin with it, I would have."

Gabriel paused for a moment. Anamaya let his words echo through her without yet trying to fathom their meaning.

"And then, in a dream, I had the strangest impression of actually *seeing* you."

Anamaya gave a start.

"It was as though I knew ahead of time what I was going to do, as though some messenger come from nowhere showed me lifelike images as clear as day of what was to come. That rope hanging from the top of the first tower, I *saw* it well before I took it in my hands. And when I did take it, I was already in a place beyond fear or courage, beyond doubt or duty: I was only doing what had to be done."

"You are arriving, drawing nearer . . . you are almost here. . . ."

"By leading the assault against your people?"

"You are here to save us."

"The night before, or even the same morning as the assault, I saw Inguill. She said those very same words. . . ."

"Accept them."

Gabriel shook his head. "Everything is still too new for me, for my mind. Sometimes I feel as though I'm separated from myself by a wall, a wall even thicker than those of the towers we took."

"You will pass through the wall."

Gabriel sighed.

"Well, for the moment, I've given up trying to understand more."

"What happened after you took the tower?"

"When your people took me prisoner, they captured a dazed man, his spirit broken, who didn't resist at all. Why didn't they kill me? To this day I don't know, just as I still have no idea why they kept me in that shack in the middle of the mountains for an entire month, feeding me those damned, shriveled-up old *papas*. You call them *chuños*, right? I'll never forget that taste of moldy earth. And can you tell me why, one fine day four days ago now, they finally decided to tear me away from that delicacy and bring me here?"

Gabriel sighed again, then said with a laugh, "Well now, Princess who knows all the secrets, can't you tell me?"

She hesitated and started gathering up their scattered clothes.

"It happened two moons ago, right?" she said eventually. "During those two moons, I often dreamed that if I saw you again, I would spend the entire night with you. And now I've had that night. . . ."

She stopped, leaving her sentence unfinished. But the time of his painful impatience was over. Bartholomew, he thought to himself, if you could see me now, you might well call me sagacious. . . .

"I want to tell you everything I have learned," she said at last, "because you are part of what I've learned. You might even be the most beautiful part of what I've learned. But you must first pass through each stage, as I did."

"I feel as though I've already passed through not a few stages," replied Gabriel with strained good-humor.

"I know, my love, I know. But there is still so much you have to learn. . . ."

"One terrible night, many years ago, we were standing by your Emperor Atahualpa's corpse. You allowed me a glimpse into that world then, didn't you?"

"I was very proud after being nominated *Coya Camaquen.* I was proud that the Powerful Lords called upon me to transmit the secrets of which I was myself unaware. I was so confused! But yes, you're right. I wanted to show you then that there was another world behind our love, another world beyond the war. . . ."

"Do you think I came near it?" asked Gabriel in a tone so beseeching that Anamaya couldn't help but laugh.

"My Puma is sometimes such a child," she said, taking his hand and holding it between hers, as if to temper the jest of her words. "But yes, of course you did, you drew near in great, furious bounds, without knowing where you were going, but always with your generous heart."

"I'm with you now, right? We're together now?"

Although separated, you will be united as one . . . She had searched for those words fruitlessly for so long. And now that she had them, she almost regretted knowing them, for they left her tongue-tied. She was no longer the little girl who knew nothing under Villa Oma's tutelage, she was no longer the proud *Coya Camaquen,* nor even the woman in love . . . but as these thoughts passed through her mind, her heart rebelled: Yes, she *was* still that woman in love, and no matter what secrets were revealed or what prophecies still lay hidden, she had to make her love live, she had to live it, gorge herself on it.

"Yes," she said, "you're with me."

Gabriel calmed down. He looked out over the magnificent land-scape being revealed by the rising sun. The face in the mountainside drew his eye more than anything else, more than the eternal snow on the peaks or the emerald rain forests below them. The face was only just visible by the weak light of dawn, but it was so prodigious that it was impossible not to look at it. Anamaya contemplated it with him.

"Who is he?" whispered Gabriel timidly.

"He's the one who brought us together."

TEN

Ollantaytambo, early July 1536

From the top of the great stairway that rose through the sacred terraces, Gabriel looked down upon an amazing sight. The *canchas* at the bottom of the valley had been built long ago. But Manco had decided to make Ollantaytambo his principal bastion, and all the narrow terraces overlooking it had been transformed into an enormous construction site. Gabriel had never before witnessed the Herculean effort that went into building an Inca city and, Manco having granted him a supervised liberty, he returned to this spot day after day, enthralled by the progress of the construction.

In the Chachicata quarry in the distance, hundreds of tiny silhouettes worked busily on blocks of stone of all sizes that had broken away from the Black Mountain. The valley was filled with the rhythmic pounding of hammers and chisels, made of hard stone or bronze, with which the tireless workers hewed the rock.

He could see people throughout the valley, from the foot of the mountain to the riverbank. Thousands of men, each one with a specific task, began work at dawn. Some chipped away at the boulders that had rolled to the bottom of the valley. They first chiseled them into a rough, unfinished shape, thus ridding them of unnecessary weight, before transporting them by raft from one riverbank to the other.

Others made rope or fashioned logs of wood with which to haul the rocks up the opposite slope, to the summit of Ollantaytambo. Hundreds of men pushed and hauled for hours on end. They levered the blocks up each section of terrain with enormous timbers, a slow, complicated system requiring great effort, but that allowed the blocks to be taken up safely and surely.

A great number of people were gathered at the end of the ramp along which the blocks were transported from the river to the construction site. Here, the work required more skill: Using only stone or bronze tools, and in a cloud of white dust, men sanded and polished the enormous blocks so that they fitted together perfectly. Gabriel watched, enthralled, as a group of men flocked around a boulder three times taller than any one of them. The block sat on a number of logs and was fastened by a web of rope.

Katari was in charge of this vast construction site. Gabriel occasionally caught sight of him supervising the erection of a temple, or the building of a wall, or the shaping of a rock, in his own sparing manner.

Gabriel never once doubted that Katari's endeavors complied with a corpus of precise rules. But they were unlike any of those in his own, admittedly very limited, knowledge of the architect's art. Katari never had a plan in his hand, for instance, and he seemed to prize the most unlikely and difficult loci on which to build his buildings. He could have expanded the town in the area between the two rivers in the valley where there were only fountains. But expanding the town was clearly not his objective. Nothing being built was designed to be lived in.

And none of the new buildings mystified Gabriel more than the temple halfway up the slope, set on a vast esplanade that had been cleared to make room for a number of blocks already prepared. Only one of its walls had been erected so far, from four enormous blocks of pink rock fitted together. The stone displayed an astonishing variety of iridescence as the sun shifted throughout the day. Between each rock was what appeared to the unknowing eye as a long stone reed.

As with all of the Incas' most magnificent buildings, no mortar held the blocks together. Each block was simply hewn to fit perfectly with its neighbor, and the walls rose up majestically, provocatively, and indestructibly. Drawing closer, Gabriel saw that three of the rocks were decorated with stylized knurls. He tried to guess their purpose.

"Do you find them beautiful?"

Katari was sweating, but his almond eyes and his face, with its protruding cheekbones, were smiling. He wore nothing over his torso, like all his workers. Gabriel admired his strong physique; his broad hands were covered in fine rock dust and seemed strong enough to snap a man's back with little effort. A stone key hung from a small gold chain around his neck.

Gabriel didn't try to hide his admiration.

"It's magnificent, Katari. I've never seen anything like it. I doubt even our best architects are capable of bringing about such wonders."

"We are not trying to build wonders."

"What are you trying to do?"

"You already know better than you imagine."

Gabriel was taken aback.

"What do you mean?"

Katari's smile broadened.

"Don't the shapes of these stones remind you of something?"

Gabriel screwed up his eyes and stared at the enormous blocks. Slowly, a shape formed in his mind. It was a blurred shape and an ancient one associated with forgotten miseries. . . .

"Taypikala!" he cried. "There were stones like these there!"

Katari nodded.

"There's more. Come closer."

Gabriel came up close to the rocks. It was midday and their shadows were short. He saw that strange reliefs had been carved on their surfaces. He thought he recognized the geometry of a double staircase. The upper flight rose up in the normal way, but the bottom one led down upside down, like the reflection of a mountain on a lake's surface. On another block set on its plinth, Gabriel brushed his hands over the relief of a T-shaped key.

"I've seen this before," he exclaimed, turning to Katari.

"In the same place." said the Master of the Stone. "Are you surprised?"

"I don't know," said Gabriel frankly. "I don't know what it means."

"I could tell you that these hollows, cut with bronze keys like this one around my neck, are designed to help us set the stones in position, and that these knurls are used to secure the stones to transport them here, but . . ."

He fell silent, his gaze wandering over the northern horizon.

"But?"

". . . it would be true. But it wouldn't be all there was to it. There's something else."

Gabriel's curiosity was piqued: not only his curiosity, but also a desire to enter another world, one he had skirted for so long without suspecting it.

"Do you see the town down there," said Katari, "with its *canchas* and their courtyards and the rooms coming off them? The alleys are set to a plan. Their lines are designed to cross. I've never seen one of your towns, Stranger, but ours no doubt didn't surprise you. But this one, on the other hand . . ."

Katari waved his arm all around him and looked at Gabriel.

". . . here, we want to pay homage to the gods with every building, every stone, every rock. We want to pay homage to the gods around us: our father the Sun, of course, but also the Moon, Illapa the Lightning Bolt, and all those mountain peaks. Look at those terraces. . . ."

All around were small terraces full of tall corn, as though the temple were embedded in them.

"As you can see, they aren't arranged in a haphazard way. They surround this temple like a jewel box. As for the temple itself, our astronomers have been watching the sky for a long time, observing the movement of the stars and planets to determine its position, as well as the orientation of each of its walls. For us, both shadow and light are a form of homage to the gods. . . ."

Gabriel thought fleetingly of the ancient abbeys and churches of his country. His mind made a tenuous connection between the Christian cathedral masons and the Incas. But he was too absorbed by Katari's tale to dwell upon it.

". . . What I'm telling you is no great secret," continued Katari almost flippantly. "All Incas know it. But what they don't know is that by approaching the stone, by looking at it and touching it, they can learn the most hidden secrets of our history, they can travel back to the most ancient times, when even the Incas didn't exist."

"You mean that the Incas haven't always been masters of this land?" said a surprised Gabriel.

Katari burst out laughing.

"The Incas are only a very few generations of men, excellent but not invincible warriors, as both you and I now know. . . ." Katari glanced at Gabriel before continuing. "They came after other civilizations of great spiritual strength. These remain mysterious even for us, and a whole lifetime is needed to understand even one glimmer."

"He who is on Titicaca is already on the road leading home," murmured Gabriel.

"You see, you know far more than you imagine! Yes, one must take the Taypikala road and the one to the Lake of Origin. The secret is in the stone and the water, in the mountain peaks forever reflected off Lake Titicaca. I was born near that lake. My father took up soldiering as a career. But my uncle, Apu Poma Chuca, the man who convinced the Inca Tupac Yupanqui to return the Sanctuaries of the Sun of Lake Titicaca to their splendor, initiated me to the art of stones. But enough of all that. I want to show you something. Come here."

Katari took Gabriel by the hand and positioned him directly in front of the two blocks on the right-hand side.

"Look carefully at those sculptures."

Gabriel had noticed them long before. There were three on each stone, equidistant from one another. They appeared to the naked eye to represent figures lying down, each one similar to the others.

"You must look at them properly, not with your eyes but with your entire body. You must enter into them."

Katari's voice lowered as he spoke these words, and Gabriel heard his voice quiver slightly. He tried to follow the Master of the Stone's instructions without really understanding them. The forms on the rock appeared to come alive.

"A . . . animals," he murmured hesitantly.

"One animal that you know well, my friend."

"The puma!"

Katari looked at him, smiling.

"You have already learned our language. And you love one of our women," he said emotionally, "but I believe that this is the first time that you have realized that your own destiny is written in the stone."

Gabriel blinked. He knew that what was in front of him was only the enormous blocks of a temple still being built. And yet, it was as if the whole world had suddenly changed. A lone cloud passed before the sun. The pink in the stones turned gray.

"Will you go farther?"

Gabriel looked at Katari, amazed. How could he go farther? Katari seemed amused by his bafflement.

"Don't worry, my Brother from Beyond. Tonight, everything that you've seen will return to you in a dream, and that will banish your fear of knowing. Come, it is time to return to the village."

Gabriel followed him down the steps that led back to the path alongside the Willkamayo. Halfway down the mountainside, they heard a deep song fill the valley. Gabriel hadn't heard a signal, but all the workers at once stopped whatever they were doing. Those in the quarry, those on the fortresses, those on the fountains or the temples, the stone workers, the carpenters, those whose job it was to carry things or to chisel, everyone in the valley turned as one toward the sun and sang a salute to it as it slipped behind the peaks of the western mountains.

Despite himself, Gabriel raised his palms up to the sky and, without opening his mouth, silently joined the others in their Song to the Universe.

ELEVEN

Ollantaytambo, August 1536

"Sometimes," said Gabriel, "I feel as though Katari has thrown his stone that stops time again."

"How do you know that he hasn't?"

They both smiled, and Anamaya's hand brushed against Gabriel's. Whenever they could be seen by others—that is, whenever it wasn't night—they were careful not to touch each other. But she nevertheless enjoyed provoking him on occasion, be it by scratching him or by surprising him with some affection, and watching the thrill in his reaction. They spent their days going from stone to stone, from the cool springs down the *collca*-lined road to the Sacred Double's temple.

In truth, they went wherever their whim took them, and wherever they arrived their love took root and bloomed.

Gabriel was enchanted.

Some days were cathedrals of silence, dedicated to the contemplation of pure beauty, to the blue of the sky, to the winds. Then there were the days when they talked endlessly, telling each other everything and anything. They switched effortlessly between languages, at times without even realizing it, carried away in each other's words.

But whether in silence or in talk, Gabriel had the impression that his heart was growing with each passing day.

Of course, there was always the mystery in her blue eyes, across which a cloud of doubt or the shadow of a secret occasionally passed for no apparent reason. He asked her no questions and was content to reflect upon her answers: He was no longer the jealous lover or the naïve, easily offended soldier. He felt like a man—not wise as such, but certainly much calmer and even happy. He surprised himself when, searching for a word to describe his state, what came out of his lips was *happy*.

His life came back to him in waves: his agonies as a spurned child, his youthful enthusiasms, Doña Francesca, prison, his dreams of freedom, of glory, his yearning to make a name for himself. He realized now that he had not once had the idea of letting happiness touch his heart. It was still such a fragile notion to him that he held back from surrendering to it completely. But when he closed his eyes and let the sun's warmth caress him, when he let himself be imbued with Anamaya's presence, it seemed to him that his life now was vastly superior to any of those in his trivial youthful dreams.

"Are you dreaming, Puma?"

"It doesn't matter which one of us is dreaming, so long as both of us are in the dream."

They were halfway up the slope, well above the long trapezoidal shape of the town below, and a little below the end of the ramp from the quarry to the site where the great temple was being constructed, the temple about which Gabriel could not ponder without remembering what Katari had initiated him to. They were facing the mountain-sculpture that he had first seen with her that dawn. He never tired of looking at it, of pondering its mystery. Although Anamaya had told him all about her life, including her closeness to the Inca at the moment of his death, she remained silent about the secrets that he had confided in her then. And with the perhaps illusory benevolence that love engenders, Gabriel refrained from questioning her about it.

"Close your eyes," she said.

He obeyed as docilely as a child. Anamaya gently caressed his hand and silently asked him with her spirit to empty his own, to empty his spirit of the war and everything associated with it, and to go with her to a place beyond desire, beyond sentiments, to the stone and the water. His body relaxed, and she sensed that he had surrendered himself completely to her.

Yet she could tell him so little. He had to travel the road himself. There was no other way. Only when he reached his destination would he know as she did, would the words come to his mouth. Until then, all she could do was show him the path of the sun and the position of the stars and hope that he would learn to ride the wind and follow the course of the water.

"Now open your eyes."

Gabriel rubbed his face as though he were coming alive for the first time.

"What do you see?"

Gabriel's eyes shone impishly.

"Why, I see that I love you, my love. I love you completely, with all I have!"

"Don't make a move, Puma! Be serious, tell me what you saw."

"I saw what one sees when one closes one's eyes. I saw dancing patches of color and a stronger light where the sun was, where I felt its heat. And although you told me to empty my mind, I saw myself on my white horse and I heard the arrows and stones whistling past me."

Anamaya's heart beat hard in her chest.

"Someone has chosen for me, haven't they? That's what I'm meant to believe?"

"I don't know the answer to those questions, Puma. You will know all that you're meant to know when they are within you."

"Please, don't speak to me in riddles."

"I know what I know by riddles. It's up to me to carry my body toward those things that will allow me to decipher them."

"Carry it, then," said Gabriel, suppressing another laugh. "Carry it over here to me, and then you'll decipher a few things. . . ."

Anamaya let herself slowly lean into him. He closed his eyes again, but this time he couldn't help but feel the pure, unadorned joy of having her against him, of feeling her passion and graceful reserve. And he found it impossible to think of anything else but love. He suddenly reached out for her, but she slipped away from him like a cat, and when his hand closed, all it clasped was shadow and wind.

She was standing up, watching the porters unload their heavy burden of *mantas* containing green and golden corn at the *collcas*.

"Villa Oma confronted Manco again this morning."

Gabriel's face darkened. The war . . . they hardly mentioned it between them, but they couldn't ignore the fact that it had almost split them apart forever. He didn't dare ask news of it, and he clung to the absurd hope that one day he would be told that it had ended in a great dance around the Aucaypata.

"Does he still want to turn me into a drum?"

"He blames Manco for not having attacked Cuzco earlier and for having sent troops to attack the reinforcements that your Pizarro managed to send, rather than concentrating all our forces on the city. He says that without some last ditch effort, the battle is lost."

"What does Manco think?"

"Manco is a warrior. The humiliations he suffered at Gonzalo's hand only strengthened his determination."

"Perhaps, but that doesn't mean that he'll necessarily win."

"He will fight until the end, even if this war cannot be won."

"And you? What do you think?"

Anamaya looked away from Gabriel to the distance.

"I think that one day the war will be over."

Gabriel laughed a sad laugh.

"Even I think that, despite not being privy to any secrets."

"Well, I am privy to the secrets, and yet my ignorance is greater than anyone else's. I know that the end of the war will set us free, Puma. But until then . . ."

Anamaya came and squatted beside him and put her head on his shoulder.

"Don't say it," he whispered.

A line of quarrymen passed in front of them. Despite their shyness, Gabriel sensed that they were watching them. He made to stand up, but Anamaya squeezed his hand, preventing him.

Yes, Katari had indeed thrown the stone that stops time. But now she saw that it was falling back to earth, and much too fast.

The rumor traveled across the valley as quickly as did the churning waters of the Willkamayo. It was shouted from summit to summit before the *chaskis* themselves reached Emperor Manco.

A regiment from General Quizo Yupanqui's army, commanded by the proud Apu Quispe, was on its way bearing a great many magnificent war prizes: Spanish weapons, clothes, and even horses. The prisoners of war were a few days' march behind.

The valley was filled with song, drumbeats, and the wail of horns.

The workers paused from their jobs to admire the victors as they arrived. No one touched the arms piled up on stretchers carried by porters with the dignity due an Inca's palanquin.

There were a dozen horses, each one surrounded by at least twenty terrified warriors holding hands to form a sort of mobile fence.

When the news reached Manco, he wanted to meet the victors, accompanied by a few of the lords from his court. He asked Gabriel to do him the favor of accompanying him, of walking alongside his litter, and Gabriel agreed before realizing the degree of the honor that had been bestowed upon him.

They waited at the bottom of the Choquana fortifications. Even Villa Oma had come along, although he hung toward the back of the train and maintained a hostile and disdainful silence.

"I would like you to show me how all these things are used," said Manco, smiling and stepping down from his palanquin, to Gabriel. "I wish to learn your people's ways."

Gabriel saw that he was looking at the approaching weapons. He said nothing. All eyes were on him.

"I'm not sure that they will prove of any use to you, my Lord Manco," he said eventually.

"Why, on the contrary, I'm sure that they'll be very useful. I don't understand what you mean. Please explain yourself. . . ."

Happily for Gabriel, who was growing increasingly uncomfortable, the troops bearing the prizes now arrived.

As Apu Quispe prostrated himself at Manco's feet, the lords silently approached the stretchers loaded with prizes. There were swords, shields, spears, morions, coats of mail, leather breastplates, and even artillery pieces. Each of these things caused Gabriel's heart to leap, reminding him of the battles in which he had participated. They banished any lingering doubt he had about the continuation of the war.

After the weapons on their stretchers came a number of porters who unfurled their *mantas,* then two more stretchers overflowing with useless riches shipped from Spain over the previous two years: brocades and silks, bolts of fine fabric, jugs of wine, preserves and other Spanish foodstuffs. There were even a number of pigs, still alive, squealing horribly, looked upon by the Indians with distaste despite their efforts to remain impassive.

But what they most admired were the horses. It had not been so long since the Incas had wondered whether the horse and its rider wasn't in fact a single being with fabulous powers. Gabriel remembered how frightened Atahualpa's men had been at Cajamarca, much to the ire of their Inca. Most of the Indians here had never had the opportunity to see a horse up close: The Spaniards had strictly forbidden them, on pain of death, from going anywhere near not only the animals but also the steel weapons. Actually owning a few of these things filled the victors with pride.

"What do you say to all this?" asked Manco.

"It isn't worth half as much as your brother Atahualpa's ransom," said Gabriel in a neutral voice, "but you can be happy for having taken them."

The conquistador's caution amused Manco, who smiled, turned away, and motioned for the victorious general to stand.

"Tell us of your victory, Apu Quispe. And be sure to speak up, so that no one among us remains ignorant of the Inca warriors' worthy deeds."

"Your army, commanded by your loyal General Quizo Yupanqui, sprung upon a regiment of Strangers comprised of seventy cavalrymen and as many foot soldiers. They were heading toward Cuzco, to reinforce their countrymen there. We tracked them for days without them ever realizing it. Then we waited for them in the narrow pass of the Pampas River. They had just crossed the Huaitara Puna.* We destroyed them under a hail of stones. We killed most of them. We took those who survived prisoners. They are following behind us, under guard. Here are their horses."

The soldier was unused to expressing himself. He spoke in short, broken sentences, and his harsh voice hardly carried at all. While he spoke he looked directly at his sandals.

"Do you hear, Villa Oma?" said Manco, visibly delighted.

---

*puna—a word borrowed from Peruvian Spanish (originally from Quechua): a high, cold, dry plateau in the Andes; a lofty, bleak region, uninhabitable due to the cold.

The Sage said nothing.

"There is more news," added the general.

"Speak."

The man hesitated, intimidated.

"Your General Quizo Yupanqui has learned that another Spanish regiment is on its way. He is preparing to destroy it also, with Inti's blessing. But messengers have reached us from the south. . . ."

Manco's face lit up. His brother Paullu was in the south with his army, under the pretext of supporting the one-eyed Diego de Almagro's expedition there. He had orders to annihilate his "new friends" as soon as he received word of the attack on Cuzco and then to return to the Inca capital and join in the general uprising.

"Is my brother on his way?"

"Yes, my Lord. But . . ."

"But what?"

". . . but Almagro and his army are with him, and he is helping the Spanish, as he has been ever since his departure. Furthermore, he has had several occasions to turn on the Spanish during battle. But not only did he not give the order, he actually allied himself with them."

"My brother, allied with the Strangers? Why, if it weren't for the fact that you have brought me the news of Quizo's victory, I would cut out your tongue and cut off your lips for uttering such an impiety!"

"In that case, you would have to cut off the lips and tongues of a great many of your lords, Manco!"

Villa Oma's dry, sibilant voice surprised everyone.

"We all know that your alliance with Paullu exists only in your own mind!"

"My brother would never betray me!"

"You're right, Manco. He has no need to betray you now, because he did so a long time ago. Only your naïveté and weakness prevent you from seeing it."

Manco trembled with rage.

"You will be silent, false sage. It is only because of our father Huayna Capac and because of the help that you once provided me that I don't tear you apart right now with my own hands for speaking so irreverently."

Villa Oma fell silent. But he did not avert his eyes. Gabriel's heart beat furiously. It was the first time that he had witnessed such explosive tension among the Incas themselves. It bode poorly on the future. The war had taken him in its grasp far more quickly than he had thought it would, and he sensed that this time it wouldn't let go.

Manco, boiling with rage, walked up to the first of the stretchers piled up with weapons. He picked up a sword and waved it about, quite comfortable handling it.

"I have learned, Villa Oma. I have learned from the story of the Great Massacre. I have learned that we were like innocents in the face of the Strangers and that we let ourselves be massacred. I promised myself that it would never happen again. I learned of the terrible war between our brothers Huascar and Atahualpa, and again I swore that it would never happen again. Before he left with the one-eyed man, my brother Paullu and I took the blood oath—we reconfirmed how it has always been between us. Now, for the first time, we are taking their weapons from them, we are defeating them in battle, we are laying siege to them, we can see the fear, a very real fear, in their eyes. And you call me weak; you tell lies about my brother!"

Manco windmilled the sword through the air, then pointed it at the sun.

"I will defeat them," he howled, "with our own weapons and with theirs. I will defeat them in the mountains as on the plains, on the rocks as on the sea, yes, I will defeat them, I will annihilate them and offer them as sacrifices to the gods in the hope that our nation will return to the peace and glory of before!"

Manco fell silent. The crowd, too, uttered hardly a murmur. Manco let the weapon fall to the ground and walked toward the horses. His men parted before him and prostrated themselves.

"I'm going to ride their horses," said Manco with eerie calm.

"Who's going to teach you?" asked Gabriel.

"You are."

TWELVE

Ollantaytambo, summer 1536

As he saddled two horses, Gabriel maintained a steady flow of soothing talk, punctuating his precise movements with a few affectionate pats. All eyes were fixed on him, and he moved carefully, wary of making any sudden movements. After girthing the big gray, he sized Manco up before adjusting the stirrups to his height. He had chosen a handsome chestnut for himself, seduced by its tawny coat and intelligent look. You'll be the third, he thought to himself, and smiled. Then he slipped on their bits and bridles before going up to the Inca.

"We're ready to go."

Manco was surprised. It was beneath an Inca to leave himself open to clumsiness in front of his lords, and especially in front of thousands of his vassals. But Gabriel spared him that risk.

"We shall first walk along, leading them by the bridle, to the bridge, which we shall have to cross on foot in any case. We shall then mount them in the bend of the road, where no one can see us, before entering the town. Does this suit you?"

Manco, who had grabbed the bridle without hesitation, nodded.

"Don't listen to him, Manco!" cried Villa Oma. "Remember who he is. It's a trap!"

"I prefer you when you're silent," answered Manco as he moved away. "Not one of you is to move from here until you see me entering the town with the Stranger!"

The road from Choquana ran in a straight line and was lined on either side by well-built low walls. Gabriel had first traveled along it as a prisoner, bound in ropes, and had admired then, through a thin layer of fog, the town, its terraces, and its temples. He reflected on the irony: Here he was now, leading a horse and alone with the Inca, a privilege that was no doubt reserved only for Anamaya and a very small group of his court.

"Allow me to thank you once again, Lord Manco."

Manco was trying not to turn around too often to check on his animal's unforeseen movements, although it was following him docilely. Gabriel noticed that he was holding the bridle neither too tightly nor too loosely and that his body displayed no tension or worry.

"I have told you already, it is not me that you should thank, but Anamaya. She spoke of you a long time ago, and I know how sad she would be were you to die. . . ."

"Then you also know that we have a common enemy."

Manco's face darkened.

"That Stranger they call Gonzalo Pizarro is a monster emerged from the Underworld, a monster that must be destroyed.

"As you probably know, I've already tried to kill him. I risked my life doing so. Now I'm afraid that, since Juan was killed, his power will grow unchecked."

"I don't understand all that," said Manco, "and I don't wish to. For me, all those brothers are Strangers who want to take everything from us. I know that Atahualpa trusted the *kapitu* Pizarro, and I know what happened to Atahualpa."

"And yet you trust me."

Manco said nothing. The two men made their way in silence. Gabriel admired the terraces rising up before them. The suspension bridge was a hundred paces ahead, supported by its unusual stone pylon set the middle of the river.

"I don't care for those men, Lord Manco. I am not their friend. I fought when I had to fight. But Princess Anamaya must have told you that I have never failed on my word, and that what I hope most for your country is peace. . . ."

"Are you their king? Do you command their armies?"

"Men like me will be needed, Lord Manco, when this war is over. . . ."

"There's only one way to end this war, and that's for us to win it."

Now it was Gabriel's turn to say nothing.

"I have endeavored to learn something of your history," he said eventually, "and I have come to believe that your wisdom is more than equal to ours. But we need time, we need to negotiate, we need to give gifts. . . ."

"I was forced to respect you, and I truly believe you to be a brave man. I consented that you keep the name Puma, bestowed on you by others. But now you speak to me of time and gifts, of wisdom and negotiation, even though your people have brought me nothing but death and destruction, pillaging, humiliation? Why should I listen to you and ignore our temples that lie in ruins, our women raped, the betrayals, the pillaging, my people made slaves? Why should I forget what I myself was submitted to?"

"Are you sure that you wish to cross this bridge alone with me?"

"You don't understand. I want you to guide me across the bridge. I want you to teach me to ride these animals. I want you to show us how to use your weapons, as well as how to make them. I want you to help us."

"I'm going to go ahead of you," said Gabriel, blindfolding the horses.

"I've crossed other bridges!"

"In an Inca's palanquin!"

"No! Before I traveled in palanquins I was a fugitive, a vagabond. Believe me, I've crossed bridges that you would never dare."

"Wait until I reach the central pylon before crossing. I'll wait there and come to your aid if necessary."

"It won't be necessary."

They passed through the two pillars marking the start of the bridge. Although impressed by Manco's determination, Gabriel nevertheless felt profoundly disturbed. That morning at sunrise, he had still felt full of serene certitude when the light in Anamaya's eyes had answered all his questions. But Manco's words had perturbed him, and he felt unbalanced. His words bothered Gabriel more than the undulations of the bridge. They were impossible to ignore. And it was equally impossible to check them with the awkward, pretentious answers he had given the emperor.

The chestnut followed, remarkably composed.

"Be sure to step evenly, so as not to frighten your horse."

"I know what to do," said Manco.

He was visibly annoyed. Gabriel didn't embarrass him with any more advice. The young Spaniard felt the chestnut's breath behind him and noticed that the bridge's movement didn't bother him as it once had. The water seething below was now familiar.

Yet when he reached the solid platform atop the central pylon, he slipped and was forced to grab the thick agave guardrope to stop himself from falling. At the other end of the bridge stood Anamaya, alone, waiting.

Sometimes, when she saw him in his Indian garb, Anamaya would forget that Gabriel wasn't one of them. Even though he spoke Quechua with an odd accent, and even though blond hairs sometimes covered his face, she felt that there was nothing of the Stranger in him.

But now, seeing him leading his horse across the bridge, she remembered in a flash their first meeting, near Cajamarca, and the impression that the horses had made then on Atahualpa and his people. She shuddered at the thought before recollecting herself.

As Gabriel drew nearer, she saw the look of surprise on his face. Manco was fifty paces behind, leading the big white horse.

"Why are you here?"

"I too want to learn how to ride a horse."

The road followed a bend that hid them from Manco's lords' prying eyes. And they were still too far from the town's gates to be seen from there.

Manco seemed unsurprised when he saw Anamaya and said nothing when Gabriel adjusted the stirrups on his chestnut to her height. Gabriel instructed them one after the other, showing them how to mount into the saddle without frightening the horse, how to hold the reins neither too loosely nor too tightly, and how to make the horse walk.

A harvested *quinua* field served as a ring. He led them around one after the other, holding their horses by tethers. "Go on!" he said. "Easy!"

Anamaya liked the tone of his voice when he gave orders, and she liked the confidence budding within her as well as the feel of her naked legs around the large, living animal—a creature utterly strange to her and with a power that she knew to be formidable. She watched as Manco, a dedicated yet impatient student, dug his bare heels into the white horse's sides, as if to show it that he was already master.

When they had perfected walking, Gabriel led them into short trots. Anamaya was surprised as she watched Manco's handling: He seemed to have naturally synchronized with his white horse's rhythm. Then came her turn and she found that she too adapted easily to the jerky rhythm, slipping along as though down a river.

Gabriel was sweating.

"I want to go faster," said Manco. "I want to go as fast as you do when you charge!"

"A gallop?"

"A gallop."

"You'll fall," said Gabriel. "You need more lessons. You need to get used to your horse first, and for it to get used to you. . . ."

"I want to gallop today!"

Anamaya recognized the stubbornness that she had encountered on the day of the *huarachiku* so many years before.

Gabriel didn't say another word but simply unclipped the tether and glanced at Manco. The Emperor slapped the horse and encouraged it with a shout, but the animal hesitated and threw its head around, as though trying to see who was riding it. So Gabriel, clenching his teeth, whipped its flank with the end of his tether. The horse, clearly irritated, immediately took off at a nervous trot down the middle of the field. Manco was jerked around like a puppet and lost his stirrups. His hands reached for something to hold on to. He grabbed on to the animal's mane, but his thighs joggled from right to left. The white horse hadn't made thirty strides before Manco slipped off its side and let out a raucous cry as he fell heavily to the ground.

"Why did you let him do it?" asked Anamaya at Gabriel's side.

"Didn't he ask to?"

Manco picked himself up, looked furiously at the horse, which had stopped a few paces farther on and was now eyeing him suspiciously. The Inca walked back to Gabriel and Anamaya, making a deliberate effort not to massage his bruised limbs.

"Well?" said Gabriel. "Do you believe me now?"

"I want to try again!"

Gabriel sighed.

Gabriel led Manco through practice until dusk. The Emperor never once wearied of being thrown, always picking himself up without a murmur or any sign of vexation.

A servant came to fetch the chestnut. He stood a little out of the way, his back to the Sapa Inca. Anamaya watched Gabriel and admired his patience and the quiet way he spoke. She sensed the violence in Manco gradually diminish, and soon he was feeling quite comfortable on the horse.

When the last of the sun had slipped behind the mountains, Manco finally agreed to stop.

"You will teach us," he said to Gabriel. "You will teach my lords as well as me. Then you will teach us how to handle a sword, then the gunpowder. . . ."

"I will do nothing of the sort," said Gabriel.

"Isn't Gonzalo your enemy?"

"I laid down my arms when the last tower at Sacsayhuaman was taken, Lord Manco. I swore then that I would never take them up again. Not against your men, nor against my own."

Anamaya looked at the two men facing each other. Gabriel made an effort to move slowly as he unsaddled the white horse, revealing its sweat-sodden barrel. Manco stood perfectly still, his eyes raging.

"What does being the Puma mean?" asked Manco, turning to Anamaya. "Does it mean eating our corn and our *quinua?* Does it mean distracting you from your duties to the Sacred Double? What kind of puma refuses to fight? I know that none such as this live in our mountains."

"He's speaking the truth," said Anamaya calmly.

"The truth?"

Manco looked at her, then at Gabriel, then back at her. He felt a violent urge rise up inside him, swiftly followed by a sense of the ridiculous. He said nothing. The evening songs were now echoing through the valley, from terrace to terrace, and the gloaming reflected off the *canchas*.

"The war is happening whether you want it or not, Stranger. The war is happening because it has to, ever since you and your people came here and violated our country. . . ."

"I don't disagree, Lord Manco."

"Then how can you be neither on one side nor the other?"

Gabriel felt oddly calm, as if a truth was revealing itself to him after having remained hidden for so long.

"Perhaps being the Puma means exactly that," said Anamaya.

Once again, Manco said nothing. He raised his hand against Gabriel, but without any real threat. He didn't understand his own motive. Gabriel remained frozen. Manco managed a slight smile.

"Put that saddle back on the horse, Stranger-who-doesn't-fight," said Manco. "Put it back on, Puma-who-doesn't-hunt, and watch!"

Gabriel obeyed, then helped Manco climb back into the saddle.

The Inca went off toward the town, first at a walk, then at a trot, and finally at a gallop, kicking up a cloud of dust behind him.

When he was no more than a black spot against the walls of the town, they heard a clamor rise up from it, louder than the chants and deeper than the trumpets and drums.

Gabriel slowly walked over to the servant holding the chestnut by the bridle. He had remained with his back turned throughout. "Go," he said to the man, who never looked at him but only at the ground, as though Gabriel were himself the Inca. The servant disappeared at a run.

Gabriel rose effortlessly into the saddle, enjoying the familiar feel of its leather and the warmth of the animal beneath him. He leaned down toward Anamaya and extended his arm. She took it, and he lifted her up to him.

They headed back at a walk, as slowly as they possibly could. As the darkness gathered and afforded them the protection of its black veil, they found no need for words to feel a mutual, powerful nostalgia.

It was the nostalgia of a cavalryman holding the woman he loved in his arms.

It was the nostalgia of the day at Cajamarca, when he had swept her up from being trampled during the massacre, and when their destiny had appeared to him for the first time, like a cool breeze emerging from the dust and the blood and the sweat.

THIRTEEN

Ollantaytambo, October 1536

In the courtyard of the royal *cancha,* shadowy figures slipped busily through the night, their straw sandals rustling along the ground. Whether it was Huayna Capac, Atahualpa, or Manco, the gods required that duty be done to the Inca—the Son of the Sun—in accordance with the rites and customs. What had been was again, and what was will be. The Inca's clothes, made from the finest vicuña wool, were made to be worn only once, he never touched his food with his own hand, and each hair that fell from his head was carefully stored away. Thus, he was always surrounded by an endless, well-ordered, and silent ballet of activity.

There was a fountain in the middle of the courtyard. It was a simple square stone from the middle of which spurted water. Four grooved channels carried the water in the Four Cardinal Directions across the courtyard. The water's energy thus passed through the center before being carried away to irrigate the Empire of the Four Cardinal Directions.

As time passed, Anamaya began to notice those things that she had formerly taken for granted. She questioned everything, even the very air she breathed. Ever since she'd had the vision, she had been aware of the secret fissure at the heart of the Empire: That which was eternal had to be, but not everything was eternal. And perhaps a symbol such as this one, the fountain, which at one time she had thought would last forever, was to exist, for the gods, only as long as a hummingbird took to flap its wings.

Anamaya heard two voices from the other side of the door-hanging: one, both tender and admonishing, belonged to Manco, and the other to his favorite son, little Titu Cusi, whose mother had died giving birth. Manco's wife, the gentle and beautiful Curi Ocllo, now lovingly cared for the child.

Manco hadn't attended to his son at all while in Calca. But once they had reached Ollantaytambo, he'd had the boy brought to him, and now not an evening passed when the Emperor didn't spend some time playing with the child.

"Faster! Come now, use your heels!" said Manco in his deep voice.

"Faster, faster!" cried the little boy in a high-pitched, overexcited voice.

Anamaya passed through the door-hanging without hindrance from the two impassive warriors standing guard at the entrance to the Emperor's private quarters.

In the torchlit room, she saw Titu Cusi riding on his father's back, urging him on with great swipes at his backside.

"Faster, horse! Faster!"

Manco bounded around on the carpets and pillows that covered almost the entire floor. The room's luxurious appointment was even stranger, in Anamaya's eyes, than that of the Inca-cum-horse ridden by a little boy bounding around amid the feathers and the finest *cumbis*.

"Look, Anamaya!" cried Titu Cusi. "I can ride a horse, just like my father!"

Manco now gently slipped his son off his back and took him up in his powerful arms, hugging him tightly.

"Go, now," he said, putting the child back on the ground.

The little boy, whose long black hair framed an impish and intelligent face, dashed across the room crying, "I will be back for another lesson tomorrow, Horse! Be ready!"

Anamaya smiled at Manco.

"Of all his brothers, he's the one, isn't he?"

Manco's face darkened.

"He's the oldest. And he's the one who has the most flair, the most confidence. He was raised by Curi Ocllo. He was nursed on the milk and strength of the woman I love. Whenever I hold him in my arms, I think of how much I love the *Coya*, and for a moment I forget about the war and about your absence."

His last two words rung out like a drum.

"My absence?"

"I know that you're here, and I know that you're looking after the Sacred Double, but . . ."

"But?"

"I feel as though you've already left with him, and that you're indifferent to the outcome of our war."

"You're wrong, Manco. I rejoice when I hear of our victories, and the news of our defeats makes my heart heavy. But your father Huayna Capac's words are ever in my mind, and they are concerned with a time after the war."

Manco laughed dryly.

"So, there's to be a time after the war? You've always been at my side, Anamaya. It was you who urged me to lead the uprising. And now you speak to me of a time after the war! Now, at this decisive moment! My beloved brother Quizo Yupanqui has failed in his attack on Lima. He died in battle. Luckily Illac Topa and Tisoc and many others have taken over. But what about you? There was a time when it seemed to me that you would hurl sling stones yourself to further the war! What happened to you that you now only want to speak about a time 'after'?"

"I will tell you, brother Manco."

Anamaya spoke to Manco for a long time. She affectionately recalled their long acquaintance, which had begun when she was a young princess who had narrowly avoided death. He reminded her of the snake that she had removed from his path; they spoke of Guaypar, his sworn enemy, and about how there was now a rumor spreading that he had resurfaced, leading an army alongside the Spaniards. But throughout their conversation, Anamaya felt a hesitation within her as she remembered Huayna Capac's words: *You will know what must not be spoken, and you will not speak it.* What was she to tell Manco, and what was she to keep to herself?

"I promised that I would stay at your side, and I have. I promised it when you found me with the Strangers. You know how I've kept that promise ever since."

"I spoke to Katari, but he told me nothing. I speak to you, and you too tell me nothing. I know that you've kept your promise. And you know that you've never heard me reproach you. Have you seen how the Sage Villa Oma looks at you? Have you ever heard me say a word to encourage his intimidation? But your silence . . . your silence makes my heart heavy, your silence echoes through my soul at night, and some-times I ask myself . . ."

As he told her of his doubts, Anamaya heard Huayna Capac's thundering voice: . . . we, the Incas, we will have to know humiliation, we will become slaves to our own shame . . . But we will not die . . . The brother's blood and the friend's blood are shed far more than the enemy's: It is the sign.

". . . I ask myself, Why am I fighting if Paullu and you—who have both been with me from the beginning—turn away from me. Even Villa Oma is thinking of making his own war. Illac Topa is in the north and Tisoc in the south, but they only rarely send me reports. Each of us on his own! It's madness!"

Anamaya wanted to give him an answer, but she realized that she didn't have one. She couldn't tell him that, by Huayna Capac's words, he was hopelessly doomed. And so her silence imprisoned him in an unavoidable war in which he was alone, like a child fighting against shadows and trees.

"You were the one who urged me on," continued Manco, "who called me 'the first knot of the future time.' But it meant nothing, it was mere noise, as empty as the wind, nothing more. . . ."

"You are brave, Manco. The flame of honor blazes within you."

"But it's useless! If I learn to ride a horse, then the horse will die. If I learn to wield a sword, then it will smash into pieces, if I send off a thousand arrows, they'll all fall back to the ground. . . ."

"What your father told me," said Anamaya regretfully, "is unclear even to me. I turn the words over and over, and they are in my mind when I'm awake and in my dreams when I sleep. They are enigmas that I decipher differently each time I think about them. The more I con-sider them, the more ignorant I feel. All I know is that the destruction has a purpose. But I don't know what comes after that."

"Is that purpose our own?"

"Ask Katari; he's the one who knows time."

Manco turned a black stone with sharp corners around in his fingers. He dropped it at her feet.

"The man who can do anything can do nothing," he sighed. "Isn't that so?"

Again, Anamaya remained mum.

"But there is something," said the Emperor.

"What?"

"The Puma."

Anamaya's breath quickened, and the anxiety that had left her now returned and almost overwhelmed her.

"If he's the Puma, then he should help us. But his words prove that he is nothing."

"He can help us without picking up a weapon."

Manco brushed aside her objection with a disdainful wave of his hand.

"What kind of friend refuses to fight when his enemy attacks? A coward, nothing more."

"You know that he's a brave man."

"Yes, I know. But I also know that if Villa Oma ever hears what your mad Puma said, he'll be executed on the spot, and I'll be powerless to stop it. You don't want to know what's being whispered about him in the terraces and in the quarry. All the men here would like to see him ritually sacrificed. . . ."

"You can't let that happen!"

Manco breathed quietly, letting a moment pass.

"That's what's so strange. No, I won't let that happen."

FOURTEEN

Ollantaytambo, October 1536

The face in front of him had screamed before dying. Now its mouth was twisted into a rictus of suffering and atrocious fear. But its eyes would never tell what had happened, because they had been torn out from their cavities and in their place was a mass of putrefied flesh and blackened, hardening crusts of blood.

Nauseous, Gabriel turned away from it to stop himself from vomiting.

The broad avenue leading from the *canchas* to the Willkamayo River was filled with the kind of hustle that one would expect in a marketplace in Spain. But instead of merchants bartering over fabrics or spices, there were only corpses.

The avenue was lined by two walls in which dozens of niches, each one about the size of a man, had been carved. And there were indeed men displayed in each one, for the admiration of all. The Indians, usually so impassive, now pointed them out to one another, talking loudly and laughing.

The most prized trophies had been placed in the niches closest to the *canchas*—the bodies of a dozen Spaniards. Their bones had been removed and they had been turned not into drums but into windbags, literally. Their skins, flayed from the rest of them, had been sewn up again and then inflated, so that they formed grotesque parodies of human bodies.

Gabriel, though sickened, couldn't help but think of the cruel irony: These men, created by God in his own image, were now re-created by foreign gods in the image of their crimes—deformed, loathsome, unnatural. And yet the human could still clearly be seen in these lifeless puppets, as though the Indian warriors' cruelty had peeled back their skin and revealed the nature of the monster within them.

Each corpse was attached to a stake and had its own niche.

Gabriel overcame his repulsion and fear and forced himself to look carefully at the faces to see if he recognized a comrade. It was true that he had hated most of them, and that by confronting the Pizarros, as well as through his relationship with Anamaya—which they had never understood—he had isolated himself from them. But now he surprised himself by suddenly feeling close to his countrymen, a belated kinship, as though he had himself been tortured and killed by bands of howling, joyful Incas intoxicated by their first taste of victory after the many bitter humiliations of defeat.

He was profoundly happy not to recognize any of the corpses. No doubt they were reinforcements recently arrived from Panama. They all had something of the astonished and terrified look of young men who had come to find gold and instead had found death.

After the Spaniards were the corpses of African slaves from the isthmus, and then those of their Indian allies, although these last hadn't received the same treatment as their masters.

They had simply been decapitated and their heads stuck on spikes wrapped in horse skin, to some of which a mane, or tail, or even hooves were still attached. Gabriel thought of pagan idols: These were grotesque versions of the demigods that some Indians had at first imagined the conquistadors to be.

Poor gods . . . the slaves' white teeth had all been wrenched out, and the multicolored feathers of one Indian, who had evidently been a chief when he was alive, were now black with dust and mud and hung down over his forehead, pathetically broken. Some of the Canary caciques still had their colored headbands, although these had slipped down past their vacant eyes to the blood-encrusted space where their necks had been.

In the middle of the loud, busy crowd, Gabriel suddenly felt brutally and inescapably alone.

He jumped into the air when a hand landed on his shoulder.

"Katari!"

The Master of the Stone wore a grave look on his face.

"Let's not stay here."

Gabriel followed him. The two men made their way through the narrow alleyways between the *canchas* toward the steep stairway leading to the Great Temple. Gabriel began to breathe easier once there was some distance between him and the macabre spectacle in the avenue.

When they had reached the temple's esplanade, they sat down on a stone block not yet hewn or fitted to the wall. Gabriel saw that two more giant monoliths had been erected since he had first seen the temple, separated from each other and the rest by a thin stone line shaped like a reed.

"You are in danger," said Katari.

"I've been in danger ever since I arrived here," said Gabriel quietly. "And in any case, I'm in no more danger than those poor souls down in the avenue. What barbarity . . ."

Katari said nothing for a moment.

"A dead man is a dead man."

"You're right. He's not any more dead because he's been chopped up into pieces, or because his balls have been sewn into his mouth, or because he's been turned into a flag or a balloon. . . ."

As he spoke, Gabriel realized that his words revealed an acerbic irony. For although he felt that he had become a stranger to his companions, he still considered himself, deep within, one of them.

"Those who did those things would like me to teach them how to use our weapons so that they can kill more people and fashion more abominable trophies for themselves. But they don't know me. I shall never again take up arms. This is how it is."

"Even if it costs you your life?"

Gabriel was surprised to hear a slight quiver in Katari's voice.

"My life . . ." murmured Gabriel> "Do I really know what it is, my life? It's been taken from me and given back without my consent so many times. . . ."

"You are the Puma," replied Katari in a serious tone. "You must survive."

Whenever he was with Anamaya, Gabriel was so suffocated by his love for her that his mind became fuddled. When he was with Katari, however, he felt unusually lucid.

"Not if I have to take up arms to . . ."

"I know, I know," interrupted Katari impatiently. "And I'm not saying that you have to. But Anamaya and I cannot protect you for much longer. Soon Manco will not be in a position to resist Villa Oma. The Sage sees this blood-sodden victory as an unhoped-for opportunity."

"Well? What should I do?"

"You must leave."

"When?"

An explosion roared out before Katari could answer.

As they flew down the stairs toward the *canchas,* Gabriel's heart beat furiously. But he wasn't sure if it was because he was alarmed by the possibility of yet another horror or because he now knew for certain that he would have to leave Anamaya once again.

Villa Oma's long, thin, corpselike arms emerged from his bloodred *unku.*

"Do you want to end up like them?" he screamed, pointing at the corpses in the niches.

He was talking to two Spanish prisoners, who were trying to display some modicum of dignity, but were both trembling from head to toe. Gabriel knew the horror that the sight of their mutilated companions no doubt inspired in them.

"What's going on?" he asked in a determined voice.

"Why, here's the Puma of the shadows!" yapped Villa Oma. Gabriel stood facing the Sage. A crowd had gathered around them, but he could see neither Manco nor Anamaya. Katari was still at his side and, more important, *on* his side—the only one in this blindly hostile crowd, the taste of blood in their mouths, spurred on by the fear emanating from the two bound prisoners.

"Our warriors tried to use your weapons that spit fire," said Villa Oma, "but all they managed to do was frighten themselves without hitting their target."

He pointed again at the niches. Not only had those Spaniards died in terror, but now they were being used for target practice.

"And these two," continued Villa Oma, waving wickedly at the prisoners, "pretended to help us. But they tricked us, and the fire exploded in one warrior's face."

"What happened?" asked Gabriel, turning to the Spaniards.

"They packed too much powder into the harquebus. It exploded," said the younger of the two in a blank voice.

"It was an accident," Gabriel said to Villa Oma.

"An accident? No, it was a trick by those mongrel Strangers. Now, they shall die!"

Some Indians grabbed the two prisoners, who offered little resistance, and shoved them toward two of the niches. The Indians pulled out the stakes on which two heads were fixed. They laughed as the heads came off and fell into the dust.

Gabriel stood in front of the two Spaniards.

"I want your men here to know who you really are, Villa Oma."

The crowd fell silent. Villa Oma was so taken aback that he too said nothing.

"When I was in the south, I saw how the most ignoble of my companions inflicted terrible suffering on your people. I tried to tell this man about it," he said loudly, pointing at the Sage. "He had the power, then, to stop it, for his opinion, along with Paullu Inca's, was important to the Spaniards. Yet he did nothing. . . ."

"Don't listen to him!" screamed Villa Oma. "He's lying!"

But the crowd remained silent and listened to the Stranger.

"Oh, he'll tell you that he was preparing for the war, that you would at last wreak vengeance on the Strangers. But I tell you that this man you call Sage is in fact a madman whose cruelty knows no limits and who will ultimately lead all those who follow him to their deaths! War is what it is, I grant you. But if you kill these two men here, than Inti will unleash his wrath against you!"

This was the last straw for Villa Oma. He cried, "Listen to him, invoking our gods! How dare he! Tie him up with the others so that he may share their fate."

Some soldiers came forth and grabbed Gabriel. Others scooped up powder from the barrel and stuffed it in the two prisoners' mouths. Still others came forward with firebrands.

Gabriel fought furiously, but to no avail. He looked for Katari.

"Enough!" thundered Manco.

The Inca had emerged through the crowd without Gabriel seeing him. Both soldiers and noblemen parted, letting him through. Only Villa Oma stood his ground, facing the Emperor. A steady trickle of green coca spittle dribbled from his lips and down his chin.

"Prostrate yourself before your Emperor!" Manco ordered Villa Oma.

The Sage had always exempted himself from the natural gestures of respect due an Inca. His bloodshot eyes stared defiantly at Manco for a moment before he bowed, very slightly, to the Emperor.

Gabriel at last saw Anamaya, half hidden behind Manco.

"Look around you, Manco!" said Villa Oma, "See that the *pachacuti* has already begun, and surrender to a force greater than yourself. Some of us used to call the Strangers gods. Look what we've done to them now."

Villa Oma pointed at the horrors that were once men in the niches, horrors held up by bronze-pointed spikes.

"It is the beginning of the upheaval, it is peace returning, for us and our people. . . ."

"The *pachacuti* began a long time ago, Villa Oma. My father, Huayna Capac, was its first victim. Yet he guides us still from beyond."

Villa Oma wasn't listening. If one listened closely, one could hear him murmuring to himself. "There is something ancient and impure in you. . . ."

Anamaya's blood had run cold when she saw that Gabriel was in danger. She took no comfort now from Huayna Capac's imprecise words, and she was frightened of visions in which she saw nothing and prophecies that prophesized anything.

Most of the Indians in the valley had gathered in the straight and narrow alleyways running between the *canchas*. They had put down their tools and abandoned their fields and had converged on the town. Anamaya sensed them baying silently for blood and death, an urge whirling within them like the waters of the Willkamayo, and she felt as if she alone was resisting it. She looked up over the crowd at the Ancestor and implored his help.

"You do not see clearly, Villa Oma, your eyes have grown as red as Atahualpa's did, and your heart is drowning in a lake of blood. You secretly cast curses, and you secretly make sacrifices, and you kill and kill, but you have forgotten that you are nothing without the Ancestors, nothing without the gods surrounding us. . . ."

"Something impure . . ." repeated Villa Oma, louder now, as though he hadn't heard a word Manco had said. "I remember the woeful day when, disregarding my advice, his spirit shadowed by illness, the great Huayna Capac refused to give the Puma the body of an impure little girl, and then even took her by his side and confided secrets to her that no one had ever or has ever known. I should have taken her from him and done away with her, because now, instead of being eaten by the Puma, she has drawn him forth from the earth so that he can consume us all. . . ."

"For the last time, Villa Oma, silence! Anamaya has never betrayed the Incas. You forget that she has never stopped performing her duties as *Coya Camaquen*, the *Coya Camaquen* chosen by Huayna Capac himself, and that you guided her along the way. Anamaya is the tradition, she is what was before and what will be. . . ."

Villa Oma fell silent. His thin body shook inside his *unku*, and the red tunic billowed like a wave of blood. Instead of words, his lips issued a froth that mixed with the green juice of the coca leaves he was always chewing. His copper skin turned gray.

Then, making a supreme effort to stiffen all his limbs and control himself, he said, with a tone of regret, "I must go. Farewell, my Lord."

Walking spasmodically, he made his way toward the river, alone.

Despite his fury and his hatred, despite all that had widened the rift between them until it seemed too great to cross, Anamaya heard in the Sage's last words the echo of the respect that he refused to give Manco and yet now did so by distancing himself. She heard the echo of an old, fraternal alliance that had soured into enmity.

FIFTEEN

Immediately after Villa Oma disappeared, soldiers surrounded Gabriel and took him through the grumbling, hostile crowd to Manco's *cancha*. Gabriel could no longer see the reassuring faces of Anamaya, Katari, or even Manco, and he felt like a flimsy basket being carried down rapids.

When he entered the *cancha*'s courtyard, its women moved away from him and he soon found himself alone by the fountain of the Four Cardinal Directions, his heart still beating furiously after his scrape with death, his mind revisiting the belligerent exchange between Manco and the Sage, and some part of him wondering whether, once again, he had been protected by some mysterious force, whether some unseen power was watching over him after all.

"Are all the Strangers like you?"

A little boy, his eyes agleam with curiosity, was staring at Gabriel without any trace of fear, despite being no more than four or five years old.

"Oh, there are many much nastier than I!" replied Gabriel with a grin.

"What's your name?"

"Gabriel."

The little boy pondered this, a serious expression on his face.

"That's a strange name. It doesn't mean anything."

"Some of your people have told me that it means puma. And you? What's your name?"

"I'm Titu Cusi, I am the son of Lord Manco and one day I will be Inca."

"Well, I'm sure that you'll be a powerful emperor and that you will also rule your people benevolently. . . ."

But the little boy was no longer listening; he rushed to his father, who had just entered the courtyard amid a guard of lords and soldiers. Manco leaned down to his son and smiled, and Gabriel saw how tenderly the Emperor hugged his boy. But when he straightened, Gabriel saw that his black eyes were once more hostile, impenetrable.

"Come," said Manco. "Follow me."

Anamaya and Katari, right behind Manco, followed him through the door-hanging into the royal chamber.

"Lord Manco," began Gabriel, "I know that you are indifferent to my gratitude, nevertheless I wish to thank you from the bottom of my heart."

Manco looked at him without saying a thing. Gabriel didn't dare look away to Anamaya or Katari.

"Had Villa Oma known what I now know, you'd have been dead before I arrived," said Manco eventually.

"What do you know?"

"Your people are coming. A powerful army, including many cavalry commanded by one of *kapitu* Pizarro's brothers, and supported by thousands of traitors."

"Gonzalo?"

Despite himself, Gabriel's heart throbbed with rage as he pronounced the hated name.

"Hernando."

He shrugged.

"You know that I'm not one of them."

"I don't know what I know about you. But I have with me here the only two people to whom your life is worth anything. Count yourself lucky that they are also the two people I value most."

"What are you going to do?"

"Let's sit down."

Manco took a seat on his *tiana*. Gabriel, Anamaya, and Katari sat at his feet, on a pile of soft vicuña and guanaco wool blankets spread over the ground. The light of the torches played on their faces, and Anamaya in particular looked as though she were covered in a fine layer of gold dust.

"Our spies have been telling us for days that they've been preparing to attack us. We are going to fight them and defeat them so completely that what few survivors remain will go to the Governor and convince him to leave us in peace . . ."

"You're mistaken, noble Manco."

Anger flashed across the Emperor's face.

"You doubt our victory?"

"Victory in battle is never a sure thing. But that's not what I mean. They won't leave. Even if you defeat those coming, others will follow, and yet others after them. Believe me, I know Pizarro better than anyone: He's a man who never gives up."

"He's the one who doesn't know me!"

"Lord Manco, no one here doubts your courage. But I beseech you, please think about it, unless you want to become like Villa Oma. You must face the reality of how strong the Spaniards really are."

"Silence!"

"Let me give you one final piece of advice, although I've no doubt you'll ignore it: Find an honorable peace, endure whatever humiliations they impose without complaint, save what can be saved, and secretly send a group of young men to learn for themselves how to use the Strangers' weapons. I'm not talking about their steel, their powder, or their horses. I'm talking about their language, their god, and their customs."

"I cannot do that."

"I know how you feel, Manco. I accept that you're going to do what you deem necessary."

"I cannot do that. . . ."

Manco repeated himself as though he were alone in a dream. Gabriel had spoken passionately and sincerely. For a moment the room was filled with silence, the torches flickering.

Then Manco turned to Anamaya and asked, "What do you say, *Coya Camaquen?*"

"Win this battle, Manco. You have no other option, nor do we. But afterward, heed those words spoken in wisdom."

Manco reflected for a moment. Then he looked to Katari.

"And you, my friend, Master of the Stone?"

Katari said nothing. He stood up, approached Manco, and took him by the shoulders. Manco stood to meet him, and the two men briefly embraced. Then Manco sat back down on his *tiana*.

"Leave me, now. I want to be alone."

SIXTEEN

At dawn, Katari wrapped Anamaya and Gabriel in *mantas* so that they were hidden up to their necks. Without wasting any words and walking quickly, they climbed the stairs to the Great Temple, hoping to avoid prying eyes. Anamaya sighed with relief as they passed through its outer wall.

They were hidden by the hill now, and no one would dare come to the little temple with the four niches where the Sacred Double was waiting for them.

Gabriel and Anamaya kissed for what seemed like time without end, with their hands on each other's faces, with the eagerness of their first kiss, and with the sadness of the last. Traveling across the other's skin was a voyage as disturbing as that of crossing the oceans or the mountains. They attached themselves to each other like two strings to form a single, indestructible circle.

When finally they separated, their eyes were swollen with tears.

"I'm leaving," said Gabriel.

"There's no other way," replied Anamaya.

The first rays of the sun landed on the Sacred Double's gold surface at the same moment as they lit the mountain crests.

"I don't want to be sad," said Gabriel.

"Nor do I. Everything is happening as Huayna Capac told me it would. The mysteries are being unraveled, and you are still here. You will be here at the end. . . ."

"I know that you're telling me what little you can. I know that I must make my own way and learn on my own. That is the lesson that sometimes I forget, sometimes I remember. When I spoke to Manco, I was no longer frightened. I knew that everything within me was as it was meant to be. Do you think I'm becoming a good puma?"

He spoke these last words with a gentle irony, and Anamaya leaned against him. He continued:

"Your love has revealed everything to me. Your love has made all this possible and bearable, even the absurdity of having to leave you once more, and once more without knowing when I'll see you again."

"He said to me: *He will only come to you when he leaves you. Although separated, you will be united as one.*"

"Your venerable old Inca was a cruel man!"

They both laughed softly, like children. They looked at the Ancestor from the same vertiginous perspective as the Sacred Double in the southern niche.

A shuffling sound startled them. Katari appeared before them.

"It's time," he said.

They climbed up the Ancestor Mountain by a narrow, poorly paved path. Both Katari and Gabriel bore a heavy stone, wrapped in a *manta,* on their backs.

They had passed through the hustling *canchas,* where every man was preparing himself for battle, without seeing a sign of Villa Oma; then they had passed by the well-stocked *collcas* before leaving the town behind. At the base of the slope, Katari had selected a stone for Gabriel, and it was this stone that was now digging into his back and shoulders, making every step he took agony.

And yet, he made no complaint and he didn't feel the need to ask why he had to carry the stone. He followed in Katari's steps, who moved with the ease and grace of an alpaca, and whose burden didn't seem to weigh him down any more than his long hair flowing freely in the breeze.

From time to time they turned around to watch the Inca troops deploy. Hundreds of fearsome archers of the Antisuyu had emerged from the forest and joined the Inca ranks. A barrage had been built downstream on the Willkamayo, and the water level had risen, making it harder to ford. The man who had forsaken bearing arms now felt a painful ache in his body, as though he shared the Spaniards' effort as they approached, as though he were only now facing the plain and peculiar reality of not being among them, on his white horse, holding his sword, sweating beneath his morion and chain mail. And another, unexpected, thought rent his soul in two: He knew that Sebastian would be among them, and that he wouldn't be there to defend his friend and even perhaps save his life.

He clenched his teeth to prevent himself from crying out in fury at his impotence, and he hooked his hands into the folds of the *manta*, distracting himself by bending forward and taking more of the back-breaking weight of the stone.

Gradually, pain and exhaustion produced the desired numbness and he felt paradoxically alleviated by his burden.

They reached a flat, rocky platform the size of an esplanade. Gabriel set down his stone and almost fell over, so great was the pain that shot through his back. Anamaya's gaze offered him some support, and he slowly straightened his body, broken by the effort as much as by the sudden doubt that had overcome him.

"We're here," said Katari.

Gabriel was completely lost. He looked to Anamaya for explanation.

"We are above the Ancestor's face," she said.

Katari squatted and took a bronze chisel from his *chuspa*. He began working the stone he had borne up the slope, precisely and meticulously. Then he did the same with Gabriel's.

"Look," he said.

On one stone, the Kolla had carved the shape of a puma, and on the other that of a snake.

"Strength," said Gabriel, "and Amaru's wisdom."

"Well done," said Katari, smiling, "you know our gods. Soon, a temple will be erected here to crown Huayna Capac's head. Those searching for the Inca's power will come here to pray and make oblations."

Now the fog scattered and the bright morning light lit the mountain slopes; a young sun brought out the colors in the terraces and put a sparkle in the water.

It was a beautiful day to die.

When the crowd down below moved suddenly and collectively, Gabriel became aware of the imminent danger. His body stiffened to such a degree that it was painful. Anamaya turned to him and said, tenderly, "You're pale."

And indeed, the blood had drained from his face, and his heart beat furiously.

"I can't," he said.

Anamaya put her hand on his.

"I can't let them die without me. . . ."

"Do you want to fight?"

"No!"

The cry had burst forth from his mouth, uncontrolled.

"Do you want to die with them?"

"I thought that I was . . . protected. . . ."

"You are, from everything except yourself."

Anamaya gazed down at the slopes and terraces covered by warriors.

"Let him go," said Katari calmly.

At that moment, the first battle cry erupted.

It was as though her blood had suddenly turned to ice, freezing her entire body. She was unable to move a limb.

Gabriel's first few steps had been slow, painfully so. At the first bend in the road, he stopped as if to turn around. But he didn't. Quite the opposite: He was almost running down the slope when she saw him last, a man become a sling stone.

She saw the Antisuyu archers on the terraces below and, on the left bank of the Willkamayo and on the slopes rising from it, innumerable warriors armed with slingshots.

She focused her mind on the stone where Huayna Capac had spoken to her, but he didn't say anything more. She had no way of knowing whether the Puma was dashing toward his death like some untamed beast or whether he was going to cross the ocean again, in the other direction, back to his people.

Katari remained at her side. He finished chiseling the two stones with which the temple would be founded.

"You had forgotten that the Puma is also a man," was all he said.

She nodded, but without believing him.

*   *   *

Gabriel hurtled down the slope, blood throbbing in his temples. It was as though the decision had been made for him without any contribution of his own will, and as he ran, breathless, he began to have doubts. As he came closer, it seemed that the mountain and the entire valley plain were growling, as though thousands of drums were being beaten within the depths of the earth, causing it to swell.

It was the voices of frightened men shouting to give themselves courage; it was the stamping of thousands of feet, the clanging of thousands of weapons.

Halfway down the slope, he suddenly found himself above the terraces where the archers from the forest had taken up their positions.

He stopped in his tracks, daunted by the sheer number of warriors; even after so many weeks in Ollantaytambo, he was amazed by how many warriors had been hidden in the mountains. Behind the archers was another mass of warriors armed with spears, clubs, and spikes. He immediately noticed that some of them had donned Spanish armor lost in battle, and he saw Indians wearing morions, leather breastplates, and even coats of mail. Some officers even carried swords.

Far away on the other side of the river, he saw the Spanish army approaching. They were still too far for him to make out their individual faces, but he recognized Hernando Pizarro by the plume in his helmet. He was riding at the head of the column. They were about a hundred or so cavalrymen, followed by at least thirty thousand Indian warriors made up of the Spaniards' usual allies: the Canaries and the Huancas. But their ranks were swollen with Incas hostile to Manco.

Gabriel felt his blood rush upon seeing them, and he elbowed his way through the mass of tightly packed warriors, swearing the whole while, until he had managed to get through a few ranks.

But when he reached the archers, he had to stop; dejected, he realized that there was no way to get through them.

He saw Manco's proud silhouette standing at the end of the terraces. He was atop his white horse, handling it well, and he bore a spear in his hand, its blade glinting in the sun.

*   *   *

Anamaya could not see the plain or the Spaniards moving across it, but she could sense their approach by the heightened tension running through the Inca ranks. She heard a tumultuous crashing of drums and cacophony of horns rise from the slopes of the mountain atop which sat the temple, the doors of which had been walled up. She realized that Manco and his battle advisers, instead of using the element of surprise that had served them well before, preferred to show their adversaries that they were expected, and to show them in such a way as to fill them with dread.

She closed her eyes and conjured up a vision of Gabriel. Where was he now? Had he managed to cross through the lines? Against all reason, she imagined him worming his way through the Inca ranks, diving into the river, and joining his people, jumping on a horse and grabbing a sword. He had often told her of how he had taken Sacsay-huaman, and she had no trouble imagining him now leading the Spanish attack.

She opened her eyes only to be blinded by the sun. "It's no longer possible," she murmured. "He swore never to take up arms again. He's come so far. . . ."

But she found no comfort in her words: Wherever he was, whatever was his will, he was in the middle of a battle, and she could not help but think of him dying.

"Santiago!"

The all too familiar Spanish war cry echoed across the valley and reverberated within her.

"Santiago!"

She recoiled with fear. Katari came up to her.

"Stay," he said. "Wait. Banish your fear."

But when she looked at him, she saw the worry in his eyes. Her heart constricted.

As soon as Manco saw Gabriel, he made his way over to him. His soldiers parted, ceding their Emperor passage.

"Why are you here?" he demanded brusquely. "Have you come to fight with us?"

Gabriel said nothing, he only stared intensely at the Inca.

"Or do you want to join your people? And die with them?"

Manco said this quietly, and Gabriel understood his confidence.

"If that's what you want to do, then I won't prevent you from crossing over to them," said Manco, pointing at the plain.

Gabriel remained frozen on the spot.

"Are you sure? You don't want to? In that case, come and join my lords," said Manco. "You've nothing to fear. Come and see what's waiting for your people. . . ."

The cry of "Santiago!" had caused some ancient instinct to boil in his veins, a call to battle that would have given him the strength to rise up, to accept Manco's provocative offer, and to break away from the mass of Incas and go to his own people. But, clenching his teeth, he said nothing.

With utmost coordination, the Incas sent a hail of stones and arrows down upon the Spaniards, causing the vanguard to halt, then retreat. Then two cavalrymen detached themselves from their company and charged at the Incas' outer fortifications. Without being able to see their faces, Gabriel recognized them both by their immense size: Candia and Sebastian, the black giant riding a white horse, and Candia a black one. His ears buzzed as he recognized Itza—of course, the mare that Sebastian had given him.

It was as though his past were galloping back toward him.

Katari removed the stone key that he wore about his neck and handed it to Anamaya. Her blue eyes were pale and distant.

A deafening cacophony rose up from the terraces, and the air was shredded with whistles. Each volley of arrows was like a cloud of stinging insects falling from the sky to devastate the earth, and the stones fell like dead birds.

Anamaya turned to the north, toward the Secret City where she had met Huayna Capac. Katari turned with her.

"Until that moment when Inti has consumed the hatred dividing us . . ." she murmured.

Katari continued: "*. . . And only women singing their grief over all the spilled blood will remain.*"

"Do you think that this is it?"

Katari opened his powerful hands, the lines in his palm crossed by scars.

"No. Not all the signs are there."

"And him? Can he die?"

"I told you, the Puma is a man, and a man must die. But that man is the Puma."

Anamaya smiled.

An explosion ripped through the air.

Gabriel watched, fascinated, as the Indian bombardment forced back Sebastian and Candia, despite their bravery. They did an about-face before a troop of cavalry headed off to attack the temple. Seeing it from below, with its formidable walls, the Spaniards had no doubt mistaken it for a fortress. Its defenders at first seemed to fall back, but then two Chachapoya Indians broke the legs of the lead horse with sling stones, sending the rest of the cavalrymen into a panic. They beat a hasty retreat and no cavalryman had since dared to charge.

Gabriel could see that the Spaniards were hesitating. For the first time, they were facing a pitched battle without the upper hand. The time when their horses had afforded them the advantages of speed and surprise was long gone, their artillery was next to useless, and Manco seemed to have taken their every move into account when he had organized his defensive lines.

Even the regiment of foot soldiers that Hernando had sent around the mountain to attack the temple's walls was repulsed by a hail of stones.

Gabriel heard a culverin fire. It came from the Inca side, from somewhere midway along the terraces, and although the explosion was no doubt harmless (and it was a miracle, thought Gabriel, that the cannon hadn't exploded and blown the heads off its amateur gunners), it provoked a proud murmur through the lines of Inca warriors.

Its rumble was heard by all the warriors waiting along the terraces and slopes, and it coincided with a roar from Manco.

The Incas surged downward toward the Spaniards, moving as one. Gabriel, powerless and unable to see anything, felt the earth trembling underfoot. He concentrated on not getting trampled by this flood of screaming men, a flood rolling down the mountainsides and taking everything in its wake, a flood laden with rage accumulated over months of humiliation and fear.

When he recovered his footing, all he could see on the plain was a fog rising. In fact, it was dust rising up from the earth, it was sweat, it was swords flying through the air, and it was the strange sight of Manco in the middle of the fray atop his white horse with his spear in hand and wearing his *mascapaicha* on his forehead, charging at the enemy like a demon afraid of nothing.

Gabriel fleetingly remembered their first riding lesson together.

"I didn't want to make war," he murmured, "and yet I make it all the same."

Despite their furious resistance and the considerable damage that they inflicted on the Incas, the Spaniards and their allies were gradually forced back. Their cavalry charges became less and less effective, no longer cutting deep behind the enemy lines. Gabriel watched Hernando's crimson feather move farther and farther back across the plain, like the shred of a red sail on a rudderless, drifting raft.

Gabriel was surprised when he noticed that the light was failing; he felt as though the sun had only just risen.

He looked away from the battle toward the peaks, the Apus that Anamaya and Katari had taught him to recognize. Then he looked back down at the two rivers. He froze in horror.

A group of around a hundred Indians was diverting the flow of the Patacancha toward the canals that they had dug weeks ago.

Gabriel immediately realized what they were doing.

They were going to flood the plain.

They were going to drown the Spaniards.

SEVENTEEN

Ollantaytambo, November 1536

Darkness fell on the mountain like the shadow of a condor's wing as big as the sky itself. The din of battle down below grew softer, as though slipping into the distance. There were fewer battle cries, but more agonized moans, and the explosions had ceased outright. Anamaya suddenly felt cold. She pulled her *manta* tighter around her shivering body.

"I wonder where Villa Oma is," she said.

Katari thought about it for a moment.

"He probably took refuge in an underground *huaca*, where he's casting curses in the hope that we are defeated, thus confirming his jaundiced and utterly wrong prophecies. . . ."

"I would have thought he'd join Manco for the battle."

"His anger imprisons him alone on an island lost in the middle of nowhere."

"He's still the Sage to me. . . ."

"And he's also just a man, like the Puma. He has never really understood why the powerful Huayna Capac confided the Secrets of Tahuantinsuyu to a strange little girl with blue eyes rather than to him."

Anamaya looked dreamy.

"Still, for me, he'll always be the Sage."

Katari's laugh carried gently into the night.

"Why are you laughing?"

"I've been trying for a while now to see, behind the *Coya Camaquen*'s façade, the little girl that you were when you arrived before the great Inca Huayna Capac. I think I just heard her for the first time."

Anamaya laughed with him.

"Why did you give me the stone key?"

"One day, when all the signs have been revealed, we too shall be separated. I will go to the Lake of Origins, whereas you will head back to . . ."

She interrupted him, putting her finger to his lips.

"Please don't say the name out loud."

"You'll need this key. With it, you will open the stone."

"How will I know?"

"You'll know."

The nocturnal breeze picked up, carrying away the sound of the men on the battlefield. Curiously, Anamaya was no longer cold.

"What about him?" she asked.

Gabriel watched the water rise with prodigious speed and flood the plain. It reached the level of the horses' girths, and now the horses could hardly move, stuck in a lake that had risen from nowhere and that threatened to swallow them up. He watched as a cavalryman fell from his saddle. In the water, he whirled his arms about, desperately trying to stay on the surface while at the same time ridding himself of his heavy gear.

As night gradually enveloped the valley, the Spanish retreat became nothing more than a dwindling noise, one that only occasionally flared up again whenever a battle cry rang out, or a trumpet, or the sudden clamor that occurred whenever the Incas caught a lagging Spaniard or managed to topple a horse.

Gabriel felt an unshakable heaviness overcome his body and weigh down his limbs.

He hadn't fought, but he felt suddenly very old, as though crippled by imaginary wounds. He closed his eyes and saw both the Inca and the Spaniard, on horseback or on foot, wielding a sword or a slingshot. He had difficulty banishing the vision, and yet he wanted to be engulfed by it, like a warrior who, surviving a battle, collapses at its end, when everything is over and he can no longer be beaten by anything but his own all-consuming weariness.

He saw Manco returning on foot, leading his mud-covered horse by the bridle. The Emperor looked Gabriel up and down without saying a word, his black eyes gleaming with pride, his being still charged with the fever of battle. Victory is a drug stronger than any number of jars of *chicha*, stronger than ten thousand coca leaves.

Manco handed Gabriel the reins to his horse and headed toward the *canchas*, an exhausted victor.

Gabriel followed in his steps.

The path was so steep and in places paved in such an irregular fashion that it was risky traveling down it, particularly at night.

Yet Anamaya and Katari descended surefooted, guided only by the occasional glow of moonlight and the instinct of those who have traveled across all the skies.

As they drew closer to the Willkamayo and the springs, they heard the clamor of the *atiyjailli*, victory songs, already being sung, in which the noble feats of the battle's heroes were lauded. The earth had not yet finished drinking the blood that had been spilled on it, and corpses still floated on the river. Anamaya saw a woman facing her from the riverbank. She was holding against her belly a *manta* containing her husband's clothes, a husband she had followed to a senseless war. Her eyes were blank, lost in a place beyond the Four Cardinal Directions.

Just outside the *canchas*, they came across men staggering along. Some were lying in the mud and their own vomit, still singing drunkenly about their famous victory over the demigods come from across the ocean. The Strangers had again become the fabulous creatures that they had been many moons ago, when they had been described as invincible, as half man, half horse, with hands that sliced through flesh, and carrying silver sticks that spat fire. But according to the legends now being invented by the drunken, victorious warriors, Viracocha himself had made the Incas from stone, and had made them so strong and brave that even with their arms sliced off they repelled the attackers and had become the masters of water and hail.

Anamaya and Katari heard this fable time and again as they made their way through the narrow alleys between the *canchas*. Even the womenfolk, gathered around the fires grilling guinea pigs, told it. Everyone spoke of the warrior who had slung the stone that had broken the leg of the first horse, and of the warriors who had diverted the Patacancha. They re-created the scene by imitating the sound of arrows or stones whistling through the air, telling how so-and-so had grabbed on to a horse and toppled its dead rider off, leaving his corpse to float down the river. Everyone spoke as though there weren't enough words to describe the joy of victory.

Anamaya was frightened.

She couldn't find Gabriel. She stared at every silhouette she came across in the dark, hoping it was him. But she didn't dare ask anyone if they had seen him. *Seen the Stranger? I hope he's buried in the Underworld.*

Her heart was pounding when they at last reached the tall, trapezoidal door that opened into Manco's *cancha*.

The Inca was standing amid a gaggle of his lords, wearing a coat of mail over his *unku*, his spear at his feet. He was waving his hands, describing some particular action, and Anamaya saw that they were still covered in blood and mud; mud covered his face, and his eyes glinted with pride and hatred. The men surrounding him laughed and smiled almost familiarly, and the great deference normally accorded an Inca now conceded a little to the camaraderie of fighting men. The room fell silent as Anamaya and Katari entered.

"Well, *Coya Camaquen*, no doubt my father had told you of our victory. No doubt that's why you've taken so long to join us."

Manco signaled for two women to bring him more *chicha*. They poured from a jug into his finely worked gold goblet. Manco drank slowly from it.

"And you, Katari? Have you been slinging stones from the top of Pinkylluna Mountain?"

The two young people said nothing. The Inca's cheeks were flushed from the liquor, and his eyes burned.

"They don't reply," he said, turning to the lords. "Either they scorn us, or else they're ashamed. . . ."

"We have laid the foundation stones for a new temple," said Katari, "which will one day crown our Ancestor, your father, Huayna Capac's head."

He spoke calmly, fearlessly. Manco lost his murderous look. He pointed at Anamaya.

"I captured an animal during the battle," he said, his rage abating. "I want to give it to you."

"What animal?" she asked gently.

"A puma. I understand that you're attached to them."

Manco motioned toward the far side of the room. Two soldiers brought Gabriel out, his face impassive.

"I'm giving him back to you, Anamaya. He's yours."

Anamaya forced herself to remain still, despite her entire body urging her to run up to him and take him in her arms.

"Your Puma can keep his life, on one condition."

Anamaya plunged her blue eyes into Manco's unflinching gaze.

"He must disappear before Inti throws his first rays on the day after our victory, tomorrow before dawn. Do you understand me?"

Anamaya remained silent. She waited as Gabriel walked unsteadily toward her. He was clearly exhausted. They stood side by side without touching, facing Manco. Then they passed through the crowd, and she felt their hostility, their lust for vengeance. They wanted to tear him to pieces.

As they passed beneath the stone lintel, decorated with a carved condor, Manco called out after them, "Tomorrow before dawn, d'you hear?"

He sounded completely sober.

Night closed in around them as they left the *canchas* behind.

She led him by the springs, then along the Willkamayo toward the condor *huaca*.

They said nothing for a long time and didn't dare touch each other. They had only been apart for a few hours, but they both had to recover their breath and slow their beating hearts before speaking.

The night was cool and clear, and as they walked they left behind all the noises and horrors of the battle. Soon, there was no defeat or victory, no fighting, no cries of hatred or triumph.

When they reached the rock, Anamaya stopped. She took Gabriel by the hand and had him lie down on the low wall that ran alongside the river. They closed their eyes together and emptied themselves of violence, letting their souls and bodies join with the water's eternal flow.

Then she stood up and led him down to the water's edge. She tenderly undressed him. His *unku*, still drenched with sweat, slipped to the ground. The water was so cold that he almost cried out from the shock. Anamaya led him toward a flat, black rock showing through the surface in the middle of the current. He stretched out on it, the cold water flowing around him, and Anamaya slowly rinsed him with her hands, washing away his exhaustion. Gabriel surrendered until he was no longer able to distinguish between her hands and the water. He felt his weariness slip away from him and sink into the river. The images haunting him slowly disappeared, and slowly he emerged from the hand-to-hand combat that he had never fought. A delicious sense of well-being overcame him, and even the first stirrings of desire. Then Anamaya had him sit up and led him back to the riverbank.

She had brought him a soft wool *unku* in her *manta*.

They climbed back over the little wall and returned to the path. They passed beneath the silhouette of the condor *huaca*.

"I didn't want to leave," said Gabriel.

"I know."

They spoke in low voices, not for fear of being overheard, but to create a sanctuary for themselves in the night. They spoke of everything except their coming separation; a separation that they knew would be upon them all too soon, despite the night's illusion of timelessness.

"I thought that I had to be close to them. I didn't want to fight your people, I wanted to be like the grass beneath their horses' hooves, within hand's reach of the wounded, within their sight. I felt as though I was *meant* to see that crimson feather in that bastard Hernando's helmet. I even felt fondness for him, and though I was ashamed of it, I couldn't help it. I knew that they were going to lose the battle, but if I hadn't come down from the mountain, I would have appeared like a traitor."

"A voice said that you weren't meant to die, but another said that you would be trampled and torn to pieces. One voice told me that we would find each other again, and another that I'd lost you."

"You were there with me. When I saw Sebastian and Candia approaching at a gallop, I turned toward you. I wanted to tell you . . ."

She laughed. Then, in a serious voice, she asked, "Are they still alive?"

"I don't know. I hope so. I saw them disappear beneath a hail of stones and arrows, and I remember willing myself toward them and wishing with all my heart that the force that protected me during the battle of Sacsayhuaman would protect them. I prayed to a variety of gods, my own, all of yours, and I said, 'Whoever you are, ignore my disbelief and save my two friends. Don't let them die now.'"

"Then they're still alive."

"You mean, I have that power?"

"I mean that power exists. Come."

They climbed through the rocks into the *huaca*. Newly sensitive to the Inca's beliefs, Gabriel felt an energy vibrating through the place. He said nothing, letting Anamaya lead him from stone to stone.

She stopped before a rock about as high as she was, its slender form indicating that it had been worked by man, although no chisel marks were visible. It was the same shape as a mountain rising in the distance, now hidden in the night.

"This is the place," said Anamaya.

Gabriel's heart skipped a beat.

Anamaya stopped herself, surprised by her own words. She had spoken without thinking, and the words had just gushed forth. The lingering remnants of her fear disappeared: Those secrets that she was meant to keep from him were now right in front of him. He had to know.

"It's a place," she said, "that is close and yet very far, and its name must remain secret. Of all those in Ollantaytambo, only Katari and I have traveled there. He carved this stone in the shape of a mountain that no one here has seen, and which rises up over there, above our secret sanctuary. On that mountain's side . . ."

Gabriel let Anamaya's words flow through him without trying to understand them. They penetrated every pore in his skin and marked him.

". . . a face is being carved. It's the Puma's face."

Anamaya paused. A moment passed before Gabriel realized that she was talking about him. Still unsure, he squinted through the darkness, trying to make out anything at all carved into the rock. But he saw nothing.

"You don't see it," she continued, "and yet it's there. Katari told you that your destiny is written in stone. Here it is, directly in front of you."

Gabriel suddenly felt an intense heat invade his body, an emotion unlike the blood-colored, ash-flavored fury of battle or the honeyed taste of carnal love. His entire body shuddered and he felt at one with the world. He felt amazingly grateful.

"I see it," he murmured. "I see it!"

He saw the Puma's fangs emerge from the rock, ready to bite, ready to tear to pieces. But Gabriel wasn't frightened. He was intoxicated with inexplicable and magnificent joy, beyond laughter, beyond tears.

"At last," he thought, "I have arrived."

EIGHTEEN

They lay naked against each other, entwined, wrapped up together as though they had been sculpted from a single block of stone. They had plunged into each other deeply, almost without moving. Their nearly imperceptible caresses brought them exquisite pleasure. They shared their breath with the breeze.

Their happiness was complete. It made all the strange twists and turns that their fates had dealt them seem obvious, even necessary. They were united in the certitude that all was well without having to explain it. Their emotions floated as though on a gentle lake by the light of the half moon.

They occasionally lay so perfectly still against each other that they almost stopped breathing. At other times, they flowed together as though they were on the river that they could hear rumbling outside, and within them as well.

They spoke without moving their lips; their words were their hands, their grammar their heartbeats. They were like light and shadow, two bodies leading a dance in the middle of the universe.

Anamaya broke away first.

Gabriel felt no pain.

He watched her gracefully slip on her *añaco* before passing him his *unku*.

She sat down beside him and gazed into the darkness at a spot on the mountain where Gabriel thought he could make out a few niches carved into the rock.

"I'm going to tell you about a trip," she murmured.

* * *

Anamaya told Gabriel about her trip through the stone and her flight as a condor over the Secret City.

He listened as she told him about the rock that spoke to her and about seeing the old face of the great Inca Huayna Capac. He remembered that she had served the Inca a long time ago.

Anamaya told Gabriel what the Inca had told her, and although not all of it afforded him insight, he engraved it in his heart; it didn't unravel all the mysteries surrounding him, but as he listened to Anamaya's soft voice, he felt a peace envelop him, a sense of abandon that he had never felt before. He was overjoyed to realize that he had not only laid down his arms, but that he had been freed from the very spirit of war.

He realized that it was war that had forced him to remain on the move his whole life, that he had been displaced by war ever since that sad day when the man he hadn't been able to call father in public had freed him from jail only to scorn him.

He felt as though he were watching his life replay itself and as though Anamaya were watching it with him. He wondered whether that was how she had felt when she flew over the mysterious valley with Katari. He saw his battles, his fights, and his outbursts. He saw them not as a Stranger, but with newfound acceptance, a sense of peace that made him want to whisper, "It was only a trifling thing." Of course, this didn't diminish his affection for his few friends or lessen the love for Anamaya burning in his gut.

He sounded the depth of his love, was dazzled by its brilliance, by its almost infinite power. He explored his own fears.

And then that landscape disappeared, and he heard Manco's severe voice echoing like a bell tower. "Before dawn, before dawn."

Gabriel thought he could make out a slight glow atop the Ancestor Mountain.

Anamaya clasped him to her.

"You know what I know," she said. "Nothing remains hidden from you. Now you must live the life you're meant to, before coming back to me. We have to wait for the signs to be revealed. . . ."

"How will we know that they have been?"

Anamaya remembered asking Katari the same question when he had given her his stone key.

"We'll know. You'll know it as soon as I do."

"Will we have to wait long?"

He said this anxiously, suddenly. She hadn't expected it. It was as though the child in him had reemerged and was demanding his happiness right away, and that he would throw a tantrum if he didn't get it.

Dawn was upon them.

A pale yellow light grazed over the mountain peaks. Night was withdrawing. Each moment was another grain of sand that slipped between his fingers. Anamaya answered his question by kissing his lips, lingering on them.

They stood up together, still holding each other, kissing almost violently, then tenderly, alternating between the extremes of their passion. And then, with an effort that wrenched the breath from his lungs, Gabriel detached himself from her.

"I love you," she said.

He looked at her. All the memories that he had of her face, all her smiles and all her tears, melted into one. He looked into the serene lake of her eyes. He thought he saw a mountain peak reflected in it.

She put her finger on his lips.

"I love you," she said again, louder now.

She looked at the Ancestor Mountain before turning away. *Remain in my breath, and trust the Puma.* The words infused her with the courage that she needed.

He turned around and began making his way down toward the riverside path, all the while sensing her standing still behind him.

He didn't turn around for fear of losing his determination, of not being able to do what must be done. He knew what that was now, he understood it and accepted it in his innermost heart.

He began walking more quickly toward the *canchas*.

As he crossed the bridge, he blinked as the sun's first rays illuminated his face.

PART THREE

NINETEEN

Lake Titicaca, March 1539

Early dawn, and a thin fog slipped slowly over the Island of the Moon. The lake was still hidden, and only the very slight sound of waves lapping at the pebble beach betrayed its existence.

Gabriel was sitting on a low wall lining the highest terrace, with his back to Quilla's temple. It was cold, and his skin was covered with goose bumps despite the large blue wool cape he had wrapped around himself. He was, as always, deeply moved by the prevailing serenity of the sacred place, a place he now knew well.

He liked this time of day, when the sky and the lake were of the same milky, fluid hue, the light gradually strengthening from its center. And although he felt profoundly alone, he also felt as though he were being carried away by the omnipotence of life now flourishing with the burgeoning day.

Now the morning breeze blew stronger; his blond hair floated on it, and it rippled his long beard. It came from the south, scattering the fog into long, thin strips and pushing it north so that it resembled a pack of white horses galloping through the blue. The little island's grass- and shrub-covered slopes appeared, and the ceremonial terraces, trimly divided by brown and ocher stone walls, now lay unveiled. They were stepped neatly right down to the somber waters of the lake, its shore streaked by the foam of small waves.

Soon, Titicaca in all its vast magnificence was visible. Gabriel could make out the vertiginous Apus to the north and east, the Ancestor Mountains, the haughty guardians of the Lake of Origin. Night's shadows gradually withdrew from the mountains' folds and ravines as the last streaks of fog dissolved in the blue sky. The sun lit with gold the cotton clouds caught on the eternally frozen peaks of Ancohuma and Illampu, clouds skimming over their rocky scree, cliffs, and seracs.

The other mountains were, in turn, very quickly crowned with gold. The lake's blue grew deeper and more dense, and its banks seemed to rise from it. Like a peacock showing its resplendent train, the thousands of geometrically arranged terraces on the western shore unfurled their variety of greens. For a brief moment, Gabriel felt as though he were witnessing the birth of the world.

The last strands of fog in the north, directly in front of him, abruptly scattered and unveiled the moon, the Moon-Mother. She was enormous, perfectly round, and hung suspended directly over the mountains reflected in the lake. She stayed there for a while, long enough for Gabriel to become absorbed in her faraway contours and shadows, and to watch her brilliance gradually diminish in the growing day.

And then the sun shot up over the big Apus and threw its blinding light over the world. The lake's surface, somber a moment before, now shimmered so brightly that it was impossible to look at directly.

The moon began to slowly fade away.

Voices began chanting behind Gabriel, startling him.

> O Mama Quilla, how cold was the night!
> O Mama Quilla, hold us tight,
> O Moon-Mother, embrace us!
> The Sun has suckled the milk of day at your breast,
> The Sun has spilled the milk of life in your womb,
> O Mama Quilla!
> May you rest in Titicaca's depths,
> May you cross through night's shadow,
> May you return to us in the unborn tomorrow,
> May you swell our wombs and breasts.
> O Moon-Mother,
> In the World Above,
> In the Underworld,
> Embrace us,
> For we are your daughters,
> O Mama Quilla!

He turned and saw a dozen old women chanting.

With their arms raised, they focused their etiolated eyes on the moon's increasingly diaphanous disc. They chorused the moon's valediction once again, their cracked lips moving together, singing from toothless mouths. They punctuated each lyric with a sway of their hips, their long capes lined with silver plaques undulating in time with their bodies. Gabriel observed, that although their faces were wizened and old, they moved their bodies with youthful grace.

They were standing in front of the Temple of the Moon, which consisted of a number of buildings set around three sides of a perfectly proportioned courtyard. Thirteen doors, with lintels and frames lined with ocher stone as delicately worked as *mantas,* opened onto thirteen small rooms, cubicles set next to the upper terraces. A young girl in a white tunic stood before each door, each one's bosom covered with a silver plate.

Gabriel shivered. He straightened himself and waited for the end of the prayer, feeling the stiffness in his muscles.

When the priestesses were finished, three adolescent girls emerged from the temple. Two of them wore vicuña wool *cumbis* over their arms, the material so finely woven that it looked weightless. The third came to Gabriel and handed him a tunic decorated with a simple red-and-gold motif.

Wordlessly he took off his coat. Beneath, he wore only a shirt and velvet breeches. The young girl helped him slip his head through the tunic's narrow neck hole. It covered him entirely, and only the toes of his boots were visible.

He could smell the animal odor of the wool and door-hangings. He took one last glance at the mountains, now iridescent in the morning light, before bowing to the oldest priestess.

"I am ready, daughter of Quilla," he murmured respectfully.

The old women surrounded him and led him into a dark room, lit only by a few candle ends. Each woman threw a handful of coca leaves into a brazier.

Fussing noisily, they urged Gabriel toward a long, dull-colored door-hanging. One priestess pulled it aside and disappeared into an unlit, narrow passage bent at an odd angle. Five old women disappeared behind her. Gabriel felt hands pushing him into the pitch-black passage.

As soon as the door-hanging had fallen back down behind him, he could see nothing. He held his hands out in front of him, feeling his way along the cold wall. Its roughcast surface was surprisingly smooth, as polished as leather by the thousands of hands that had felt their way along it.

The passage forked off to the left and narrowed considerably. Gabriel stopped, but an old woman behind him, so close to that he could feel her breath on the back of his neck, impatiently ordered him to continue. Gabriel had to shuffle sideways to pass. His chest brushed against the wall. He advanced cautiously, still feeling his way with his leading arm, before passing through a barely large enough gap into another room, much larger than the first and filled with smoke.

On one of its walls were four arched niches pierced with little square holes through which thin beams of daylight passed. A huge, slightly bulging silver disk, twice as large as a man, gleamed on the opposite wall. Its convex surface distorted the mirrored images of the women moving about the room. Thick smoke billowed from two large, baked clay braziers, painted in rich colors, standing below the disk. They used dried llama dung as fuel, and its acid stench was mixed with that of burned flesh and guts, the heady odor of burning coca leaves, and the acrid reek of sacred beer. The smoke was so thick and the stench so old and well maintained that the walls themselves seemed to give off the smell.

Gabriel covered his mouth and nose, and stepped back despite himself. But now the old women crowded around him. Some grabbed his hands, his arms, or even his neck, others took hold of the folds of his long tunic. They led him to the center of the room, moving as a large, single body. The acrid smoke eddied around them. It irritated Gabriel's eyes, but he nevertheless watched the women's grotesque reflection in the silver disk as they began chanting:

> O Mama Quilla, hold us tight,
> O Moon-Mother, embrace us!

The senior priestess stoked the embers in the braziers, and only then did Gabriel realize that they were shaped like roaring pumas. She threw more coca leaves onto them, and then some small plant roots. The smell of these last was very strong, not unlike incense, and it overwhelmed all the others. But the smoke the roots gave off greatly irritated Gabriel's eyes, and tears formed beneath his eyelids. The women tightened their grip on him and began swaying from side to side, leading him along in their dance so strongly that he felt like a doll in their hands. They sang plaintively:

> O Moon-Mother,
> In the World Above,
> In the Underworld,
> Embrace us.

The senior priestess broke away and stood to face them. She raised her right hand and touched the silver disk. Their distorted image in it moved with increasing frenzy. She picked up a jug of *chicha*. Still swaying, she tilted it forward and spilled the bitter liquid all around, even on the embers in the braziers, and chanted:

> O Quilla, drink for us!
> O sweet Mother, drink for him!

The air in the room had become quite unbreathable. Gabriel gasped for air, his mouth wide open, tears rolling from his smarting eyes. He felt as though he had sand grinding under his eyelids. He wanted to rub them to stop the burning, but the old women holding on to him never gave him the chance. He could barely see the senior priestess put the resplendent fabrics woven by the virgins on the braziers, their bright colors reflecting for an instant in the silver disk.

The smoke lessened for a brief moment before returning twice as thick, heavy, and black, and the old women's swaying grew increasingly frenzied.

The *cumbis* on the braziers twisted as they burned, their delicate wool fibers decomposing into tiny green and blue flames that consumed their ornate geometric designs. Their beautiful colors crackled and burned. One after another, the bolts of fabrics in the braziers turned to ash. Gabriel felt the smoke fill his mouth like some abrasive paste and burn his throat and lungs. Each breath required enormous effort. He clenched his fingers on the women's shoulders, and they supported him with amazing strength, considering their great age, never once ceasing their chant.

Gabriel opened his eyes with great difficulty, but he could barely see the silver disk or the priestess through the smoke. Although he was choked by nausea, the old women held him ever tighter.

And then, suddenly, they fell silent and stopped swaying.

He watched the smoke dance before Quilla's silver disk. The smoke rose up in volutes of various colors. One whorl was pure white, another yellow, another brown, almost black. Some were gray at the bottom of their spiral, green in the middle, and red at the top. The smoke danced irregularly, arrhythmically. The heavy smoke toward the top of the room twisted back down toward a thick, smooth, rising bank, then twisted up again before dispersing into diaphanous strands, their mottled colors mingling together. Opaque wisps spiraled up against the silver disk as though trying to bore a well into it.

The room was dark and menacing; its walls seemed to be moving in on them like a giant fist closing. Gabriel felt his throat constrict, as though he were being strangled. All the muscles in his legs, his back, and his shoulders suddenly felt so heavy that he could barely lift his feet. His heart beat as though it were trying to burst out of his chest. He kept his eyes open despite the pain, and he thought he glimpsed a face in the silver disk. But a moment later there was nothing, and he was convinced that he was about to die. He saw blood flooding his eyes and mouth. He saw himself falling into the abyss.

Unable to cry out, he tore himself away from the hands holding him. He pushed aside the old women, flinging them to the ground, and rushed at the gap in the wall and so out of the room. He scraped his palms and forehead as he moved too quickly through the narrow passage. He bolted toward the temple's exit and, gasping for air, emerged into the cold, bright morning.

*   *   *

Gabriel lay on the temple's grass-covered esplanade, recovering.

When he eventually looked up, he saw the oldest of the priestesses standing a few paces away. A gaggle of young girls stood behind her, in front of the temple's doors. They were all, oddly enough, smiling and laughing, and the old priestess wore a broad, toothless grin and uttered a high-pitched laugh.

"I warned you, golden-haired Stranger!" she guffawed. "I told you that you wouldn't be able to take the Smoke of the Encounter! Only very old men and women can stand it and travel into the silver disk."

Gabriel ran his hands over his throbbing head. He sat up and glared at the woman.

"Well, maybe I failed the test," he grumbled. "Or maybe it's rather you who can't produce the Smoke of the Encounter?"

The very old woman laughed again. But this time, her laugh was as short as it was dry.

"Your words are nothing more than a ripple on the lake," she flung back at him in a serious tone. "You asked me to take you through the smoke to the *Coya Camaquen;* I told you that you wouldn't make it. Thrice you've tried, and thrice you've failed."

"Maybe the *Coya Camaquen* can't hear me. Maybe she's gone to the Other World."

The old priestess grimaced contemptuously as he voiced his fear.

"You are arrogant, golden-haired Stranger. You cannot stand the smoke, so you pretend to know what Quilla's silence signifies better than I do! Know that had she wanted to, she would have drawn your last breath from you in there. Quilla's domain has always been denied to men still in their prime. It has been thus since the dawn of time! And yet the *pachacuti* has begun building, and our Mother the Moon needs you."

Gabriel shrugged. He turned from the old woman and her criticisms and walked away, taking off his long tunic as quickly as he could. But the priestess ran after him, grabbed his wrist, and commanded:

"No! You cannot leave like this. You must serve Quilla until she has forgiven you your impiety."

"What do you mean?"

The woman said nothing, but simply pointed at the young girls.

"Follow the Daughters of the Moon and do everything that they ask of you."

"No," protested Gabriel, "I've had enough of this stupidity for today!"

"Follow them," repeated the priestess, not releasing his hand. "It is Quilla's will. She will answer all your questions."

"Apinguela! Apinguela!" cried the young girl in the prow.

"Apinguela! Apinguela!" chorused the twenty young women in the vessel, pointing at a gently sloped little island, very low in the water.

Gabriel stood up awkwardly to see what they were pointing at. He took hold of the long reed vessel's mast. But the vessel's motion on the short, choppy waves forced him to sit down again. His useless effort was met with a teasing laugh. The women began fervently chanting:

> The Sun,
> The Moon,
> Day and night,
> Spring and winter,
> Stone and Mountains,
> Corn and cantuta.
> O Quilla,
> You are the milk and the seed,
> You open your legs
> To receive the passion of the night,
> O Quilla, it is your will that
> He who leaves Titicaca
> Is already on the path home.

The wind blew from the south and filled the strange-looking sail made of tightly braided *totora*, a fine and supple reed. It was almost as efficient as a Spanish canvas sail. The hull was made of the same material bundled together in large bunches on which the young women lay. The vessel had no keel, no rudder, and no oar, and it moved forward by fits and starts, steered only by the set of the sail and with long poles where the lake was shallow enough. It took them almost an entire day to reach the little island that the Daughters of the Moon called Apinguela. And not once throughout the day did they stop their laughing and singing.

Gabriel was the only man aboard. For hours, he had been the focus of their attention and the butt of their jokes. And not one of his shipmates gave him a straight answer when he pestered them with: "Where are we going? To do what? What does Quilla want with me?"

"You'll see, you'll see," they replied, chuckling. "Mama Quilla is thinking only of your happiness!"

Nor had they allowed him to help steer the vessel. They stuffed him with *chicha* and fruits of the jungle. His belly full, and oppressed by the sun beating down on the lake like a white flame, he had fallen asleep for the better part of the day, only to wake with his heart in his mouth.

The wind now carried the evening's coolness to them, and the shadows of the rocks on the little island's approaching shore were long in the light of the low-slung sun. All the women were silent now. The only sounds were those of the creaking rigging on the mast and the reed hull cutting through the waves. Their faces were taut, serious, watchful.

Gabriel, surprised, stood up again. He ran his eyes over the island shore, looking for some sign of life or some boat coming to meet them. But there was nothing on the island's slopes but confused slabs of rock from the cracks of which grew tufts of *ichu* or bushes worn down by the wind.

"Apinguela!" cried the girl in the bow again.

The girl closest to Gabriel pointed to the island's eastern point.

"There," she said quietly, pointing at a shadow bigger than the others on one of the rocks plunging into the lake. "Apinguela! Our Mother the Moon's womb is open."

Gabriel made out a yawning cave on the water's edge, a giant fissure in the rock leading into the island's heart.

The Daughters of the Moon began busying themselves even before they entered the cave. While some dropped the sail, others began navigating the vessel with long poles. Still others took out some glowing embers that they had brought along in a leather gusset, and with them lit a dozen torches. In the middle of the vessel, meanwhile, four women removed the *cumbis* that were wrapped around a stone urn, and fifteen gold figurines of llamas and small-breasted women, their arms across their bosoms.

As the bark slipped into the cave, Gabriel felt a warm breeze coming out of it. The flames of the torches flickered for a moment, and then they were inside. The interior was calm, mild, and warm. Its walls, from the waterline to the top of the natural vault, were smooth and covered with a thin layer of moss. The water was perfectly still, without a single ripple, and was so translucent that they could make out its shallow bottom by torchlight alone.

All the women were standing silently and facing forward. Gabriel tried to stand as well, but a number of firm hands forced him back down.

The large bark moved deeper into the cave, the women pushing it along with their poles. They reached a point where the cave split into two tenebrous passageways. The Daughters of the Moon took the one on the left, which was larger and which grew suddenly deeper so that the bottom could no longer be seen through the emerald water.

The unexplained heat grew more oppressive here. Sweat beaded on Gabriel's forehead and streamed down his spine. The passageway grew narrower, and the rounded edges of the *totora* vessel squeaked quietly against the moss.

They went another eighty *codos* or so, then stopped. Gabriel was stunned to see an enormous silver disk, at least as large as the one in the Room of Sacrifices in the Temple of the Moon, blocking their way.

The women wordlessly placed their torches in holders carved into the mossy walls. They began quietly chanting again.

Then everything happened so quickly that Gabriel didn't have time to protest or even understand.

In no time at all, the youngest of the Daughters of the Moon whipped off their clothes and dived into the water. Then those still on the vessel undressed. Gabriel, embarrassed, sat up and leaned against the wall of the cave. He wanted to look away, but the women, instead of being embarrassed, came to him and removed his tunic, then didn't hesitate to tear away his shirt and yank off his breeches.

"Hola!" he cried, pushing them away. "What are you doing?"

His voice echoed loudly throughout the cave. The silver disk seemed to tremble. But he was answered only with laughter. The women were more forceful now, and tore away his remaining clothes. And because he was still resisting, they bound his wrists together with a thin but strong-fibered rope.

"God's blood, you're all mad!" cried Gabriel, again causing the air in the cave to shudder.

Yet his surprise, his embarrassment at his nakedness, and the intoxication still throbbing through his temples made his resistance as futile as that of a newborn babe.

As he clumsily tried to free himself from the rope binding his hands, the women deftly tied its other end around the stone urn's long, chiseled neck.

Gabriel saw two Daughters of the Moon lift it up and realized, too late, that they intended to throw it overboard.

It went over with a splash. Gabriel made one last-ditch effort to hold up the urn, but the rope cut deeply into his wrists. He let out a furious, desperate cry as he was yanked over the side behind it. He had just enough time to take one last gulp of air before his face slapped against the water and he was dragged under.

He was surprised to find the water as warm as the air in the cave. The farther down he went, the hotter it became. His descent didn't take long. A few fathoms at most. He touched the rocky bottom with his fingers. Looking up through the clear water, he could see the light of the torches on the surface. But they seemed far out of reach.

He tried again to untie his hands, but in vain. And then, they appeared all around him: all the Daughters of the Moon, swimming like mermaids. Some were holding the little gold figurines, which glinted in the water like fish scales.

His lungs were running out if air. His chest was burning, and he began to panic.

The women continued darting about him, brushing passed him, stroking him, touching him. He wanted to cry out for them to release him. But the women just danced around, their underwater ballet became slower and slower. He saw them lift the cover off the urn and put their statues into it.

His temples were pulsating furiously, and the fire in his lungs now spread throughout his body, ripping through his muscles as though his blood were boiling. Asphyxia dulled his senses. He thought he could still feel them stroking his face, his buttocks, and his belly. He struggled and kicked, banging against them. But they simply pressed in closer to him. He felt their thighs and arms around him.

Then, something gave way.

He stopped thinking about life or death. He felt a woman's body against his, and he recognized Anamaya's warmth. He surrendered.

Immediately, he felt relieved, transported, protected.

He searched for his lost but never forgotten beloved's face.

But before he managed to find it, the tongue of fire licked the interior of his lungs once again. A raucous cry tore his throat.

His eyes closed, he realized that he was breathing once again.

His cheeks slipped wetly against the girls' arms and breasts as they passed him along to the vessel.

He found that breathing caused as much pain as being asphyxiated had.

I didn't see her face, he thought with grief.

He shuddered and convulsed. His teeth chattered. He felt himself being wiped down, he felt their hands stroking him and bringing the blood back to his veins. When he opened his eyes, his vision was blurred by the tumult of his heart. But he could see the faces smiling down at him.

I didn't see her face, he murmured.

"Mama Quilla only reveals herself when she deems it fit," replied one of the women gently.

"Not Quilla's face," protested Gabriel, "Anamaya's!"

"Quilla is every face," replied another woman.

At last, warmth returned to his body, and he could feel the women caressing him.

He made a final mental effort to conjure up Anamaya, to gather together all her features in his mind's eye and make her real enough to touch with his fingers.

But in vain.

All he could feel was the Daughters of the Moon's insistent caresses on his body, and their lips as they moved across his flesh, seeking to pleasure him. He felt their fingers tightening around his erection, and without looking he knew that parted thighs were descending upon his loins.

He surrendered to them, seeking solace from Anamaya's absence.

TWENTY

Vilcabamba, March 1539

"Listen! Listen!"

Anamaya stood up in the river, the water eddying around her waist.

It was a moment of great beauty. The distant sky glowed lambently in the gap between the canyon's walls, gold merging into red like a perfectly woven *cumbi*, and yet at its zenith lingered a very pale blue.

It hadn't rained for the first time in many days, and the jungle's humidity was less stifling. Dusk brought life back to the riverbanks set between the steep, densely vegetated sides of the canyon.

"Listen," whispered Anamaya again, looking intently upstream.

Curi Ocllo, Manco's young and very beautiful wife, had been cavorting in the streaming water not far from Anamaya. She gained her footing on the river's pebbly bottom and stood stock-still. Her body was more thickset than Anamaya's, but perfectly proportioned. She squinted, put her hands over the brown areolas of her breasts, turned toward the valley, and then shook her head with incomprehension.

"What do you want me to listen to?"

Anamaya waved to her to be quiet. She stared intently at the uppermost foliage hanging over the little stream in which they were bathing. She saw branches bend, and long, hanging strands of leaves shiver as though from a gust of wind. But she realized that it was only a group of impish monkeys made playful by the coolness of dusk.

And in fact, the jungle was resonating with noise, but only the ordinary, reassuring noise that always precedes dusk in a jungle. Weaver orioles gave their gurgling cry in short bursts, and their song rose above the ceaseless patter of the blue-white waterfall that pierced through the green in a cloud of mist. A flight of green parrots passed over the river emitting ruffled squawks, much to the annoyance of a dozen local red-

and-blue macaws. For a moment, they released a furious cackle from their nests hidden in a crevice in the cliff. But then silence returned, save for the murmur of the water.

"I'm listening. But I hear nothing," said Curi Ocllo.

She slid down up to her neck in the cool water as Anamaya, still tense, ran her eyes over the riverbanks where a group of tortoises lay basking on fallen logs.

"It was only a bunch of parrots, that's all," said Curi Ocllo, smoothing down her thick hair.

"No," said Anamaya, "I'm sure I heard something."

Anamaya let herself slip into the water and watched Curi Ocllo's round, finely-featured face as she approached. Anamaya felt the young woman's hands rest tenderly on her shoulders.

"Well then, what you heard was audible only to a *Coya Camaquen*. Something that doesn't reach the ears of an ordinary woman like myself."

"Maybe."

"Not maybe, absolutely!" declared Curi Ocllo, vexed. "Everyone knows that you and the Master of the Stone can accomplish marvels!"

She waved away a cloud of tiny white butterflies. Then she floated gracefully on her back over to the shallow, muddy bank. With her eyes closed, she surrendered her splendid naked body to the current's caress.

Anamaya smiled. She was about to answer when suddenly her expression changed once again and she looked up, her eyes searching, her ears listening intently.

She felt a kind of breath or murmur come down the river and envelop her. It was nothing tangible, just an inexplicable sensation. It could simply have been a cool gust, the barely audible whisper of the wind singing through the dense jungle. But she couldn't stop herself from thinking, from hoping, that it was something else. She sensed a presence. Was it the Puma's breath?

Gabriel!

For a few seconds, her whole being was filled with him. A shudder passed through her belly, and she wrapped her arms over her breasts, her nipples hard. She strained to hear as clearly as possible. The invisible murmur enveloped her again. She thought she felt Gabriel's hands and breath on her quivering skin. She was so overcome with emotion that she closed her eyes involuntarily.

She whispered his name without realizing it.

And then, the spell lifted as abruptly as it decended upon her. Its coolness evaporated into the jungle's warm, humid air in an instant, like a reflection flashing across a mirror.

Anamaya relaxed and opened her eyes. Everything was as it had been before. The sky had grown redder, and the shadow between the green-covered cliffs had grown. The monkeys were welcoming the coming night with excited cackles, the parrots were squealing at the macaws to keep them away, and little clouds of butterflies were gracefully rising up in the mist of the waterfall.

"What did you feel?" asked Curi Ocllo nervously, now curled up on herself in the water.

Anamaya laughed lightly, bringing herself back to reality. Manco's young wife, her eyes dark and warm, looked at her with a mixture of curiosity and fear.

"You did see something!" she exclaimed. "You were so strange just now, so absent. . . ."

With an embarrassed laugh, Anamaya slid into the water. She felt the unreasonable fear that Curi Ocllo could see on her skin the mark of Gabriel's mysterious caress sent to her by the Ancestors of the Other World, so she hid her nakedness.

She scooped up water from one of the many eddies around her and splashed it over her shoulders and the back of her neck.

"It's difficult to explain."

"You mean it's forbidden to talk about it."

"No, it's not forbidden. Just difficult to explain and difficult to understand."

Curi Ocllo curled her beautiful, still childlike lips into a sulky pout. She tilted her head back so that her thick hair streamed in the current like black seaweed, and her round breasts emerged from the water like two golden water stones.

"We should go back now," said Anamaya.

Curi Ocllo uttered a little laugh, both teasing and jealous, and her belly shuddered.

"I know what you don't want to tell me, *Coya Camaquen*. You thought of the Stranger you love, didn't you, the one that you call the Puma?"

Anamaya hesitated for a moment, then smiled and admitted, "I didn't *think* of him. I felt him."

"You felt him? Felt him as though you were in his arms?" exclaimed Curi Ocllo, standing upright now, wide-eyed.

Anamaya only laughed and nodded. She took the young woman's hand in hers and led her to the riverbank where their clothes hung from the low branches of a ficus tree.

"Does he often come to you like that?" asked Curi Ocllo.

Anamaya waited until she was out of the water before replying. Her voice was slightly muted, as though the confidence that she was about to impart was more of a confession.

"He doesn't really come to me. But his presence surrounds me. He's searching for me, thinking of me."

"I don't understand."

"I told you that it was difficult to explain. Wherever he is, he remembers me; he wants to be close to me. So he tries to pass through the Other World to reach me."

"How is that possible?"

"It's possible because he's the Puma . . . and no doubt he has priests and priestesses helping him!"

Anamaya laughed at her own words. Curi Ocllo finished dressing and glanced at her, both suspicious and confused.

"I'm not making fun of you, Curi Ocllo," continued Anamaya quietly. "There's much more to the world than what's visible. The Powerful Ancestors are watching over us. We must trust them."

"Yes, yes, I know. You all say that, you, the priests, the Master of the Stone. But it seems to me that the Powerful Ancestors don't watch over everyone equally. Maybe they've even turned away from Manco and me . . . and almost all Incas!"

The young woman's voice quivered with anger, and she began crying. She dashed suddenly toward the path cut through the jungle, as though she were about to flee.

"Curi Ocllo!"

"How long have you been apart from the Stranger, Anamaya?" asked Curi Ocllo in a hard voice, her back to Anamaya.

"Twenty-eight moons."

"And during those twenty-eight moons, you've never known where the one you call the Puma's been?"

"No, I haven't."

"And yet, despite all the time that's passed, he's never forgotten you nor you him. Despite all that time, you still feel close to him and he to you."

"Maybe."

"Not maybe, certainly! I'm sure that you see him in your dreams, and that you even lie with him in your sleep! Twenty-eight moons! I'm sure you're right: The Powerful Ancestors are protecting you both and don't want you to be apart. You and a . . . a Stranger!"

Curi Ocllo turned on her heels and stood defiantly before Anamaya.

"And why? Will you tell me why, *Coya Camaquen*?" she shouted, and for a few moments the jungle's din ceased.

"I don't understand your question, Curi Ocllo," replied Anamaya gently.

Pain and despair racked the young queen's beautiful face.

"I've only been apart from Manco for four moons," she sobbed, "and yet I sleep without dreams, and when I swim, I swim alone. Wherever I go, my beloved's presence is absent. The Powerful Ancestors wrap me only in cold solitude. They ignore me, *Coya Camaquen*, and I think that they don't even support Manco anymore."

"Manco is doing what he must do," said Anamaya quietly. Her heart constricted from understanding only too well the truths overwhelming Curi Ocllo. "He loves you," she continued. "He loves you more than any of his other wives."

"He loves me, but I cannot reach him. My bed is empty. He loves me but I don't feel his hands or mouth on my skin. He loves me, but my tomorrow appears as cold and frozen as a winter's day atop the highest mountain."

"He's fighting a war, Curi Ocllo. Manco's fighting the Strangers. He's fighting a terrible war."

Tears streaming down her cheeks, Curi Ocllo shook her head.

"No, Anamaya, and you know it better than me: Manco's not fighting a war, he's losing one."

"Curi Ocllo!"

"Who can deny it? Emperor Manco, my husband, is alone, and his strength is diminishing. His brother Paullu has joined the Strangers. Sage Villa Oma is waging his own war on the side. You and the Master of the Stone, you're both here in Vilcabamba, hidden in this newly built jungle city, and you're both always dealing with the Powerful Ancestors and are far from Manco, far from my beloved. And I'm here too, even I'm not at his side!"

"Curi Ocllo," murmured Anamaya, taking the woman in her arms. But she couldn't deny what the Queen was saying.

"He's so alone! The Strangers have captured his son Titu Cusi, the one he loves most! He's surrounded by traitors! They even took the mummies of the Powerful Ancestors from Cuzco. . . ."

Anamaya was deeply saddened. She couldn't think of anything to say to soften these terrible realities. She simply stroked the young woman's wet cheeks and murmured, "Don't think that I'm abandoning Emperor Manco, Curi Ocllo. I've always been close to him; he's always been like a brother to me. Nothing that we're doing here in Vilcabamba is against him. Quite the opposite: The Master of the Stone has built a city where your beloved Manco will one day be able to live, and to live as a Son of the Sun should."

Curi Ocllo shivered and broke from Anamaya's embrace. Recovering her pride, she wiped away her tears. But then she grimaced with pain once again. Like a lost child, she cried, "Oh, Anamaya, I'm so frightened of what tomorrow might bring!"

The sun was at its nadir by the time Anamaya and Curi Ocllo reached Vilcabamba's outer walls. The newest Inca city had been built to Katari's precise plans, and it induced a mysterious sense of serenity.

Its terraces and *canchas* were meticulously arranged around the great ceremonial square in front of the Temple of the Sun, a long building with ten doors. The walls of the rooms were coated with ocher roughcast that glowed gold in the failing light. Like a jewel, it captured the setting sun's blaze even as the nearby river and agricultural terraces disappeared into night's shadows.

And night had already descended upon the mountains to the north and upon the sinuous valleys of the Pampakona to the east, valleys covered in forests of cedars and giant *caboas* from which rose ribbons of fog.

The two young women heard the faint cry of birds, and slowed their pace through the wet grass. They kept their eyes fixed on the peaks still aglow on the southern cordillera. And then the light brusquely disappeared, leaving the ferns and glaciers and the two women in darkness.

They heard frogs croak loudly from nearby and then fall silent just as abruptly. Curi Ocllo jumped and grabbed Anamaya's arm. Wordlessly, she pointed toward a thick clump of bushes beside a wall. The broad leaves moved unnaturally, and a young puma emerged. Its still light-colored coat gleamed in the darkness.

It moved toward them supplely, skipping lightly on its powerful paws.

Anamaya involuntarily held her breath. She heard Curi Ocllo let out a little cry of fear.

The puma was so close now that they could make out the white rims around its eyes and the pale edging around its ears. It stopped two paces from Anamaya and looked into her eyes. It opened its jaws slightly and let out a long, soft growl.

And then it turned and bounded away into the bushes.

Anamaya and Curi Ocllo stood absolutely still for a moment, petrified, listening to the soft padding step of the feline as it headed off into the jungle.

When Curi Ocllo, her bosom still raised from having held her breath in fear, turned toward Anamaya, she saw the happiness on her friend's face.

"You were right," she whispered. "He *was* there. He stayed close to you."

TWENTY-ONE

Lake Titicaca, Copacabana, April 1539

"Lord Gabriel!"

The child standing in the doorway was no more than twelve years old. Yet the severe expression on his face aged him by a few years.

"Leave me be, child!" growled Gabriel. "Let me sleep or else I'll slice you into pieces and feed you to the pumas."

"Lord Gabriel, you mustn't sleep anymore," replied the child, utterly unimpressed.

Gabriel sighed and opened his eyes.

"By all the saints! It seems that my slumber does indeed displease you, Chillioc. Why do you wake me, child, when it is not yet day?"

"Someone's coming, Lord Gabriel, someone's coming to see you."

"Indeed?"

Gabriel now focused his attention on the child, who still stood at the threshold. He could hear the noise of the women out in the courtyard preparing the morning meal.

He sat up in his hammock, careful not to set it swinging, and asked the child, "Who is it, and how do you know?"

"The *chaski* said, 'A Stranger is coming on a horse. He is old and tired. He is already past Copacabana and is coming from Cusijata!'" The child shrugged, then added, "If a Stranger's coming all the way here, then it must be to see you."

Gabriel couldn't help but smile. He got up, the hammock swinging gently behind him.

"Fetch me my tunic, Chillioc," he ordered. "An old and tired Stranger, you say? Does he have white hairs on his face?"

"I don't think so. The *chaski* only said that you couldn't see his face because it was entirely covered in cloth. And that also he wasn't far and that he would reach your *cancha* before his shadow had shortened even by a hand."

Gabriel finished dressing and looked at the child, intrigued. When he came out into the long courtyard, the servants, busy around the hearth set under the sloping roof, greeted him with smiles and invited him to eat. He declined and grabbed the child by the neck, drawing him near.

"Well now, Chillioc, I'm going to have to thank you for waking me. Come and meet the Stranger with me."

What they saw first was so strange a sight that it took even Gabriel a few moments to realize that it was a horse and rider. The approaching figure looked more like a pile of blankets, both Spanish and Indian, moving along the terraces overlooking the lake of its own accord.

"Whoever he is, he doesn't seem to be in the best of health," said Gabriel to the child hurrying behind him.

When the strange rider was no more than thirty or forty *codos* from them, he stopped. The man hidden beneath the pile of *mantas* looked like he was about to fall from his saddle.

"*Hola!*" cried Gabriel, approaching him quickly now. "*Hola, compañero!* Who are you?"

But no reply came from the pile of blankets. Gabriel, suddenly cautious, slowed down and urged Chillioc back.

"Stay here, child. Don't come any closer. The rogue might have a crossbow hidden under his rags."

The boy reluctantly obeyed and gave Gabriel a reproachful look. Gabriel looked at the man and horse for a moment, both so utterly still that they might have been dead. But he could make out no sign of a weapon, and in fact not even a glimpse of the rider was visible beneath the blankets. Gabriel, worried, wondered whether the exhausted hack had been carrying a corpse all these leagues.

"*Hola! Hola, compañero!*" he shouted, louder now.

His cries startled the horse and it shied back a few paces and turned slightly. Only then did Gabriel notice the long monk's cowl hanging over the rider's boots, their heels worn through, and a hand clenching the reins, an instantly recognizable hand, the ring and middle fingers joined together.

"By God! Brother Bartholomew! Chillioc! Quick, Chillioc, come and help me!"

Gabriel approached the horse, reassuring it with soothing words. As he stroked its cheek with one hand, he took its bit firmly in the other.

"Come closer, Chillioc, don't be frightened."

"I'm not frightened, Lord Gabriel."

"Good. Come and take a hold of this strap. Stand still, don't yank on it."

As the child held the animal still, Gabriel pulled off the blankets. What he found horrified him. Bartholomew sat slumped over the saddle; he had either fallen asleep or was unconscious. His cowl was torn to shreds, and his face was barely visible through swaths of old bandages, brown with coagulated blood.

"In the name of God," growled Gabriel, grabbing Bartholomew's hand. "Brother Bartholomew! Brother Bartholomew, wake up!"

But the monk's eyes didn't flicker. The hand that Gabriel held between his own was so thin that it seemed devoid of flesh. Gabriel considered for a moment. Then he let go of Bartholomew and turned to the boy.

"Come here, Chillioc."

He took hold of the boy by the waist and lifted him up onto the horse's rump, just behind the saddle.

"Hold on to my friend, make sure he doesn't fall," he explained, guiding Chillioc's hands to the pommel. "There, hold on to that. And hold on tight. I'm going to lead you to the *cancha*."

Gabriel looked at the child: Chillioc was grimacing with disgust, his face pressed against the foul-smelling blankets. Gabriel smiled wanly.

"Don't worry, boy, he stinks, but then all Strangers stink when they first arrive at Titicaca!"

* * *

It was only long after the women had carefully cleaned his wound that Bartholomew came to. His eyes, set deep in their sockets, searched his surroundings. Eventually he emitted a hoarse sound from between his chapped lips.

"Gabriel?"

"I'm right here, my friend."

Gabriel waved the women away and took Bartholomew's emaciated hand. They smiled thinly at each other, and Gabriel sensed his friend's relief as the monk's breathing grew more regular.

He had never seen Bartholomew naked before, but what he had seen while helping the women cut away his rags quite simply shocked him. The priest was so thin that the skin on his ribs and hips was stretched to splitting point. His legs and arms were covered with bruises and unhealed wounds.

They had carefully unwrapped his old, begrimed bandages and revealed his face. They had found a long gash from his temple to his left cheek, cutting through his flesh and gray-speckled beard. The suppurating, infected wound had smelled awful, was poorly cicatrized, and had a few translucent worms wriggling beneath its crust. The servant girls had screamed at the sight of it.

Now it had been thoroughly cleaned, treated with ash and the acidic sap of a jungle root, and covered with a green plaster, which gave the monk the appearance of having two faces.

"I don't know what happened, old friend," murmured Gabriel affectionately, "but they did their worst to you."

"I made it! Thanks be to God, I'm here with you; that's all that matters." He smiled briefly and shut his exhausted eyes before adding, "I thought that I'd never make it. But God knows when to intervene. . . ."

"Perhaps he could intervene less violently next time," quipped Gabriel, picking up a bowl. "Here, a little *quinua* broth. You must eat. Your stomach is as thin as a feather in the wind."

But Bartholomew swallowed only four spoonfuls before pushing Gabriel's hand away.

"I've been traveling for eleven days to reach you. We were coming back from the south, where the Pizarros crushed Manco's general Tisoc's insurrection. He was taken prisoner, and . . . oh, it's unspeakable! Such horror, Gabriel, such horror day after day!"

He spoke in a dry, halting voice. Gabriel knew that Bartholomew needed to talk. And he knew too well what images were haunting the monk. Had he not been haunted by the same for months and months?

"Children, women, the old!" said Bartholomew hoarsely, "Massacres and humiliations day after day. And when Tisoc was taken, his troops defeated, Gonzalo ordered an even more horrendous repression. He had deep ditches dug and lined with sharpened spikes, and he threw men into them, and women too, after raping them. He set houses full of people alight, burning them alive! Oh, Gabriel . . ."

"I know, Bartholomew, I know. I saw all that when I went south with Almagro a few years ago. I've never forgotten it. It cannot be forgotten."

Bartholomew clenched his bony fingers around Gabriel's tunic and clung to him as though frightened of plummeting into the horrors plaguing his memory.

"I remembered your words, Gabriel: 'I didn't add to the suffering, but I didn't prevent it either, which is the same thing.' I understood what you meant, and like you my inaction filled me with shame. Oh, Lord, I think I even insulted you when you tried to open my eyes to the horror. . . ."

"Bartholomew . . ."

"No, let me finish. My throat is infected from the air that I breathed there, my nose is still full of the stench of children burned alive. If I sleep, I see them . . . Oh Christ! Christ! The flames that consumed them burn within me; they're scorching me. . . ."

Gently, Gabriel and the servant girls wiped Bartholomew's forehead and torso down with clean and fresh sponges. But nothing could stop the monk from raving.

"I found them chained together. All women, not one older than twenty. But I was caught. The beasts, the beasts! Being a servant of God saved me from nothing. No doubt the Lord wanted to infuse the suffering of all his children into my flesh. Jesus did it! Yes, he wanted to mark me, Gabriel! Because they are his children too. Everyone must realize that the Indians are also God's children. . . ."

"Easy, Bartholomew, easy . . ."

". . . But at least the women got away before the sinners beat me and called for my head. I succeeded, Gabriel! A few, at least, managed to escape. Too few. Only twenty children. There are so many more, Gabriel, so many more!"

Bartholomew was almost delirious, his voice a high-pitched screech. Gabriel set his hand on his friend's forehead to appease him.

"Be still, my friend. I'm here. You're being taken care of."

"I fled. I traveled only by night, so that they wouldn't follow me. Beasts. They are beasts from hell. . . ."

"We're going to give you a potion, Bartholomew, you're going to sleep."

"No, no, I have to tell you everything!"

"We'll have time for that tomorrow. You must rest now."

"I've come to ask something of you, Gabriel, something important. Only you can . . ."

But Gabriel signaled to the women, who had in any case already understood what they had to do from the feverish pitch of Bartholomew's voice. They lifted the priest by the shoulders and gently propped him up. They passed a little brazier of burning herbs under his nose. Almost immediately, he slumped back, docile, and they poured a liquid down his throat. He was asleep in moments.

It was only in the evening two days later that Bartholomew at last recovered his spirits and was able to eat a proper meal.

Gabriel had had his friend's bed set up in one of the rooms looking out onto the lakeshore. Women had watched over him day and night through his coma, administering potions to him until his fever began to subside. And as soon as the monk opened his eyes, Gabriel had fruit and coca leaf tea brought to him, making sure that his first foods were easy ones. Bartholomew was so hungry that his fingers trembled as he devoured everything that was given to him.

"I owe you my life, Gabriel," he declared in a raspy voice, breaking a long, slightly awkward silence and wiping his mouth.

"In that case, we're even. I would have been roasted alive in that Cuzco prison long ago if it weren't for you."

"I suppose I said a lot of cretinous things during my delirium?"

"Unfortunately not. You spoke only the truth. But forget about all that. I am delighted that you're here with me, and to see you eating with such appetite."

"These fruits are one of God's wonders," murmured Bartholomew, nodding, "as though they were plucked from the Garden itself."

The women had carefully wrapped a bandage around the monk's head, and he now yanked it aside unthinkingly to better taste the juicy mangoes and guavas. The fruit seemed to bring life back to his emaciated face. As he ate, Bartholomew let his gaze wander over the shimmering blue of the lake.

At that late hour of the day, the mountain peaks were linked together by an unbroken layer of thick clouds. The reflections of the vertiginous slopes had become indistinct in Titicaca's surface, the color of which had grown darker and more opaque.

"I'm beginning to understand why you came here," said Bartholomew with a thin smile. "You were right when you told me that it was hard to imagine a more beautiful or peaceful place."

He fell silent for a moment, with a pained and serious expression on his face, before continuing. "After having seen what I saw these past few months, it's as though God has at last accorded me some rest and wants to show me that there is still peace and harmony in at least some parts of our world."

Gabriel glanced at him, astonished. The thick bandage distorting the left side of the monk's face and wrapped around his skull only accentuated his weariness. Gabriel smiled wanly and nodded.

"I was in no better condition than you are now when I discovered this earthly paradise, Bartholomew. And I thought much the same thing myself, although without any consideration of God. And indeed, it seems to me that Titicaca is in fact meant to be our refuge from a world turned too inhuman. . . ."

"Inhuman!" spat Bartholomew bitterly. "Inhuman is the right word!

I'm saddened to admit, Gabriel, that you were far wiser than I. How right you were to leave us and stay away from the Pizarros after that horrific battle that destroyed Cuzco. May the Lord forgive me. You tried to warn me, but I didn't want to hear. It's only now that I understand what you said to me when I came to you in your cell and the Incas were about to destroy us: 'For the peoples of this country, there are no longer any good Strangers or bad Strangers. In their eyes, we all deserve to be annihilated. This is what Hernando's diplomacy has brought upon us; this is what giving free rein to Almagro and hellhounds like Gonzalo has caused.' You were so right, so right. And now three years have passed, and things have only become far worse."

Bartholomew's chest shuddered with emotion, and he fell silent for a moment, closing his eyes. Then, he asked in a barely audible murmur, "Gabriel, how can God allow such a thing? When will he end his chastisement? Dear friend . . . sometimes I wish that I were the one through whom he would administer his punishment to those monsters!"

Gabriel saw the tears welling up in his friend's eyes, and his sense of propriety urged him to look away. They were united in a brief silence, contemplating the lake. Outside on the shore, children's cries and adult voices accompanied the departure of a vessel leaving for the islands.

Gabriel took up a sliced mango and stared at its flesh as though its sweet flavor concealed some obscure, unidentifiable poison.

"This country is like this fruit. It only wants to diffuse its richest flavors. Here, on Titicaca's shore, I sometimes feel that I am at the threshold of a wondrous, open world, one that is expecting us, even offering itself to us, but one that we obstinately refuse to see. I feel that peace would enrich each Spaniard more than cartloads of stolen gold."

"Oh, peace!" exclaimed Bartholomew sarcastically. "For my part, I don't ask so much. I would be satisfied if Don Francisco and his brothers conducted themselves with a little restraint instead of endlessly exacerbating the suffering. As though the war with the Incas weren't enough, there's now a civil war raging among the Spaniards!"

"I knew that one-eyed Almagro had been condemned by Hernando."

"The truth is that Don Diego de Almagro was murdered. He

made a fatal mistake. After the siege was lifted, when the Governor's brothers were greatly diminished, he took the city under his control and imprisoned Hernando and Gonzalo. I can assure you that I tried to dissuade him, not because I wanted to help Hernando, but because I knew that Almagro's coup would be a disaster. But alas, what is the word of a man of the cloth worth to an obstinate old man convinced of having been the Pizarros' dupe for years? Not a night passed when Almagro didn't have nightmares about Atahualpa's ransom, about all that gold portioned out at Cajamarca, gold that the Governor had disallowed him. His hatred and lust for vengeance blinded his reason. To take Cuzco for himself was one thing, but to throw the Pizarro brothers in jail, well that's just like picking up a scorpion by the tail. They got rid of him as soon as they could, and when they did they showed about as much emotion as if they were slaughtering a chicken."

Gabriel shook his head.

"I've too many bad memories of Almagro to grieve for him. And I see that Hernando and Gonzalo haven't changed their ways at all."

"They're mad! All of them are utterly mad! Their side immediately took the lust for vengeance that had been Almagro's as their own, as though it were a ball stolen from the other team! And indeed, two sides were formed: those supporting the Pizarros and those thinking only of acquiring their own fortunes. And all anyone thinks about is annihilating the other side."

Gabriel couldn't help but laugh sardonically. Bartholomew looked at him reproachfully and prodded at his bandage as though beneath it was all the suffering of Peru.

"The truth, Gabriel," he sighed, "is that soon, we, the Spaniards, are going to destroy ourselves. And we're going to do it far more effectively than the Incas ever could. May God Almighty forgive us. Unless he has decided that it's time to punish every man who has contributed to the horror here in the New World."

Bartholomew spat out these last words vehemently. Gabriel said nothing for the moment, but only stared at the sparkling lake. Then he asked, "Does that mean that war against Manco is subsiding?"

"Manco is losing the war. During his brief dominance, Almagro confused the Incas by naming Paullu, Manco's brother, as Sapa Inca. Many Indians rallied to Paullu. Now Manco is alone, and his position is weak. He lost a series of battles, and he retreated farther and farther into the forest, as though its trees were his only defense. Furthermore, he suffered two terrible blows. . . ."

Bartholomew hesitated for a moment, even though Gabriel was giving him his full attention.

". . . His son was captured: A young boy named Titu Cusi. . . ."

"Titu Cusi!" murmured Gabriel. He remembered the look on the child's face playing in Ollantaytambo. He remembered the child asking him, "Are all Strangers like you?"

"Also, Inca Paullu took all the mummies of Manco's clan with him to Cuzco. No doubt you know better than I do what effect that had on Manco."

"For the Incas, whether lords or peasants, if the mummies are with one Noble Lord rather than another, it means that the former has the Ancestors' support," grumbled Gabriel, frowning. It was a very important factor.

Bartholomew closed his eyes and squeezed the juice of a blackish-brown prune between his cracked lips. Immediately, his expression relaxed almost to one of well-being.

"Paullu is an odd character. I'm not sure whether we should admire the wisdom of his pragmatism or be heartbroken by his cowardice. But in any case, he always seems to be on the side of the strong: first Almagro, now the Pizarros. And no matter who he's allied himself to, he never hesitates to make war with his brother Manco. He never reveals what he's thinking. He was with us during that horrific expedition to the south. He didn't once try to stop the massacre of his own people, nor did he take issue with the capture of Tisoc, Manco's general leading the rebellion."

"So," murmured Gabriel, "Manco's alone."

Bartholomew stared at him intently, a question hanging on his lips. But he decided otherwise, and said merely, "I heard it said that he's founded a new Inca city, very far to the north of Cuzco. Apparently it's in the jungle rather than in the mountains, and is utterly inaccessible to us. But to tell you the truth, after what I've seen these last few months, I think that his reign and his rebellion will soon be nothing more than a memory."

A heavy silence fell between them. Bartholomew broke it first, asking hesitantly, "Is my impression that you've had no news of Anamaya correct?"

Gabriel shook his head and attempted a thin smile.

"It's been almost thirty months since I saw her last. I don't even know if she's still alive, if she's still in this world."

Another silence, then Gabriel continued with feigned lightness:

"But it's not surprising; we had agreed upon it. I accepted it for a long time. I told myself that our separation wouldn't last forever, that the war would soon be over, or that Anamaya would come to me because she wanted to. And then the truth became clear to me. Much time has passed, and I'm beginning to forget what her face looks like. It's unbearable, and yet I have to accept it. If I tried to find her, I'd be endangering her. She still can't leave her people, not the way things are, and she can come to me even less."

"The way things are?" asked Bartholomew in a low voice. "Are you referring to that gold statue that she calls her husband?"

"Certainly, the Sacred Double," said Gabriel, smiling. "You know, Bartholomew, despite all your efforts to respect the Incas, I doubt that you understand what it means to them."

"What does it matter whether I understand?" answered Bartholomew, somewhat ill-temperedly. "What matters is that Gonzalo and Hernando still covet that . . . that object. The mere idea of all that gold drives them mad."

"Their madness to the Devil! They'll never have it."

Gabriel spoke with such serene confidence that Bartholomew looked at him closely once again, as though he were hearing a new, unfamiliar voice speaking from his old friend's mouth.

"You seem very sure of that. You know as well as I do that they're capable of leaving no stone unturned in the whole of Peru to find it."

"They'll find nothing under every stone they turn," said Gabriel, still smiling. "We Spaniards can heap suffering on the peoples of this

land. We can kill them and rob them. But look at that lake, Brother
Bartholomew. Look at those mountains. . . ."

Gabriel waved toward the slopes which, in the play of the light,
seemed to dissolve into the pale blue sky at their peaks, just as their
bases melted into Titicaca's cerulean glitter.

"It is indeed very fine," said Bartholomew, "and yet . . ."

"No," interrupted Gabriel, "it's not about beauty. All of what you
see lives. Mountains, stones, water . . . everything here exists in a world
parallel to our own, just *like* our own, and yet you and I don't know how
to see it."

"What do you mean?"

"I mean that the Incas can see the invisible. More than that, they
know how to sense its breath and receive its support. They can sense life
wherever it is and however it manifests itself. It's true that they're no
stronger than chickens under the sword's iron blade, and indeed, one
day they may well be exterminated like chickens. But the essential will
remain; it will live on. Nothing will prevent them from taking away
their knowledge of the world that exists in the mountains, the stones,
and this very lake, a world that we can neither see nor hear. There are
forces at work here that are far greater than anything any Pizarro can
hope to match."

This time, Gabriel spoke with passion. Bartholomew had a sad and
gloomy look in his eyes.

"Well, that's not a very Christian way of seeing the world. Gabriel,
I've heard that since you've been here, you've been participating in their
pagan ceremonies."

For a brief second, it seemed like Gabriel was going to lose his temper. But he laughed ironically instead and shook his head.

"It doesn't matter what people say about my life here. It suits me
perfectly."

"Are you sure about that?"

"Are you starting an inquisition?"

"I'm a man of God, Gabriel, and I'm your friend. But don't imagine for a minute that I am willing to accept that you abandon, and
maybe even scorn, the work of Christ and the hope that it brings each
one of us!"

"I will abandon my respect for neither mankind nor for life itself. That should be comforting enough for you."

Bartholomew scrutinized Gabriel. Tension racked his emaciated face. Then, as though overcome by exhaustion, he nodded.

"No doubt you're right. But it's a strange thing to admit."

Gabriel put his hand on his friend's arm.

"I am at peace with myself, Brother Bartholomew. My soul is at peace."

The monk shuddered feverishly. His lips began trembling violently. He shut his eyes and murmured, "I don't doubt that your soul is at peace, dear Gabriel. But alas, mine is not. Far from it. I am exhausted, and I think I'll sleep a little now. But will you do me a favor? While I sleep, open those leather saddlebags. In them, you'll find some pages I wrote. For the love of God, please read them."

"I'll not do it for the love of God, Brother Bartholomew, but for your friendship, certainly."

Bartholomew didn't emerge from his deep sleep until nightfall. He opened his eyes and saw Gabriel sitting by the light of a brazier a few paces away. He was contemplating the lake and the mountains, already veiled in darkness. He had a large leather case on his knees, containing a bundle of papers covered in a small, tightly packed hand.

"Gabriel . . ."

Gabriel turned around and smiled. And yet, it seemed as though some of the shadows that he had been contemplating had remained in his eyes. Bartholomew pointed at the leather case and said, "Did you read it?"

"I read it. There are so many horrors and injustices chronicled in these pages that the world it paints could be Hell itself."

"And yet, and I can swear it to God, I have written about only those events at which I was personally present. I have written down everything that I have seen since setting foot here in Peru, omitting nothing. I have listed every injustice and humiliation inflicted on the Indians, every violation of the laws of God, of Rome, and of our own country. Everything!"

Gabriel looked down at the leather case, perplexed. Then he set it at Bartholomew's side.

"Yes, everything. But you are reckless, dear Bartholomew. Should the Pizarro brothers or their friends find these papers, you're a dead man."

"That's precisely why I traveled only by night coming here," sighed Bartholomew.

Gabriel smiled, but his tone was serious.

"I'm afraid that it won't be enough. Burn these pages, Bartholomew, burn them now in this brazier. Or at least hide them somewhere very secure. They don't serve you now in any case: Who wants to read such melancholic prose!"

Bartholomew sat up and uttered an enraged yap. He crawled from his bed and grabbed the leather case, waving it over his head. "Burn them? Hide these truths from our King Charles, who must be made aware of them? Spain must know what is happening here! Rome will be horrified when he reads these pages!"

Gabriel shook his head, smiling sardonically.

"Your fever has made you delirious, friend. Have you forgotten the gold? Do you really think that anyone across the ocean cares how it's obtained? Do you imagine that the King or the Pope will cease covering their palaces in gold merely because the savages here are being ill-treated? Come now, Bartholomew! You know very well that Don Francisco and his brothers can continue playing the tyrants so long as they continue sending treasures back to Europe!"

"You are mistaken! You are utterly mistaken, Gabriel!"

Bartholomew stood up unsteadily. His indignant cries were so impassioned that two servant girls and Chillioc, carrying a torch, came rushing in. Gabriel nodded to them to assuage their alarm, while Bartholomew, beside himself, grabbed hold of Gabriel's hands.

"No! No! I will not have you say such things! Not you, Gabriel! There *are* good men in Spain, there *are* men of good will in Rome! There are good men in court and in the church! There are men who believe that the Indians are children of God just as we are!"

"Perhaps. But alas, they are over there, not here."

"That's why they must be told!"

"And even if they would know . . ."

Beneath his bandages, Bartholomew looked demented. He blinked continuously, as though involuntarily, and a thick vein pulsed visibly in his neck. He was as taut as a bow, and Gabriel worried that he was going to faint at any moment. But instead, the monk put his hands on Gabriel's shoulders.

"Listen to me, Gabriel. There is someone in Spain, a man of the church, who is trying to ensure that all the people living here in these mountains are treated with respect, that they're allowed to live with dignity. This man is a Dominican called Las Casas. He is the kind of educated man that you and I like and admire. He has read Erasmus. . . ."

"One man, Brother Bartholomew! He's but one man alone, like you, like me. And he is so far from these mountains. . . ."

"No, he's not so alone. His influence is far reaching. He has the ears of some important people. He has already managed to have Pope Paul III issue a bull declaring that all the Indians on earth be treated as humans. . . ."

When he saw Gabriel's sardonic smile, Bartholomew threw back his shoulders with rage. With his skeletal hand, he pointed at Gabriel's servants standing at the back of the room, wide-eyed with incomprehension, and declaimed:

"We consider that the Indians are truly men and that they are capable of understanding the Catholic Faith. We declare that, notwithstanding whatever may have been or may be said to the contrary, the said Indians are by no means to be deprived of their liberty or the possession of their property, even though they be outside the faith of Jesus Christ; and that they may and should, freely and legitimately, enjoy their liberty and the possession of their property; nor should they be in any way enslaved; and we declare that the said Indians and other peoples should be converted to the faith of Jesus Christ by preaching the word of God and by the example of good and holy living."

Short of breath, his bandaged head nodding slightly, Bartholomew finished his declamation and grabbed young Chillioc, pushing him before Gabriel.

"Such are the words and the will of the Holy Father! I swear, on this child's head, that it is true. I swear it solemnly to Almighty God that the Sacred Office wants what we want!"

Gabriel reached out and stroked Chillioc's terrified face.

"Don't be scared, Chillioc," he said in Quechua. "My friend is taken by fever. Help me put him back to bed."

Bartholomew protested, but his exhaustion was greater than his fury, and he could hardly stand. As the child and Gabriel urged him back to bed and pulled a blanket up over him, he asked in a broken voice, "Do you believe me, Gabriel?"

"I believe you."

"Then take these pages to Spain. Take them to Las Casas. He needs them."

Gabriel froze, taken aback.

The torchlight played on their faces, distorting them. Bartholomew's bandages looked like a mask.

"Me?" he asked.

"Who else but you has the will and the courage to do it? See how this child looks at you, Gabriel," insisted Bartholomew, taking Chillioc by the hands. "If you take these pages to Spain, then he will have a future as an adult."

Seeing Gabriel frown and turn away, the monk continued:

"What are you waiting for here? For Anamaya to come back to you? You know that it won't happen like that. You are alone. You're wasting your time here, contemplating the landscape of Titicaca while those you pretend to defend are being destroyed. Take these papers to Toledo, take the truth to where it will have the most effect. Who better than you to tell the King about this country? Help me, Gabriel. Not for God's cause, I know that you've forsaken him. But for the cause that you cannot forget, and which fills your heart with sadness."

Gabriel stared unblinkingly at the monk for some time. He said nothing. But Bartholomew saw the look in his friend's eyes and knew that his words had had their effect.

A milky dawn spread over Lake Titicaca. The morning fog fragmented into strands. In the gaps, the gray water of the lake could be seen, as well as the gray walls lining the terraces. At the bottom of the large bay facing the sacred islands of the Sun and Moon, a few plumes of smoke rose from the houses of Cusijata.

Gabriel stood halfway down a steep rocky hillock cropping out into the lake and admired the enchanted place one last time. It was the only place he had managed to find peace since that March day in 1532 when, after having almost perished in the South Sea, and accompanied by Sebastian, he had first trodden on the beach at Tumbez, and had been one of the first conquistadors to step on Inca land.

That had been seven years before, almost to the day. Seven years of hope, of battles, of glory sometimes. Almost seven years of love. And yet, in those seven years, so little happiness, just a few fleeting moments stolen from the war and the tragedy.

Anamaya! Even just whispering her name to the gentle morning breeze made his body tremble as though the entire surface of his skin were tattooed with the his beloved's magical name: Anamaya!

And now he was going to return to Spain an entirely different man from the one who had left it seven years before. He was going to go back to Spain without looking back, without even kissing Anamaya's lips one last time. He was going to leave and slowly forget the smell of her skin, the warmth of her thighs. His memories of her guiding him on voyages into the strangeness of the world were going to slip irretrievably away.

He couldn't believe that he could even do it.

But the monk's words had harrowed his soul throughout the night. They had been reasonable and utterly persuasive words, despite Bartholomew's overexcited state. Gabriel had rebuffed them as best he could, but to no avail. And then, suddenly, other words had crossed his mind, words spoken by Anamaya. They were words that she had addressed to the Puma and that had carried the incredible and bizarre message of a long-dead Inca emperor.

> You will see the Puma; he will bound here from across the ocean.
> He will only come to you when he leaves you.
> Although separated, you will be united as one,
> And when everyone has left, you will remain, and the Puma will remain at your side.

Together, like your ancestors, Manco Capac and Mama
Occlo,
You will beget new life on earth.

They were words that had been heard but not understood, words
kept in his mind the way a strongbox holds a mystery. But now the
meaning of the words became crystal clear to him: Yes, he had to leave.
At last, he understood how he was going to get back to Anamaya. Not
by diving into Titicaca, but by crossing the ocean, by going back to
Spain, by surrendering to what appeared to be a coincidence but which
was in fact his destiny bestowed upon him unwittingly by
Bartholomew. Bartholomew, he realized, was the servant of the Inca
Ancestors as much as he was of Christ!

A sound of something moving in the bushes startled Gabriel out of
his thoughts. He turned around but saw nothing. Then Chillioc
emerged hesitantly from a clump of bushes. He seemed reluctant even
to look Gabriel in the eyes.

Gabriel smiled tenderly and extended his hand.

"Come here, Chillioc."

The child placed his little hand in the Stranger's, and Gabriel had
him sit down at his side.

"You should be sleeping," he reprimanded the boy affectionately.

"I couldn't. I saw that you were awake, and I followed you."

Gabriel squeezed the child's hand. They sat together in silence
watching the fog's slow dance over the lake.

"Are you going away, Lord Gabriel?"

"What makes you ask?" said Gabriel, surprised.

"I saw it in your face when you were talking with the sick Stranger."

"Yes, I'm going away, Chillioc. You saw right. I'm going to miss you."

"Why do you want to leave? Aren't you happy here with us?"

"I am happy," said Gabriel with a smile, "very happy."

"Well, then?"

"Well, it's time that I leave and return to someone. And there's
something I must do."

The child looked at him, his eyes full of sadness and incomprehension.

"If you leave," whispered Chillioc, "the Strangers who hate us will come here. Everyone will be so frightened."

"That's one of the reasons why I'm leaving," said Gabriel, his voice constricted, "so that you'll never again be frightened of Strangers."

"Do you think that's possible?" asked the child, wide-eyed.

"Perhaps. I don't know. But I do know that it's impossible to live without trying to make it so."

Twenty-two

Vilcabamba, June 1539

"I love being in your presence, Sacred Double," whispered Anamaya. "I've been your wife for ten years now, enough time for the four seasons to alternate the heat and the cold of our world ten times. Ten times has another year been added to the distance between now and the day of my birth. I was a child when Emperor Atahualpa ordered me to accompany you forever, to become the *Coya Camaquen*. Now I'm a woman older than Emperor Manco's wives and concubines. And yet when I'm with you, I feel as though time passes without touching us."

Anamaya smiled tenderly. She was squatting on her heels at the gold statue's side. The Sacred Double had been set before the Great Temple of the Sun at Vilcabamba on a pedestal built by Katari. She spread the offerings at his feet, as she had done a thousand times before: honey, fruit, river fish, and young corn. Then, and adhering to strict ritual, she scattered coca leaves on the embers glowing in a painted bowl shaped like the serpent Amaru.

O beloved husband, she thought, bowing to the statue, accept these offerings brought to you by your devoted *Coya Camaquen*.

The bitter, dry smoke rising from the coca leaves plumed upward, slowly twisting around the gold statue like a long and lazy caress before disseminating into the new and warm day.

The little city in the middle of the jungle gleamed resplendently in the dawn, as it had every morning since the rainy season ended. Beyond the tip of the Sacred Stone to which the sun hitched itself every morning, the great ceremonial square and the walls lining the terraces attached to the royal *canchas* emerged from the opulent jungle. Soon the maze of alleys, stairs, and bridges would in turn emerge from the shadows. Not a day passed when Anamaya didn't admire the perfect harmony of the city's design, a design that Katari seemed to have created out of nothing, as if by magic. The temples, the houses of both the aristocrats and the common people, and the warehouses were so well proportioned and laid out in the jungle that if one walked only a quarter of an hour from Vilcabamba, it disappeared from sight as though a mirage.

"I love your company, Sacred Double," continued Anamaya quietly. "It appeases me and fills me with hope: I feel that Emperor Huayna Capac protects us through you, protects us while war rages all around us, destroying everything. For a long time, Sacred Double, I didn't know how to love you, or even hear you. I was too young. I feared you. I feared your silence and your body made of gold. I feared my duties as your wife. I feared the wisdom that your presence gave me and which infuriated the Powerful Lords and filled them with jealousy."

Anamaya paused and reflected. A group of chosen virgins, carrying *cumbis* destined to be offered to the Sun Father, passed by the temple's high, trapezoidal door. When they saw the *Coya Camaquen* in prayer, the young girls bowed their heads, and out of respect kept their eyes fixed on the flagstones.

"Your presence, O husband," continued Anamaya, smiling tenderly and a little wryly at the young *acllas*, "has turned a simple, mixed-blood girl into a widely feared woman!"

Now a serious expression returned to Anamaya's face, and she stroked the statue's shoulder.

"The thing I fear most, Sacred Double, is that you prevent me from loving the one who was designated to me by Emperor Huayna Capac. I fear your jealousy. I fear that you'll try to keep me from the one who, despite his long, long absence, makes my heart beat and my body melt like snow under Inti's caress. Yes, O Sacred Double, I dread your jealousy!"

Anamaya anxiously scrutinized the gold face before her. Its dark gaze grew lighter in the growing light of day. Its shadow stretched away beneath its powerful nose and over the fine contours of its lips, which seemed to suddenly and faintly smile. Anamaya closed her eyes and, in one breath, surrendered her confession to the statue:

"O Sacred Double, how many times I feared your wrath whenever my mouth or soul spoke his name, Gabriel, or whenever his hands or lips touched my skin! Forgive me my stupidity, beloved husband. I now know that that fear was needless. Three moons have passed since the Puma's breath touched me that evening by the river. Since that moment, and ever in your presence, Sacred Double, not one night has passed when the Puma hasn't come to me in my sleep. We are together in every dream, Sacred Double. We caress each other and love each other as a woman and man blessed by Inti's light. I run my fingers through the hairs covering his cheeks; I feel his face quiver beneath my touch; I see the fire in his eyes when he desires me and when he enters me with as much strength as he did during the nights we shared in Cajamarca, Cuzco, and Ollantaytambo. Night after night, Sacred Double, his heart caresses mine. In every dream I have, I see him change into the Puma, and I know that he hasn't forgotten me. Every morning, I wake up feeling serene and confident. At last I understand Emperor Huayna Capac's words. Yes, the will of the Ancestors is being fulfilled. And I, the *Coya Camaquen*, will soon accompany you to them, where you will be at peace."

Anamaya remained absolutely still, deep in her devotion. Her eyes were still closed, and she had bowed deeply to better receive the gold statue's silent reply.

It was only after some time had passed that she became aware of someone's short, halting breath and ululant sob nearby. She straightened herself quickly and found Manco's young wife prostrated a few paces away, her face wet with tears.

"Curi Ocllo!"

"Help me, *Coya Camaquen*! Please, help me . . ."

"Curi Ocllo!" Anamaya exclaimed again, getting to her feet and reaching out to Manco's wife. "What's wrong?"

"A *chaski* announced last night that Stranger soldiers have left Cuzco. They're advancing through the Sacred Valley. They're coming here. . . ."

Curi Ocllo's large, dark eyes searched Anamaya's desperately, as though trying to impart all her fear to the *Coya Camaquen*. Anamaya simply frowned. Curi Ocllo sobbed louder now, bent double, and cried, "The thing I feared most is becoming reality, Anamaya! Oh, it's too terrible! May Inti save us!"

Anamaya urged the young woman to her feet and wiped the tears from her face.

"I don't understand your panic, Curi Ocllo! Manco is in Vitcos with three thousand warriors. He'll repel the Strangers, just as he's done before. They don't know how to fight in the jungle."

But Curi Ocllo, far from being reassured, simply sobbed louder. Anamaya could feel the young *acllas* behind her looking at them surreptitiously. She wrapped her arms around the young queen's trembling shoulders and led her out of the temple.

"Calm down, Curi Ocllo," she whispered tenderly. "It won't do for the Daughters of the Sun to see you in this state."

Curi Ocllo mumbled an apology. The two women walked out onto the great ceremonial square. Anamaya headed toward the broad stairway that led out of Vilcabamba and toward the cornfields alongside the river.

"Tell me what's bothering you so much," she said as she invited Curi Ocllo to sit on a little wall.

Curi Ocllo took a few moments to gather herself.

"Five moons past, Manco again wanted to take Cuzco from the Strangers. But he didn't even get close to the City of the Puma because his brother Paullu was returning there with thousands of soldiers from the south, where he had just defeated old and faithful Tisoc."

"Yes, yes, I know all that," interrupted Anamaya impatiently, "I even warned Manco that his offensive would prove useless. He mustn't try to fight Paullu."

"But it's not Paullu who wishes Manco the most harm," murmured Curi Ocllo, looking away. "It's my brother, Guaypar."

Anamaya stiffened as Curi Ocllo continued in a muted voice.

"Guaypar gathered a large force of northern warriors some time ago, and now he's offering them to Paullu. He doesn't care that Paullu submits to the Strangers the way a woman submits to a man who doesn't love her. For years, he's hated Manco as much as I've loved him. All his thoughts focus on one thing only: destroying Manco. And I don't even know why."

Anamaya shuddered and shut her eyes. She reached for Curi Ocllo's shoulder and clasped it affectionately.

"I know why," she whispered.

Curi Ocllo's words had transported her back into the past, and she now relived those cold, bright days during the *huarachiku* in Tumebamba. All of them—Manco, Paullu, Guaypar—had been little more than children then. And at the time she had been too, and Villa Oma had barely started educating her, although it was true that she was already under Atahualpa's protection. She remembered the terrible race. She remembered Manco's fear when he came across the snake, and she remembered Paullu's deep, fraternal love for his brother. And she remembered also Guaypar's violent and hateful nature, already manifest. She remembered Manco and Guaypar fighting around the fire, two mere boys consumed by rage, baying for blood, drunk on *chicha*, brawling through the night, each prepared to actually kill his opponent, until one of Manco's uncles separated them.

"The lesson has been given, and none shall forget it," Manco had said, to which Guaypar, consumed by hatred and shame, had answered: "You are damned, Manco! You will burn before reaching the Other World. Your soul will never be free!"

And she remembered more: She remembered Huamachuco, where Guaypar had asked her to become his wife as the Strangers were advancing on Cajamarca. She remembered Guaypar telling her, "My soul lives only for you, Anamaya! Just thinking of you makes me burn up inside."

"Yes," she repeated, "I know what divides them."

"I want to stop them from killing one another, Anamaya. Manco is my beloved husband! I have never wanted any other man. But Guaypar is my brother. I love him too."

Anamaya said nothing and couldn't bear to look into Curi Ocllo's horrified eyes.

"Please, help me, *Coya Camaquen*," implored the young woman.

"But how? How can I help you? How can I stop what must be?"

"Let me go to Manco. He needs me. And I want to be at his side when Guaypar confronts him. I'll stand between them if I have to."

"No, Curi Ocllo," said Anamaya gently, "I won't allow you to do such a foolish thing. What Manco and your brother face is too ancient and too strong for you to ward off. You cannot prevent them from opposing each other if that's what must be."

"No! Never! I will never abandon them!" screamed Curi Ocllo. "I'll go to Vitcos without an escort if I have to! Shame on you, *Coya Camaquen*! Shame on you for abandoning your lord. . . ."

"Curi Ocllo!"

But Anamaya wasn't quick enough to hold back the young woman, and Curi Ocllo now bolted away toward the center of Vilcabamba, screaming the whole way. Anamaya took off after her, but gave up after only a few paces.

O Inti, she prayed silently, tears streaming down her face, this day began with such hope and happiness, yet already it is heavier than the clouds atop the mountains.

TWENTY-THREE

Cuzco, June 1539

Gabriel was shocked as he approached Sacsayhuaman. Most of the fortress for which so many men had fallen, and in which he had forged his legend, had been destroyed in the flames of battle. The towers now lay in ruins, and the hordes of warriors that had once sent a storm of arrows and stones down upon him had disappeared. But the gargantuan blocks still stood proudly, although they guarded nothing but wind and a mystery.

Bartholomew halted his horse and pointed.

"Do you see that?"

There were children playing in the quarry overlooking the fortress, little figures running after one another, catching one another and rolling around on the ground. Their strident cries could be heard across the hills.

Gabriel smiled.

"There are no victims in a children's war."

"Yes, but they grow up quickly. And there's nothing easier than learning how to kill one's fellows."

Gabriel nodded.

They passed through fields in which wheat, barley, and oats were now being cultivated in addition to the native corn and *quinua*, and they were surprised to discover small and enclosed cabbage patches lining the road into town.

The City of the Puma extended from the foot of the great walls, which now had grass growing on them. Gabriel remembered how deeply enchanted he had been the first time he laid eyes upon it. It called to mind Anamaya's face, now so distant, when she had stood at Manco's side. And he remembered Pizarro's subsequent triumph.

Bartholomew drew some clothes out of a saddlebag and offered them to Gabriel.

"We're about the same size," he said shyly, "and I thought that . . ."

"I don't need them."

Gabriel spoke quietly, but firmly. He felt Bartholomew's stare upon him. But he knew that this time he would not be disguised as an Indian, as he had been when he had returned to Cuzco determined to kill Gonzalo. This time, he wore his simple tunic as a mark of his solidarity with this new world. He wore a dun *unku* on which the women of Titicaca had, on his request, woven a black puma.

"It took time for me to become what I am now, Brother Bartholomew, and I'm not going to start disguising myself as what I am no longer."

Bartholomew's silence belied both respect and curiosity. A few moments passed before he made one last attempt.

"You know what they're going to say, don't you?"

Gabriel didn't bother to reply.

"Let's press on," he said, digging his heels gently into his horse's sides.

He was untroubled in a way that only a man who's decided on doing what must be done can be.

As he entered the town, Gabriel immediately noticed everything that had changed since he had last been there.

The most noticeable, even spectacular, thing was the filth. The canals running down the middle of the roads, in which limpid water had once flowed, were now clogged with every conceivable kind of refuse; he saw potato peelings and half-eaten cobs of corn. The stagnant water gave off a nauseating stench, as did the horse and pig dung covering the streets.

"The gifts of civilization," said Bartholomew sardonically, noticing the look on Gabriel's face.

Gabriel looked up.

Cuzco had been set alight, and all the thatched roofs that had burned had been replaced with tiles. It made for an odd architectural combination, these noble Incan palaces covered with Spanish tiles. Gabriel also noticed that some of the trapezoidal Inca doors had had doorsills added to allow wooden doors to be set in them in the Spanish style, each door equipped with a large lock.

"They never knew theft," said Bartholomew, "and they used to bar their doors with a simple pole only as a sign that they were absent. The lock and key, another one of our gifts . . ."

Two pigs chased a rabbit at full speed down the street and passed through Gabriel's horse's legs. The animal sidestepped nervously. Gabriel noticed the stares he was drawing, and he reflected that he, a Stranger in Indian garb, caused more of a murmur than did the Indians who had taken to wearing Spanish accessories over their traditional clothes: here a pair of gloves, there a leather belt, another wearing breeches. He noticed that only those Indians of the Inca race still proudly wore their traditional dress unaltered.

When they arrived at Aucaypata square, a great many memories came flooding back to him: the time the mummies had been solemnly brought here, and Manco's coronation. But his voyage into the past was interrupted by the sound of a bell ringing, and he froze upon hearing that deeply familiar and even ancient sound. He looked at Bartholomew, stupefied. The priest pointed to the spot where the Sunturhuasi, a mysterious building, used to dominate the square.

Where there used to be a tower crowned with a conical roof, there was now a construction site. Not a single stone had yet been placed, but the scaffolding had already been erected. The workmen had hung a single bell from one of its beams, and its ring echoed across the square, causing all the Indians to turn and face it.

"*El Triunfo!*" said Bartholomew. "They've started work on it already and have named it after their victory during the siege. Apparently a painter is coming from Spain to commit to canvas the miracles that took place here. . . ."

"What miracles?"

"The miracle of the Sacred Virgin putting out the fires, accompanied by an invincible knight on a white steed."

"Oh yes, I vaguely remember that miracle," said Gabriel.

"Few are the men who have no need to believe in miracles to give themselves the will to live."

"So I'm beginning to realize."

Gabriel led Bartholomew to the road leading to Hatun Cancha. They stopped before a modest palace with a guanaco hide hanging over its door. Gabriel dismounted and handed his reins to an old man, who had clearly made horse-minding a profession.

"What are you doing?" asked Bartholomew.

"Someone's expecting me," said Gabriel calmly.

"When did you set up this meeting?"

"In another life. After all, you're the one who wants me to believe in miracles. Do you want to come with me?"

Bartholomew waved his joined fingers in the air, declining Gabriel's offer, and smiled before wandering away at a slow pace.

Passing through the palace was like parading through an extravagant theatrical production. What with its antechamber, its long corridors, its Indian valets in livery, and its young servant girls, Gabriel had the comical impression of having been suddenly transported onto a stage and charged with playing a role for which he hadn't been given the lines. He was waiting impatiently in a room crammed with wall hangings when a thunderous laugh made him turn around.

"Sebastian!"

"Don't you recognize this place? Ha! I must admit, it was in far worse condition then. . . ."

Gabriel conjured up the image of the palace's fire-blackened walls and burned-out roofs, the condition it had been in when Sebastian had brought him here to equip himself after freeing him from jail.

"I was the one who was in a far worse condition," he sighed.

The two friends embraced affectionately. No matter how perceptive and understanding Brother Bartholomew might be, Gabriel knew that he would never share this kind of intimacy with him, the intimacy of brothers-in-arms who have lived through many an adventure together. After a long embrace, the two men released each other, laughing and slapping each other's back. Gabriel looked at his friend.

He was dressed in the most extraordinary manner: He wore brightly colored breeches and a fine lace ruff of the sort favored by Pizarro. But Sebastian looked upon Gabriel with equal astonishment.

"What strange things you wear," they said almost simultaneously before breaking into laughter again.

"I have to make an effort to stand out from the black slaves arriving here from Panama," said Sebastian. "And what about you? Have you been crowned Inca?"

"I'll be Inca the day you're named governor."

"And why not? Ours would be a fine alliance: First we would celebrate our victory by roasting Gonzalo on a spit, then we would design a prosperous reign of peace, after having first filled our pockets, of course, as insurance against hard times!"

"You seem to me pretty well insured now."

Sebastian made a face.

"You can't imagine how difficult it is," he said. "A daily struggle. I'm utterly exhausted."

He snapped his fingers and, without his having to say a word, two young servant girls hastened forward with a carafe of liquid that glowed deep red by the torchlight and two silver goblets on a silver platter.

Gabriel's palate had lost its discrimination for wine, but his face flushed when he swallowed a mouthful.

"Not so bad," he said, clicking his tongue, "but it has nothing on what we drank at . . . what was that inn called?"

"The Bottomless Jug!" roared Sebastian. "Ah, I remember that dear charlatan of an innkeeper and his unforgettable wine well . . . but you're right, nothing could match it."

There was a note of nostalgia in Sebastian's voice. Gabriel let a moment of silence pass between them.

"Tell me about yourself," said Sebastian eventually. "There's a rumor about that you've become some kind of great Lord over there on Titicaca's shores. . . ."

"I'll tell you all about it later, Sebastian. First, I need you to bring me up-to-date with events . . . I know only what Bartholomew has told me. You might begin by telling me about your fortune."

"Well, I'm a rich man, as you can see, yet I feel as threatened as I did when we first met, when I was still but a poor slave, protected only by the good Candia. . . ."

"Why do you feel threatened?"

"Almagro was my protector, even though I was a somewhat reluctant protégée—he had his failings, but he could never forget that I had saved his life! In any case, ever since his death, I've felt the noose of hatred and jealousy tighten around me. And like I told you, there are more and more penniless blackamoors arriving every day, and when a good Spaniard sees me in my splendid garb, when he sees my three concubines, he tells himself that I am an insult to the natural and divine order of things. No doubt there'll be one who, soon enough, will take it upon himself to set upon me in some dark alley, chop me into pieces, and feed me to his foul swine."

"Can't you be more . . . discreet? Can't you keep all your wealth hidden under that flagstone, in that cave where it used to be?"

Sebastian burst out laughing.

"To hear this from you, of all people!"

"What? It's not the same thing."

The African grinned at him.

"You're right. It's not the same thing. I don't know what your motives are, but I cannot forget what I told you once: There's an ocean between us that no pilot, no matter how able, can cross. That's how it is."

He drank slowly, enjoying his wine. He extended his goblet to one of the young girls, smiling at her tenderly. She filled his cup.

"I refuse to change my ways, even if I have to die. It cost me too much effort to get what I have; I had to suffer too many humiliations and play too many tricks. I'll never forsake it for a poor and uncertain life. If I have to die tomorrow, then it will be with my steel Toledo sword in my hand, and my blood will run onto my lace ruff."

"I understand."

Sebastian waved his hand through the air, as though sweeping away all his pessimism.

"Bah, you haven't come here to hear about my blighted destiny. You've come for her, haven't you?"

Gabriel stiffened.

"The blue-eyed princess, I mean," said Sebastian redundantly. "You've heard the news then. . . ."

Gabriel's heart beat like the bell on the *Triunfo*.

"I've heard nothing. Brother Bartholomew told me nothing about her. What's happened?"

"The expedition, by the blood of Christ! You haven't heard about the expedition?"

Gabriel sat up on his chair and knocked over his goblet. The wine splashed over the thick wool carpet.

"Tell me, by God!" he said, almost shouting. "Tell me what's happened?"

"They left at least two months ago, on the Governor's orders," said Sebastian somberly. "Three hundred men under Gonzalo's command, plus a large number of Indians led by Paullu and other Inca captains hostile to Manco. They went into the jungle with one aim: Capture Anamaya and the great gold statue that they know is always with her because she's married to it, in some way or other."

Silence.

"Why her?"

"They believe that Manco is weak, now that he's separated from his generals, and they think that taking her will be the final blow. They think that all they'll have to do then is track him down and finish him. But the truth is that they're all obsessed with that gold statue. Surely you've heard tell of Candia's misadventure. . . ."

"No, but save it for a later time. I'm sure it's very amusing. Do you know if the expedition achieved its goal?"

"I doubt they have, or we would have had news of their triumph. And Paullu wouldn't have returned to rally reinforcements from Don Francisco. He's here at this very moment."

Gabriel seized Sebastian by the hands and said, "I must see them. Where are they?"

"No doubt at the Governor's place, at La Cassana. Unless they're at Paullu's palace at Colcampata, which he acquired at his coronation."

Gabriel headed for the door, preceded by the two young servant girls. He pushed them aside gently.

"Sebastian, might I ask a favor of you?"

"What?"

"I don't want to talk about it now. But if I did, would you do it?"

He heard his friend sigh, and quickly stopped himself.

"Forgive me. Pretend I said nothing."

"I cannot pretend that you said nothing. I don't know what mad scheme you have in mind, but unfortunately for me, yes, I will help you."

The two friends briefly embraced. Then Gabriel darted away, leaving behind the servants in their livery and the servant girls, who looked suspiciously like concubines.

Bartholomew was waiting for him outside. Gabriel jumped onto his horse, saying nothing.

"Where are we going in such a hurry?" asked Bartholomew.

"To Colcampata. Why didn't you tell me?"

"I don't . . ."

"Don't lie to me, Brother Bartholomew, and don't lie to yourself! Don't tell me that you didn't know about Gonzalo's expedition!"

"You know very well that you can't do anything on your own, Gabriel."

"I'll be the judge of what I can and cannot do."

They headed off, their horses' hooves clacking on the stones. Gabriel did his best to control his anger and to curb the fathomless dread that had taken hold of him.

TWENTY-FOUR

Cuzco, Colcampata, June 1539

A crowd had gathered on the square at Colcampata.

Although he mostly kept his eyes focused on Don Francisco Pizarro, Gabriel glanced around at the thick vegetation in which the City of the Puma was set here in the heart of the mountains. He now understood its eternal force better than ever, and how it remained and would remain far from the stench of swine and the other stains brought by its conquerors. He could feel its powerful life force, dormant for now, but ready to leap forward and roar at any moment.

Mummies had been installed in the niches carved in the palace's perfectly built walls. Gabriel was moved when he recognized the mummy of Inca Huayna Capac.

"Paullu asked for them," whispered Bartholomew in his ear. "He felt that the 'legitimate' Inca should not be separated from his Ancestors."

Gabriel nodded, but kept his eyes fixed on Don Francisco Pizarro, his old protector.

The Governor was older and bonier than ever; but although he seemed to have shriveled with age, he still emanated the energy that had always been his. His dress was entirely black except for his white hat and stockings. The only sign of his immense wealth was the very fine lace ruff that he wore around his neck. With his black eyes, he was focusing all his attention on the person facing him, who was sitting on a *tiana*, as befitted an Inca. Gabriel recognized Paullu.

Cuzco's latest Inca was of the same size and age as his half brother Manco. But the similarities ended there. Whereas the rebel in the jungle had features that seemed to have been chiseled in stone by a sculptor, Paullu was round. And although it wasn't fat, his face still gave the impression of a flabbiness that comes from surrendering to life's easier pleasures. Only his eyes revealed his strong will and his quick mind.

The two men conversed without the aid of interpreters: Paullu spoke perfect Spanish.

As Gabriel and Bartholomew joined the circle of Indian lords and hidalgos, Pizarro turned his head toward them.

Gabriel met the old captain's gaze and felt a wave of old emotions come over him. He looked into those black eyes deeply embedded in their sockets, stiffened, forced a smile, and bowed very slightly.

"What I need to know before I help you, Lord Paullu," continued Pizarro, "is the likelihood of the expedition being a success."

"It is very likely, Governor; it is almost a sure thing. . . ."

Paullu's voice retained the raucous intonations of Quechua. Gabriel heard a hidalgo behind him spit and mutter: "This mongrel would have us all killed in that damned jungle. . . ."

"I hastened back here, at your brother Gonzalo's insistence, to rally reinforcements. Manco's troops are powerful and well organized."

Pizarro's eyes flashed at the mention of Manco's name.

"Are you sure that you can destroy that dog?"

"I cannot call my own brother a dog," said Paullu politely, "even though I think that he's made a terrible mistake by leading his rebellion beyond what is reasonable. But to answer your question: Yes, we can defeat his army. But on one condition. . . ."

Paullu, sure of himself, paused for effect.

"What condition?" asked Don Francisco impatiently.

"Your Governorship knows how dependent your men are on mine to guide them through the forest." Paullu looked defiantly at all the Spaniards present. "You know that your brothers Hernando and Gonzalo, were they here, could testify that my loyalty to you has been the decisive factor in a great many battles. . . ."

"I have no doubt of it, Lord Paullu. We know what we owe you. And you know what you owe us. . . ."

Pizarro let his eyes linger on the royal fringe hanging over Paullu's forehead.

"A good alliance—a good *friendship*—is based on a good equilibrium," said fearsome Paullu, softer now. "What I want to say to you,

Governor, is that it is absolutely imperative that I return to the forest with my troops and with reinforcements. I must return to your brother Gonzalo and make sure that the expedition achieves its aims."

"When do you want to leave?"

"Tomorrow or the following night. Time is running short. But think for a moment, Governor: As soon as victory has been obtained, you can go back to building Lima, your beautiful City of Kings. . . ."

"And you can return to ruling over your beloved Cuzco."

"Certainly, I'm not indifferent to the city of my Ancestors," replied Paullu, gesturing discreetly at the mummies watching them from their niches.

"So be it, Lord Paullu. You may proclaim that, by order of the Governor, you are free to recruit as many men as you deem necessary."

"I need Yungas, Governor, more than mountain men. Yungas from the coast, used to a humid climate. . . ."

Pizarro made another impatient gesture.

"Do as you see fit, my dear Sapa Inca. You know your Indians better than I do. Just make sure you win."

Pizarro was the first to rise from his seat. He gave the merest flicker of a bow to the Inca, who remained utterly impassive. Gabriel reflected that the slightness of the Governor's gesture captured all the ambiguities of the relationship between the two men.

The Inca dignitaries moved away.

Murmurs immediately rose from the Spanish ranks: ". . . can't trust that traitor . . . he was a friend of Almagro . . ." But Pizarro restored silence by simply raising his hand. His authority was more absolute than ever. No one openly contested it.

"Enough," he said. "We need him, but he also needs us. He's too cunning to betray us at this stage. He wants us to get rid of his beloved brother first. . . ."

He spoke these last words with an amused irony.

"Now leave, the lot of you. I want to be alone with . . ."

He turned to Gabriel. Fresh murmurs rose from the assembly. Not everyone present had met the Spaniard dressed as an Indian, but everyone had heard the legend about the proud knight protected by Santiago who had taken the fortress single-handed.

The old conquistador and the man who had been like a son to him were left alone on the square.

"Well then," began Pizarro, "what kind of thing is that to be wearing?"

Gabriel couldn't say how many hours they spent together.

Noon came and went, the sun slipped down the warm blue vault of sky, the mountains turned gold, evening's shadows grew longer—and still they talked.

The Governor showed real pleasure in rediscovering Gabriel's company. He asked him all about life on Titicaca's shores, and teased him about the native women; Gabriel had him tell about his beloved Lima, the founding of which had so absorbed him. They talked of the past, of Seville and Toledo, of the audience with the King and the terrible crossing to the new world. The reserve between them dropped as they talked, and the Governor relaxed and waved his white hat about like a rag or flag or sail, emphasizing some point that he was making.

"I've been asking myself a question, Don Francisco."

"What is it, my boy?"

"I've heard tell that, during your first expedition, your men were on the point of abandoning you, and that you drew a line in the sand to show where poverty ended and fortune began, where the past was buried and where the glorious future could be found. . . ."

"Yes, on Gallo Island," murmured Pizarro dreamily.

"They say that twelve men crossed that line over to you."

"Yes. What is it that you want to know?"

"I want to know if it's true. If that's the way it really happened."

Pizarro said nothing for a moment. Then a smile broke the severity on his face.

"Aren't you friends with some of them?" he asked. "Haven't you asked Candia?"

"Yes, but he only laughs. I want to hear it from your mouth."

But Pizarro gave nothing away, or else he was enjoying the conversation too much to end it by giving an answer.

"Well, I've heard something too," he retorted. "I've heard that a cavalryman with features exactly like yours, although not dressed in the odd manner that you are now, galloped on a white horse through a storm of Indian arrows, passed through blazing fires and, with the Sacred Virgin's protection, who appeared at his side, took the three towers of the fortress on his own. Is it true?"

Now it was Gabriel's turn to smile.

"Why, you have so many friends, Don Francisco. Haven't you asked them?"

"Yes, and they all swear to me that it happened just like that, by Christ. With the notable exception of my brother Gonzalo, of course."

Gabriel burst out laughing, and the old conquistador joined him.

"These legends," murmured Pizarro, "which of us can say if they're true or not? So many memories come to me as though from out of the fog. Sometimes I wake up in the morning convinced that I'm in my village in my beloved Extramadura, building a bell, absolutely sure that that's what I'd done all my life. Then I remember where I am and what I've seen, and I become old again."

"And yet, here you are."

Gabriel waved at the country surrounding them. Night was falling and torches were being lit here and there. The two men shared a moment of silence together, each lost in his own thoughts, each privately dwelling on the shared past that brought them together.

Then Gabriel heard the Governor almost whisper to him, "I need you, son."

His body stiffened as though he had been slapped in the face. Despite the affection that bound him to Don Francisco, despite the respect that he had for him, he sensed a dark, unbearable menace in those words.

"I'm alone once again, as you know very well. Hernando murdered the one-eyed Almagro and has gone to Spain to justify himself to the King. God knows what his fate will be. I don't pretend not to know that you hated him, but he's the only one who has more brains than *cojones*—forgive me the expression—but you know my opinion of the others."

"Then why did you leave Cuzco in Gonzalo's hands?"

Gabriel tried to say this as calmly as possible, but he couldn't hide the reproach in his words.

"Because despite all his failings, he's one of my own people, and the only one I can trust. All these captains arriving from Spain with their ten horses and fifty foot soldiers, they think that they can do whatever they want, and they expect the treasures of Peru to be simply handed to them."

Pizarro set down his hat on a little wall overlooking the town. He took Gabriel by the arm and leaned toward his ear, as if to share a secret.

"You know that I'm living in concubinage with an Indian princess . . . we've baptized her Doña Angelina . . . well, you can't imagine the lengths that I have to go to to hide my love for her! And as for my darling little Francesca, my daughter by Doña Inés Quispe Sisa, why, not a day passes when I don't want to run to her and take her up in my arms. I haven't seen her for weeks now, and I miss her, Gabriel, I miss her so much."

Don Francisco's eyes glistened with tears.

"I only want one thing," he continued. "I want to live with them, eat simple meals with them, wash it down with a goblet of wine diluted with water, keep my old body going by playing children's games in the country, teach my daughter the games I used to play as a child, skittles and royal tennis . . . do you think that I enjoy riding from dawn to dusk down impossible roads, leading these armies, winning over *caciques*, racking my brain about whether I should trust Paullu or not. . . ."

"Then make peace!"

Silence. Pizarro picked up his hat and rolled it like a clod of earth between his hands.

"Peace! You use grand words these days, I find."

"Don't you see, Don Francisco?"

"I see some kind of demon, my boy, a Spaniard disguised as an Indian who throws words about above his station. . . ."

The old man's face grew taut with cold fury, and it was hard to believe that this was the same man who just a moment before had been the sincere, doting father. But Gabriel felt overcome by a force that he had never felt before, and all his limbs relaxed and his body was filled with a soft euphoria. He said confidently:

"Have you ever listened to the words of those who don't tremble at the mere sight of you? Do you know that your soldiers respect none of your laws? That they persist in pillaging this country, killing its inhabitants, and reducing them to slavery? Do you think that this will bring peace with the Indians?"

"First I have to win the war against this damned Manco. We'll establish peace and harmony afterward. . . ."

"No, Don Francisco, you don't see at all. The lust for war is everywhere. It infects all your men. You allowed Almagro to be murdered. . . ."

"I didn't know . . ."

"Come now, you didn't know. Just as you didn't know that Atahualpa was going to be executed? You knew, Don Francisco, but you turned your head away and averted your eyes until the deed was done. And now, the desire for vengeance corrupts the air. Each man hates his neighbor and dreams only of grabbing as much as he can; everyone feels that an injustice has been done them and that violence is the only law! And now you are so blind that you cannot see in your lieutenants' docile eyes which of them is going to betray you, which ones are perhaps already plotting to take your life. . . ."

Pizarro tried many times to interrupt, but Gabriel's impassioned tirade left him no opportunity. But now he raised his voice and said mockingly, "Come now, my boy, they would never dare!"

Gabriel paused for breath. "You had—you still have—the chance to be remembered in history books as the man who conquered a land and made a nation of it! But you're squandering it."

"I cannot, Gabriel!" cried Francisco in despair. "I know your courage, and I know your generosity, and I'm prepared to listen to whatever you have to tell me. I don't deny that much of what you say is true, and sometimes, when I'm alone at night, I pray to the Sacred Virgin, I cry and beg for mercy for the crimes that are being committed. I have no harsher judge than myself, not even you. No one, apart from Almighty God, knows what I know! But what you're proposing is impossible, don't you see, it's simply impossible. . . ."

"Is it true that the purpose of Gonzalo and Paullu's mission is to capture Anamaya and the gold statue?"

"Yes, and Manco as well. But Gonzalo convinced me that he would be easier to take if we have his priestess in our hands, as well as that gold statue with god-knows-what magical powers. . . ."

"And then there'll be peace, you say," said Gabriel sarcastically, almost hissing it through his teeth. He continued:

"Do you really think that by simply destroying what they hold most precious, you'll make peace? No, it'll be the opposite, Don Francisco: You will simply cause more war. When—or *if*—you get rid of Manco, you'll have to deal with Villa Oma, the Sage turned warrior, and then with Illac Topa. And when they fall, others will rise behind them. And when, in turn, you're finished with them, you'll have to face your own men, you'll have to remain forever on your guard, unable to trust anybody at all. Don't you see that by behaving like this, you're leaving everybody, both Spaniards and Indians, with a legacy of war, one that they'll never give up?"

"You don't understand, Gabriel. You're still too young. I know all that. But I also know things that you don't. Over there," he said, pointing to the west, "they're growing nervous, and news has reached me that they plan to send a viceroy here. If I don't take Manco and crush his rebellion first, then it'll be finished."

"What will be finished? Your power? The extortions and murders?"

"My dream. My dream will be finished. . . ."

Don Francisco's pale, thin lips quivered as he spoke these last words, and Gabriel held back from continuing his castigation. He had nothing to say about the substance of an old man's dream, a man who had risen high above his humble origins; he knew that each man has his own secret, his own pathetic and magnificent dream.

Both men gathered their breath. Their anger subsided, evaporated into the night, was absorbed in the stones, absorbed, perhaps, by the wisdom of the mummies that had been observing them.

"Let me go to them," said Gabriel. "Let me take them the order to immediately negotiate a peace with Manco. You know that I know him well. I'm probably the only Spaniard that he'll agree to talk to."

"No."

Gabriel tensed. He walked a few steps across the square. All his emotions had fused into a deep fatigue, a weariness that was the sum of all the years in Peru, of the immense sadness of being unable to convince the man whom he had both hated and most admired.

He stared at the mummy with the broken nose: Huayna Capac. A wave of long-forgotten emotions passed through his body, and he shivered as though he had suddenly been transported through the night to the terraces overlooking Ollantaytambo.

He turned around.

Francisco Pizarro hadn't moved.

"Adieu, Don Francisco."

The Governor didn't move. Gabriel turned away and made to head back into town. Suddenly he heard the old man's voice from behind him.

"What are you going to do?"

Gabriel turned to face him, but he could no longer make out Pizarro's features through the darkness.

"I've thought about the story of what happened on Gallo Island, Don Francisco. I believe that you really did trace that line through the sand with the tip of your sword. And I believe that every man has to choose: Which side is he on?"

He paused and filled his lungs with the cool night air.

"I believe that there comes a point in every man's life when, like you, he can draw his sword and trace a line in the sand. I think that every man has a choice."

"What are you going to do?"

"What I must."

Gabriel disappeared into the night.

TWENTY-FIVE

Cuzco, June 1539

"You've lost your mind!" howled Sebastian.

Gabriel raised his hands to appease his friend. He had never seen him so enraged.

"Calm down."

"You're telling *me* to calm down?"

"Let me explain it to you again. . . ."

"Do you take me for some stupid slave?"

Gabriel lowered his arms in surrender.

"I take you for my friend."

Bolts of fury passed across Sebastian's eyes. A single torch and a few candles on the little inlaid table at which the two men were sitting were the only sources of light in Sebastian's palace. His servants and women had gone to bed, and the two men spoke in low voices.

"Does a friend," continued Sebastian, calmer now, "wish the death of his friend? Does he commit suicide alongside him?"

"All I'm asking . . ."

"All you're asking is to bankrupt me by having me finance an expedition into the depths of the jungle to save one Indian girl—I can get you fifty much prettier ones simply by snapping my fingers! Oh, and to forge a peace that no one wants. Oh yes, I was forgetting, and to help a gold statue escape, a gold statue that will in any case end up at the forge at La Cassana anyway, or else in one of those noble hidalgos' palaces. Let me tell you again, my friend: You've lost your mind. And if I listen to another word from you, then I'm as mad as you are."

"And so am I," said a third voice from the shadows, "struck with the same insanity, or one very like it. But I still want to believe it."

"You do, Bartholomew?"

The monk came into the light. He stared at a sketch of the Sacsay-huaman fortress.

"Can it be," began Sebastian, "that since Bishop Valverde's return, you have lost your position in this fine city's religious hierarchy?"

"What do you mean?"

"Doesn't your office make you their ally?"

"My friend, my office—and its burden—have made of me the wit-ness and, for far too long, the accomplice of horrors and those who carry them out. I didn't come here to help massacre the natives in God's name. And this man—your friend—represents my opportunity to end it. Two years ago, when his Holiness Paul III issued his papal bull, I believed that we had won a decisive victory. But that hasn't turned out to be the case. I wanted Gabriel to go to Spain and bear witness to what is happening here, to insist upon the King's intervention in the name of God's law. Yet I understand what you call his madness, and I would go with him if I could. . . ."

Sebastian looked from one man to the other.

"And may I know how—purely out of curiosity—you're going to find men to go with you?"

"I've a few friends," said Gabriel, smiling.

"Who? Our old comrade Candida has already lost half his fortune trying to get into that damned forest! If I'm to part with my gold, may I at least know the names of these friends?"

"Wouldn't it be better for you not to know, so that you can enjoy your prosperity all the more?"

"How kind of you, Your Grace! He gives me permission to enjoy my prosperity! What touching generosity . . ."

"Sebastian . . ."

"Never mind 'Sebastian.' You would ruin me and have me killed, and you want me to thank you."

Gabriel and Bartholomew fell silent. There was no more space left in the night to argue, to convince him, to cajole, to complain, to joke around. All that they could do was to look at the ex-slave's face and see the expressions of anger, of doubt, of temptation, and of refusal pass across it.

"What if I refuse?"

*   *   *

It was a moonless night. Gabriel and Bartholomew hurried through the darkness along Cuzco's alleys. They crossed the Aucaypata and headed down toward the Temple of the Sun. Hurrying alongside it, Gabriel had his breath cut short: Its walls had been demolished, and only the heavy stones of its foundations remained, no doubt because its conquerors hadn't had the courage to destroy them, or else because they planned to build on top of them.

"What have they done with the garden of gold?" hissed Gabriel. "Turned it into a trough for their pigs?"

Hidden in the night, he remembered the Inca's prophetic words that Anamaya had revealed to him on their last night together, the meaning of which had remained a mystery to him. But he knew that it was his faith in that prophecy as much as the love in his heart that now made him prepared to defy anything.

When they reached the Pumachupan *canchas,* he put his hand on Bartholomew's shoulder. The monk said nothing, but simply turned to him and smiled. His scar was a dark shadow across his face. He didn't hesitate as he headed toward a door leading into a modestly built *cancha.*

"It's here," said the monk.

The *cancha*'s courtyard was dark and deserted. They woke a few guinea pigs as they entered, and the animals darted through their legs, squealing.

Then a torch came toward them at chest hight. Its light blinded Gabriel, and he shielded his eyes. A familiar, throaty voice spoke to him in good Spanish.

"Welcome, my Lord."

Gabriel made out the dwarf silhouetted behind the torch. He followed him, fearing nothing, feeling as though he had come across an old friend. They had only ever met by night and had never spoken more than a few words to each other, but the dwarf had always been there to help him get closer to Anamaya. And now, once again, he was going to help.

The dwarf led them through a door, the humble door-hanging of which belied the luxury that lay behind it. It was as though the dwarf had been crowned Inca of a miniature kingdom created for and ruled by him, and destined to be known by him only. Everything in the room was exceptionally valuable: the goblets, jars, and trays were all of gold or silver and decorated with jewels. There were vicuña wool carpets and a table made of precious wood and inlaid with emeralds, as were the two chairs and the bench around it. Gabriel noticed the familiar shapes of llama and condor figurines in the room's niches, but he also saw some that were far more terrifying than anything he had yet seen in the Incan world. The most surprising was an icon of the Virgin. What's more, everything was particularly small, as though it had all been made on a scale befitting the dwarf by artisans working in his court.

The dwarf invited them to sit, which they did as best they could. The time when he had worn a long red robe, the only robe he owned, its fringe always dragging in the dust, was long gone. He now wore yellow linen breeches, a yellow doublet, and a four-pointed hat of the sort that Gabriel had seen on Kollas by Titicaca's shores.

"I'm afraid this place is far humbler than my house in Yucay," said the dwarf, "but I am happy to welcome you here nevertheless."

"Your destiny has brought you good fortune, it seems," said Gabriel with a smile.

"A slave I was, and a slave I shall always be. But in the meantime, I allow myself to enjoy—discreetly—what Fate has given me, and I watch my sons grow. They are five and seven years old, yet they are both already taller than me. Which proves that Fate knows how to be seduced. But you haven't come to listen to my life story."

"We have come to ask you for help."

The dwarf laughed and slapped his thighs with his disproportionately large hands.

"Who would have thought it? Who would have thought it indeed?" he said over and over.

When the dwarf had finished laughing, his last "who would have thought it?" lost in a hiccup of mirth, Gabriel explained that he needed a guide and a dozen men to take him to Ollantaytambo and through the impenetrable forest where Gonzalo was hunting down Anamaya and Manco.

The dwarf asked no questions. He looked seriously at Gabriel for a long while.

"I have always taken you to her," he said.

Gabriel nodded.

"When do you want to leave?"

"This very night."

The dwarf whistled between his teeth.

"We will go to my house in Yucay. I'll gather the men we need there. But do you have enough gold?"

"Yes, he does."

The door-hanging lifted and Sebastian's giant shape appeared.

"He has it," said Sebastian, lowering his head as though the smallness of everything surrounding him obliged him to shrink himself. "He doesn't want to waste any time, I assume?"

Sebastian laughed at the surprised look on Gabriel's face.

"It's worth risking torture just to see that look on your face, your Grace. Come on, let's hurry, my neck hurts merely standing here."

The four men went outside. Gabriel, moved, took Bartholomew's arm and squeezed it. The two ex-slaves walked side by side in front of them, not speaking a word. The dwarf trotted along but the giant still had to hold his gait. They passed by a number of silent *canchas* before coming out onto the paved road to Collasuyu.

When they had passed the last of the houses and they could see nothing before them but crop fields and the dark outline of the mountain behind which lay Yucay, Bartholomew and Sebastian stopped in their tracks. Sebastian whistled softly between his teeth.

Two Indians appeared, leading a white shape through the night.

"Itza!" cried Gabriel.

"I told you that I'd keep her for you."

"Itza!"

"Your range of expression amazes me. Will you say it a third time, I wonder?"

Ignoring his friend's jibe, Gabriel stroked the mare's muzzle affectionately. When he turned to face his friends, his eyes were aglow.

The monk raised his joined fingers toward Gabriel.

"You'll allow me to bless you," he said with a smile. "May the One True God be with you!"

"And don't forget your big *cojones,*" muttered Sebastian. "Keep them tucked well between your legs."

Gabriel looked at his two friends before embracing them briefly. He opened his mouth, about to thank them.

"Don't say a word," growled Sebastian. "You bore me already. You're going to sob like a woman, I know it, you're going to cry, 'Itza! Itza!' and I hate that kind of thing. Now hurry."

Gabriel hesitated, then turned away and rose effortlessly into the saddle. He sped away into the night.

Twenty-six

Vilcabamba, Vitcos, July 1539

Anamaya observed the men and women busy working on the terraces below Vilcabamba for a moment before approaching them. Under Katari's watchful eye, women were kneading clay before carefully spreading it inside wooden molds. Then, men would carry the gleaming, thick plaques to a spot a little farther away, where they would sit and fold the plaques over themselves on their thighs, before carefully setting them to dry in the sun on a bed of leaves. Farther away, other men put the dried, light gray plaques in a round furnace.

Anamaya joined Katari. He watched as he called to one of the workers to bring him a clay plaque that he had just folded over itself. The Master of the Stone quickly etched a little snake into the still soft clay with a reed stylet.

"What are you doing?" asked Anamaya. "What are these earth plaques for?"

"To cover your roof, *Coya Camaquen*, and to keep you dry from the coming rains."

Anamaya bunched up her face and looked without understanding.

Katari etched another snake on another plaque. He worked so quickly and easily that the snake appeared as suddenly as the real reptile does from the grass.

"These are what the Strangers call *tiles*," he explained, his eyes agleam. "Once these clay plaques have been baked, all we have to do is set them over the frame of a roof for the building to become absolutely rainproof. I decided to do your roof first, *Coya Camaquen*, as homage to you. Then we'll set them over all the *canchas* of Vilcabamba and make our Emperor's new royal city truly beautiful."

Katari showed her the tile that he had just decorated and added,

"My only worry is that our men's thighs are smaller than the Strangers', so our tiles are smaller than those I watched being made in Cuzco. We're going to have to adjust the frameworks of our roofs to size."

"You surprise me, Master of the Stone," said Anamaya with a smile. "You, the guardian of our Ancestors' knowledge, the custodian of our traditions, are going to replace Inca roofs with something invented by the Strangers?"

"Why not? Are we not to learn from others? We learned how to work gold and silver from Chimu goldsmiths after all, and pottery from their ancestors, the Mochicas, and weaving from the people of Paracas. These tiles are a wonderful invention. They do away with the tiresome work of cutting *ichu* and replacing rotted roofs every four seasons. Should we ignore this knowledge merely because the gods haven't yet taught it to us? They won't diminish the beauty of our buildings and walls in any way, because everyone knows that we, the Incas, build better and more beautiful buildings than any other of Viracocha's peoples!"

Katari's face and voice betrayed uncharacteristic enthusiasm. Anamaya was moved. She watched the workers' efficient ballet.

"What you say makes me happy, Katari. It means that you believe that our people must continue to evolve and live in hope despite the war, despite Manco's weakness, and despite Emperor Huayna Capac's dire predictions."

"Let me address the two questions that you are asking me as one, *Coya Camaquen*," replied the Master of the Stone in a serious tone. "Firstly, I believe that it's baneful to ignore new knowledge and new skills. It can only displease the Powerful Ancestors, who will everything to exist in this world as a mark of their presence."

Katari raised his arm and pointed beyond the muddy terrace they were on to a gang of children squatting and admiring a dozen horses grazing in a field.

"Manco captured those animals during the battle of Ollantay-tambo. He was very proud of himself when he brought them here. But what can we use them for? Only he knows how to climb on their backs. And now, unfortunately, this jungle is our only territory, and these animals cannot move through it. What's more, we don't know how to make the metal soles they need for their feet. So how can those horses serve us, other than filling our children with wonder?"

"Well, they serve Manco's pride," said Anamaya tenderly. "They show that our Emperor isn't always the victim of the Strangers' strength."

A thick and odorous smoke was now rising from the round kilns nearby. Anamaya soberly contemplated the men and women around it, who remained unaware of Katari's artwork on the tiles.

"I'm flattered that you should want to decorate my roof first," she said, "but I won't see the result for some time. I have given Curi Ocllo permission to join Manco, and I've decided to go with her."

Katari gave her a surprised, worried look, and Anamaya answered his question before he had even asked it:

"For almost a whole moon, I have been forbidding her from leaving Vilcabamba. But she cries more than she eats and is wasting away. In any case, she may be right: Manco may well find comfort in her company."

"But why are you going with her?"

Anamaya hesitated for a few seconds. She watched as some workers called to one another and fed green branches into the furnace in order to keep the temperature even on the tiles.

"I promised Manco that I would stay at his side. We've been apart for some time now. Also, Curi Ocllo fears that her brother Guaypar will confront Manco; there's an old enmity between them for which I feel partly responsible. But will I be of any use to the Emperor?"

Katari, doubtful, shook his head.

"That is not your proper place, *Coya Camaquen*. Manco's enmities are like the *ichu* roofs in this town: They are old methods that don't keep either the rain from dampening our beds or the Strangers from winning battles. And in any case, traveling through the jungle now, while the Strangers approach, is unsafe."

"We'll have a strong escort," interrupted Anamaya, placing her hand affectionately on the Master of the Stone's wrist. "Katari, I'm entrusting you with the Sacred Double. Take good care of him. I shall return as soon as I can. I have the feeling that soon we will have to take him to the secret place."

*　　*　　*

Their small expedition advanced cautiously through the jungle for three days, following the river, before sighting the fortified palace set on a rocky spur at Vitcos. Despite Katari's anxiety, they had met with no trouble other than finding a way through the thriving tangle of vegetation so thick it had very quickly swallowed up the path that had been cut by the previous expedition.

Curi Ocllo had shown real courage and had never hesitated to step out of her palanquin whenever the narrowness of the path demanded it. And now that they could see the walls of Vitcos looming over the valley, her impatience was so great that her hands trembled. Her face had lost the ugly, anxious furrows that had beleaguered it in Vilcabamba, and she had recovered the beauty so loved and desired by Manco. Her eyes beamed and her lips were in full bloom. She had the qualities of both a very young girl as yet untroubled by experience of the world and of a woman who knew that her beloved would soon look upon her and call her to him.

When they reached the bottom of the set of stairs leading up to the fortress by its steep northern slope, the column came to an abrupt halt. As the officer commanding the fifteen warriors escorting the women approached their palanquin, Curi Ocllo called out, "Why have you ordered us to stop, officer? We're almost there. . . ."

The officer bowed respectfully and, with the skill of one long accustomed to this type of ceremonial gesture, twisted slightly so that his bow was addressed to Anamaya as much as to Curi Ocllo.

"It's true, *Coya,* that we are almost at Vitcos," he said, "but that is exactly why I wish to ask for the *Coya Camaquen*'s permission to send an advance party of two soldiers to the fortress, to warn the Emperor of your arrival."

"It's unnecessary," whimpered Curi Ocllo. "His sentinels will warn him. Anyway, it would be marvelous if I could surprise him!" She giggled, turned to Anamaya, and pleaded, "There's no point wasting any more time, right?"

"Officer," asked Anamaya, "do you think it absolutely necessary to send scouts? The *Coya* is right: The Emperor's sentinels will warn him of our coming."

The escort's commander, troubled, hesitated before bowing again and answering.

"In truth, *Coya Camaquen,* I want to make sure that Emperor Manco is actually in the fortress."

"Why wouldn't he be?" cried Curi Ocllo. "We would know if he'd left it. He would have sent a messenger. Oh please, Anamaya, we're so close!"

"It would be stupid to take unneccassary risks," Anamaya said.

Tears immediately appeared in Curi Ocllo's black eyes. Anamaya couldn't help but smile at the girl's caprice.

"Officer," she sighed, "send a scout with news of our arrival. But let us not linger here; we shall press on without waiting for his return."

Curi Ocllo, as uninhibited as a spoiled child, threw her arms around Anamaya's neck and held her tight.

"Thank you, Anamaya, thank you! You can't imagine how happy I am to be with Manco at last!"

The expedition was within two slingshots of the fortress when the scout returned at a run. The officer again halted the column.

"*Coya Camaquen,*" he announced, "there's no one there. Vitcos is empty."

"Empty?"

Curi Ocllo cried out in despair.

"The Emperor and his men seem to have left several days ago."

"But why?"

"Perhaps there are Strangers in the area, *Coya.*"

"In that case, officer," ordered Anamaya, "we mustn't linger on the path. Let's get to the fortress as quick as we can. We can stay there since it's empty, and defend ourselves in it if we have to."

When they passed through the bailey, they found that the buildings and courtyards were indeed empty.

Anamaya and Curi Ocllo were worried. They stepped from their palanquin and walked across a perfectly square courtyard lined with low buildings. The soldiers accompanied them as they made their way toward the buildings facing the palace's entrance. A narrow passage leading off at a right angle led them to the fortress's most outlying point.

The spot afforded them a splendid view. The building here had been built on a rocky outcrop atop a steep slope that fell away to the river. It was a long, heavy building, punctuated by fifteen magnificent doors with white granite lintels, and with a raised patio. The snow-covered peaks and slopes of the Apus towered around it, and the place seemed imbued with an indestructible quality, as well as with a curious serenity.

"I don't understand!" cried Curi Ocllo, her voice breaking. "Why would Manco leave without sending even a *chaski* to meet us?"

"It's only a slight setback," Anamaya assured her, staring at the forest on the surrounding slopes. "Most likely he has retreated to the little fort at Machu Pucara."

"But why? Why didn't he warn us?"

"Perhaps the officer is right: The Strangers are closer than we thought. We must be extremely careful. I'm going to send a messenger to Machu Pucara so that Manco can—"

Just then, terrifying howls erupted all around them. Their blood ran cold.

They could see nothing at first, as though the howls had risen spontaneously.

And then they appeared.

A hundred or two hundred warriors from the north. They wore the colors of Quito on their tunics and leather helmets on their heads. Holding their shields out before them, they surged forward from behind the long building where they had been hiding.

They brandished bronze-headed clubs and axes, and twirled their slingshots. Their spears were pointed menacingly forward.

The officer commanding the escort quickly screamed orders to his men. His handful of soldiers formed a pathetic barrier around Anamaya and Curi Ocllo and held their spears out before them. But they had hardly taken up their positions when a volley of sling stones whistled down upon them, killing two of them on the spot. Curi Ocllo's scream rose above all the others and seemed to catalyze the assault.

The fight was so quick and violent that Anamaya no time to realize

what was happening, much less to flee. The officer was the last to be killed, his skull split open with a studded club.

Silence fell upon them.

The northern soldiers surrounded them. Curi Ocllo fell to her knees. The warriors looked upon them blankly, and the young Queen grabbed hold of Anamaya. The men parted, their shields clanging together, allowing a passage. A high-ranking Inca officer appeared. He wore fine ear plugs, a cape threaded with silver, and a short fan of blue and gold feathers attached to his helmet. His face was hard and bony, and his eyes appeared particularly small and set well back in their sockets. Both women recognized him, and Curi Ocllo jumped up and dashed toward him, crying, "Guaypar! Oh, Guaypar, my brother!"

She collapsed at his feet, overcome with emotion. Guaypar dodged her without even glancing at her trembling shoulders. A thin smile stretched his well-defined lips. He came up close to Anamaya, who simply looked at him with utter contempt.

"We've been waiting for you, *Coya Camaquen*. To be honest, we came all the way here just for you."

"If that's the case, your welcome was atrocious, Guaypar."

Guaypar's smile broadened. Anamaya could see Curi Ocllo sobbing behind him. Soldiers were already tying her hands.

"I don't worry myself too much about blood relations, Anamaya. My sister disowned me a long time ago when she married Manco, that traitor and usurper. . . ."

"Know that my fate is tied to hers, Guaypar!"

"That's for me to decide, *Coya Camaquen*! But I'm sure you'll understand my impatience. I've been dreaming of this moment for so long."

His eyes gleamed with self-confidence and hatred and, for the first time in a long while, the twin venoms of doubt and fear coursed through Anamaya's veins.

"Do you remember that night at Huamachuco? It was before the coming of the Strangers, when Emperor Atahualpa was waging war against Huascar the Mad."

Guaypar smiled as he asked his question. But his smile was as icy as his voice. Anamaya returned his smile and replied, "Yes, I remember."

She was half-sitting, half-squatting on the ground in one of the fortress's smaller rooms, where Guaypar's men had put her. They had tied her arms and legs to a heavy log without undue brutality, but without respect for her rank either. The log dug into her back and forced her to maintain a twisted, uncomfortable position. She felt a sharp pain all along her spine, and it was spreading through her shoulders. Yet she forced herself to smile as she said again, "I remember. You had just been made a captain for having captured Huascar's generals at the battle of Angoyacu."

A surprised look passed over Guaypar's dark eyes. Anamaya could see his chest rising with his heavy breath. He looked away from her, toward the patio where his troops were noisily settling themselves. A thousand questions sprung to Anamaya's mind, but she held back from asking them, forcing Guaypar to spit out his long-harbored resentments.

"That night, I told you that you were the most beautiful woman in all of Tahuantinsuyu. I told you that no other woman could boast half your beauty, and that no mouth or eyes could be compared to yours. . . ."

Although he was firmly on his feet and stood tall over Anamaya, who remained bound below him, Guaypar nevertheless gave the impression of defending himself rather than dominating her. His ceremonial axe, made of silver and gold, trembled slightly in his hand. He was ashen faced, as though the poison of his memories were polluting his flesh. He continued, "I gave you more than words; that night I asked you to become my wife. You refused."

"If you remember that, then you also remember why," Anamaya replied quietly.

Guaypar laughed bitterly and said, "Oh yes, the Sacred Double! You told me, 'I can't because of the Sacred Double!' But now there isn't a single noble lord in all the country who doesn't know how the *Coya Camaquen* displays her fidelity to Emperor Huayna Capac's Sacred Double by spreading her legs for a Stranger! A Stranger who disguises himself as an Indian and who is scorned by his own people as much as he is hated by ours! And if it weren't for your protection, then . . ."

Guaypar didn't finish his sentence. But he made a slicing gesture through the air with his hand, showing what fate he had reserved for Gabriel.

The pain in Anamaya's back forced her to close her eyes for a moment and gather herself. Outside, she could hear noises and shouts; more troops had arrived. When she opened her eyes again, she saw officers on the threshold of the room waiting for Guaypar's orders. But none of them dared interrupt him.

"What do you want of me?" she asked, trying to mask her agony.

Guaypar paced the room twice without answering, as if he hadn't heard her question. The he stopped in his tracks, stared blankly at the activity outside, and declared in a muted voice, "I said something else to you back then. Don't you remember?"

"You always said a lot, Guaypar. If you're asking me what my memories of you are, I can sum them up in only a few words: Yours were always words of hatred and violence. It was that way from the beginning."

"No!"

His rage twisted his features and startled the officers waiting just outside.

"No!" he cried again, squatting down to Anamaya's level. "I loved you from the beginning. But you, Anamaya, you who were nothing, not even a princess with Inca blood, you who were but a girl from the forest, you rejected me time and again the better to seduce Atahualpa and Manco!"

"So jealous for so long," sighed Anamaya, shaking her head, "poor Guaypar. How can anyone live so long consumed by so much envy?"

"I told you a long time ago, Anamaya! I couldn't have forgotten you even if I had wanted to. Not one season, not one battle passed when I didn't think of you! Every woman I've taken to my bed has brought only you to mind. I never once fought the Strangers without keeping an image of you in my head. And I always knew that this day would come, a day when I could at last make you suffer the same torture that your contempt for me has caused me to endure!"

Every part of Guaypar's face was taut with hostility, and his violence made his words as heavy as stones. Moving with the deliberate slowness of a madman, a blank look in his eyes and his lips quivering, he raised his hand to caress Anamaya's cheek. Yet he didn't touch her. He simply let his fingers hover just above her skin, and he moved them over her body from her hairline down to her breasts.

"What do you want of me?" whispered Anamaya with great difficulty.

"First, I want to use you to catch Manco and kill him. Then it'll be your turn. Then I'll take Paullu's place and become Emperor."

"You're both mad and stupid," murmured Anamaya, shutting her eyes. "You have no idea about the future. Your hatred is leading you to the Underworld, and you will never return to your Powerful Ancestors."

"Nonsense, *Coya Camaquen*! I've never been duped by your impressive words, Anamaya. I don't believe in your magic. Huayna Capac was too sick and senile to impart the slightest power to you. It was all a hoax invented by Atahualpa to dupe the Cuzco clans. And you made the most of it, didn't you?"

"What does it matter what you believe, Guaypar? You can kill me. You can weaken Manco and maybe even defeat him. But don't delude yourself into thinking that you can alter your own destiny, and even less the Empire's. You will never be Emperor. Inti has already decided what paths his sons shall take."

Anamaya stared into Guaypar's eyes. Her blue gaze belied nothing of the pain searing her arms, back, and shoulders. Guaypar, nonplussed by her calm, stood up and moved away. His face had grown even grayer, and his eyes seemed to have retreated farther into their sockets.

"What have you done with your sister Curi Ocllo? Do you want to kill her too? She loves you almost as much as she loves Manco, but your contempt blinds you to it."

Guaypar waved his hand through the air as though sweeping away Anamaya's reproach, but he didn't have time to offer a reply. Guffaws rose up outside, and they could hear the sound of steel clanging together and Spanish boots on the flagstones.

"Why, I find you already at your task, Lord Guaypar!"

Anamaya immediately recognized Gonzalo's voice, long blond hair, and fine features. The years had inflicted on his beauty only a few crow's feet around his eyes, and perhaps the turn of his mouth had grown more severe. When Gonzalo Pizarro sniggered, she noticed that he was also missing a tooth on one side. He looked at her with the pride of a hunter looking at his prey, vanquished at last.

A dozen Spaniards milled about behind him, each with metal helmets and high-legged boots, their breeches dirty from the passage through the jungle. Each man rested his hand on the hilt of his sword. The little room filled up very quickly. Sensing that all eyes were on her, Anamaya forced herself to keep an impassive expression on her face, even though she was at eye level with their boots.

"Allow me to congratulate you, Lord Guaypar," continued Gonzalo in the same cheerful tone. "You've done an excellent job. I had imagined it would prove far more difficult to flush this precious Princess out of this godforsaken jungle."

Guaypar's stony expression showed no reaction to the Spaniard's unctuous words. Gonzalo leaned forward, took Anamaya's chin between his gloved fingers, and brutally tilted her face upward.

"I see that you cannot hide your joy at seeing me again, my lovely Princess!"

Anamaya said nothing. But she didn't show a trace of fear when she looked directly into the Governor's brother's eyes, and stared with such intensity that Gonzalo was startled and looked away, uttering a discountenanced snigger as he did so.

"She's always been like this," he explained to his companions as he puffed out his chest like a peacock, "provocative and sure of herself. It's going to be a real pleasure interrogating her. Lord Guaypar, have you asked her where she's hidden the gold statue yet?"

A chill ran down Anamaya's spine. Everything became instantly clear to her: Guaypar and the Strangers were looking for the Sacred Double. They hadn't captured her by accident. She saw her fear confirmed in Guaypar's hate-filled gaze.

"When Manco is deprived of both you and his father the Sacred Double," he murmured to her in Quechua, "he'll be as helpless as a child."

"I thought that you had only contempt for my influence over Manco," mocked Anamaya.

"What does it matter what I think! Manco is the one who believes in your powers, although they haven't helped him much up till now. When he hears that we have you, he'll be terrified. He'll take it for a sign that the Powerful Ancestors have forsaken him. And then I will finish the fight that we began that night of the *huarachiku*."

"Guaypar!" cried Anamaya. "Guaypar, you can't! Atahualpa called you his brother. Inti's blood passes through your heart. You are an Inca: You cannot allow the Strangers to desecrate the Sacred Double! You know very well what they'll do with it: melt it down into ingots that they'll carry away across the ocean. It will spell the end for our people. Guaypar! If that happens, no Son of the Sun will ever again stand tall in the light of day! Not you, and not anyone else. Kill me, Guaypar, and kill Manco, if that's your aim. But do not lead the Strangers to the Sacred Double, lest you destroy that from which you yourself were born! I beg of you, Guaypar! I'm not the one asking this of you: The Powerful Ancestors are begging it of you through my mouth. . . ."

"*Hola*, enough!" growled Gonzalo, raising his hand as though to catch Anamaya's words. "So much talk, so many words, Lord Guaypar! I'd prefer it if they were in Spanish. What's she telling you?"

"I told him that I look forward to dying," replied Anamaya before Guaypar had a chance to open his mouth. "And that I prefer death to helping you find what you're looking for."

"Oh, my pretty little friend," Gonzalo retorted with a wink to his companions, "those are words spoken in ignorance. You cannot imagine how much I'm going to enjoy convincing you to change your mind!"

"Lord Gonzalo," interrupted Guaypar slowly in Spanish, "let me take care of the *Coya Camaquen*. I believe I know where the gold statue is. Soon, I'll lead you there, just as I led you here. . . ."

"Indeed?"

Gonzalo raised a suspicious eyebrow. His face twitched nervously, and he tried to appear defiant as he declaimed, his voice breaking:

"That is not how I see things, my dear friend. I know that you've found your sister here, Manco's pretty wife. Let her take you to him. I'm sure that you'll find a way to convince her to do you this little favor! And when you meet with Manco, you can tell him that this one is with us, and that I'm . . . I'm making conversation with her. I'm certain that he'll pay you close attention."

Gonzalo pointed at Anamaya as Guaypar shook his head.

"What's the point of finding Manco if it isn't to do battle with him?"

"Why, nothing's preventing you from killing him, if you can, Lord Guaypar," chaffed Gonzalo. "But didn't you explain to me that, without this girl, Manco is like a worm lying on a rock heated by the sun?"

As the Strangers ushered him out of the room, Guaypar looked at Anamaya. This time, there was less hatred in his gaze than there was weariness.

TWENTY-SEVEN

Vitcos, Machu Pucara, July 1539

It was late into the night.

A dark lantern had been placed at Anamaya's side. She hadn't had anything to eat or drink since her capture. The pain racking her body hadn't let up once and made it so difficult to breathe that she put all her effort into doing only that. She had quickly forgotten her hunger and thirst.

Anamaya forced herself to keep her eyes open despite everything that she had endured. She wanted Gonzalo to see in them her indifference to him.

He had returned alone to the room in which she was being held. He was in his shirt and held a dagger, and she could barely make out his face by the lantern's scant light.

"I like you when you're silent," he murmured, fondling his blade. "My pleasure will be more intense and last longer."

He sniggered as he straightened, stepped back out of the light, and slid behind her.

"Did you know that Gabriel's disappeared? He's gone, he's flown away . . . some say that he's already back in Spain, others that he drowned himself in the lake."

Anamaya didn't flinch. She concentrated all her effort into being still, denying Gonzalo the pleasure he was seeking. She said nothing and showed not the slightest emotion.

"I might have taken you as my wife years ago. I didn't find you displeasing then. I even spoke about it with my brother Juan. Do you know that your beloved Gabriel led Juan to his death?"

He slipped his blade between her skin and her tunic.

"I loved Juan. Wherever he is now, whether in heaven or hell, I want him to hear your screams when you feel the kiss of my blade."

He jerked back his knife and cut through her tunic. It slipped away and left her shoulder and one breast bare. Still, she remained absolutely still.

"You're strong," whispered Gonzalo into her neck, "but now you're going to learn that I'm stronger than you."

He walked around in front of her again and looked her in the eyes.

"I'm going to do to you what your warriors did to my *compañeros*. But I'm going to do it my way. . . ."

He pressed the point of his blade against her shoulder and slid it down to her breasts.

"First, I'm going to remove some of your skin, here," he said in an even voice, "first one nipple, and then the other . . . they say that a woman won't die from such a cut, but that it's incredibly painful. Especially if one fills the wound with salt."

He smiled. He waited in vain for her to react.

"There's another technique that I've seen: You spread a little gunpowder over the wound, then set a match to it. The advantage of that is that it stanches the bleeding."

Anamaya was no longer listening. She let his words buzz around her like the pointless noise they were. Gonzalo spoke more and more, becoming excited by his own litany of tortures. But Anamaya felt an inexplicable serenity fill her heart and soul. Her fear was lifted from her, and even the pain in her back seemed to diminish. Gonzalo vomited an endless stream of words, revealing all his vilest thoughts and desires, yet he remained as impotent as a child who wants to hunt and kill animals that exist only in his imagination.

"But before I indulge myself in any of these pleasures," said Gonzalo, picking up the lantern and standing tall, "I'm going to let my dear companions enjoy you. You will give them your pretty body before I whittle it away. I'm sure that at least twenty of them will find you to their taste before your vagina becomes worn beyond use."

With a smug laugh, he raised the door-hanging and added, "Of course, Princess, you can avoid all these troubles. All you have to do is lead us to the gold statue. You have my word that once we have the statue, you'll interest me no more than does my horse's shit. So, what do you say?"

She hadn't said a word since he had come in with his taunts and threats. With all the refinement of a princess, and with a drop of sweat pearling above her lip, she said:

"No."

She woke and realized that she had dozed off.

She could hear a sound through the complete darkness of her prison. It sounded like something moving through the bushes.

Her arms and legs were so numb that she could no longer feel them. But she could still feel the sharp, needling pain in her back and shoulders.

The rustling became louder. It stopped suddenly, then began again, slowly.

And then a few clumps of *ichu* fell on her, and she understood. What good fortune that the roof was made of *ichu* and not of the tiles of which Katari was so proud.

"I'm over here!" she whispered. "Over here! I'm the *Coya Camaquen*. . . ."

Bigger clumps of straw now fell through the darkness. She felt the freshness of the nocturnal breeze caress her naked shoulder. Tied as she was, she couldn't look up properly; nevertheless she caught a glimpse of a silhouette in a hole in the roof.

Suddenly she grew fearful. What if it was one of Guaypar's men?

She said nothing and held her breath as the man jumped to the ground as supplely as a cat.

Nothing happened for a moment. Silence reigned.

Why was he staying so obstinately silent?

She felt his fingers touch her naked flesh, and with one hand he found the ropes holding her while he caressed her neck and temples with the other. She trembled, terrified, about to scream, when he whispered in her ear.

"Anamaya."

She almost fainted. Her heart melted like a lava flow.

O Noble Lords, thus have you willed it!

The voice whispered again: "Anamaya!" She felt strong arms wrap around her. She felt an indescribable happiness rise up and explode in her chest.

"Gabriel? Gabriel!"

"Yes, it's me. Shh! Don't make a noise, there's a guard outside."

"Oh Puma, my Puma! I knew that I should trust you!"

"Shhh, wait a moment . . . I'm going to cut these ropes . . . gently now . . . those bastards didn't skimp on the rope. . . ."

"How did you know?"

"Quiet, don't be impatient."

When she felt the ropes slacken, she tried to kneel and take Gabriel's face in her hands, but her legs gave way under her. And as the blood rushed back into her veins so that she felt a sensation in her legs as though they were being pricked by a thousand agave needles, she collapsed into his arms.

"Gently now," he repeated, and she could hear the smile in his voice. He kissed her temples, her eyelids, his lips searched for hers.

But when his hands found the tear in her tunic he stiffened and said, "Are you hurt? What did they do to you?"

"Nothing," she said, smiling also, "all they did was talk. They want the Sacred Double and they tried to frighten me."

"Yes, I know. I set out on Gonzalo's trail as soon as I heard what their goal was," Gabriel explained as he tenderly massaged Anamaya's stiff muscles. "I caught up with them in four days. As I didn't know where you were, I thought it best to let them lead me to you."

"It's been so long," breathed Anamaya, taking his face in her hands again, "so long! But I never once believed that we had been separated forever! And a few days ago, I began feeling your presence near me. . . ."

Gabriel put a finger to her lips. They heard someone walking outside and remembered the guard. Gabriel held Anamaya tightly in his arms and murmured in her ear.

"I refuse to be apart from you ever again. Ever. Don't ask me to do it; I'll refuse."

Anamaya, cuddled against his chest, uttered a little laugh.

"I won't ask you," she replied. "From now on, we shall stay together forever."

And in the ensuing silence, they remained in each other's arms as though all eternity were concentrated into those few moments and their wish was being fulfilled.

Then Gabriel pointed at the hole he had cut in the roof and said in a low voice, "Gonzalo is so sure of himself that he put you in a very inadequate cell. There's a thick branch hanging over the roof. It leads to a tree outside the outer wall. We'll climb down it and be outside the fortress. The dwarf is waiting for us there. He'll guide us to Manco at the little fort at Machu Pucara."

"I thought that's where he was."

"If we walk all night, we can reach Manco's camp before Gonzalo and his henchmen find out that you've escaped."

"Yes," agreed Anamaya, slowly rising to her feet, "we must hurry. Curi Ocllo was with me. But Guaypar took her prisoner and wants to force her to take him to Manco. We must get there before they do."

"You're right," said Gabriel. "There's not a moment to be lost."

Yet he took the time to clasp her to him once again before leading her away.

Emperor Manco wore a gold breastplate over a black-and-white check-ered *unku*. His elongated gold ear pieces dangled over the shoulders of his long vicuña cape. He wore the *llautu*, the royal fringe, on his fore-head, and from his gold-covered, woven-reed helmet rose the three feathers of the *curiguingue*, marking him as Inti's son.

He was standing upright on his battle palanquin, itself held up by ten men. He held his ceremonial spear in his left hand, and his right rested on the pommel of the sword hanging from his waist. It was the most finely worked of all those brought to him by his warriors. His stare was as stony as the peaks of the highest mountains. His lips and eyes were so still that it was impossible to tell if he was breathing or not.

The officers and troops around him hadn't seen their Emperor don all his finery for many moons. They knew that it meant something important was going to take place that day.

At dawn, when the night's fog was still hanging over the river's cold waters, Manco had given his generals the unexpected order to muster the men into ranks outside the old fort's outer walls as if they were on the great ceremonial square, the Aucaypata at Cuzco. Intrigued, they quizzed him with their eyes as he stood before them, smiled, and said:

"Last night I learned that the Strangers are sending us an important envoy. I wish to give him the proper reception."

And as soon as Inti's first rays pierced through the forest canopy, trumpets erupted, announcing the visitor's arrival.

The thousands of warriors had formed five ranks. Their lines stretched right into the forest and bristled with spears, pikes, standards, and long-handled clubs. Behind Manco stood a dozen officers around harquebuses taken from the Spaniards.

They all remained absolutely still as Guaypar approached with Curi Ocllo a few paces behind him.

When they were a hundred paces from Manco, the *Coya* collapsed to the ground, tears streaming down her face, and shouted loud enough for all to hear.

"Forgive me, my Emperor! Beloved husband, you are the only one that I love and obey. I beg you, forgive my brother Guaypar. He wishes you no harm!"

Some of the soldiers saw a smile flicker across Guaypar's face. But Manco's officers were already swarming around him. They grabbed him by the arms and, although he resisted with all his strength, forced him to prostrate himself before Manco. A grizzled old general fetched a heavy stone and dropped it on Guaypar's shoulders, growling:

"Pay homage to your Emperor or die, filthy traitor!"

"You're nothing but a coward, Manco!" shouted Guaypar in response. "You need your thousands of men to meet me, whereas I come alone."

Manco said nothing, but simply looked down upon Guaypar, snarling contemptuously. Two of his officers held the butts of their spears against his neck, forcing him to look down at the ground. Yet he continued, shouting.

"You are not your father's son, Manco, you're not his match! If it hadn't been for the *Coya Camaquen*'s plotting and Villa Oma's madness, you would never have placed the *llautu* on your forehead. My brother Atahualpa would never have designated you as his successor. . . ."

As he continued screaming, Curi Ocllo rushed to him. Her whole body was trembling and she clenched her silver *tupu* so tightly that blood trickled from her hands. Terrified, she cried, "Shut up, Guaypar! Shut up! You cannot speak to my husband the Emperor like that!"

Curi Ocllo tried to cover Guaypar's mouth with her bloodied hands, but Manco signaled to a soldier with his eyes, and the soldier grabbed Curi Ocllo by the arms and dragged her away.

"Anamaya is my prisoner," growled Guaypar, still looking at the ground. "She will lead me to the Sacred Double. It's over, Manco! The Powerful Ancestors are with me now!"

Manco stepped forward and drew his sword from its scabbard in one smooth movement. Curi Ocllo's wails grew louder.

"Anamaya no longer has your father Huayna Capac's support," Guaypar continued, "but the Strangers have made me a promise. If you end the war and return to Vilcabamba, they will let you live."

Manco waved his men away with his sword. He smiled and said, "Stand."

Guaypar rose, letting the stone fall from his shoulders. Manco's menacing smile grew broader.

"Poor Guaypar. You still haven't learned the lesson I gave you all those years ago at the *huarachiku*. Look here."

Manco stepped away from him. The ranks opened and allowed Anamaya and Gabriel passage.

"Poor Guaypar," mocked Manco, still wearing that sinister smile, "your words echo through the forest, as loud and as terrifying as a parrot's squawk!"

At that moment a trumpet sounded a long wail. An officer bolted up and shouted, "There are Strangers approaching, my Lord! They are only a hundred slingshots away."

As Manco raised his sword above his head, Curi Ocllo rushed forward and collapsed at his feet and crying, "Don't kill my brother! Oh Manco, spare him, spare him out of love for me!"

"You should never have brought him here, *Coya*," growled Manco. "it is better that I cut off his head than he mine. Your brother is fond of the Strangers' steel: Well then, let him swallow it!"

The blade of his sword whistled as it described a large arc through the air. Guaypar's head shook oddly. He had a surprised look in his eyes as his head fell from his shoulders and a jet of blood burst forth from his neck.

Curi Ocllo let out a horrified, animalistic scream. She clasped her brother's convulsing body to hers, his blood covering her face and chest.

Anamaya and Gabriel rushed to her. Manco was already ordering his generals to scatter the men into the forest. Utter confusion reigned for a few short minutes as thousands of warriors broke their silence and their perfectly formed ranks, and bolted toward the north.

"Come, don't stay here," begged Anamaya, shaking Curi Ocllo by the shoulders, who remained huddled over Guaypar's body. "Don't stay here. The Strangers will take you prisoner. Come with us. . . ."

But Curi Ocllo had buried her face in her brother's chest, and she remained there, shaking her head and uttering little cries like a badly wounded animal.

"She can't hear you," said Gabriel, unable to prize Curi Ocllo's fingers from Guaypar's.

They heard harquebuses being fired in the forest.

"Come on, Anamaya!" cried Gabriel, taking her around the waist and wrenching her away from Curi Ocllo. "We must go or else they'll take us too!"

And as they ran to the north amid the tail end of Manco's troops, Gabriel turned around one last time and saw Curi Ocllo, her hair drenched with blood, still wrapped tightly around Guaypar's headless body, as though she wanted to slip into the abyss with him.

PART FOUR

TWENTY-EIGHT

Chuquichaca, March 1540

The afternoon light cascaded through the treetops. The thick canopy hid the blue of the slowly darkening sky. Animal cries and bird songs echoed through the forest's immensity, auguring the coming dusk and plunging Anamaya back into the world of her childhood.

She sat on the bank and watched the river run by. She thought about her mother.

The rumble of the rapids upstream carried her into her dream. She became almost unaware of Gabriel sitting to her right. They sat on a narrow stretch of sand amid a tangle of long, dead branches polished smooth by the water. She saw herself running barefoot toward her mother's open arms. It was a recurring dream, and it usually ended as a nightmare: The memory of the sling stone striking her mother's forehead, and of her mother's body suddenly becoming a dead weight in her arms. She would wake in a cold sweat and be overwhelmed by her loneliness.

"Where are you?"

Gabriel's voice was like a cool breeze come from the water, and it drew her gently out of the daydream of her childhood. Since leaving Curi Ocllo to her despair and her brother's corpse, they had traveled for six moons together alone in the forest, far from Manco and far from the war. Their understanding of each other had grown deeper with every dawn and every dusk. They had reached a point where they could dispense even with words to realize the fullness of their love, and they remained simply and perfectly in each other's company. A mere glance or slight brush of the hand was enough to fill either one of them with happiness.

"I was taking a long trip. . . ."

"Was I there?"

Anamaya smiled.

"No. I was with my mother."

The sun disappeared behind a cloud and a shadow fell upon their faces.

"You've often mentioned your mother," said Gabriel, "and I know that you meet her sometimes in the Other World. But why don't you ever see your father?"

Gabriel had never before asked her that question so directly, and Anamaya's throat grew dry.

"I don't know. His face remains indistinct in the night."

"Anamaya . . ."

Gabriel reached for her hand, and she surrendered it to him before continuing.

"It's as though my mother's death has erased everything that I lived before. What's left is very hazy. . . ."

"'Only one secret will remain hidden within you. You will have to live with it.' Isn't that what Emperor Huayna Capac told you?"

"Yes. You remember his words well."

"To me, they're your words. And perhaps that's the secret. Or perhaps it's something else. While I was waiting for you at Titicaca, I tried to reach you on the spirit plane. I asked the Daughters of Quilla to help me. One of them spoke of you as *the girl with the eyes the color of the lake.*' She said, *'There's no great mystery. Our mother the Moon dropped water from the lake into her eyes because the one you seek unifies the beginning and the end of time. She carries the Origin in her eyes. And as for you, you're going to have to learn to see if you want to find her!*'"

Gabriel chuckled at the memory of the priestess's displeasure with him. A fragile smile lit Anamaya's face as a quail called from nearby.

They had taken off their *unku* and *añaco* and were bathing in the river. The silt-laden water was delicious in the warmth of the sun. Two tortoises sat on a branch sticking out of the water, their heads extended far out of their shells toward the sun, absorbing as much heat as they could. Six little tortoises sat beside them, completely immobile.

The blue streak of a kingfisher passing overhead sometimes flashed across the water's surface, and the occasional catfish slapped the water with its tail. Butterflies pirouetted about above a pool of water on the riverbank and filled the air with color.

Anamaya and Gabriel took turns diving underwater, their laughter mingling with their splashes. They wrapped themselves around each other like two water snakes coupling, and the trail of foam that they left behind was carried away by the current.

They saw a dugout canoe coming up from downstream, profiting from the countercurrent that ran alongside the riverbank. The two men standing at the two ends of the canoe, each holding a long pole, often had to duck to avoid the overhanging branches hampering their progress. When they were level with Anamaya and Gabriel, they looked briefly at the couple in the water and nodded before carrying on and bearing off to the bank, where they would disembark and carry their pirogue beyond the rapids.

Gabriel stretched out on the sand. Anamaya leaned over him and rubbed his back and shoulders with some leaves that produced an odor both sweet and peppered, and which provoked a mild lightheadedness. Gabriel surrendered to her long, gentle massage, as gentle as a caress. Anamaya had taught him that his body was more than just a mass of bones and nerves, a powerful body eager to conquer; she had shown him that it was also a river of gentleness, one that flowed with tenderness before it shuddered with desire.

Evening brought with it a cool breeze, and Anamaya pulled her *manta* up over the both of them. She brought her knees up to her chest and cuddled up against him, and he put his lean arms around her, his muscles as streamlined as blades.

"I feel that the time is coming," she whispered.

"How do you know?"

"Everywhere, everything is fading. It's the time of signs. I'm frightened and I'm happy. I'm so eager to take you there."

"Where?"

"Over there."

"You can't leave Manco yet. You have to stay with him."

"He's the one who's leaving us, Gabriel. He's the one who's leaving and going into the forest with all his rage. Guaypar is dead, of course, and Gonzalo has returned to Cuzco. But others will come, and then others after them. We don't know what's happened to Villa Oma, but we know that his war is leading him nowhere. Illac Topa is still resisting, but he's alone and spends most of his time on the run. Manco has ruled over nothing but shadows for many moons now. The Empire of the Four Cardinal Directions no longer exists. Vilcabamba is a capital without a country; the Incas have no more peoples to subjugate, no more lands to conquer. They are far from their mountains, far from the land first turned by Manco Capac and Mama Occlo's sickle."

"But it can't just disappear without a trace!" protested Gabriel.

Anamaya nodded.

"Oh, there'll be a trace. We must wait for Katari," she said. "It was he who advised us to leave Vitcos for a while, and it will be he who calls us when the time has come. We must trust him."

Suddenly they were interrupted by cries rushing down the riverbank. They sat up to look and saw children holding sticks and running toward them from a hundred paces upstream. They were chasing a piece of wood that was floating gently down, following the caprices of the current. Every now and then one of the children would jump into the water and direct the piece of wood back toward the bank before another would strike it with his stick, sending it back out into the middle of the river. It occasionally disappeared into an eddy before reappearing and continuing its slow descent.

"It's a basket!" exclaimed Anamaya.

"Let them play . . ."

"Wait, there's something in it."

When the basket was level with them, some of the children dived into the water. Encouraged by the laughter and urgings of those who had remained on the bank, they grabbed on to the sides of the basket and dragged it out onto the stretch of sand. Curious and smiling, Anamaya went up to it.

The basket was unusually large and its cover solidly latched with an agave rope. As Gabriel joined them, the overexcited children pulled on the cover with all their strength.

The cover snapped open with a loud crack. Anamaya screamed in horror before the children had even realized what they were looking at.

TWENTY-NINE

Vitcos, March 1540

Anamaya shuddered when she saw the elegant lines of the Vitcos palace atop its rocky outcrop. She remembered only too well the empty fortress and Guaypar's terrible surprise attack, her capture, and Gonzalo's threats. Her body remembered the cold touch of his steel dagger on her skin. Gabriel, as though sensing her discomfort, wrapped his arm around her shoulder and shared his warmth and strength with her.

"I refuse to be apart from you ever again," he had said to her when he set her free. Since then, the full meaning of those few words had become only clearer to her, along with a horrible vision that haunted her and which she couldn't shake: that of Curi Ocllo's crumpled skin in the basket, flayed from her corpse and bunched up in the fetal position as though she had been trampled to death. Her face had been intact despite the macabre vessel that they had found her in. What had been most sickening was the echo of the beauty that had once been hers lingering in her profaned skin.

They had set the heinous basket on a litter of branches and reeds and had set off for Vitcos, escorted by a few warriors.

What had happened for Manco's adored wife to be so atrociously mutilated? Who had had the sinister idea of sending her floating down the river, with the absurd, and now rewarded, hope that she would be discovered and taken to Manco?

Manco! Even just thinking about his suffering wrenched Anamaya's gut. Despite all her efforts, she hadn't been able to protect the Inca from this horror, and it was impossible to know what its consequences would be.

Despite the great exertions that the forest exacted from those traveling through it, they had made sure, every evening, to submit offerings to Curi Ocllo's soul wandering through the Other World. They had burned coca leaves and beseeched Mama Quilla to support her during her difficult journey to the Underworld. One time, Anamaya discovered Gabriel with his hands joined together, his eyes closed, and his face tilted up toward the forest's thick canopy.

"What are you doing?"

"I'm praying to a god in whom I don't believe."

"If you're praying, doesn't that mean that you do believe?"

"I'm praying for her, for her soul to find peace."

Anamaya didn't press him. But she could see a light in the darkness of his grief, and she knew that the Puma and she were closer than ever. Neither the war nor the gods would separate them again.

As they drew nearer the palace, with its fifteen doorways held up with white granite lintels, Anamaya saw a group of soldiers, spears in hand, coming to welcome them. They had recognized the *Coya Camaquen.*

They passed through the narrow door that led to the top of the hill where the palace and the fourteen buildings attached to it were assembled in a single *cancha.* The soldiers led them in silence, their faces impassive, to Manco, sitting on a large patio.

As they passed through the palace, Anamaya instinctively tightened her grip on Gabriel's hand.

"Where have you been?"

Manco's voice thundered through the courtyard dotted with orchids, their dizzying perfume permeating the air. A young puma, captured in the forest, grew restless in its bamboo cage set in an enormous recess in the wall.

Manco ignored the porters as they set the basket at his feet. His eyes, sunken into their cavities, remained fixed on Gabriel and Anamaya. Everyone, his servants and soldiers, lords and concubines, lowered their heads and held their tongues. Fear rose from the stones.

"We were where the Willkamayo and the Vilcabamba meet," replied Anamaya.

There was an infinite calm in her voice that troubled Manco. He looked away and considered the basket at his feet.

"What have you brought me?" he asked.

Bowing with the submission that every Inca subject owed his or her Emperor, Anamaya approached. She didn't say a word as she raised the wicker cover.

Manco froze, his mouth agape, as though all the air were rushing from his lungs. He fell to his knees and grabbed the edges of the basket.

A howl tore through the air.

It wasn't a human cry. It contained no words. It was the cry of a wounded animal spewing out the pain that was tormenting its guts. Everyone present in the courtyard bent almost double, as if trying to disappear into themselves. They often had cause, in these troubled times, to fear their Emperor's ire or distress. But what they were listening to now was unlike anything that they had yet witnessed.

When Manco at last recovered his breath, his whole body succumbed to a series of spasms. He grabbed Curi Ocllo's face and raised it above him, the flaccid hide of what had once been his wife's magnificent body and the joy of his nights dragging behind it. He screamed again.

Anamaya reached out to him. She brushed his neck and felt the tension in it. But just as her fingers touched his skin, he jerked away from her as though her touch had burned him.

"Manco . . ." she whispered to herself.

He didn't cry. He was like a storm that rumbles through the night, shredding the darkness with bolts of lightning, causing the world to tremble unto its very foundations.

"No! No!"

Those were the first words in a human language that emerged from his mouth. But they brought no relief, no salve, and they were as animalistic as the involuntary cries that rose from his throat.

"No! No!"

All his defiance was concentrated in those words, his refusal to submit, his refusal to lose, his refusal to be taken, his refusal to give up, his refusal that life should be so cruel; but despite all this, he remained like a hunted animal, surrounded by a scraggy horde. He was a mass of flesh and bone still attached to life only by the fiber of his unequaled and atrocious rage.

His people slipped out of the courtyard one by one, going as quietly as possible in the cowardly hope that he wouldn't notice them, sticking close to the walls as they headed for the doors, their faces covered in sweat and fear.

Only Anamaya remained, squatting in front of Manco, who lay on the ground still screaming, but less loudly now.

Gabriel brushed his hand over Anamaya's back and left as well. She glanced at him tenderly before looking back at Manco.

"Manco," she murmured again.

She looked at him. The young Inca looked like an old man. His body and face were older and more exhausted than Huayna Capac's had been when she had kept him company in his time of dying. And whereas Huayna Capac had known the secrets, Manco knew nothing anymore, and wanted nothing. He had driven his eyes back into his skull with blows from his fists, and his skin was riddled with agitated, trembling lines. His skin had turned a lusterless gray.

"Manco . . ."

He sat up slightly and stared at her.

"I . . . I can't . . ."

Then, with only Anamaya as witness, he surrendered to the bitter and futile tears of despair.

That night, the courtyard filled again. Manco didn't move, despite the rain that began falling. He had let Anamaya dress him in his finest clothes, and now the drizzle caused the feathers in his *curiguingue* to droop slightly. A silver platter lay before him, and a pretty concubine stood by, ready to fulfill a command that wouldn't come.

"Speak," he said.

The dwarf overcame the fear in his gut, remembering that ever since the great Huayna Capac had found him under a pile of blankets, he couldn't die.

"Two women came to me in Yucay and told me what you must hear, my Lord."

"Why did you wait so long?"

"I was frightened, my Lord. I was frightened of this secret that is too heavy for me."

Driven by his powerlessness, the dwarf spoke the truth. All those present feared an outburst of rage from Manco, but he only sighed through his thin lips.

"Speak now," he said, pointing to the basket. "Your secret is not yours to keep."

"Governor Pizarro had received your messages of peace. As a reply, he had sent you a mare, a black slave, and other precious gifts. Fate had it that one of your commanders came across the convoy and, thinking that it would please you, sacrificed the mare, the black slave, and a few others. Those who escaped returned and complained to their *kapitu*, who became enraged."

Anamaya felt raindrops trickle down her neck under her *añaco*. But she could no more move than could the others.

"He gave Curi Ocllo to be raped by his brother Gonzalo, then by his secretary, and then by some Spanish soldiers, and perhaps even by some Indians allied to the Strangers. When they saw that her thighs were covered in blood and sperm, they were satisfied. He then ordered that she be executed."

Gabriel was chilled to the bone, horrified by the dwarf's words. He remembered the Governor's voice and the affectionate way he had squeezed his foster son on the shoulder. Now he felt sick at the thought of every moment he had shared with his old tutor.

Manco wasn't looking at the dwarf. He wasn't looking at anyone. His eyes gazed blankly into the falling night, to the snow-covered peaks, to the Apus that had forsaken him.

"Curi Ocllo distributed her jewels and all her things to the Inca women in her entourage. She didn't say one word in anger or resentment. She only asked that her body be placed in a basket and released on the river, so that it would find its way to you."

The dwarf's cavernous voice was the only sound in the courtyard.

"One of my women gave her a band of fabric, and Curi Ocllo thanked her and embraced her. Then Curi Ocllo blindfolded herself. As they tied her to a post, she said: 'If I have spoken even one false word, let my still-beating heart be fed to the puma. You would harm a woman to assuage your rage? What could you do to a woman such as I? Hurry, so that your appetites be satisfied.' They say that many were cry-

ing, even Spaniards. Then some Canary Indians let fly their arrows into
her and pierced her with their spears, and she didn't let out even one cry
of pain during her agony. Afterward, they lit a giant pyre to burn her,
but it was against Inti's will, and her body remained intact despite the
flames. That night, my women collected her and put her in this basket,
as she had requested."

Katari slipped through the crowd until he reached Gabriel. He
gripped his arm discreetly and whispered, "We must go immediately!"
Anamaya turned around and looked at them quizzically.

"And then?" asked Manco.

"Sage Villa Oma was there. He had been captured at Condesuyu,
and they had brought him to Yucay also. He cursed them, although he
was shackled in chains, and he called them worthless dogs for what
they had done to your wife. So they burned him alive. . . ."

Unlike the dwarf's description of Curi Ocllo's end, which had met
with silence, the description of the Sage's death met with groans and
curses. Manco raised a hand, restoring silence.

"Even as the flames licked his feet, the Sage called for support from
Huayna Capac and all the Sapa Incas, Chalkuchimac and Atahualpa. . . ."

"Did he call for me?"

The dwarf hesitated for the first time, and his voice lowered a
notch.

"No one heard your name, my Lord, but no doubt he died too
quickly to call on all those he needed. After the Sage, they burned your
General Tisoc. . . ."

Katari led Gabriel away, and Anamaya saw them disappear through
the crowd. No one noticed them in the confusion provoked by the
dwarf's litany of executed Inca commanders.

"They burned Taipi and Tanqui Huallpa, Orco Huaranca and Atoc
Suqui . . ."

Manco's face didn't flinch once, and he didn't once look away from
the darkening sky. While every other person in the courtyard shuddered with shock at the name of each warrior enunciated, the Emperor
seemed to retreat further into himself, almost disappearing. But Anamaya noticed his clenched hands. Although she didn't know where
Katari had taken him, she was glad that Gabriel had left.

". . . Ozcoc, Curi Atao," continued the dwarf, compounding the horror shared by all, and it was as if each star in the sky had gone out and had left the world in a deep and final darkness.

"Villa Oma was right," said Manco at last, "we should have destroyed them before they destroyed us. Chalkuchimac was also right. They often showed weakness, yet we never exploited it. We deluded ourselves with false signs, we believed in comets and pumas. . . ."

Manco wasn't looking at Anamaya, but his hatred and deception were almost palpable.

"Leave me," said Manco, lowering his eyes onto them. "I am alone."

In a bedlam of spears and pikes, shields banging together, sandals shuffling along the ground, and rising and falling voices, they left.

Only Anamaya remained.

"You too," said Manco.

"I've never left you. You know that I've never left you."

"Once, I believed that you were going to help me build the Empire of the Four Cardinal Directions, and to expand it as no previous Inca had ever done. I believed, as my father had said you would, and as the Sage had convinced himself was true, that you were an omen from the Lake of Origin, sent to make us aspire to greatness. But you were none of that, and the prophecies that you bore in silence brought me only humiliation and destruction. Leave, now!"

"You refused to heed wise words and follow the path, Manco. You listened only to your anger, just as you did that very first day, when you unleashed it pointlessly against Guaypar. . . ."

"And now Guaypar is dead, Villa Oma is dead, Tisoc is dead, my beloved Curi Ocllo is dead, they're all dead, and I shall soon die too. Is that your prophecy? Are you a woman sent from the Underworld to make me suffer?"

"Your son Titu Cusi lives yet, and you carry the hope of so many others. . . ."

"So many others?"

Manco brought his hand up to his forehead and tore the royal band from it.

"My power is like this feather," he spat, waving it contemptuously, "brought to me on a gust of wind, and taken away on another."

He laughed a short, bitter laugh.

"See what remains of my power!"

He jumped up and approached the cage. The young puma was asleep. He considered it in silence. Then he murmured, "You must grow up first before you can help us, right? You weren't found by chance, were you? Who knows, perhaps you're an omen."

He opened the wooden door and grabbed the sleeping animal. In one fell thrust, he plunged his *tumi* into the puma's heart, then snapped its spine and broke its neck with a fury that had risen uncontrollably from the bottom of his soul. He broke each of its legs, tore out its eyes, ripped its jaws apart, and turned around, his arms covered in entrails and blood.

"Do you still want to stay at my side, lover of pumas?"

Anamaya was struck dumb with horror. But she forced herself to say, "I cannot abandon you. Yes, I want to stay with you."

"No!"

Manco raised his bloodied hand at her. There was little menace in his gesture, but it marked their definitive separation. Yet Anamaya overcame her repulsion, went up to him, and took his hand between her own.

"I will leave if you wish it. But remember that I never once left you. Remember that ever since that first day, when your father Huayna Capac confided in me, I have done nothing but obey."

Manco said nothing. He withdrew his hand from Anamaya's. She didn't know if he had understood her words, lost as he was in his lonely, violent trance. His voice was like one spoken from the Underworld when he repeated:

"No."

And as Anamaya left the patio, leaving behind the gathering pool of puma blood mixing with the rain on the ground like red mud, she thought about how Manco the rebel's entire life had reached its end in that one word, a word that he had spoken calmly and from the depths of his soul: no.

Katari and Gabriel had dashed through the empty *cancha*, dodged the soldiers patrolling the fortress's bailey, and reached a path leading into the forest without exchanging a single word. When he felt that it was safe, under night and the shelter of the trees, Gabriel asked, "What is it?"

The Master of the Stone shook his long black hair.

"Your friend Bartholomew arrived three days ago. He was wise enough not to go to the fortress and to send me two messengers instead. We've hidden him in a *huaca* an hour's walk from here."

"Bartholomew . . ."

"He's a wise and knowledgable man," continued Katari, "and we spoke about the origins of the earth, of its creation, and also about its strangest creature, Man."

"Don't tell me that he crossed through the forest just to have a metaphysical conversation with you!"

"We talked about what was before, and what will be."

Gabriel lost his sarcasm and said, "I know my friend the monk. No matter how deep his friendship for you is, he wouldn't have crossed through the forest without good reason."

"He'll tell you his reason."

The rain dampened the usual sounds heard in the forest at dusk.

"And Anamaya?"

"I had to get you away before Manco's rage turned against you. She will join us soon, along with the dwarf."

The two men made slow progress. Although it had stopped raining, the forest was wet through and through, and water dripped on them endlessly, as though the trees and sky were sweating.

They came to a glade in the center of which a wall built of a few blocks of hastily hewn stone stood around a simple bamboo cabin.

Bartholomew's familiar figure stood in the doorway. The gray-eyed monk gave Gabriel a long embrace. He seemed to be trembling feverishly.

"You're unwell, Brother Bartholomew."

"Don't worry about me. I feel much better now that you're here. Where is she?"

He turned to Katari, who pointed to the forest.

"She will come with the dwarf as soon as she can."

"Good," said Bartholomew, "I need her."

A break in the clouds allowed the last light of dusk through, and the three men spent a moment looking at the brilliantly colored butterflies darting about the glade. Monkeys created a hullabaloo in the forest, and they could hear two vividly feathered macaws perched in the nearby trees calling to each other.

The monk looked fondly at Gabriel and said, "You've made great progress since I saw you last. There is no trace of anger left in your face, and you no longer seem like a man haunted by the Devil."

"Was it that bad?"

Bartholomew touched Gabriel's forehead with his joined fingers.

"Love has taken a hold of you, my brother. I mean the kind of love that nourishes and kindles one's heart, a love that gives, that shares."

"That's the love that I know."

The three men sat down on tree trunks set out before the cabin and conversed quietly in the splendor of the falling night. Gabriel didn't grow impatient, but every now and then he glanced at the forest's edge, watching for any movement in the foliage that might signal Anamaya arriving.

There was a peace between them, a peace shared by three men who had each seen much in their lives, and who had managed to avoid the ravages that the war had instilled in the hearts of others.

Anamaya and the dwarf appeared only with the last rays of the setting sun, when Katari was already lighting a fire.

Bartholomew contemplated her with admiration and respect.

"Here you are together," he said, his gray eyes burning feverishly. "Seeing you side-by-side, I see what is noble about each of your peoples, and why your union, brought about by mysterious forces, is more important now than all the destruction it has weathered."

Anamaya sat by Gabriel. The two young people were holding hands and listening to Bartholomew in silence, both sensing the solemnity of his words and wondering what he was leading to.

"You remember, Gabriel, how I wanted you to carry dispatches describing what is really happening here to Spain. Well, I learned something a short while ago that I can only interpret as a divine sign."

A smile creased the monk's weary face, as though he were mocking the depths of his own faith.

"King Charles the Fifth is sending a permanent judge to this country. His name is Vaca de Castro and, as far as I know, he's a just and moral man. Perhaps he's even at sea at this very moment, on his way to Lima. It is an unhoped-for opportunity for us, one that may well never happen again. We wanted to go to Spain, and now Spain is coming to us!"

"How do you know this?"

"I know it, Gabriel. Oh, I can hear the doubt and caution in your voice, and believe me, I share them with you. But there are some signs that cannot deceive: for his crimes, the vile Hernando has been imprisoned in Spain."

"Yes, but surely not for his crimes against the Indians. Most likely they jailed him for having murdered Almagro."

"It doesn't matter. The time of impunity is over. Everywhere, in the church as much as at court, voices are denouncing the conquest's excesses, and clamoring for justice for the crimes done to the people of this land!"

Gabriel sighed. "One needs a faith like yours to hope that it will come to anything, Bartholomew. For my part . . ."

"Forget about my faith in God, and forget about my faith in the nobility of the Spanish soul," interrupted Bartholomew. "Don't you share my faith in Man? Don't you think that this man must hear, as soon as he arrives, something other than the rants of two sides determined to destroy each other and to pillage as much as possible so long as there remains a single ounce of gold or silver in this land?"

Gabriel threw his hands up. "I don't know . . ."

"Heed him!"

Katari had spoken so loudly that he startled Gabriel.

"What do you mean, Master of the Stone?"

"I mean that his words are true and just. I mean that we cannot spend our entire lives in the forest, hunted like animals, fearful of the slightest rustling in the bushes, weakened by the forest's humidity and diseases, and always at the mercy of hostile forces. That is the life that Manco has chosen, but it cannot be ours."

"And Anamaya?" asked Gabriel, turning toward the Princess.

"She must go with you," said Bartholomew, looking for Katari's nod of agreement. "She must go with you and bear witness that the Indians are not ignorant beasts but human beings whose history, religion, tradition, and way of life deserve our respect and protection."

"And what if she falls into their hands?" said Gabriel, his voice breaking. "What if this permanent judge is not a sage or a saint, but another Gonzalo? What if they take her and do to her what they did to Curi Ocllo?"

"It's a necessary risk," said Anamaya calmly. "You too might be arrested and imprisoned. Bartholomew and Katari are right. We must try."

"And the Sacred Double?" It was Katari's turn to speak. "If the *Coya Camaquen* agrees, I will take care of the Sacred Double and prepare him for his voyage."

Gabriel looked at each of them in turn.

"Apart from Sebastian, you are the three people in this entire country whom I trust more than myself. Why, then, am I plagued by doubt?"

"So are we, Gabriel," said Bartholomew. "I'm not talking about the certainty of success, but about the chance, however slim, of founding a nation."

"Over a hundred moons have come and gone since your arrival," said Katari quietly, "and you'd have to be blind not to see that the Strangers are here to stay. You can seize this opportunity to ensure that future generations will have your face and not the hateful one born of destruction and looting."

"What if we fail?"

No one offered a reply. They could all hear Gabriel's agreement in the gentleness of his voice.

"I'll go," he said.

He took Anamaya's hand and held it between his own.

"We will go, since you consider that it's the path we must travel. I will ignore the feeling of danger that I have within me. You shall have to pray for us, my brother."

Bartholomew grinned.

"You're always in my prayers, whether you like it or not."

Gabriel turned to Katari.

"And you, Master of the Stone, don't abandon us."

"We will meet again soon."

"How will we know it?" asked Anamaya.

Katari pulled some cords from his *chuspa* and deftly rolled a series of knots in them with his strong fingers. He handed them to Anamaya and said firmly, "Take this *quipu*. When the time has come, it will direct you to where I am. And the stone key will open up space and time to you. I will be reunited with you as I am separated from you, I will bury myself while you raise yourselves up, I will sink where you rise. But together, we will be in the eternity of Viracocha's way. Now go."

As Katari set off back to Vitcos alone, without even a torch, Bartholomew, the dwarf, Anamaya, and Gabriel set off into the forest on their journey of hope and doubt.

THIRTY

Lima, June 24, 1541

Seabirds soared off the fog-laden ocean and on their long white wings glided over the newborn city. They wheeled around in the air over the city square and the unfinished cathedral, then headed off toward the verdant hills along the coast, squawking as they went.

Anamaya looked up and watched them. The mild morning breeze caressed her forehead. The strange veil covering her hair fluttered gently against her cheek and lips, and she pushed it away with a surprised gesture.

Everything that she had seen since arriving in Lima had amazed her: the birds, the houses, and the immense ocean, which she had never before laid eyes on.

Gabriel had taken her to the top of the scaffolding around the cathedral, and from there she had seen the entire plan of the city. She saw that the Strangers arranged their houses with as much systematic order as the Incas did their *canchas*. Each was exactly the same size and perfectly square. Their roofs, here, had no tiles. They were flat and covered with a thick layer of earth, and the houses sat between identical courtyards and perfectly straight streets down which the Strangers came and went all day long, as if that was all they ever did.

Like the cathedral, which still had no bell tower, its nave hastily given a temporary vault of planks and straw, most of the houses were unfinished. Some were nothing more than a few beams and some shingles. Undefined plots here and there served as enclosures for pigs or poultry and sometimes even for those strange things that the Strangers called "carriages"—wooden contraptions consisting of a box set on four wooden circles on which the Strangers sat and had themselves pulled along by their horses.

The building across the square from the cathedral was far bigger than any other. Its walls were evenly covered with a perfectly white roughcast, and wooden balconies and louvered shutters painted blue jutted out from them. The building included two courtyards and a bushy garden the size of a house. This was the home of the Governor, Don Francisco Pizarro.

"Do you remember the letter I sent to Bartholomew to read to you, when I was on my way to join Almagro in the south?" Gabriel asked Anamaya in a low voice, holding her hands in his. "Do you remember? It must have been seven, eight years ago now. I think it was also in June. Well, this is where I wrote it, just before nightfall. The sun was already low over the ocean. There were no houses then, only a stand of trees ripe with fruit. There were a few huts in a clearing from which children stared at us, flabbergasted. It had all the elements of paradise that one can imagine."

He pointed to the spot where the river met the ocean in a whirl of yellow water, and then beyond it, toward the opulent orchids, and then at the still empty plot beyond them.

"Don Francisco very solemnly declared to me: 'It shall be here!' The next day, a few stakes were driven into the ground and everything was decided: The square would be here, the church there, over there the houses and the streets. Nothing could have been simpler! Each plot four hundred and fifty feet square and to contain four houses, and each street forty feet wide. And so it was done; the capital of Peru was born!"

There were notes of both pride and bitterness in Gabriel's voice. Anamaya gently remarked, "It displays the power of the one who has conquered a nation. Emperor Huayna Capac did the same at Quito after having defeated the northerners. His Powerful Ancestors did the same before him throughout the Empire of the Four Cardinal Directions. But all that's over now. It's no longer for us to build cities."

She said this with real sadness, but also with a serenity that put Gabriel ill at ease. He felt her shiver, even though the breeze off the ocean was warm.

"Are you cold?" he asked, worried.

"No," she said with smile, "no, it's nothing."

In truth, it wasn't cold that made her shiver but the unnatural silence reigning over the city that morning. Apart from the birds, not a single sound rose from the city, and it felt as though the day were holding its breath so that it could better scream later. Very few people were hurrying through the streets. The wind caused little whirlwinds of dust here and there on the empty square.

She had heard silence like this before. Every time, it had preceded an upheaval. Anamaya thought of Emperor Huayna Capac's words despite herself: *The Strangers, in their triumph, will know misery.* She noticed the concerned look on Gabriel's face and said with an amused smile, "It's only that I'm not used to these clothes!"

Less than a week earlier, before they entered Lima and despite Gabriel's protestations, Bartholomew had forced them to don Spanish clothes. "Can you imagine the reaction were Anamaya to go into town all dressed up like an Inca princess? In less than an hour, all those gentlemen would be interrogating her about what purpose she has in coming here! And it wouldn't take Don Francisco's henchmen any longer to begin asking her about the whereabouts of the gold statue. No, dressed in the Spanish manner, with her hair curled and her blue eyes, no one will suspect her to be an Indian. There are already many well-dressed, young, mixed-blooded women in Lima. And the same goes for you, too. You've been forgotten; try to remain that way, at least for a while."

"These damned clothes," grumbled Gabriel, unbuttoning the collar of his shirt, which he had become unused to wearing. "I guess we're going to have to wear these disguises for a while. There was bad news yesterday. Bartholomew heard tell that the vessel carrying Judge Vaca de Castro was wrecked before reaching Tumbez."

"Does that mean that he's not coming?"

"For the moment it means nothing at all. Except perhaps that this city seems to me more ill than Bartholomew, and that I'm beginning to regret agreeing to his request."

Gabriel looked at the houses around the square, then shook his head and said, "No, that's not right. The city isn't sick; it's stuck between Pizarro's people and those loyal to Almagro, now dead. It's stuck in the mire of mutual hatred. I don't like this silence, and I don't

like the emptiness in the square. I don't like being here and I like even
less having brought you here. And I don't like this disease that is consuming Bartholomew. It could well be contagious, particularly for you.
I've heard that vast numbers of Indians are dying from the fevers that
we have brought with us."

"Don't worry, I'm safe," reassured Anamaya, "and if your friend
would accept my help, I could cure him."

"Bah! Bartholomew is as stubborn as a mule. He grows worse with
each passing day, yet he accepts no other remedy but his prayers! I've
never seen him like this, both so impassioned and so doubtful about his
god—not even when he arrived in Titicaca in tatters. Indeed, if he
wasn't so consumed by fever, I wouldn't stay here."

"We must do what we must do," said Anamaya quietly.

"I'm not so sure that we can do anything at all!"

She was about to answer when a sudden gust lifted the hem of her
long Spanish skirt. She cried out in surprise and slapped it down, and as
she did so, her shawl slipped away, undoing her hair.

Gabriel laughed a tender, teasing laugh. He helped her set herself
right, and each time he looked at her, he felt stirred by her beauty. Her
innate grace was accentuated by the long, large-pleated silk dress that
followed the curve of her waist, and by the cambric camisole she wore
beneath a velvet blouse, revealing the curves of her bosom.

"How beautiful you are," he said, moved. "Sometimes I feel like
nothing can touch you, that your beauty protects you and me with you."

Gabriel was about to pull her to him, but he remembered where he
was and refrained. A man was walking quickly across the square. He
was a tall man whose gait Gabriel instantly recognized. Before entering
the cathedral's shadow, he looked over his shoulder, as if he feared that
he was being watched. His hat hid his face and his hands were hidden
beneath an old, faded cape that fell down from his shoulders, but
Gabriel knew exactly who he was.

Gabriel grabbed Anamaya by the hand and led her toward the
wooden stairs.

"Come," he said. "It appears that we have an unexpected visitor."

*   *   *

"Sebastian de la Cruz!"

The brim of his broad hat tilted upward, revealing the dark shadows beneath Sebastian's eyes. His face was marked with more lines than when they had last met. But his eyes still had that familiar twinkle, glowing brightly in his black face. The former slave flung his cape over his shoulder and warmly extended his strong hands toward Gabriel.

"God's blood, it's true, then! You're here!"

They embraced strongly albeit briefly, and Sebastian's happy, welcoming grin quickly gave way to a furious expression.

"Damn the Devil," he fulminated. "What has corrupted your mind so that you return to the wolves' den? And, what's more, accompanied by a . . ."

He stopped short, dumbfounded as he recognized Anamaya.

"Damn my eyes, it's you! Forgive this fool, Princess," he guffawed, bowing gallantly. "Your disguise is most effective. I had taken you for one of those gold diggers who are arriving here by the boatload. Indeed, I was asking myself what our dear Gabriel was doing with a woman like that."

"Bartholomew wants Anamaya to meet the judge Vaca de Castro when he arrives," Gabriel explained, smiling.

"If that's the case, you're going to be waiting for a long time."

"What do you mean?"

"I mean that the judge won't be here until hell freezes over."

"Those are hardly appropriate words to speak in this place, Don Sebastian."

All three turned around at the same time. Sebastian chuckled about having been addressed as "Don."

Leaning against the post of the door leading into the sacristy was Bartholomew. His skin was pallid, his forehead glistened, and his eyes were strangely dilated. The scar across his left cheek was swollen and seemed as though it had been caused by a branding iron. Anamaya went to him, but he held up his hand to stop her and protested, "I am fine, my girl. My appearance is deceiving. It's like this every morning, but the fever abates after a few hours. I must simply be patient; the day will come when God wills that I be cured."

"You've been saying that since we left the mountains," said Ana-maya gently, "and yet it seems as though your god cannot hear you. I have some herbs here that will cure you in just a few days, and . . ."

"Quiet," interrupted Bartholomew. He took Anamaya's hand and brought it up to his lips, much to Sebastian and Gabriel's surprise.

"Quiet, don't say another word, *Coya Camaquen.* I know what you can do; I've seen you at work. But you are in a house where it's best not to mention those things."

He crossed himself and uttered a little laugh, which set off a fit of coughing. When he had recovered, he waved at Sebastian and said, "Let's forget about all that. Don Sebastian has more important things to tell us. What do you know about Judge de Castro?"

"He's dead, drowned."

"By the blood of Christ! Are you sure?"

"Whether it's the truth or a rumor? It's hard to tell. Don Juan Her-rada spent three hours last night assuring us that the sinking of Judge Vaca de Castro's vessel was no act of God. The waves and currents had nothing to do with it, according to him. He claims that the Governor sent a ship to sink the judge's."

"Does he have proof?" asked Gabriel.

The question made Sebastian smile. He shrugged and said, "We're beyond needing proof, Gabriel. In any case, there's another rumor going about town as well: That the judge's vessel was damaged beyond repair in Panama and it will never reach Peru. Whatever the truth, everyone is convinced that the judge is dead, and as a consequence the Pizarros' tyranny will last so long as the Governor lives."

"So," said Bartholomew, running a bony finger along his scar, "Don Herrada fans flames from the embers, knowing full well what his fire shall burn."

"Do you mean to say that Herrada and his followers are plotting to kill Don Francisco?" exclaimed Gabriel.

"At this late hour, it's more than a plot: It's a commitment," said Sebastian.

"Be careful, Don Sebastian," mumbled Bartholomew, opening the door behind him and glancing out. "Your voice carries far, and the unfinished walls of this church will not hold your words in. Let us go into my cell."

"May I ask what you're doing here?" Gabriel asked Sebastian as they passed through the sacristy toward Bartholomew's tiny room.

"Oh, playing the fool, like you. Three months ago, I decided that I'd had enough of this continent, and particularly of its inhabitants."

Sebastian put his hand on Anamaya's shoulder, walking between them, and clarified.

"Its Spanish inhabitants, I mean. Those whose skin remains white despite the mountain sun. Whether they're part of the Governor's clan or allied with Almagro's son, I cannot condone what they've done to Peru. I continue to see clearly, despite having become a free and rich African. And what I see is entire boatloads of slaves being unloaded here, and sold for half the price of a pig or mule. So I sold my house in Cuzco, with the intention of moving to Panama. I sold it for a good price, I'll admit, and I've bought myself a lovely boat with some of that glittering gold, big enough to carry all my treasure."

"Panama?" said Anamaya. "Where's that?"

"North of here, Princess. It's the country where I was born and where we were when we discovered that yours existed. But my plans may shift like the wind. After all, who knows? Perhaps Panama will prove itself to be as nasty a place as Lima, and I too will have to discover my own country!"

Sebastian's laugh sounded a little forced, and his eyes revealed more emotion than he wished.

"Why haven't you left yet?" asked Gabriel.

"Ah, as for that, it's a long story. My caravel lies at anchor three cable lengths from the port. But for the past eight weeks, Don Francisco has forbidden any boat belonging to Almagro's people to take to sea. He's worried that they'll sail to meet Judge de Castro. And although I did my utmost to distance myself from Herrada and Almagro's son, I will forever remain 'Almagro's African' in the Pizarros' eyes. As for Almagro's people, they never miss an opportunity to show that I belong to them."

"What do you mean?"

Sebastian sighed a deep, heart-rending sigh. He watched Anamaya as she left through a little side door, the hem of her dress floating along the stones. He smiled and murmured to Gabriel, "One almost regrets that she's not always dressed like that. The fashions of Spain suit her like a glove."

"Don Sebastian," interrupted Bartholomew abruptly, pushing him into his tiny study, "we're safe from indiscreet ears here. Let us speak about fashion some other time. Are you sure that a plan is in motion to kill Don Francisco?"

"Don Herrada is not the only one rousing dissent. The weapons have already been ready for two days. Even the moment has been chosen."

"Where and when?"

"Later, when the Governor crosses the square on his way here."

"Before mass?"

"Herrada hopes that the Governor will find his place in hell as soon as possible, despite Don Francisco's daily devotions. He doesn't want to allow him the opportunity to repent in mass."

Bartholomew shook his head and sighed, as though the last of his strength were draining from him. He slumped into a high chair and closed his eyes before murmuring, "What can I do? Don Francisco knows that I had something to do with the judge's coming. And he even holds his brother Hernando's imprisonment against me. Even if I tried to warn him about the plot, he would never listen to me. No doubt he'll even suspect that I'm part of it."

"Forgive me, Brother Bartholomew," said Sebastian, "but there is one person who can warn the Governor, and who even has an excellent reason for doing so."

Sebastian and Bartholomew looked at Gabriel at the same time.

"No!" protested Gabriel, raising his hands before him.

"Gabriel . . ."

"No, Bartholomew! Whatever quarrel there is between these murderers, it's no concern of mine. The time when I lent support to Don Francisco, and even justified his actions, is long gone. And what's happened over the past few months, including Curi Ocllo's horrendous death, has done nothing to change my mind."

Sebastian grabbed Gabriel's open shirt with his right hand and clamored, "Why do you think I'm here, Gabriel, your soul to the Devil! Your name was mentioned in Almagro's house last night. Herrada and his men know that you're here in the church. Someone must have recognized you. And do you know what they concluded?"

Gabriel said nothing. Sebastian released him and hammered his finger into his chest, emphasizing each word. "They concluded that Don Francisco felt in danger and that he summoned you to save him! You, his follower from the beginning of the conquest, the one he called 'son' for so long. Gabriel de Montelucar y Flores, the 'Santiago' of the siege of Cuzco! Don't you realize how terrified they are of you?"

"They're insane."

"No. They angry and they're frightened. They see threats and traps everywhere. And not always without reason."

"What he says is true, Gabriel."

"Of course it's true, Brother Bartholomew. And what will happen, my dear Gabriel, is that if you don't hurry as fast as your feet will carry you to the Governor and warn him, they will kill you along with him. Unless they decide to kill you first, so that they feel safer."

The door hinge creaked, startling them all. Her dress rustling, Anamaya entered carrying a bowl containing a hot, dirty brown liquid. She smiled and handed it to the monk and said, "Come, drink this. Your god will not hold it against you. There's nothing in it that he didn't make himself."

"I'm pleased to see that you haven't remained immune to the teachings of Christ."

Bartholomew smiled waggishly. He was about to push the wooden bowl away, but then changed his mind and, with a shrug, took it.

"Since it means so much to you," he murmured.

Anamaya turned to Gabriel as he drank and said, "Sebastian is right. You must go and warn the Governor."

"Anamaya," protested Gabriel, "I told you before, the only intelligent thing for us to do is to leave Lima immediately."

"No. Everything begun must be finished. Only then may we return to the mountains."

Gabriel scowled gloomily. Sebastian leaned close to him and said in a deep, serious tone, "Please, my friend, I beg you."

Gabriel was startled by the solemnity in his voice.

"As I told you," continued Sebastian, "they're harrying me to join them. Herrada made it clear that if I didn't join them, sword in hand, then my boat and my plans were finished."

"Then I shall go," said Gabriel.

Gabriel had to insist that the Governor's door be opened to him. It was only after he had announced his entire name—"I am Gabriel Montelucar y Flores!"—and then waited a little while longer that the heavy studded door creaked open. Two peasant faces appeared above bodies dressed in bloodred livery and charily scrutinized him before letting him pass.

"His Lordship the Marquis is waiting for you in the garden," said the younger of the two pages.

Gabriel walked out into the courtyard and saw a dozen other faces staring at him from the gallery. He recognized some of them, old companions from Cajamarca or more recently arrived courtesans he had briefly met in Cuzco. But none of them doffed their hats in greeting, so nor did he. The heels of his boots clacked against the courtyard's round flagstones, and he followed the page down a corridor. He saw him as soon as he passed through the low door leading into the garden.

His shoulders were perhaps a little more stooped, but on the whole his tall figure remained upright beneath the long, black garb he wore draped down to his ankles. He wore a gold-studded belt around his waist from which hung a silver scabbard holding a dagger. His felt hat was as immaculately white as his deerskin boots. He had his back to Gabriel, and he held a copper watering can from which he slowly trickled water onto the base of a young fig tree. Old age had marked his hands with large brown stains, which clearly suffered only slightly from rheumatism. His voice hadn't changed at all, and it remained slightly abrasive but with a note of tenderness, as was evident when, without turning around or even a greeting, he declared:

"This is the first fig tree planted in this country. I water it every day and even speak to it a little. Did you know that plants like to be spoken to as they grow?"

"Don Francisco," said Gabriel dryly, "Almagro's people have decided to kill you as you make your way to the cathedral later."

Don Francisco didn't react; he showed no sign that he had even heard Gabriel's words. He kept pouring the trickle of water onto the base of the fig tree, creating a little hole in the loose, crumbly earth.

"Governor, did you hear what I just said?" asked Gabriel in a harsh voice. "Don Herrada has been rousing his troops all night. They have unsheathed their swords."

The trickle of water ended. Gabriel heard someone opening the louvers of a shutter in one of the windows, and he could sense eyes watching them both, studying their every move.

Don Francisco turned around at last and looked at Gabriel with his faded eyes, his pupils as pointed as daggers. Gabriel searched them in vain for some flash of truth. Although the Governor still trimmed his beard neatly, it no longer hid the lines that had gathered on his face. And when he smiled, parting his lips, Gabriel saw only three bad teeth jutting out of gums as pink as a baby's.

"No one calls me 'Governor' anymore," he almost whispered, "rather, they call me 'My Lord Marquis.'"

"God's blood, Don Francisco, this is no time for simpering airs! Two hundred men are bent on killing you!"

"Nonsense!"

"You know very well that it's true! Half the Spaniards in this country hate you and are furious with you; they're baying for your blood!"

"They've no reason to be furious. It's nothing more than spitefulness and treason."

"They have very good reasons, Don Francisco," said Gabriel, raising his voice with irritation, "as you know very well!"

"What reasons? Haven't I been like a father to everyone? Do you know what I do when I see someone destitute? I invite him to a play skittles!"

"Don Francisco . . ."

"Listen to me, Gabriel! I invite him to play skittles. Ten pesos a game, sometimes more, twice as much if he can afford it. Sometimes, if he's a man with a name, for a gold piece. And then, I lose. I take my time, because I like playing, but I lose. I always lose, do you see? That way, the poor man is no longer poor, he keeps his honor, I haven't condescended to him with alms. People speak ill of me and no one lets me have a moment of peace. I have no other concern than the good of all, and yet people spread lies about me, they twist my words, they betray me!"

"Allow the boats belonging to Almagro's people to leave, and you'll have peace."

"Why have you come to tell me these things, my boy? And dressed, I see, as the good Spaniard that you are?"

"I didn't come to Lima to see you, Governor. I came to meet the judge sent by the crown."

"Ah?"

"But apparently you drowned him."

"That's a lie! Another damned lie! I offered to bring him here on one of my galleons, but he preferred his leaky boat. But he will come. He's not drowned at all. What do you want to say to him?"

"That it's time to give the Indians of this country the respect that is due all human beings. I will tell him that they are humans just like us and that the Pope shares this opinion."

"You know the Pope's opinion?"

"Do I know yours? I will tell him how you and your brothers inflicted suffering on hundreds, on thousands of innocent souls."

"And you're innocent?"

"Oh no, I did too, foolishly following your orders. I followed blindly until the cries of agony and the horrors that we brought everywhere we went opened my eyes for good."

"In that case, my friend, you will tell him how you and I had to fight those savages to make this land a Christian land. You will tell him how the Very Blessed Virgin saved us from perdition a thousand times, and that without her, nothing would have been accomplished. You will tell him how, at Cajamarca, we were nothing more than Almighty God's instrument!"

"No, Don Francisco."

"Well then, you will be a liar, like the rest of them! You, who God favored among all others. Have you forgotten how he protected you during the siege of Cuzco?"

"I don't know what it was that protected me."

"You dare to renounce us!" shouted Pizarro, brandishing his water-

ing can about. "You dare to renounce your God, and to renounce me? Who brought you here? Who gave you a name when you were nothing more than a louse on the surface of the world?"

"You're talking about a story that isn't mine to tell, Don Francisco. Those gentlemen over there, leaning at your windows listening to us, who shower you with compliments every day, will tell it, I'm sure. I can't play that tune anymore, Don Francisco: my eyes and my heart remember too many things that you never wanted to erase, too much suffering that you never tried to check, and some that you even caused!"

"So, you too are angry with me, my son?"

"That word means nothing anymore between us, My Lord the Marquis. What's more, it is useless. I got used to having no father a long time ago."

"And yet you worry about me. You don't want me to die, you're prepared to draw your sword to defend me."

"I didn't say that. I won't fight for you. I came to warn you because your death could very well lead to mine, and I still have much to do before leaving this world."

"Ha! What could you possibly have to do that's so important?"

Don Francisco's bitter sarcasm took Gabriel by surprise, and his surprise restored his calm. He smiled and stepped away.

"I don't believe that I could explain it to you, My Lord Marquis. It would take a lifetime."

Don Francisco's face closed like the door of some very old, isolated, and dilapidated cottage. The furrows on his face deepened, and his eyes spoke nothing but a haughty contempt.

"I'm going to have mass given here, in my room," he announced in an even voice. "Then we'll see if Herrada and his bums dare to come for me here! As for you, you can drink some juice from my oranges while I pray. They're the first ever to be picked in this country."

"I'm not thirsty, Don Francisco."

The Marquis extended his hand toward Gabriel's shoulder, a gesture he had made many times before, one that coupled a mark of friendship with his demand for submission. But there was something new in Gabriel's eyes, a determined calm, that caused him to stop himself.

He remained like that, his hand suspended in the air between them, his black eyes desperately searching his "son's." Then he slowly let his hand fall.

"It shall be as you wish," he grumbled, his voice mute.

Gabriel was moved more by this powerlessness than he had been by all the words that had preceded it.

"Be careful not to die."

The hint of weakness and of doubt that had appeared on the Marquis's face immediately disappeared. And it was with a straight spine and a firm voice that he declared arrogantly:

"A man such as I doesn't die."

"Long live the King! Long live the King! Death to the tyrant!"

About thirty of them emerged from an alley and made their way across the square in front of the cathedral. Anamaya had taken Bartholomew to the top of the scaffolding, and though she was too far to make out their features, their fervor electrified the increasingly muggy air of Lima.

Again they howled: "Long live the King! Long live the King! Death to the tyrant!" and thus increased their frenzy, waving their weapons about. They had crossbows, partisans,* spears, and lances, and even two harquebuses.

"They've gone mad," murmured Bartholomew, almost involuntarily tightening his grip on Anamaya's arm. "Are they trying to bring about a pitched battle?"

Anamaya was scanning the square for Sebastian's giant figure, and she didn't answer the monk right away. But before she had spotted him, a thunderous clamor shook the scaffolding. Two or three hundred men, most of them on horseback and wearing breastplates or coats of mail and all of them shouting, emerged from the alleys that had been empty just a moment before and from the houses surrounding the square.

---

partisan: a spear or pike with two opposing axe blades or spikes.

"Sweet Jesus," exclaimed Bartholomew, his face pale and beading sweat.

"Are they so frightened of the Governor that they have to be so many to kill him?" asked Anamaya.

"Certainly they're frightened of Don Francisco. But they fear Gabriel, the 'Santiago of Cuzco,' and his magic powers far more."

Anamaya couldn't help but giggle, surprising Bartholomew.

"That makes you laugh, *Coya Camaquen*?" he murmured anxiously. "I find you unreasonably calm."

He was interrupted by the sound of a blank being fired from a har-quebus, and he was almost shouting as he continued.

"Just look at them! If things continue at this rate, Pizarro will be dead within the hour, and maybe Gabriel as well. That doesn't worry you?"

"Don't worry, Bartholomew, my friend. Gabriel isn't going to die."

"How can you be so sure?"

Bartholomew looked up angrily. But when his eyes met Anamaya's, he instantly realized that she was right and that he could never know from whence came her knowledge and her certainty.

He closed his eyes and fervently crossed himself. Down on the square, the mob rushed Don Francisco Pizarro's house.

"To arms! To arms! They're trying to break down the door! They want to murder the Marquis!"

The page's alarmed cry echoed throughout the enormous building and caused a panic in the courtyard. Gabriel saw the courtesans stumbling over one another up in the gallery, desperate to flee rather than draw their swords. An iron fist grabbed his arm and pulled him back. He turned around and found himself so close to Don Francisco's face that he could count the number of furrows leading away from his eyes and into his beard.

"Follow me, come to my room, you can at least help me put on my breastplate. They'll all have run like hares soon enough, and we won't be many left to defend."

And indeed, only three or four men joined Don Francisco in the antechamber at the corner of the building, a room that had the advantage of having only one point of access.

"Stand by the door," Pizarro ordered two lords, each of whom had a dagger in one hand and a sword in the other.

He took off his long coat and said to his ever-present page, "My dear Diego, watch what they're doing and tell me everything."

As he opened the chest containing his old breastplate wrapped in a cotton sheet, he glanced at Gabriel, who was certain that he saw a smile flash across the old man's face.

"My Lord, my Lord!" cried the page. "They're in! They've broken down the door and they're in the outer courtyard!"

"How many?"

"Ten . . . no, fourteen, maybe fifteen. They're rushing about, I can't count them exactly."

"The poltroons. D'ye hear, Gabriel? Two hundred of them out on the square and only fifteen who dare to enter. They've got balls like peas."

"My Lord! Lieutenant Velásquez and Secretary Salcedo took fright and jumped through the window to the garden."

"Ah! Two more with nothing but air between their legs!"

There was mirth in Don Francisco's roar.

"In the name of God, Gabriel, undo these straps while I put on my armor. They don't know what they're in for, trying to murder me!"

"My Lord, Don Herrada and his men are coming up the stairs of the inner courtyard. They're fighting . . . oh, my Lord, Don Hurtado and Don Lozano are wounded!"

"It's happening quickly. Shut the doors to the gallery and post three men behind each of them."

"Impossible, my Lord. Many of their lordships are hiding under the beds and in the cupboards!"

"The damned cowards! May they eat dust and swallow their own bile! Gabriel, my boy, pull! Pull it tight!"

Gabriel yanked on the straps that joined the front and the back of the breastplate. With growing distaste, but also with a calm that surprised even him, he felt as though he was entombing the clamorous old man in an iron grave. Meanwhile, the sound of fighting drew ever closer.

"Oh, my Lord, his Lordship Chávez has been killed! They've stuck knives into his neck! My Lord, they're killing everyone!"

"The mongrels! In the neck, ten against one! The whoresons! Shame on them!"

The shouts and curses grew suddenly louder, and the door was forced open so hard that it bounced off the wall. Pizarro's loyal page stumbled wordlessly backward, his throat open, and fell to the ground never to rise again. For a brief moment, everybody was frozen, wide-eyed and holding their breath. Then the cry "Death to the tyrant!" bounced off the Governor's iron chest.

Gabriel instinctively jumped to the side, and although he had promised himself to leave it in its scabbard, his blade was bare. The room descended into chaos. There was a whirlwind of sword striking sword, of men screaming ferociously, their stinking breath mingling in the air. In the mêlée, no one paid Gabriel much heed as Don Francisco defended himself like a demon disguised as a man. He waved a partisan about with his left hand as his right whipped his sword through the air, parrying blows and slicing through the enemy. He showed no sign of age, no sign of weakness. Even his beard seemed to be made of metal sharp enough to cut. He furiously forced back the conspirators, who seemed to be weakening.

"Death to the tyrant!" screamed Don Herrada, pale faced and shoving his men ahead of him.

"Traitors! Buffoons! Your souls to the Devil!" answered Don Francisco.

A second wave of conspirators rushed into the room. Gabriel saw Sebastian's tall figure enter with them, awkward and stiff in the confusion.

"Sebastian!" he shouted. "Don't stay there! Get out of the way, let them fight!"

Sebastian deflected Pizarro's partisan with an awkward flourish, but one of the Governor's men struck his arm. Grimacing with pain, blood already spurting through his sleeve, he turned toward Gabriel, who moved toward him. But Don Herrada, as though he had guessed

Sebastian's intention, used both his hands to shove Sebastian forward onto Don Francisco's deadly sword.

"Sebastian!"

Gabriel whipped his sword through the air in an attempt to deflect Don Francisco's. But the Governor had thrust with all his might. His sword, a veteran of so many battles, found the gap at the bottom of Sebastian's coat of mail. It pierced into Sebastian's flesh so easily that Don Francisco stumbled forward into his chest as the African giant let out a long, quiet groan.

And then everything happened at once. As Sebastian collapsed, Don Francisco's sword still in his side, the Governor froze with surprise. And in that instant, ten daggers landed on him simultaneously, with ten voices crying as one:

"Kill him! Kill him! Death to the tyrant!"

Gabriel grabbed Sebastian's shoulder, and with great difficulty managed to drag him back. As Gabriel pulled the blade out of his friend's guts, Don Francisco collapsed onto the floor not two paces away, his toothless mouth agape in a silent cry. Blood streamed from his mouth as he breathed:

"Confession! I beg you, let me confess! For mercy's sake, let me kiss the image of the Very Blessed Virgin one last time!"

Gabriel felt Sebastian's body convulse in agony in his arms.

"Hold on!" he begged, pressing his hand over his friend's gaping wound and noticing without feeling it that his own hand had slipped on the blade, leaving a large gash across his palm. "Hold on, don't die, Sebastian. Anamaya will fix you."

"Let it be, Gabriel. It's better this way."

Sebastian placed his hands on his friend's, smiled, and looked over at the Governor's twisted face. In response to Don Francisco's final plea, one of his murderers had smashed a jug into his face, ripping his mouth apart, and with it, his prayers.

"He's already dead," breathed Sebastian, "and soon I will no longer be a slave."

"Hold on, hold on."

Gabriel felt tears stream down his cheek and mingle with his sweat as the words came out of his mouth.

"I'm going to ask you yet another favor, Sebastian."

"Ha! I know you, your Grace. You want to win a little more time. . . ."

"I promise you, I need you!"

"You've always tended to sob like a woman at farewells, Gabriel. Shut up and hold my hand."

And as his friend closed his eyes and boarded the vessel that would carry him to his final and absolute freedom, Gabriel never once let go of his hand.

A tenacious, muggy fog rolled in from the ocean and blanketed the coast's meandering line of ocher rock. The fog repelled the assault of the hard sun that set the immense desert to the north of Lima ablaze.

It took only a three hours' ride on horses and mules for the green opulence of Lima to disappear behind them, along with the madness that had reigned over the city since Don Francisco's death. The cries of hatred had become demented dances, farandoles of revenge that demanded satisfaction. The old Governor's slashed body had been paraded through the great square like some old rag, as though it were a tattered banner taken from the enemy on which to wipe one's old grudges and fears brought on by too many years of lawless living.

As the Pizarros' palaces were looted amid a cacophony of sinister laughter, Bartholomew pressed Gabriel to leave town before Don Herrada came after him.

"I must bury Sebastian first," he had protested, his eyes completely bloodshot.

"It's impossible. They won't spare you the opportunity. You're the last remaining person who frightens them. Don't think that they're going to forget about you just like that."

Then Anamaya had suggested that they leave and take the former slave's body with them.

"Why not?" Bartholomew had murmured with a shrug of his shoulders. "I'll consecrate a plot to bury him in, and he won't be any less at peace there than he would be here."

And now they were at that plot, having dug a grave between two stones standing like two giant, welcoming arms. They had erected a cross as tall as a man from two pieces of driftwood, and its shadow shrouded the plot of dusty earth. Bartholomew was on his knees, murmuring a prayer, but Gabriel didn't join him.

With his uninjured hand, he held Anamaya's, and he let the memories come back to him like a flight of dark-feathered birds. He remembered the first time his friend had smiled at him, at the inn called The Bottomless Jug, in Seville, and he remembered his first words: "We've discovered a new country." He remembered Sebastian repeating: "Never forget, my friend, that I'm black and a slave. Even if things look like they've changed, I'll never be anything else." He remembered Sebastian tightening the garrotte that killed Atahualpa. He remembered Sebastian saving his life, protecting him, mocking him, unfailingly faithful until the very last.

"He will be well here," murmured Bartholomew as he stood up and stared at Anamaya as though he didn't dare cross Gabriel's eyes. "This was another of your good ideas, Princess."

"Yes," agreed Gabriel, his face twisted with bitterness. "For a man who lived his life like another's shadow, he's definitely on his own here. No doubt Herrada and his people have already seized his boat. He will have vanished from their minds in only a few days, as though he had never existed."

His lips quivered with rage. Bartholomew looked at him with his gray eyes.

"I'll never forget that it was I who baptized him," he murmured.

"Baptized? Sebastian?" said Gabriel, astonished.

"Yes. He asked me to baptize him shortly before I left Cuzco. But I promise you, I didn't bother examining his faith too closely. Let's just say that he wanted to put his mind at ease."

Bartholomew wrapped his hand with the joined fingers around Gabriel's and Anamaya's.

"I baptized him with as much love as I married you two."

Gabriel was startled.

"I don't remember any marriage ceremony, Brother Bartholomew."

"Be at ease, my friend. Wasn't I the first person to urge you to go to her? And didn't I come to fetch you both in the heart of the forest? I married you privately that day, in my heart, although I do believe that my friend Katari assisted me during the rite. There have been times when words have stood between us, Gabriel, but I don't want to leave you without first having given you my friendship and a sign of divine love as well as human. Will you agree? Will you both agree?"

"Thank you," said Anamaya, and Gabriel nodded his head.

"No, *Coya Camaquen,* it is for me to thank you. And for much more than you can imagine. I know that, if it weren't for you, the shame and suffering in this land would be far greater than it is. I will never forget you. And when I speak to Judge Vaca de Castro, and when I go to Toledo and plead your case, and that of all of Peru, it is your face that I shall see in my mind."

They shared a moment of silence together, joined as much by their shared emotion as by the touch of their three hands. The heat of the desert and the crashing of the surf on the nearby coast enveloped them in a solitude as immense as the sense of peace they shared. Gabriel was surprised to feel his sadness ebbing away, as though the vastness surrounding him were absorbing him and revealing to him the true beginning of his life.

Bartholomew drew his hand away first. He ran his joined fingers along his scar, a gesture that had become automatic to him whenever he was embarrassed by emotion. He laughed and said, "As you can see, my fever has been lifted. We'll never know whether God answered my prayers or whether it was the Princess's brew. But it doesn't matter. Know that I intend to live for a long while yet!"

And with that he clambered atop his mule and headed north. Anamaya and Gabriel stood in each other's arms, watching him. She said, "Don't you think it's strange that he also talks about a sign from his god?"

Gabriel knew what she was referring to. The Emperor Huayna Capac's words were running through his mind as well:

War visits the Sons of the Sun and war visits the Strangers: It is the sign.

The brother's blood and the friend's blood are shed far more than the enemy's: It is the sign.

The Stranger who worships a woman rather than his Ancestors is killed: It is the sign.

Yes, each thing had now reached its end.

"Come," murmured Anamaya, "it is time to go to the mountains and free the Sacred Double from our presence."

"Never doubt me. Remain in my breath, and trust the Puma," replied Gabriel, looking one last time at Sebastian's grave.

THIRTY-ONE

Machu Picchu, Caral, 1542

They had said little since leaving Lima.

Each was lost in his or her thoughts, reliving the chaos, the passions, and the amazing events that had occurred in their lives. Gabriel would stare at the stone ribbon of the Inca royal road stretching before him and imagine that he was bobbing on a rising sea; Anamaya would gaze at the mountain peaks and occasionally stretch her arms to remind herself that she was only a human being. Any pride that they might have harbored had disappeared: The *Coya Camaquen* and the White Knight of Santiago were now only a woman and a man traveling along a road, accompanied by a few porters. Their love required no words: It lived with only gestures and glances.

They had remained in their Spanish clothes. Gabriel looked at his wounded hand by the morning light. It was slowly cicatrizing, and a strip of young skin, as smooth as a child's, had formed next to his hardened, adult skin. He thought about Sebastian: His death had torn the fabric of Gabriel's soul and, like the wound on his hand, he knew that it would never fully heal. It was strange to be alive after Sebastian had died, thought Gabriel. It had taken so many deaths for him to realize such a simple thing.

They had reached the Apurimac Valley, and Gabriel turned every now and then to look at the perfect triangle of a mountain rising over the steep-sided valley that they now journeyed through.

They were one day away from Rimac Tambo.

Constant reminders of battles haunted Gabriel throughout the trip: a rushing river here, a mass of fallen rocks there. Beyond them was the unknown.

Yet he didn't feel the need to ask where they were heading.

He knew.

He knew that, when they reached the *tambo*, the porters would leave them and they would remain alone.

He knew that they would take off their Spanish clothes, which they would never wear again, and that he would once again don his *unku* and she her *añaco* of fine white wool.

He knew that she would look to the north and show him where the comet had appeared to her; that they would then take the road into the thick forest that the sage Villa Oma had first led her down.

She would say: "This is the place."

Night was coming, and a thick fog rose up and blanketed them so that they were almost invisible. Gabriel couldn't help imagining her disappearing in the fog, and his fingers tensed involuntarily. He twirled around like a drunkard, only stopping when she took him by the hair. He stood still, his heart pounding. She took his wounded hand and brought it to her soft lips.

Katari felt the thousands of drops of water brought by the sea wind gather on his forehead.

Everything receded from sight.

The sky, the sea, and the earth were all shrouded in the same mother-of-pearl whiteness. He had to touch his skin to be sure of its texture, to be sure of his own tangibility. His other senses had been all but annihilated, as though the three Worlds had merged as one, as though all the elements had been concentrated into one.

Yet he continued walking toward the north, guided only by the light within him.

He had walked every day since leaving Vilcabamba and Manco's vacant eyes. The Inca hadn't even noticed him leave, and hadn't paid any attention to the preparations that took place for the Sacred Double's voyage. He only interrupted his solitude by uttering the occasional brief order, and the only signs of life he showed were in the middle of the night, between the legs of one or another of his concubines. What had once been gestures of respect were now reduced to marks of fear. He woke every morning screaming at the top of his voice, and he ordered all his soothsayers to his bedside to interpret the dreams and visions that terrified him and twisted his features. His lips had been trembling uncontrollably when Katari took his leave, as though the Inca were trying to say something, but the effort was too great, and he had found it impossible. Oblivion was consuming him from within.

Katari had entrusted the Sacred Double to his Kolla kinsmen, who obeyed his commands without demanding any explanations, and who, since boyhood, had maintained an untouchable tradition of saying very little. They would escort the statue's palanquin through the forest, making as little noise as an anaconda. They would take it to where it was to go, in keeping with Huayna Capac's words, to meet with Anamaya and the Puma, and so to its eternal resting place.

Katari had preferred to leave on his own.

The mere presence of another human being would have disturbed his thoughts, and perhaps even led him astray. For almost a month, he had lived with only the sounds of nature, had breathed only the perfume of orchids, their leaves dripping dew, and had conversed only with birds.

He had slept very little, but he always had the same dream: He knew exactly where he was, despite never having been there before. He woke happy and full of a certainty that made him bound to his feet and push on ever faster. His strong legs had led him through many landscapes, from heat to cold and back to heat.

He had left the forest for the undulating plateaus of the puna, where the hills receded to the vanishing point of the horizon. He had gazed upon the yellow tufts of *ichu* growing under the pure blue sky. Whenever he had seen a dust cloud, he had known that it wasn't men who had kicked it up but a herd of vicuñas, the ground trembling with their collective step.

Heading down toward the coast, he had crossed stony deserts, occasionally intersected by streams on the luxuriant, green banks of which sat almost completely naked Indians, perfectly immobile, who watched him approach without uttering a word.

As he had approached the sea, he saw an increasing amount of fog streaked across the sky, filling the air with humidity and penetrating his skin. Now it was so thick that it surrounded him entirely, and though it blinded him, he could see everything. It gave the impression that the atmosphere was made of wool, and that it absorbed all sounds. But he could hear everything. The fog brought with it the odor of the sea, but he could smell scents from far farther away.

"You have arrived," he whispered to Anamaya and Gabriel. "You are far, yet you are very close to me. We are together."

The fog lifted as they progressed into the mountains, leaving the Apurimac behind them. They had walked throughout the night and now, in the cool dawn, she was in his arms. He surrendered to the blue in her eyes, the blue of the sky, the blue of the night, the blue of the sea, and the blue of the lake into which he had dived to find her again.

When they had passed the stone columns rising up toward the sky, Anamaya had passed her hands over Gabriel's eyes, compelling him to close them. As they continued climbing the stairs suspended between sky and earth, he was overcome by a profound apprehension. Then Anamaya squeezed his hand, signaling that he could now open his eyes.

The sight that greeted him was more beautiful and more powerful than anything he could have imagined. It was as though, here in this secret place, a covenant had been struck between Man, the sky, the mountains, and the river to build a temple in which to glorify the gods on nature's, rather than man's, scale.

"Picchu," murmured Anamaya.

His eyes shone, and his lungs were filled with an exalted, serene breath. He knew that he was where he was meant to be, that he had reached the end of his way. He let his eyes slide over the stepped terraces, over the houses and temples, he let them follow the murmuring water and air, the smoke spiraling in gray volutes from the *ichu* roofs, beyond which he could see a vast square. But his eyes were repeatedly drawn to the mountain looming over the place, a slight, slender mountain. His heart thudded as he recognized its shape. It was the same as the rock with four niches in Ollantaytambo, and he saw in its rock the form of a puma coiled up about itself, looking down over the city, dozing yet terrifying and watchful.

There were so many questions to ask yet no answers to be had: Everything was there.

Anamaya radiated at his side.

"I made a promise," she murmured. "I promised that I would never reveal the secret, that I would never pass through this door with a Stranger."

"Isn't that what you're doing now?"

"You're not a Stranger. You are the Puma. The secret belongs to you. You are home."

Gabriel felt happy and free, and the young child asleep within him would have hurtled down the terraces, would have darted through the narrow alleyways that came out onto the vertiginous slopes beneath which shimmered the silver ribbon of the river. But the place emanated such solemn dignity that he contained his excitement and stilled his soul.

Anamaya descended the stairs that led to the monumental door through which, many years before, she had watched Villa Oma disappear. The same heavy wooden palisade was in place, hermetically sealing the access to Picchu's center. She placed her hands on it and it immediately swung open, revealing a street lined with low-roofed houses. Three impassive guards bearing spears welcomed them, their faces completely neutral, and wordlessly led them to a huge house with carefully roughcast walls and a steep-sloped gabled roof. Two trapezoidal windows offered a view over the entire valley.

An old man sitting on a *tiana* greeted them. His long hair was as white as the snows of Salcantay.

"Many years have passed, Huilloc Topac," said Anamaya slowly, "but you're still the guardian of this place."

The snow-haired Indian's eyes were covered in a film the color of mother-of-pearl, like those of a blind man. Yet when he turned to face them, Gabriel felt as though he were looking into his very soul. The guardian said simply:

"I've been waiting for you."

Set in the middle of an immense cradle of hills, the whole bathed in a gray light, the six mounds formed an almost perfect circle. The sea was many days' walk behind Katari now, and yet he could still smell its scents. A river snaked along at the bottom of the slope, both its banks crowded with vegetation.

Katari's heart beat hard.

To the uninitiated eye, the mounds were nothing more than piles of dust and dirt that stood out only because they were of a darker tint than the rocks and stones surrounding them. For the Master of the Stone, however, who had traveled from farther afield than his own lifetime, this was the end of the road.

Here, time ended and began.

He slowed his pace and let the winds resonate in his ears as though they were seashells; a trumpet echoed throughout his body, a horn from before time began that told Katari the legend of what had been and what was to come.

This is where it had all begun, well before even the time when Viracocha had emerged from Lake Titicaca, well before he had headed north and waded into the Great Sea at Tumbez, now desecrated for all time by the coming of the Strangers.

It was here that the monolithic *huaca*, the *Stone of Origins*, lay, marking Man's link to the Andes.

The stones had told him this, and the ancient *quipus* saved from the rape of Cuzco had confirmed it.

He drew the *quipus* from his bundle and ran his fingers along the knots on the cords, and with his eyes closed he chanted a wordless invocation. A very ancient *amauta* had given him the key. They were the memory of the Andes, and he knew how to invoke them. He could smell the smell of the river mixing with that of the sea in his nostrils. His long black hair swept across his face. He headed unhesitatingly for the highest of the mounds.

Its shape became clearer as he approached, and he could see the regular staging of terraces hidden beneath the pile of earth. He was standing before a pyramid.

His *quipus* still in hand, Katari didn't waste any time looking for the access beneath the pile of stones. He slowly walked around the pyramid, letting himself be inspired by its presence and that of the generations that had practiced their rituals here.

When he was at the base of a ramp that he could make out beneath the mass of earth, he saw that he was within a vast circle.

His face lit up.

"*Urku Pacha,*" he whispered, "the passage to the Underworld. It is here. Come."

He sat down in the center of the circle and spread his *quipus* out before him. Then he lay down on the ground and spread his arms and legs, and a rumble from the heart of the earth rose up in him.

They had spent the entire previous day and night with Huilloc Topac. The old man hadn't wanted to know anything about the wars or what was happening in the Outside World. He had none of the contemptuous hostility that Anamaya remembered from their first meeting. He was as level and unadorned as a stone polished by centuries of rain.

At dawn, just as first light was grazing over the uppermost terraces, he had led them silently through a series of steep alleyways until they reached a stone platform with an open cave at one end. Prevailing there was the stone shadow of a condor, its beak plunging into the earth.

Huilloc Topac set out a few coca leaves, and Gabriel felt oddly in harmony with him as he helped him light a fire and pour *chicha.*

"Soon," said Huilloc Topac, his eyes rolled back, his head spinning like a star lost in the sky.

They left him and wandered freely through the city. They came across young girls and priests, goldsmiths and weaver-women. They saw the peasants already working in the corn terraces off in the distance. A heavy, black stillness had fallen over the city, the calm before the storm.

They spoke to each other only sporadically, saying very little, occasionally only a word or two.

At dusk, they returned to the house overlooking the valley and watched the evening fall.

All of a sudden, a voice rose up and reached them, and soon the entire valley was in song. The song's beauty was tragic and mysterious, a penetrating, monotone song in which human voices, trumpets, and drums all merged as one.

Anamaya and Gabriel got up and followed it.

The entire population of Picchu had gathered out on the square below the temple with the five niches. They all wore white *unkus* and *añacos,* and those lining the way to the center of the square held torches. The song increased in volume, all their chests rising and falling, a song that echoed endlessly across the valley. Gabriel and Anamaya drew nearer.

He had arrived.

The Sacred Double was there, waiting for them, the sun setting behind him.

The people of Picchu bowed their heads, and some were even prostrated on the ground to show their reverence.

Anamaya approached the Sacred Double alone. When she touched his head, the song instantly ended, and the only sounds that remained throughout the entire valley were that of the wind and the Willkamayo's rumble from down below.

> Nothing exists in vain, O Viracocha!
> Everyone leaves from the shores of Titicaca,
> Everyone arrives at the buried pyramids,
> Everyone returns to the place that you have accorded them!

They prayed slowly, each word flowing out of their mouths. When they had finished, Anamaya spread the *quipus* out before her and ran her fingers along the knots as Katari's spirit passed through her. To Gabriel, she appeared more beautiful, more luminous than ever as she straightened and said:

"A long time ago, the Sapa Inca Huayna Capac confided the secrets in an inexperienced young girl from the forest. Since then, many have fought to possess them, many believed that they could find them in war and endless destruction. That time is now over. There is but one secret—that the Sacred Double must now find his home so that the eternal soul of our mountains and the unity of all the worlds—this one, the Other World, and the Underworld—are conserved for the rest of time, which is itself the soul of our people."

They began chanting again when Anamaya fell silent, and the people of Picchu now moved their bodies in a slow, undulating dance, a solemn, trusting dance. The porters raised the Sacred Double onto its palanquin and Anamaya led them through the three levels of terraces below the square, where the throng remained, chanting and swaying. They went to a small, steep-sided platform the edge of which fell away into the Willkamayo ravine, and where tunnels pierced into three rocks seemed to plunge into the very bowels of the earth.

"*Urku Pacha,*" said Anamaya, taking the stone key given to her by Katari. "This is the place."

The sun's last rays hitched themselves to the *Intihuatana* and remained there for a moment as the Sacred Double disappeared into the central tunnel.

The chant stopped once again, and now the entire earth trembled as though everyone in the world were stamping their feet, or ten thousand drums were being beaten beneath them.

Seeing that the sun was about to slip behind the mountains, Katari sat down and prepared to throw the stone-that-stops-time one last time.

He saw a ray of light hitch itself to the top of the pyramid, then slide down its side like a bolt of lightning. It landed at his feet, at the spot where the circle of the underground temple opened.

"This is the place," he repeated, and took out his bronze key.

A muffled hammering sound emerged from the ground, and it began to tremble. He felt its vibrations penetrate into his feet and move up his legs, as though a thousand armies were on the march and converging on him. The age-old gangue of the *Stone of Origin* at the top of the pyramid cracked, then crumbled away. The wind come from the ocean carried away its dust. As the bare point of the pyramid emerged from the ground, drops of rain exploded against its granite skin.

Katari raised his face and offered it to the rain.

The sun had disappeared behind the mountains, and Gabriel had joined Anamaya on the terrace at the ravine's edge.

The people of Picchu slowly walked away and were swallowed by the night. They walked in long, silent columns, leaving the city forever. They left toward the Four Cardinal Directions, carrying torches, and they appeared from afar like enormous snakes of fire slipping down the mountainside. Stars were beginning to appear in the sky.

They had spent years building the secret city of Picchu so that it would be a final resting place worthy of the Sacred Double. His gold entrails contained the entire history and power of the Incas, the past and the future of the Andes, the memory of the glories they had built and the tests that they had endured. Did those leaving now know it? Most probably not, thought Anamaya, yet they're still proud of the work that they accomplished. They left without a word, and without looking back: What had to be said had been said, what had to be done had been done.

Anamaya and Gabriel watched Huilloc Topac leave with them, his long, snow-white hair fluttering on the night breeze, before he too was gone.

Nothing remained but silence.

The air was heavy, and they felt a humidity suddenly stick to the skin on their faces. They looked up and saw storm clouds, blacker than the night that they were traveling through, fill the sky. It began to rain. They could make out the silhouettes of the mountains by the pale, silent flashes streaking through the sky. They very quickly surrounded Machu Picchu like a pack of wild animals, fangs gleaming through the dark. The thunderbolts struck here and there with raucous yaps.

Anamaya instinctively huddled against Gabriel, whose breathing had accelerated. She reached for his hand and held it against her belly. As though attracted by her gesture, a thunderbolt landed right near them, on the highest of the terraces. They trembled together, their eyes closed, expecting a roar of thunder. With a sound like that of dead wood cracking, all the flames in the sky converged into one dazzling ball, and now it hurtled down the slope, spitting sparks of molten gold, and exploded into a multitude of blazing rivers, which seeped into the slightest cracks in the stone. An acrid, sulfurous odor filled the water-laden air. Only then did the thunder begin rolling from peak to peak and into the depths of the valleys, so intense that it echoed in their chest cavities. It fell like a fury from the sky above and rose like a wrath from the earth, shaking the entire world.

They weren't frightened.

The storm ended and a fresh wind came up and blew away the clouds, clearing the sky.

Once again the wind rustled the leaves.

The night was so absolute that it seemed as the world consisted of nothing but sky.

When the rain ended, Katari traveled through the stars. From the horizon, he followed the way of the *Mayo,* the celestial Sacred River, and when he stopped before the hazy cloud of the Lama, he smiled. The Powerful Ancestors of the Other World were thanking him for what he had accomplished. The cloud broke open, and he clearly saw the *lla-macñawin,* the lama's eyes. The two stars twinkled softly. Theirs was a regular, slow, harmonious pulsation, the eternal couple sharing the beat of one heart.

"You have arrived," he murmured within himself, "and I am with you. Time is unified. We have come from before and we will come again in the future. All is well."

Gabriel and Anamaya spent the entire night wandering through the constellations.

Anamaya called the Pleiades *collca,* and said that, together, they were the Mother of all the other stars. She pointed at the three stars of Orion's belt and whispered in Gabriel's ear.

"The condor, the vulture, and the falcon."

He flew with her and discovered, delimited by stars, the shapes of the Bird, the Bear, the Snake, and, finally, the Puma.

By the half light of dawn, Anamaya pointed out Venus to him, calling it *Chasca Cuyllor.*

The world had been swallowed up, and now the world was reborn.

Like a snake, time had coiled up, and time was now unfurling itself.

They kissed for a long time.

Then they climbed back up the terraces, made their way through the city's alleys to the stairs leading out of it. Anamaya led him up the steep and slippery slope through the forest to the summit of Machu Picchu where, years before, she had held the hand of a little girl who was meant to be sacrificed, but wasn't.

They climbed through the lush vegetation, their eyes bedazzled by the sun of the new day. They passed through the stone doors and looked up, feeling as if the vault of the sky was within reach of their fingers.

The wind played with the clouds and fog, and they went fearlessly to the rock at the peak. Hand in hand, they unfurled their arms as though they were wings, as though they were about to launch themselves into the void.

The wind strengthened. The blue on the horizon grew deeper. They held each other still, two bird-men filled with love, facing the rising sun.

Down below, there was nothing but rocks and, already, ghosts.

"We're alone!" Gabriel shouted to the wind.

Quietly, she replied:

"We're together."

Around 1520, a decade before Peru was discovered by Francisco Pizarro, the Inca Empire faced invasion along its eastern borders by hordes of Tupinambas. Leading these Indians from Brazil was a European called Alejo Garcia. The Sons of the Sun managed to check the invaders, who nevertheless established themselves at the base of the Cordillera and came to be known as Chiriguanos.

A legend tells that Alejo Garcia, a Portuguese of Flemish descent, captured an Inca princess and took her as his companion before disappearing to the east. Garcia had eyes as blue as porcelain.

After having first rescued his son, Titu Cusi, who had been captured by the Spanish, Manco managed to survive for a few more years in his refuge at Vilcabamba. He was killed at Vitcos in 1544 by seven men loyal to Almagro whom he had received as friends. The men were hoping that their cowardly murder would earn them a pardon from Gonzalo Pizarro.

Along with the most important members of his family, Paullu was baptized as Cristobal in 1543. In 1545, a title was conferred on him and he became a hidalgo. During those dark times, he was one of the few main players to die a natural death, in 1549.

The dwarf, Chimbo Sancto, most probably spent his old age on his land in the Yucay valley. Of his many children, only two daughters inherited his dwarfism. But all trace of them has been lost in the shadows of the past.

Hernando Pizarro spent twenty years in captivity in Spain. From his prison in the de la Mota castle in Medina del Campo, he carefully and tenaciously managed the Pizarro clan's immense and ultimately useless fortune—

a position he earned thanks mainly to his marriage to his brother Francisco's daughter. When he was released in 1561, he built a palace in his native Tru-jillo. He died there in 1578, almost completely blind, at the ripe old age of seventy-one—something of an accomplishment during that era.

Gonzalo Pizarro never changed his ways, and life appeared to reward his undiminished ambition. In 1544 he declared himself Governor of Peru, in open rebellion against the Spanish Crown. He spread terror among his enemies for four more years, especially through the armed forces of his lieu-tenant Francisco de Carbajal, nicknamed the "Demon of the Andes." In 1548 Gonzalo was finally defeated by royal troops and was beheaded on the battle-field.

Manco's successors resisted from their base at Vilcabamba until 1572. Throughout that time, periods of guerrilla war alternated with peace negoti-ations. In 1572, Tupac Amaru, the last legitimate Sapa Inca, was captured in his forest refuge, taken to Cuzco, and beheaded on the square of the Inca Empire's former capital, by order of the Viceroy Francisco de Toledo.

His head was nailed to the pillory. But instead of putrefying, it grew more beautiful every day, and became the object of growing veneration. Unto this day, a myth predicts that the Inca will return the day his head is again joined to his mutilated body.

Acllahuasi—House of the Chosen Women (*acllas*).

Amauta—A sage, a learned man.

Añaco—A long, straight tunic reaching the ankles worn by women.

Apu—Quechua word meaning "Lord" or "Governor"; also used as a title preceding the names of mountain divinities.

Ayllos—A throwing weapon similar to a bola; it consists of three leather strips ballasted with rocks, designed to entangle the legs of a running quarry.

Balsa—A wooden raft made of balsa wood.

Borla (Spanish) or *mascapaicha* (Quechua)—Along with the *llautu* and the feathered *curiguingue,* this woolen fringe makes up the royal headpiece of the Sapa Inca.

Cancha—An open inner courtyard; also a collection of three or four buildings around such a courtyard, forming a single living area.

Chaquiras—Small pearls from pink shells (*mullus*) that are made into necklaces or woven into ceremonial costumes.

Chaski—Runners who carry messages by relay.

Chicha—A ceremonial beverage; also a fermented beer, usually made from maize.

Chuño—Naturally dehydrated potatoes that keep for months.

Chuspa—A small woven pouch decorated with religious motifs and used to carry coca leaves.

Collcas—Circular or rectangular buildings made up of a single room and used as warehouses to store foodstuffs, weavings, weapons, and luxuries.

Coya—Title accorded to the Inca's principal wife.

Cumbi—The finest quality of woven cloth, usually made from vicuña wool.

Curaca—A local chief or official.

Curiguingue—A small falcon; its black-and-white feathers were used to decorate the Sapa Inca's headpiece.

Guanaco—From the Quechua *huanaco*, an undomesticatd Andean member of the Camelidae family, related to the llama.

Hatunruna—Quechua word meaning "peasant."

Huaca—Quechua word meaning "sacred." By extension, any location or sanctuary in which a divinity is kept.

Huara—Shorts. Boys were given a pair of these during the initiation rite called the *huarachiku*.

Ichu—A type of wild grass that grows at high altitudes and is used mainly to thatch roofs.

Inti Raymi—One of the major festivals of the Inca calendar; occurs during the winter solstice.

Kallanka—A long building with doors that usually open onto the square of an administrative center.

Kapak—Chief.

Llautu—Long, woolen plaits wrapped several times around the wearer's head to form a headpiece.

Manta—Spanish word meaning "blanket," but used to denote the cape worn by Inca men (*llacolla*) and women (*lliclla*).

Mascapaicha—See *Borla*.

Mullus—Shells from the Pacific Coast, usually of a red or pink color. They were widely used during Inca religious rites, either in their natural state or after having been worked.

Pachacuti—A great upheaval signaling the beginning of a new era.

Panaca—Lineage from an Inca sovereign.

Papas—Potatoes.

Plateros—Spanish word denoting those metalworkers who specialized in precious metals.

Pututu—A large seashell used as a trumpet.

Quinua—An Andean cereal rich in protein.

Quipu—A device of colored strings in which knots were tied. The knots served as a mnemonic system for keeping records.

Sapa Inca—Literally "Unique Lord." The title of the Inca sovereign.

Tambos—Inns set at regular intervals along the Empire's roads. In such places the traveler could find food and shelter, as well as fresh clothes, all provided by the state.

Tiana—A small bench or stool reserved exclusively for the Inca and for *curacas*, which was a symbol of power.

Tocapu—A geometric motif with symbolic meanings used to decorate Inca weavings.

Tumi—A ceremonial knife, the bronze blade of which is set at a ninety-degree angle to the handle.

Tupu—A long needle made of gold, silver, bronze, or copper, used to clasp a cape, or *manta*, together.

Unku—A sleeveless, knee-length tunic worn by men.

Ushnu—A small pyramid set on the square of an Inca settlement and reserved for the use of those in power.

Viscacha—A rodent of the genus *Marmota*, with a tail similar to a squirrel's, which lives in scree.